Blessed Are The Peacemakers?

The destruction of Paradise.

Also by Samson Soledad:

In The Beginning, There was. . . ME!

Fifth Sunset

If I Give You A Fish

Blessed Are The Peacemakers?

The destruction of Paradise.

**Constantine Papavasiliou
&
Samson Soledad**

BOOKS
InAmerica
California, U.S.A.

Published in the United States by InAmerica Press
a division of InAmerica, Inc.
POB 2645, Valley Center, CA U.S.A.
InAmerica and colophon are registered trademarks of InAmerica, Inc.

The author and publisher would like to thank the following
for permission to reproduce illustrations:
Mr. Gordon Stewart
Mr. John Elkington
all contributors of Creative Commons

Library of Congress Cataloging-in-Publication Data

ISBN 978-1-934613-24-5
Papavasiliou, Constantine; Soledad, Samson, authors.
Blessed Are The Peacemakers?: The destruction of Paradise/
Constantine Papavasiliou & Samson Soledad.
Includes bibliography.

First U.S. Edition
[First Printing]
Copyright © 2013-14 by The ProtoGnosis Institute
All rights reserved under International and Pan-American Copyright Conventions.

InAmerica Press website address: www.inamericapress.com
Printed in the United States of America.

Cover Design by David Sean Stringer

For my father, who survived this hell,

. . . so I wouldn't have to.

Acknowledgements

We wish to thank a few individuals who were instrumental in the transformation of an idle threat into a reality.

It is the amazing life story and breadth of knowledge of Mr. George D. Koulaxes that inspired the decision to pursue this work. A tireless promoter of Hellenism, George never mentioned any of his incredible feats and experiences until it was necessary to hear them in the context of our discussions. He is a true gentleman and the model of an ordinary man armed with extraordinary humanity.

A man who truly bears the burden of a powerful endowment, I stumbled onto Roger L. Jennings, grandson of Asa K. Jennings the protagonist of this story. He provided an insider's view of his grandfather as well as a look at his personal papers. Roger continues his family's legacy to seek solutions to the difficult relationship between Greece and Turkey.

In another inquiry into a key character in the book, that of British Vice-Consul Edwyn Cecil Hole, I managed to be acquainted with his granddaughter, Ms. Valerie Nield. Valerie was tireless in her wish to help me bring her real grandfather to the story. She too, provided me an insider's look into her grandfather's experience as a British authority who, in surviving the holocaust, tried to walk a narrow line between his official duty and his humanity.

Fortunately, we were able to impose on Dena Sarris to point out all of the tortured logic that only made sense to the authors. Her experience as an educator and patience as a classy lady, likely prevented much scratching of readers' heads to understand what's going on in the story.

And finally, Archbishop Chrysostomos Kalafatis, a saint and martyr of the Greek Orthodox Church, a source of veneration to millions of Orthodox Christians and a source of a humble author's profound pride as a blood relative. Agios Chrysostomos remains a legendary priest who personified the concept of dedication of a shepherd to his flock.

A Note to the Reader

The story you are about to read is technically considered historical fiction. I say 'technically' because there are a few events that actually are fictional in that they were inserted and dramatized so that the story would flow more smoothly. But aside from these dramatic insertions, all of the characters, events and the timeline in which they occur, are true and consistent with credibly-sourced historical records, so that the materially significant events in the story are all **non-fiction.** All of the characters are real people that actually experienced the events. A short bio of each character is provided as an appendix.

While I have used literary license to dramatize the characters with what the real individuals might have been, or likely were thinking at the time, or perhaps which restaurant they patronized or what they ordered for dinner, the relevant actions and crucial events that comprise the compelling nature of the historical record are preserved and occur in the actual timeline of history.

Where possible, the dialogue is taken from actual quoted statements of the real people who lived these events. There has been some compression of the events into the available characters, only because without doing so would require an even larger cast of characters, and perhaps complicate and obscure the point of this historical calamity. In every case, however, each event is the result of eyewitness testimony from those who lived it, and in many cases, related or experienced by American relief workers, military, or travelers who happened to be in the wrong place at the right time. Witnesses that collectively had no reason to color the narrative in favor of their own prejudices or against someone else's.

I will readily stipulate to an obvious bias in the telling of this story since I believe that once exposed to the facts, there is no way to remain objective about it. However, in spite of that bias, no portion of the story is presented without having found a factual basis in the historical record so that a historically-accurate account can be read.

At its core, this is a story of the actions of ordinary people raised in the atmosphere of western democratic principles, who in spite of political duplicity at the top, stood up for humanity and refused to sacrifice their God-given spirit to dark side. Behind all of the horror, arrogance, corruption and greed, it is a story of uncompromising faith, hope and goodwill. In the end, it is also a true story about how one man's faith and strength of purpose can trump the apathy and greed of nations.

CONSTANTINE PAPAVASILIOU
& SAMSON SOLEDAD

Prologue

'BLESSED ARE THE PEACEMAKERS,

FOR THEY WILL BE CALLED CHILDREN OF GOD.'

Matthew 5:9

Clearly, the character of peacemakers, as revered in the Beatitudes, couches them in a state of sanctity. Yet, this story reveals more than anything else, the wide chasm between the ideal and reality of men who take on the role. It is formulaic of how arrogance, corruption and greed necessarily caused the destruction of the paradise that is the subject of this story. Therefore to fully understand it, we must comprehend the preceding conditions that spawned its destruction in the first place.

Ever since mankind has had the ability to read and write, historians have chronicled human vanity by celebrating one tribe's conquest over another. For millennia scribes have lauded and stroked their exalted leaders- emperors and kings - to elevate their decisions or actions to some morally-justified imperative.

The nineteenth century would take the conquering of one's neighbors and elevate it to a new political concept known as the 'Age of Imperialism.' The absolute monarchs of Great Britain, France, Germany, Italy and Japan, plus the United States, developed a new game wherein the world map was the playing board to display who controlled which peoples and what territory. Emperors, kings, dictators and political leaders who thought themselves worthy, apparently only considered the niceties of claiming more geography and people.

As the field of despots became more and more crowded, a series of European alliances were set up between strange bedfellows as a deterrent to a perceived aggressor. Hence, the Holy Alliance between Austria, Prussia and Russia; the Three Emperor Alliance between Austria-Hungary, Germany and Russia; the Dual Alliance between Austria-Hungary and Germany; the Triple Alliance between Austria-Hungary, Germany and Italy; The Reinsurance Alliance between Germany and Russia; the Franco-Russian Alliance; the Entente Cordiale between Great Britain and France; and the Anglo-Russian Alliance.

What proved to be a confused network of bizarre alliances failed to pacify aggressive imperialists. The Balkan Crisis of 1908-09; the First Balkan War of 1912-13; and the Second Balkan War of 1913, were child's play compared to what the continental European leaders had built-up in their delusional obsession to increase the size and power of their realm to match their monumental egos. The consequence would come to be known as the Great War, and later to be codified as World War I.

What started the war in the first place? Perhaps it's the bubble that supreme leaders reside in where their inner circle praises their every action and reaction. Or perhaps it's the arrogance that accompanies the narcissism of the ruling classes. Essentially it comes down to arrogant men trying to demonstrate militarily whose manhood was the most prominent.

What was the metaphorical trigger? An eighteen year-old student, Gavrilo Prinzip (Princip), and his coffeehouse mates, devised what they thought to be a novel idea to advance the radical mission of the Young Bosnian nationalist movement.

What did he do? He assassinated Archduke Franz Ferdinand of Austria and his wife Sophie, the Duchess of Hohenberg.

Within a month of the assassination of the heir to the Austro-Hungarian throne, Emperor Franz Joseph, in his final act as emperor, invaded Serbia. Not to be outdone, Germany invaded Belgium, Luxembourg and France. Russia joined the madness by attacking Germany. In the end, sixteen countries would sacrifice much of their human and monetary resources as a consequence of the arrogance of a handful of chosen or unchosen leaders.

Of the sixty-five million soldiers mobilized to defeat or destroy their perceived enemies, almost fifty percent, were either killed, wounded, held as prisoners of war or went missing in the exercise. Over eight million died and twenty-one million were wounded. In other words, more than five thousand human lives were lost <u>each and every day for almost five years</u>, just so a few moronic heads of state could satisfy their addiction to power by sending their constituencies out to capture more territory and people to rule over.

Once the shooting stopped, there would have to be a winner and a loser so that the winner could bask in the glow of victory and prescribe the appropriate punishment for the loser. The irony of it all is that with the glorious end of the Great War, or as H.G. Wells described it, 'the war to end all wars,' the world still could not agree on the question of whose male member was the most prominent.

On 11 November 1918, to the relief of most people on the planet, the Germans finally signed the armistice agreement. With the end of hostilities the political leaders of Great Britain, France, Italy and the United States, (who would become known as the Supreme Council and the 'Big Four') gathered in Paris to decide the peace terms and punishment for those vanquished countries making up the Central Powers: Germany, Austria-Hungary, Bulgaria and the Ottoman Empire (Turkey). Then, as was the European tradition, once the victors had agreed on the terms they would demand, they would meet with the losers and negotiate the actual terms of a peace agreement.

France, a dubious member of the winning side, had successfully lobbied to have the conference in Paris. Then, she had lobbied for the opening of the Paris Peace Conference, to begin on the anniversary of the Unification of Germany, forty-eight years earlier, when the princes of the various German states gathered to create the German Empire. A profound date in the French consciousness, 18 January marks the date France surrendered in the Franco-Prussian War. Clearly, the proposal of this particular opening date was meant to erase the earlier emasculation of France and to return the favor, by hosting the disappearance of the German Empire.

Such were the circumstances in January 1919 as we begin our story.

Chapter 1.

If there's ever a month of the year that Paris is not considered cheerful, it's the rainy month of January - and in 1919, January proved to be particularly dismal. Repeated rain showers cast the city in a darkened grayness, producing a wet cold that could be felt down to the bone. There was so much rain that earlier in the month the Seine rose nearly twenty feet above flood stage, forcing residents along its banks to evacuate. Even the bear population at the *Jardins des Plantes* had to be let out of their cages to avoid drowning. As if the skeletal image of leafless trees lining the avenues wasn't depressing enough, many leafless trees were now stumps that remained as Parisians had been forced to cut them down for firewood.

While Paris had avoided the brunt of destruction that devastated much of northern France, signs of the war were everywhere. The city took on the look of a ghostly version of itself. Bombs had been lobbed into the city producing some destruction, and in the aftermath the cleanup produced piles of rubble that stood as depressing reminders. Even the famous thoroughfare *Avenue des Champs Élysées*, bore some unmistakable scars of the Great War.

A short walk from the *Champs Élysées* across Paris' lowest bridge, the *Pont des Invalides*, intersected the street known as the Quai d'Orsay, historically known for the artists who paint along the banks of the river Seine. At this intersection stood the grand French Ministry of Foreign Affairs building, also known simply as the Quai d'Orsay.

Stéphen Pichon, the amiable French Minister of Foreign Affairs, made his way to the side entrance of the Quai d'Orsay. Pichon's title was somewhat deceiving in that his likability was his most significant asset. He was otherwise considered lazy and indecisive. In other words, he was a typical government bureaucrat that spent most of his career sitting on the fence in order to avoid being accused of a wrong decision. He followed instructions to the letter insuring he could always blame a misstep on his superior.

Looking out through the glass doors, a realization struck him. He was standing within a few feet of the four most powerful men in the world.

To his right stood David Lloyd George, the Prime Minister of the great British empire, representing its vast global network of

1. *"The Big Four" posing for a photo. (left to right: David Lloyd George, Vittorio Orlando, Georges Clemenceau, Woodrow Wilson).*

colonies and the world's mightiest navy. Unlike his predecessors, Lloyd George was not a child of breeding within the British aristocracy. Coming from Wales, which suggested humble beginnings, Lloyd George often used that impression to make him seem all the more remarkable. In truth, he was raised in an educated family environment. Perhaps due to the fact that he lost his father at a very early age, to be raised by an uncle who was a village cobbler, his circumstances propelled him to aspire to a far greater stage. He was an exceptional orator, debater and thrived on challenge. He was keenly aware of what people were thinking and was able to manipulate his audience by virtue of his personality. Naturally optimistic, he always believed he could find a solution to a problem. Predictably, from his modest beginnings, his favorite targets were landowners and the aristocracy.

Next to Lloyd George, stood Italy's Prime Minister, Vittorio Orlando. Also a liberal politician, Orlando was the obvious weak sister of the group. Having become Prime Minister immediately following Italy's humiliating defeat at the hands of the Germans at Caporetto, his political strength remained in question. Although an accomplished professor of law and author of more than one hundred writings on legal and judicial issues, Orlando was severely handicapped in Paris by the fact that he couldn't speak English.

Pichon marveled at how Lloyd George and Orlando seemed to converse without understanding what each other was saying.

Next to Orlando stood the old Tiger, France's elder statesman and Prime Minister, Georges Clemenceau. At seventy-eight years old, he was significantly older than his counterparts. But he was by far the wittiest and most cynical of the group. Clemenceau who also was known to his citizens as 'Father Victory' was given the name for leading the nation to victory. He was both fiercely patriotic and ever on guard against his lifelong enemy, Germany. Born into the privileged class, he was only twenty-eight years old when the Franco-Prussian War began. Stubbornly fearless, he had continued to fight the Germans in Paris after the French had already surrendered. Having experienced two invasions in his lifetime, his allies were faced with his staunch intransigence and vindictiveness towards Germany. Like his father, Clemenceau was a trained doctor, but chose not to practice medicine. His passion had always been politics and France. He was openly hostile of Lloyd George and the American President Wilson when they attempted to soften the punishment of Germany. In his mind, they could not comprehend the extent of the French suffering and he was resolute in his vengeance.

Lastly, Pichon studied the American President Woodrow Wilson. Like most Europeans, Wilson appeared as the American savior who had come to Paris armed with his idealistic *Fourteen Points* program and his vision of a League of Nations that would end war forever. Certainly, it was the hardship suffered by Europe throughout the war that would elevate Wilson to that of a demigod. Of the four, Wilson was the most handicapped by his own ideology that would never be able to stand up to scrutiny or reality.

Born into privilege as a southerner from Virginia, Wilson predictably was paternalistic to women and blacks. He was ambitious and supremely idealistic, thus nurturing radically progressive views. He openly opposed big business as evil and supported the dispossessed and downtrodden. He was the embodiment of contradiction in that he often quoted from the Bible while simultaneously ruthless to anyone who crossed him. He clearly wanted power and justified it by his desire to do good works. The son of one of the founders of the Presbyterian Church in the United States, his views were unrealistically liberal, to the point where some thought he had no appreciation for, or comprehension of reality.

Pichon contemplated these four masters of the universe. In another setting, they would just be four arrogant old men propelled by their own personal weaknesses. In this setting, they were further handicapped by their complete ignorance of the disastrous potential consequences of their acts. Acts that would ultimately inflict pain and suffering on the entire world over the next one hundred years and beyond. But Pichon was incapable of seeing their inadequacies. He, like everyone else, was blinded by the image of the four men who were about to decide the fate of the world.

Pichon opened the glass doors. The cold and wet January air sent a chill through his body, as his attire was better-suited to the eighty-plus temperatures maintained in the ministry building. His mission was to retrieve the celebrated world leaders who stood outside for a photograph honoring the historic Paris Peace Conference due to begin the following week. Standing around like actors vying for a part in a movie, each of them consciously trying to project the image he believed would maximize his stature in the eyes of the world. Eyes that would be anxiously following newspaper and newsreel accounts of the proceedings. After all, they were on a world stage and they represented the winning tag team.

Pichon shivered as the temperature difference between his office and the outdoors exceeded thirty degrees. He cleared his throat to get their attention.

"*Pardonnez-moi, messieurs!* My office, it is ready for you now. Kindly follow me, so we may begin *la discussion préliminaire*."

The quartet, chilled from posing for the historic photo acknowledged Pichon with some indistinct grumbling. They turned and swaggered through the doors as they followed him into the building. They labored to climb the stairs of the ornate rotunda to the double doors of Pichon's office which would become the preferred meeting place for the Big Four. While each of them had a staff of assistants, this initial meeting was to be a private ceremonial gathering without staff, suggesting the importance of the group and the moment.

As they entered Pichon's office the heat coming off the blazing fireplace was a temporary welcomed change to the gray winter chill. They gathered in front of the hearth with hands outstretched. Once the heat overcame the numbness, they all turned like a family of formally-dressed penguins to thaw their posteriors. With backs to the fireplace, they could see the ornate, upholstered regency chairs strategically placed with an obsessive adherence to head-of-state diplomatic symbolism. As the host country, France's armchair sat alone in front of the hearth. The United States, being the only country represented by a head of state, had a chair a few inches taller than the others, flanked by the chair of Great Britain, with Italy's chair off to the side by itself.

The room was a perfect setting for such a historic meeting. The high-domed ceiling, the carved-oak wall panels, the ballroom-sized *electric* chandelier, the large hanging seventeenth-century Catherine de Medici tapestries, the Aubusson carpets, all contributed to the importance of the occasion and its celebrated participants.

Once seated, a white-jacketed server silently approached with a tray of four fluted champagne glasses. He held out the tray so that each dignitary could take a celebratory glass of Moët & Chandon champagne.

As host, protocol demanded that Georges Clemenceau speak first.

"*Je suis heureux*. . . I am pleased we can begin. At least we have survived the photo that will no doubt make us the most easily recognizable targets all over the world."

The elder statesman addressed the group in excellent English, learned from his travels to the United States. The others offered a perfunctory if not tense laugh, realizing that the comment had a disturbing truth attached to it. He then raised his glass with a gloved-hand that he wore to hide a severe case of eczema.

"Welcome gentlemen to the Quai d'Orsay! Perhaps it is because we are here on a Sunday, but there is nothing on the agenda today other than the photo we just endured and to toast the commencement of the Conference. I suppose that is one of the burdens we must endure as world leaders."

Lloyd George quipped, "At least we can say that the meeting was a resounding success."

Wilson shot a look at Lloyd George and thought, *You idiot! Don't you even sense the profound importance of what we are here to accomplish?*

Clemenceau was not about to let this first gathering go to waste.

"I do have one request before we toast our momentous victory. Since our discussions in the larger working plenary sessions will be in front of many delegates and the world press, I would like for us to agree here and now, that when we do meet in this office alone, that we all can be frank and candid between one another without fear of. . . *punition*. . . *How you say*. . . *ahhhhhhh!*. . . castigation. Can we all agree on that?"

Lloyd George lifted an index finger as if to interject a thought.

"To your point, Georges, I remind you that only three of us speak English," looking over at Orlando with a smile and thereby producing a returned smile from the Italian.

". . . and from the tortured smile on his face, he has no idea what I'm talking about. Either our group needs to be expanded to include Mr. Sonnino, who can translate, or we keep him out of the loop and decide on what the world will look like between the three of us. I, for one, would prefer the latter."

Lloyd George, smiled again, this time nodding at Orlando, who smiled and nodded back. "I doubt he could grasp a nuance if he tripped over it."

America's President Wilson ignoring Lloyd George's comment, looked over at Clemenceau.

"I have no intention of being other than candid, in this room or outside of it."

Clemenceau had a compulsive urge to roll his eyes as he thought, *You fool! You should save this crap for your American audience.*

Wilson then turned to look at Lloyd George.

"David, you already know I have certain reservations about the fluctuating nature of the Italian position. Perhaps we could agree on certain matters between the three of us and then together, hopefully garner a unanimous agreement from Italy."

Clemenceau glared at both Lloyd George and Wilson. He didn't care for either one of them. In fact, he thought Wilson was intellectually stunted. Out of frustration, he spoke more slowly and deliberately at Wilson.

"Mr. President, I expect that *all* of us are *capable* of candid conversation. Surely, as President of the United States, you can see that your statements made in public must be carefully parsed, as opposed to a private conversation between us, behind closed doors. My point is for us to appear to the world as voices of reason instead of alley cats scratching at each other."

Wilson smiled and nodded as the light finally went on.

"Oh yes, of course! I thought you meant something else."

Clemenceau still holding his glass up, "Before I forget, I want to thank you all for agreeing to the official opening date we established for the Conference. It is an important date in that it must remind the Kaiser that Germany is the vanquished remnant of an evil offensive and must accept her punishment."

Lloyd George raised his glass.

"Georges, as you know from our earlier conversations, I was very much opposed to the idea of tying the opening session to Germany's unification anniversary. For that matter I opposed the Conference being held in Paris. There's no sense rubbing their noses in it, while we make them pay for their sins. All it does is make the wound turn septic. I only agreed to the date because you made such an issue and if we can't agree on an opening date, how will we be able to get anything done? But I caution you to see that the French press does not make too much of this orchestrated coincidence. Other than that, 18 January is as good a date as any."

Distracted and still trying to analyze whether Clemenceau's last comment was casting an aspersion on him, Wilson only caught the last bit of Lloyd George's comment, and raised his glass.

"Gentlemen, I too, did not feel this Conference should set an opening date that would be viewed as retribution for France's earlier difficulties, but in the interest of moving on, I did not object to it."

Grasping the moral high ground, Wilson was still glowing from the adoration of the crowds that welcomed him last month on his arrival for the Conference. His name was on the lips of most Europeans who inappropriately attached great value to his idyllic and unrealistic *Fourteen Points* program, and his equally idealized League of Nations that would somehow magically keep peace in the world.

Finally, Orlando shrugged his shoulders in silence, lifted his glass and forced another smile.

"*Al nostro successo . . . Salute!*"

Without his English-speaking Foreign Minister, Sidney Sonnino, Orlando was stoic and more closely resembled a mustached floor lamp. He was begrudgingly in Paris strictly to secure the territorial gains Italy was secretly promised in order to support the Allies in the war.

Even though all four glasses were now raised for the toast, Clemenceau's blood pressure was boiling as the slow-thinking Wilson was belittling France's push for the significant opening date. He was especially distrustful of Wilson's ignorance magnified by his progressive dogma.

"Mr. President! We are in complete agreement that the actual opening date is a minor consideration in the outcome. But to the people of France, who were attacked by Germany, this is retribution exacted for the injuries they suffered. We did not start this war! It has cost us all dearly. If I may be candid though, France has suffered more than anyone. The war was fought on our soil. I will not allow the defeated to negotiate what their punishment will be for their provocative action. I am confident, what we decide will be the fair and proper punishment. And..."

Clemenceau looked over at Wilson and slowed his speech for effect,

"Mr. President, I believe the League of Nations is the perfect forum to accomplish our mission."

Shaking of his head from side to side while he uttered the words betrayed his true feelings about Wilson's foolish League. But he knew he must walk the fine line between his need to maximize France's position and the knowledge that his beloved country could not survive another war without the participation of Britain and the United States.

At this point, Lloyd George couldn't stand it any longer.

"Gentlemen, my arm will soon be too tired to hold up the weight of the champagne. Can we complete the toast and *then* make our little speeches?"

Everyone donned an uncomfortable smile as they raised their glasses higher in the air.

Lloyd George prompted them. "Hear, hear!"

They all took a sip of champagne and then set their glasses on their side tables.

Clemenceau needed to make his final point.

"Gentlemen, starting next week we will have more than thirty countries coming to us to gain favor for their demands. Most of them are just selfish little demands from selfish little countries. I want to make it clear in advance that none of their issues are worthy of discussion relative to our terms for Germany. It doesn't really matter how we redraw any border for these little countries in that they will continue to blame their difficulties on those next door. But

Germany as we have seen twice in the last fifty years, cannot be trusted to be a peaceful neighbor. We must ensure that France is protected from her at all costs."

Ignoring Clemenceau, Wilson recalled the adoring, cheering masses, believing he would serve as the ultimate arbiter of the final peace plan and that peace agreement be a product of his own utopian League of Nations. Having a limited attention span, he was instantly impressed with Clemenceau's expression of approval for the League. Conversely, he was offended by Lloyd George, who had refused to rush over to Paris last month to welcome his momentous arrival. He wondered how the senior British minister could consider the British general elections as more important than the historic arrival of the first U.S. President ever to travel to Europe while in office?

Chapter 2.

Due east of the Quai d'Orsay stood the magnificent Notre Dame Cathedral - looking more like a nicotine-stained copy of its former self - as all the stained-glass windows had been removed in anticipation of German bombs and replaced with cheap yellow glass. But images such as these were insufficient to diminish the new optimism that had infected Europe upon commencement of the Paris Peace Conference. Hundreds of thousands had flocked to the streets to welcome the American President who won the war and would now end war forever.

The decision to meet in Paris had been a function of Clemenceau's wish to humiliate the Germans. He doggedly fought against Lloyd George's preference for a neutral site like Geneva, Switzerland. But, Lloyd George was a negotiator, not an ideologue. Actually, Wilson had not been opposed to Paris until he met with his most trusted advisor.

Colonel Edward House was not really a military colonel. But the honorary rank somehow became attached to him. House had advised Wilson, "It will be difficult at best to make a just peace but it will be almost impossible to do so while sitting in the atmosphere of a belligerent capital."

Wilson then joined Lloyd George in preferring a more neutral setting like Geneva. But Clemenceau refused to back down from his position. Strangely, reports spontaneously emerged convincing Wilson that Geneva had been infiltrated with legions of German spies. Consequently, the stubborn French Premiere got his way and Paris survived as the setting for the Conference.

The city was inundated with kings, premieres, presidents, diplomats, military officers, industrialists, journalists, translators, secretaries, and every conceivable service provider that such an event would foster. As a result Paris would again see signs of life. After weeks of pre-conference lavish parties, meetings, dinners and yes, even work by the legions of young diplomats establishing possible peace scenarios, the calendar finally arrived at the opening of the Peace Conference.

From his left-corner seat at the head U-shaped conference table, Colonel Edward House looked out over the crowd in The *Salle de l'Horloge* (The Clock Room) at the Quai d'Orsay, the site for the opening plenary session of the Conference. At one end of the hall was a magnificently ornate fireplace, but without a glowing fire. Most of the heat would come from the humanity crowded into the room. Large crystal electric chandeliers hung from the ornate molded ceiling but were somewhat obscured by the abundance of cigarette smoke hanging in the air. Since cigarette filters wouldn't be invented for another six years, the aroma of tobacco coated everyone and everything.

The conference consisted of the delegates of thirty-seven nations - who were filing into the meeting room that would soon be filled to capacity. House watched delegates upon walking into the room, mill around the conference table until they spotted their own place card. Along the walls stood the various journalists and moving-picture cameramen preparing their equipment to record an event of momentous importance. The temperature in the hall had risen sufficiently already melt the ice in the water pitchers. Considering that most of the people sitting or standing were men in business suits, the heat seemed all the more stifling.

This was a historic occasion and everyone in attendance knew it. One could feel the gravity of what would transpire in the weeks that would follow. Everyone was convinced that the fate of mankind and the future of the world now hung in the balance. The air was electric with excitement - which translated into a low roar of discussion as the attendees awaited the banging of the gavel.

Colonel House again scanned the room looking for any signal of something out of the ordinary. Noticeably missing were the five delegates from Japan, but that was expected as they had not yet arrived in Paris. The Russians weren't part of the seating arrangement, but that was because the Russian ally had been Czarist Russia, and the surging Lenin communists were not considered allies. But straight down the leg of the 'U' on his side, House noticed two glaring empty seats. Looking for potential problems, House leaned over to his colleague General Bliss who had a better view. "General, can you see who is missing from the table? There are two empty chairs down this row."

General Tasker Bliss had been recalled out of retirement to become the American Plenipotentiary at the Conference. Bliss looked down at his seating chart. "Oh, that's the Greek delegation. That would be . . . Venizelos, Greece's Prime Minister and Politis, the Foreign Minister."

House sensed a problem. If anyone should be present, it would be the Greeks. It was believed, but not spoken that the Greek force had won the deciding battle against a heavily fortified Bulgarian position at *Skra di Legen* on the Macedonian front. Many believed it was this victory that convinced the Germans to sign the Armistice. He stood up and walked over to Lloyd George, with whom he had developed a close working relationship over the last few months.

House leaned over Lloyd George's shoulder and whispered into his ear. "David! The Greeks are not here. Is there a problem?"

Lloyd George looked over at the table where the Greek delegation was supposed to be. He saw the empty chairs. "Ed, there's nothing we can do about this now, but after this circus ends, meet me and we'll get to the bottom of it. There must be a problem."

"I'm not going to wait." House stayed bent over Lloyd George's shoulder. "I'll have someone go over to their hotel and ask what's wrong."

House went back to his seat and motioned for one of his military aides. He whispered into the young lieutenant's ear. The aide sped off through the crowd.

Finally, Count Luigi Aldovandi Marescotti seated behind the main table at the Conference Secretariat desk, stood and banged the large polished oak gavel on its matching disk. The high-pitched crack echoed through the hall, bringing the room to an immediate silence. It was beginning!

"*Signore e signori, accoglierete favorevolmente il presidente degli Stati Uniti, presidente Woodrow Wilson . . .*

Mesdames et messieurs. . . veuillez accueillir le président des Etats-Unis d'Amérique, Le Président Woodrow Wilson . . .

Ladies and gentlemen, would you kindly welcome the President of the United States, President Woodrow Wilson!"

The hall thundered with applause as Wilson stood at his chair, looking down at his prepared remarks. He waited until the crowd sat in silence for a full minute using every bit of drama he could. Finally he spoke.

"I have the great honor to propose as definitive president of this conference the French Premier, M. Clemenceau. I do so in conformity with usage. I should do it even if it were only a question of paying homage to the French Republic, but I do it also because I desire, and you certainly desire with me, to pay homage to the man himself . . ."

Wilson continued to read and parrot the remarks that had been prepared for him. As he read them, he felt discomfort that his true feelings were completely contradictory of his words. He could hardly stand the man. But he was certainly willing to make these remarks in exchange for France's support for his signature League of Nations.

". . . Thus, gentlemen, it is not only to the Premier of the French Republic, it is to M. Clemenceau that I propose you should give the presidency of this assemblage."

Before Wilson could be seated, the crowd roared with applause and cheers. He bowed to the seventy delegates and all of the attendees and then sat down. The BBC cameraman at the side of the hall kept turning the crank handle on his new moving-picture camera. This would be an historic newsreel that would be carried all over the world.

Before the applause died down, Lloyd George stood and waited for silence. He thought, *Now it's my turn to lie!*

"Gentlemen, it is not only a pleasure for me, but a real privilege, to support in the name of the British Empire the motion which has been proposed by President Wilson. I shall do it for the reasons which the President has just expressed with so much eloquence. It is homage to a man that we wish to pay before all . . ."

As he read his notes, his eyes involuntarily returned to the empty Greek chairs. He had developed a special relationship with Greece's Prime Minister Eleftherios Venizelos. He believed the Greek politician was extraordinarily gifted and would be the British Empire's new partner in the Near East. Suddenly, he was worried.

". . . He represents the admirable energy, courage and resource of his great people, and that is why I desire to add my voice to that of President Wilson and to ask for his election to the presidency of the Peace Conference."

Before he sat, he looked to his right and saw House staring back at him. He sat down as the applause continued.

While Italy was a member of the Supreme Council, she was not given a place at the head of the table. In fact, instead of being closest to the head on the side opposite France, she was delegated to a less important position between France and Belgium. Since Prime Minister Orlando didn't speak English, it was Baron Sonnino who stood up after Lloyd George sat down.

With a heavy Italian accent, Sonnino read his notes.

"Gentlemen, on behalf of the Italian Delegation, I associate myself cordially with the proposal of President Wilson, supported by Mr. Lloyd George, and I ask you to give the presidency of the Peace Conference to M. Clemenceau. I am happy to be able in these circumstances to testify to my good will and admiration for France and for the eminent statesman who is at the head of her Government."

As staged, Clemenceau was voted in as the President of the Conference which was followed by a selection of mind-numbing speeches all applauding the goals and virtue of the assembled group. After what seemed a lifetime, with no actual work being performed, the plenary session finally expired. Everyone at the event seemed to think they were performing the critical work of peace. In reality, however, thirty-five nations, with thirty-five different agendas and thirty-five different demands were now starting a zero-sum board game, where the Big Four would decide how to divide that game board.

After the room cleared out, House returned to update Lloyd George.

"My aide inquired as to the reason the Greeks have stayed away. Apparently, Venizelos decided not to attend after he received the seating arrangement. He's upset over the fact that Greece only received two seats, while Serbia was given three. He didn't seem to have a problem with Serbia, as he views them as friends. His problem is definitely with us."

Lloyd George was openly upset. He thought his relationship with Venizelos was solid. He believed Greece's history, culture and customs were complimentary to Great Britain, and more importantly, he needed Greece's army to get the Turks out of Anatolia. He decided to go over to the Hotel Mercedes immediately to mend things. His aide put a call into Venizelos.

The official British staff car whisked Lloyd George over to the Hotel Mercedes. He was not about to let this problem linger. He had built a close relationship with Venizelos during the war. Otherwise, Greece would have probably remained neutral.

He knocked on the door. Venizelos personally opened the door to his friend.

"Lefty. . ." Lloyd George said as he entered the room. "Where were you? Why weren't you at the opening session?"

Lefty was the name that Lloyd George created for his friend. When they were first introduced years before, he was faced with nine syllables that made up the very Greek name. E-lef-ther-i-os-Ven-i-zel-os. There was no way Lloyd George was going to manage that on a casual basis. So he just called him what he thought it sounded like. Venizelos was not left-handed, but that didn't seem to make a difference.

Eleftherios Venizelos was born on the Greek island of Crete, part of the vast Greek territory that had long been under Turkish rule. Son of a wealthy merchant in a long line of partisans fighting for Greek independence, he was the consummate product of heritage, history and character to evolve into a passionate Greek nationalist. A natural leader schooled in law, Venizelos would become a self-assured, idealistic, informed and convincing politician. Part of his indefatigable energy would come from his study of the greatness of classical Greece. What would become an obsession, he believed his country should reemerge as the great empire it was in the golden age of classical Greece. This obsession would come to be known as the *'Megali Idea'* (Big Idea).

Venizelos remained silent as he followed Lloyd George into his suite, who turned and looked at his Greek friend.

"Well?" Lloyd George asked.

Venizelos went over to his lounge chair and waved his arm toward the chair opposite him. "Sit, David! Can I get you some refreshment?"

"No thank you!" Lloyd George said. "Obviously something is wrong. What is it?"

"David, I think over the years, we have developed a good relationship; one that is built upon friendship, goodwill and the rule of law. We probably have these sentiments because Great Britain is a democracy that is based upon the foundations of classical Greece. This mutual sentiment was the basis of my effort to break neutrality and bring Greece into the war on the Allied side. As you well know, when I sent the Greek forces to *Skra di Legen*, I did so because our Allies, the French were unable to defeat the Bulgarians. Yet, I placed three-hundred-thousand men under the command of a Frenchman, General d'Espèrey. You more than anyone understand it was the capability of the Greek forces that overwhelmed the Bulgarians, and we both know that is why the Germans surprised you all by signing the Armistice early. So without the Greek assault, you would still be at war with Germany and there would be no opening session for me to attend."

Lloyd George remained silent as he had no valid comeback.

"Now, you ask me if I have a problem. Surely you've heard that when Monsieur Clemenceau sent his forces into Odessa last month, he found that he didn't have sufficient troops to fight the Soviets either. What did he do? He came to me and asked if I would send our men to help him in Russia. The war is over, yet he asks me to help him invade Odessa. Did I say no? The war is ended. But our Allies have asked for our help," he paused for effect, "and two Greek Divisions are on their way or already arrived in the Ukraine to support France. Greece has no stake in that dispute and yet we are there to support our ally."

Lloyd George avoided his friend's stare.

"Does it surprise you," Venizelos asked, "that our friends and neighbors, the Serbs, with whom we have many cultural and religious ties, did not have any practical effect in bringing the war to an end, and yet," Venizelos paused again, ". . .and yet, somehow you and Monsieur Clemenceau decided the Serbs should have three votes at the Conference while Greece was only worthy of two."

"Now wait!" Lloyd George stuttered. "You have to understand there are other pressures." Venizelos closed his eyes and raised his hand showing his palm for Lloyd George to stop.

"David, did you think that with all the blood our people spilled to rescue your French friends that we were entitled to fewer votes than a country that had no participation in your victory?"

"No, of course not!" Lloyd George said with much discomfort. "Please! You must keep your eye on the goal. Seats at the table in Paris have nothing to do with the outcome. You have your *Megali*

Idea and you know I agree with you completely. You and I must get rid of the Turks and replace them with Greece in Asia Minor. That is the goal. Whether or not Serbia has three seats or ten seats, it doesn't matter. They were given three seats because there are so many competing interests in Europe, we had to settle on something we could get all those interests to agree on. I am committing to you as your friend. Great Britain is looking to make Greece our powerful ally for the future of Asia Minor, Thrace and the Mediterranean. You have *my* word on that. Do not look at these political musical-chair games as meaningful."

Venizelos, shook his head. "But do you not think that my countrymen will see how you have belittled our accomplishment? Do you think that might have an effect on their support of me?"

Lloyd George smiled at his friend. "Lefty, you are my friend. . . my colleague! I will make certain the world knows that Greece was instrumental in ending the war. They will see that Great Britain and Greece are bound together as one. I give you my word!"

Having placated his friend, Lloyd George headed back to his hotel. He really didn't have time to deal with Greece or any of the other fires that were starting around his ankles. The Balkans, Asia, Asia Minor, all of these disputes were essentially an annoyance, in that the thrust had to be Germany and the reparations that would compensate England and France. He could see no sense in repairing the hinges on the front door when the house was on fire.

Chapter 3.

A week following the opening session, a second plenary session was called to create Wilson's League of Nations. Already, Czechoslovakia had been created, Poland had been re-created and some Baltic states were close to becoming independent of their former masters. In spite of the perceived progress in that first week, events had now exposed a troublesome reality. With so many nations in attendance, the peace process would take much longer than originally thought. During that same time, the revered "peacemakers" (Wilson, Lloyd George and Clemenceau) also realized just how much they disliked each other. While they could all be accused of being liberal politicians, they were from completely different worlds with completely different views. In fact, the only characteristic they shared was an inflated ego.

It was still too early to reduce the enthusiasm that greeted the Peace Conference. In predictable political theater, the delegates unanimously adopted a resolution calling for the creation of the League of Nations. They seemed to ignore contradictions of their advertised global peace, like the French invasion of the Ukraine and the Czech invasion of Teschen just two days before the vote.

Yet President Wilson was ecstatic over the unanimous approval of his pet project. Unfortunately for those in his sphere of influence, as a consequence, Wilson became all the more inflexible and arrogant in his new role as world savior. He smiled openly as the delegates appointed committees to draft a constitution, deal with reparations and respond to territorial disputes. His exuberance would be short-lived.

Things were not as rosy for Wilson back home. He was informed about strong opposition to his League of Nations coming from Republican Senators. Focused more on his world stage in Paris, Wilson appealed to his Senate to delay any discussion of the League until he returned to the U.S. the following month.

Once the League was created, however, the psychology of the peace process began to change. The original purpose of the Conference was to bring together delegates of the victors in order to prepare the terms that would be offered at the real conference with the enemy - which was supposed to follow in order to negotiate the final terms of peace. After all, it had always been done that way in Europe. But it quickly became clear that the problems between the participants were mammoth. There was no longer talk about it being a preliminary to the real conference. The concern now focused on the mountain of problems obstructing their vehicle for peace and, more importantly to these four masters of the universe, the consequence of failure. The preliminary conference of the victors somehow morphed into becoming the real conference.

With tensions and stress rising to crisis levels hardly a month into the Conference, as Clemenceau was being driven to a scheduled meeting with America's Col. House and Britain's Foreign Minister Arthur Balfour, an anarchist, Louis Emile Cottin, jumped alongside his car and fired seven shots at point-blank range. Clemenceau instinctively turned away from the gun allowing one of the bullets to enter his back passing between two ribs but missing any vital organs.

Conscious through the entire incident, Clemenceau was carried back into his house. He was alert when his assistant came to attend to him. Clemenceau looked up at him. "They shot me in the back! They didn't even dare to attack me from the front!" Of course, had Clemenceau not turned away from the gun, he would not have been shot in the back. But the assertion did fit his image of choice-- heroic and larger than life to those who would hear about his comment.

The assailant was seized by an angry crowd who were there to watch Clemenceau's departure. Cottin was carried off and nearly lynched. Word was sent on to Balfour and House who had been waiting for his arrival. When told, with a worried look on his face, Balfour turned to House, "Dear, dear, I wonder what this portends."

With his keen focus on the pulse of the Conference, House replied, "If Clemenceau dies, we'll be back at war within a month."

Both Balfour and House rushed over to Clemenceau's residence. By the time they arrived, he was sitting in an armchair, being attended to by a pretty young nurse. As they entered the room, Clemenceau looked up at his visitors.

"I guess I should celebrate the fellow's marksmanship. A Frenchman who misses his target six times out of seven at point-blank range should seek a different vocation."

Balfour smiled at Clemenceau seeing he was his witty self. "I can see your assailant hasn't diminished your normally rosy disposition."

The nurse trying to comfort him said, "Minister Clemenceau, I thank God for this miracle."

By now, the doting nurse was becoming an annoyance. "Stop it!" Clemenceau said, "If heaven intended to perform a miracle, it would have been better to have prevented my aggressor from shooting me in the first place."

House smiled. "I think he's too mean to die."

Within a week of the attempted assassination, Wilson returned to the United States, arriving in Boston, where he was scheduled to lobby for support of the American people and face his detractors. Meanwhile, Lloyd George returned to London to face his own people and the British Parliament.

Wilson addressed the Boston audience about his fabled League of Nations and how the world would soon enjoy perpetual peace. He used the same idealistic rhetoric he had used in Paris. Neither the American public nor the Senate was impressed. Ignoring the President's earlier appeal, the Senate had in fact met and discussed Wilson's League in his absence. Perhaps because there was a large ocean separating them, the American public was unconvinced that Wilson's League of Nations would or could maintain peace in the world.

With Wilson still in Boston, Senator Henry Cabot Lodge, chairman of the Senate Committee on Foreign Relations, released a 'round-robin' statement, declaring that the composition and workings of his League of Nations were unacceptable, and that the proper time for discussing it would be after the peace treaties had been signed. A round-robin is a statement prepared by a senator and circulated among his colleagues for their consideration. Those who support the stated position indicate their support by signing the paper around the edges of the document, disguising the authorship and the order of signing. By releasing it signed by 39 senators, the statement demonstrated sufficient support to deny Wilson the mandated two-thirds majority required for the ratification of treaties.

After a bruising two weeks of negativity back home, Wilson sailed back to France arriving at the port of Brest. He was despondent over the resistance he was getting back home. As if to depress him more, he was met at the dock by Marshall Ferdinand Foch, the Allied Supreme Commander of the Western Front. Clemenceau had sent him as the French attack dog.

As Wilson disembarked from the ship, Foch handed him a list of demands.

"Mr. President, welcome back to France. I have been working with Premiere Clemenceau and we have prepared this list we believe should be included in any agreement that follows in the working sessions of the committees. The people of France deserve these things and they demand it."

Wilson couldn't believe it. "Couldn't this have waited until I arrived back in Paris? Was it necessary to give me the list the moment I stepped onto French soil?"

"I believe it makes the point of the seriousness of the matter."

Wilson was annoyed. He read the list containing all the lamentations he had heard before: crippling, yet undefined, reparations from Germany for the destruction of French property; an Allied occupation of Germany; and an establishment of a Rheinland buffer zone forbidding any German troops entry in the future. Wilson thought, *You horse's ass!*

"Marshall Foch, I will deal with these matters as they come up in the working sessions. I'm surprised you came all the way up here to tell me what M. Clemenceau has already told me several times. I would think you would be a bit less bold or the world press might be informed how much the Greek victory at *Skra di Legen* led the Germans to quit. To hear the French Press, you singlehandedly masterminded the Allied victory over Germany. Perhaps we should just leave this to be discussed at the Conference."

David Lloyd George sat in on the Council of Ten working session, but his mind was elsewhere. On his first day back in Paris he was troubled by what he witnessed in London a few days earlier. His government had enacted two anti-sedition laws which enabled the state to intern agitators without a trial. As if that wasn't troubling enough, the laws gave judges the absolute power to try cases without a jury. The new laws were meant to respond to discontent in India where Hindus, Muslims and Sikhs were uniting in their opposition to

British rule. Lloyd George was troubled because history had taught him that without a check on power of this sort, abuse would follow. The activist, Mahatma Gandhi had already proclaimed a campaign of passive resistance and non-cooperation. It would only lead to more confrontation.

Once the session was called to order, President Wilson opened with his most recent annoyance aimed at Clemenceau, but addressed his comments to the entire group.

"I find it disturbing that with all we must deal with, the very moment I step on to French soil, I must be accosted by a French delegate who feels he has the authority to hand me a list of demands." Wilson looked at Lloyd George for support of his admonition. But Lloyd George was still thinking about what the new anti-sedition laws could precipitate at home.

"David... David..." Wilson raised his voice, "David, are you with us?"

Lloyd George snapped back to the present. "Sorry! I was trying to work something out in my head. You were saying..."

"There's no sense repeating my episode with Foch. We need to come to some conclusion on the German peace treaty. There are so many diverging interests and claims, I don't see how we can come to an equitable solution with ten members trying to reach a conclusion. I would like to recommend we replace this Council of Ten with a Council of Four. I believe the four of us can better deal with the German issues, rather than resort to endless disputes between the ten of us."

Lloyd George still not totally engaged nodded. "I agree completely. Four reasonable minds can come to a decision more quickly than ten. This thing is beginning to get away from us."

Clemenceau nodded as well "I agree."

The three members looked over at Orlando. Sonnino translated what they had just proposed. Orlando also concluded that four could arrive at a decision more quickly than ten. Since Italy was a major ally in the war, he presumed his claims would be approved by the other three major powers. Orlando smiled and nodded to the group. "*Acconsento!*"

With a bit of arm-twisting, the other members of the Council of Ten conceded the point and with a quick vote, ten became four.

On the seventy-ninth day although they all had made their speeches to the world about the everlasting peace that would come from the Conference through the mythical League of Nations, essentially no progress had been made on the issue of Germany, its reparations, the loss of its colonies, its territories, etc. Meanwhile, the armies of nations in the Conference were invading each other with abandon, as if occupying new territory would entitle the invader to keep his new territory when the treaties were finally signed.

Orlando opened the session which was translated by Sonnino immediately afterward. "Gentlemen, in two weeks, Europe will be celebrating Easter Sunday. And yet, even though we've eliminated six members in order to simplify matters, we have not resolved any claims. More specifically, before we begin to deal with the claims of others, we need to establish and agree on the claims of the major powers. All I hear is talk about fairness, but in the case of Italy, there doesn't appear to be any desire for fairness."

Clemenceau quipped, "I agree with Minister Orlando's assessment. As I have mentioned time after time, Germany must pay for the damage and suffering that she caused. She must pay not only the cost of the war, but the damages to our people. I am demanding that France be permitted to annex the left bank of the Rhine and the Saar Basin. We must be allowed to have a buffer from Germany's aggression in the future. We must decide on these issues before we do anything else. Otherwise, Germany will rise up once again and wreak havoc on the world."

Lloyd George chimed in. "While I'm not prepared to burden Germany with sufficient reparations to bankrupt itself or just take land that is occupied by Germans, I agree with Minister Clemenceau that we must decide on how much Germany must pay."

Wilson kept shaking his head. "I cannot agree with France's aims to destroy any chances of Germany restoring its economic vitality. It would lead to a worldwide recession. I would agree to a measured response on reparations, but not so harsh as to destroy its viability as a sovereign nation."

Clemenceau became agitated. "My dear President Wilson. You sit there with the Atlantic Ocean protecting you from Germany and you begrudge the people of France for wanting security from a repeat of what has already befallen them. I suspect you would have a completely different attitude if, for example, your neighbor to the north, Canada, and therefore Great Britain, had attacked the United States and destroyed half of your country."

Wilson smirked. "I understand your outrage Georges, but that is why my opinion is valuable here. We have not been attacked by Canada. You were attacked by Germany and my opinion is one of objectivity. You are more interested in revenge. Minister Orlando is correct. We have not accomplished anything since we began, and I don't see any improvement coming. I must therefore state, that either we come to a reasonable decision or the United States delegation will return to America and deal with our own problems."

Always the negotiator, Lloyd George thought this was going to a place no one wanted it to go. "Hold on for a moment. I have a suggestion. Let's compromise with a short term solution. We can show the world the progress it needs to see, and not create a worldwide panic. I suggest that the Council allow France to occupy the regions it is concerned with on a temporary basis. We can also state that Germany will be forced to pay reparations for the war and the damage, but the amount will be determined at a later date. Will that be enough to keep our group together?"

The indiscriminate mumbling and nodding prompted Lloyd George, a seasoned negotiator, to verbalize their inaudible gestures. "From your reactions, I conclude that this is acceptable and we have an agreement."

The bold statement seemed to satisfy the group. Clearly, the council's attention was fixated on what to do about Germany. No one seemed to give any notice the issues raised by the rest of the world. The French expected the old tiger to make Germany pay dearly. Lloyd George had won his election based on that promise as well.

Chapter 4.

In Punjab India, more than five-thousand miles away, Brigadier General Reginald Edward Harry Dyer of the British Indian Army stood before his bathroom mirror staring at his ample mustache, his face just inches from the hanging mirror. He had cultivated it for most of his adult life. He very carefully snipped the few hairs that chose to deviate from his desired configuration. Unconsciously, he hummed the *British Grenadiers Song* as he thought about the current brewing dilemma under his watch. Although his current rank was considered temporary, Dyer had enjoyed the rank of Brigadier General for three years now. He was an important military officer in the British Indian Army with the obvious advantage of having been born in Punjab. An Irishman, he entered the British military service upon graduation from the Royal Military College.

As he dressed, he contemplated the new command he had assumed just two days before. He knew there were troubles in Punjab and he was fearful of a mutiny in this region of India. The problem stemmed from the crowds that had been protesting the deportation of agitators from the province. A magistrate acting on orders from the Punjab government had arrested two doctors who were vocal about non-violent protest. When a crowd formed in protest to the arrest, the troops panicked and several protestors were shot. The shooting resulted in a mob that attacked Europeans in the city. Three British bank employees were beaten to death and a teacher, Marcella Sherwood, was injured but rescued by local Indians.

General Dyer was outraged that a European woman had been attacked by local Indian peasants. He had absolutely no patience for anyone who resisted British rule and he was adamant about carrying out the new anti-sedition laws prohibiting public association. His first order was to establish martial law in the city of Amritsar.

Upon arrival at headquarters, he learned of the *Baisakhi Festival* that came to Amritsar each year, in which people from the surrounding villages poured into the city. The festival was being held at *Jallianwala bagh*, which was a six acre enclosed courtyard with five entrances. Even though his official proclamation of martial law had yet to be put into effect, General Dyer decided that this festival was a flagrant violation of the law.

Dyer gathered fifty riflemen and two armored cars outfitted with machine guns arriving at *Jallianwala bagh* in the early evening. He positioned the armored cars and the riflemen in a formation that completely blocked one of the five exits. Although the meeting was a peaceful gathering, General Dyer stood at the gate incensed that the crowd before him was flagrantly assembling in violation of the law. Without any advance warning, he turned his head toward the formation of riflemen and in a calm but stern voice issued his command.

"Open fire!"

The riflemen seeing the crowd was unarmed and orderly, began firing above the heads of the crowd. Dyer immediately noticed that while the crowd began to disperse, no one was falling as the result of being shot. He became quite agitated. His command was being intentionally evaded.

Dyer shouted, "Aim lower! That is the only way these people will learn a lesson about British authority."

Once innocents began falling from gunshot wounds, Dyer calmly watched the panic that ensued. The screams intensified as the crowd desperately ran away from the direction of the guns. But he clearly wasn't satisfied by the lesson. He then instructed his riflemen to aim for the exits toward which most of the frantic civilians had been running.

Dyer then shouted another order. "Machine guns ready!" The gunners atop the armored cars looked nervously at one another as they cocked the guns.

"Fire at will!" he ordered.

Seeing no way to avoid his orders, the two machine guns began firing at the crowd. Much more efficient than riflemen firing one shot at a time, the machine guns cut down rows of screaming people trying to run away from the direction of fire.

The festival attendees had either managed to escape through one of the gates or they were lying dead or wounded on the ground. With no one left to shoot, the guns ceased fire without an order to do so. Dyer seemed quite pleased that the lesson was now appropriate for the violation. In the end, three hundred seventy nine unarmed civilians were slaughtered with no defense other than their outstretched hands. Twelve-hundred more were wounded although there was evidence to indicate the number of casualties was far greater.

On Monday morning, as the working session began, an aide silently handed a note to Lloyd George. Unconsciously, he opened the note and read it. His face went pale. He crushed the note in his hand. He was visibly upset.

Clemenceau seeing his reaction asked, "David, are you alright?"

Startled. Lloyd George looked up at him. "Oh it's just some distressing news from India. It doesn't affect anything we do here today."

Vittorio Orlando did not like what he was hearing from Sonnino's translation of the discussion. It was becoming clear to him that he was mistaken in thinking he would have more influence with four instead of ten delegates. Both Lloyd George and Wilson seemed to be more receptive to the charisma of Greece's Prime Minister Venizelos than to his own claims as promised in the secret Treaty of London. The territories promised to Italy were critical in that Italy was essentially broke and that the fertile lands of southwest Asia Minor would help Italy's ailing agricultural economy. Furthermore, without that promise of land from the Allies, Italy would have sided with Germany in the war. Just because he wasn't a schooled orator like the Greek, he was not about to see Italy get squeezed out of its due.

The main problem was that Greece was promised some of the very same territory that was promised to Italy. Orlando was vehement that as one of the four major powers, Italy's claim should take precedence and be accepted. In Orlando's mind, Greece was just another small country like Romania, or Serbia. Those promises did not hold the weight of his claims. He even questioned whether Sonnino was correctly translating his concerns. The more he took exception, the more they seemed to discount his position.

Faced with his own inability to speak English and his lack of understanding as to how these men could ignore his claims in the face of the Treaty they signed during the war, Orlando stood up and glared at the group. He looked at each one and then spoke.

"*Sto andando! Chiamimi quando siete pronto ad onorare le vostre promesse.*"

He adjusted his suit jacket, stiffened his back and stormed out of the room.

The stunned three Council members simultaneously looked over at Sonnino, perplexed. Wilson shrugged his shoulders. "What on earth did he just say?"

A stunned Sonnino, translated.

"He said. . . 'I'm leaving. Call me when you are ready to honor your promises.' "

Wilson looked at Lloyd George, then at Clemenceau. "I told you he was going to be a moving target. He cannot get his wish, so rather than discuss it, he storms out. Sidney, please go out and retrieve M. Orlando. This is highly irregular."

"I'm sorry," Sonnino replied, "but knowing Minister Orlando, I fear it would be better to let him cool down. He is Sicilian. He is from the old school. When you make a promise. . . you keep it. If not, then a promise is meaningless. He is upset over President Wilson's position that the Treaty of London is no longer valid. I will try to convince him to return tomorrow, but I doubt that I can. I suspect you will have to honor your promise if you intend for him to return."

Finally, no longer willing to hide his contempt for Wilson, Sonnino stood. "President Wilson, after ignoring and violating your own *Fourteen Points* with Tyrol and the Polish, you want to restore your virginity by applying them vigorously where they refer to Italy. Frankly, Mr. President, we expected better from you."

Sonnino left the room.

Lloyd George smiled. "Well, we can't do much about Italy's refusal to continue. I suggest we work things out on our own and then we can deal with Italy when and if she returns to the Council."

Chapter 5.

The morning after 1919's annual May Day celebrations seemed to bring color back to the streets of Paris. Spring was finally in full force and the city was on its way back. At the Quai d'Orsay, the Great War seemed a remote detail next to the work of the peacemakers. Everyone was either busy or looked that way. The nightly parties provided low hanging fruit for the gossip columnists. Delegates were parading around openly with their mistresses, and suddenly there was a new relaxed morality that made Paris even more exciting than before.

This particular Friday working session of the 'Big Three,' now that Italy had walked out, seemed merely a prelude to another entertaining friday night in Paris. For the younger Harvard and Yale-nurtured diplomats assigned to the less-than palatial wing of the Hotel Crillon, the secret trap door that connected to the rear second floor of Maxim's restaurant saw increased traffic. The private rooms on the second floor of Maxim's that had long facilitated secret trysts of its wealthy patrons, now could serve as the *de facto* 'lovers' lane' for American diplomats.

The weighty issues of drawing up new borders of countries were not quite sobering enough to limit the excesses that would follow after the sun set. Unlike the legions of American diplomats, President Wilson, still brooding over Sonnino's parting observation, decided he would openly lobby against Italy. Upon the opening of the session, Wilson presented a report he had received about Italy.

Wilson was indignant. "I guess Minister Orlando's departure was more theater than outrage. I've warned you about Italy's fluctuating loyalties. I see that they're sending ships to both Fiume and Smyrna. Apparently, they've already landed troops at Adalia in southwestern Asia Minor."

Lloyd George egged him on, "What do you propose we do?"

"I can send our largest cruiser, the *George Washington,* to either place. If I do that, it could produce a result. . . and far be it from me to desire that this result should be war. But the attitude of Italy is undoubtedly aggressive; she is a menace to the peace."

Lloyd George added, "I've received a dispatch from Mr. Venizelos where he indicates that there is an understanding in Asia Minor between the Italians and the Turks, who are resuming their policy of terrorism against the Greeks. Mr. Venizelos asks us to send a warship to Smyrna. He proposes to send a Greek ship himself. My opinion is that we should, all three of us, send ships to Smyrna."

The ever-cynical Clemenceau shrugged his shoulders. "A fine start for the League of Nations! Perhaps we should return to the discussion of the German reparations. These issues between Italy and Greece are of minor consequence to what is at stake."

As diplomats dressed up in their finery to celebrate another completed week of work on world peace, one of the young British diplomats was prepared to delay his weekend celebration in order to have dinner with the Greek Prime Minister. Harold Nicholson, born in Tehran to the British Ambassador, Sir Arthur Nicholson, was a bright, Oxford-schooled, wunderkind. While certainly willing to dance the evenings away with young pretty socialites, Nicholson was openly bi-sexual. Intellectually elitist, he was sufficiently savvy to see and understand the ugly unintended consequences of the decisions being contemplated by the three old men in pushing the world toward destruction.

As they dined, Nicholson listened to Venizelos discuss the significance of Italy's provocative act against Greece's claims in Asia Minor. Venizelos was concerned that by unilaterally invading the territory, Italy would steal the prize through unauthorized occupation. Venizelos lamented, "I have received assurances from both Lloyd George and Wilson of their support and comfort, but this can force them into saving face and letting Italy have its way."

Nicholson who spent most of his waking hours truly analyzing the political dance, shook his head from side to side as he sipped his vintage bordeaux. "Mr. Prime Minister, I can see what you fear, but I believe you are quite mistaken. I believe that the Italians have made a foolish wager.

"Even in the Balkans, I can't understand the Italian attitude. They are behaving like children, and sulky children at that. They obstruct and delay everything and evidently think that by making themselves disagreeable on every single point they will force the Conference to give them fat plums to keep them quiet.

Nicholson's eyes were sparkling in that he was confident in the advice he was giving the Greek. "By landing troops on the Asia Minor coast, they've unwittingly handed the prize to Greece. I can assure you neither Wilson nor Lloyd George favors the Italians. In fact, they're quite hostile to Italy. This act will lose them the prize they seek. I suggest you offer up the Greek forces to the Council immediately."

Nicholson's prediction was confirmed on Monday morning's session. President Wilson announced his receipt of a petition from the Greek population of the island of Rhodes, complaining of Italian brutality and massacres.

In a confirmation of his earlier warnings, Wilson said, "We are going to find ourselves in the presence of a *fait accompli*; the Italians will be in Anatolia. The only way to stop them is to settle the question of mandates as soon as possible and to settle the question of the occupation of Asia Minor at once. We should let the Greeks occupy Smyrna. There are massacres starting there with no one to protect the Greek population."

Clemenceau chimed in to help the case, "Do you know how many ships Italy has off Smyrna at the moment? She has seven."

"The best thing, " Lloyd George added, "is for us to decide all this between ourselves before the Italians come back to the conference. Otherwise I am convinced they will beat us to it."

Clemenceau stipulated, "I am quite willing to do so."

Wilson raised his hand to emphasize his point. "It will be impossible for the United States to direct any American troops to occupy any part of Asia Minor. We have a policy of neutrality which would be broken."

The council had been informed that Italy would return the following day. Since no one had reacted to his earlier walkout, Orlando was now forced to return under the stigma of reduced influence.

Lloyd George offered a warning. "I must insist again that we do not let Italy confront us with a *fait accompli* in Asia. We should allow the Greeks to land troops at Smyrna."

President Wilson suggested, "The best methods to stop the Italians are financial. . ."

Lloyd George, shaking his head, interrupted. "Have we ever prevented the Turks from making war, although they have always suffered from lack of money? My opinion is that we should tell Minister Venizelos to send his troops to Smyrna. We will instruct our admirals to let the Greeks land wherever there is a threat of trouble or massacre."

Wilson asked, "Why not tell them to land as of now? Have you any objection to that?"

Lloyd George smiled at the suggestion, "None!"

Clemenceau again chimed in, "Nor have I. But should we warn the Italians?"

Lloyd George replied, "In my opinion, no!"

Clearly, no one in the room had given any thought to consider the unintended consequences of sending the Greek armies to occupy a land where the Greek people had endured more than half a millennium of abuse at the hands of the Ottoman Turks. Their only concern seemed to be fixed on keeping the Italians out of Smyrna.

Clemenceau wrapped it up in a bow, "Concluded! David you should contact your friend, M. Venizelos as soon as possible. Now please, may we return to the details of France's temporary occupation of the Rhineland?"

Once out of the morning session with the decision reached, Lloyd George telephoned Venizelos and instructed him to come to the Quai d'Orsay and attend the afternoon plenary session that was called to approve the terms of the all-important German treaty.

As the hall filled with delegates, Lloyd George spotted Venizelos. He quickly walked over to the Greek and dragged him off to a corner.

"Do you have troops available?" Lloyd George asked.

Venizelos nodded, "We do. But for what purpose?"

"Wilson, Clemenceau and I decided today that you should occupy Smyrna."

Venizelos grew a broad smile. "We are ready."

Lloyd George gave his friend a knowing look as they both understood the importance to Greece of this decision. Then he hurried back to his chair. Venizelos remained in the hall in order to watch the decision materialize. From his chair, Venizelos searched the crowd and spotted Nicholson standing at the back of the hall. He stared at Nicholson with eyes of admiration as Nicholson nodded back with a smile.

Once the session was called to order, Lloyd George stood to speak. "Before we proceed to the subject of the German treaty terms, I have an announcement. We have reached a decision with regard to the occupation of Smyrna. The Council has decided that M. Venizelos shall order his Greek forces to occupy Smyrna as sole agents of the Allied Powers to protect the population and restore order."

A shocked British General Sir Henry Wilson reacted with jaw-dropping surprise. He maneuvered himself to sit down right behind Lloyd George, and whispered in his ear.

"Pardon me sir for this interruption, but I must protest this decision. I believe it is ill-advised and will create devastating consequences. I beg you to reconsider."

Lloyd George smiling, "Nonsense Henry! The Greeks will put a stop to these massacres we've been hearing about."

General Wilson, shaking his head, "Sir, you don't understand. If you send the Greeks to occupy Smyrna, you'll be starting another war for sure."

Lloyd George turned and looked at Wilson in disbelief, "Again, nonsense Henry! Once the Greeks stop the massacres, they will oversee the peace in addition to helping us keep the Straits open. The Turks cannot stand up to the overwhelming Greek force. Don't worry about this. I'm on top of it."

With the approval of terms for the German treaty now behind them, the Council allocated some time to address the Ottoman problem as there were additional outcries from the staffs about the decision to allow a Greek occupation of Smyrna. Harold Nicolson was one of those called to the session to produce the Asia Minor maps he had created.

Forced to be a silent minor party at the session, Nicholson watched in amazement as the bizarre scene played out in front of him. Arthur Balfour, Britain's Foreign Minister seeing it was Nicholson's maps that had mesmerized the group, whispered to Nicholson standing next to him, "Those three all-powerful, all-ignorant men sitting there and carving continents, with only a child to lead them."

Nicholson was so taken by his own disbelief, and Balfour's comment once the session ended, he rushed back to his hotel room to write down in his diary, the incredible scene he had just witnessed. He wrote:

'A heavily furnished study with my huge map on the carpet. Bending over it (bubble, bubble toil and trouble) are Clemenceau, Lloyd George and PW (President Wilson). They have pulled up armchairs and crouch low over the map. . . They are cutting the Baghdad railway. Clemenceau says nothing during all of this. He sits at the edge of his chair and leans his two blue-gloved hands down upon the map. More than ever does he look like a gorilla of yellow ivory. . . It is appalling that these ignorant and irresponsible men should be cutting Asia Minor to bits as if they were dividing a cake. . . Isn't it terrible, the happiness of millions being discarded in that way? Their decisions are immoral and impracticable. . . These three ignorant men with a child to lead them. . . The child, I suppose, is me. Anyhow, it is an anxious child.'

Nicholson recalled another moment after the council moved to the dinner table. He wrote:

'I spread out my map on the dinner table and they all gather 'round. Lloyd George, A. J. Balfour, Milner, Henry Wilson, Mallet and myself. Lloyd George explains that Orlando and Sonnino are due in a few minutes and he wants to know what he can offer them. I suggest the Adalia zone, with the rest of Asia Minor to France. Milner, Mallet and Henry Wilson oppose it: A.J. Balfour neutral.

'We are still discussing when the flabby Orlando and the sturdy Sonnino are shown into the dining room. They all sit round the map. The appearance of a pie about to be distributed is thus enhanced. Lloyd George shows them what he suggests. They ask for Scala Nova as well. 'Oh no!' says Lloyd George, 'you can't have that. It's full of Greeks!' He goes on to point out that there are further Greeks at Makri, and a whole wedge of them along the coast towards Alexandretta. 'Oh no,' I whisper to him, 'there are not many Greeks there.' 'But yes,' he answers, 'don't you see it's colored green?' I then realize that he mistakes my map for an ethnological map, and thinks the green means Greeks instead of valleys, and the brown means Turks instead of mountains.'

Once he was done with his diary, Nicholson immediately wrote a note to his wife:

'Isn't it terrible, the happiness of millions being decided in that way, while for the last two months we were praying and begging the Council to give us time to work out a scheme?

Their decisions are immoral and impracticable. . .

The funny thing is that the only part where I do come in is the Greek part, and here they have gone beyond, and dangerously beyond, what I suggested in my wildest moments.'

Chapter 6.

The day dawned with a clear, sunny sky suggesting a fine spring day to commemorate an important milestone in history. The entire city of Smyrna on Asia Minor's western coast was tinted blue and white from all the Greek flags that hung from windows and every conceivable post on the streets, especially the quayside. For today would mark the milestone when Smyrna would once again fall under the control of Greece.

It had been almost six hundred years since the city had been conquered by the Ottoman Turks. Before then, it had been a Greek city since the eleventh century B.C. The Turkish overthrow ended twenty-five hundred years under Greek rule. These last six hundred years had been especially difficult for the culture that essentially civilized the ancient world.

Under Ottoman rule Greeks, Armenians and Jews were considered second-class citizens. Perhaps not as humiliating as slaves or criminals, they were technically considered citizens of the Ottoman Empire, but were not equals to Muslims. They did have a right to worship their own religion but beyond that were subject to discrimination. For example, a Greek, Armenian or Jew could not testify against a Muslim, as such testimony was legally inadmissible. They were forbidden to carry weapons or even to ride on the back of a horse, making them taller than a standing Muslim. They could not live in a house that overlooked the house of a Muslim. They were heavily taxed in order to enjoy their second-class status and if they violated the Ottoman rule, the punishment ranged from heavy fines to execution. Any Christian could convert to Islam, but conversion in the other direction was punishable by death.

But today was different. In Smyrna, today would once again mark the date where a Greek, an Armenian or a Jew was legally equal to a Muslim in every way. To the Greeks of Smyrna, it was a deeply moving occasion. The fulfillment of a dream dreamt by countless generations of Anatolian Greeks. From the thousands of Christians

2. *Greek Smyrniotes celebrate the arrival of Greek occupation forces on 15 May 1919.*

gathering on the quayside, the city had the feel of a public holiday. The crowd was giddy with anticipation of what was about to happen.

The day before, a detachment of Greek troops had arrived to serve as crowd control. But as the first plumes of smoke on the horizon came into the crowd's view, those troops were unable to hold back the excited Smyrniotes, as they pushed to get a better look. By 7 a.m., the now visible Greek transport ships, led to cheers and tears of joy from the crowd.

By 7:30 a.m., the English-built Greek ocean liner *Patris* approached the quay with the first Greek soldiers. The *Patris* had been shuttling Greek emigrants from Piraeus to New York's Ellis Island since 1909, but today she would land the first Greek occupation forces in Smyrna. A bugle sounded from the bridge of the *Patris* and was responded to by blasts from the ship's horn and cheers from the jubilant crowd.

As the first soldiers emptied onto the quay, owing to the significance of the event, Chrysostomos, the Greek Orthodox Archbishop of Smyrna, dressed in his finest vestments, approached them. The regiment's commander, Colonel Stavrianopoulos, ordered the troops to stand at attention. With tears in his eyes, the Archbishop blessed the soldiers, as thousands of onlookers made the sign of the cross over and over again. Clearly moved by the occasion, Chrysostomos knelt and embraced the regiment flag of the troops he had blessed and openly wept. Then he rose and smiled through his tears to wish them success in their efforts.

Chrysostomos had ample grounds to be overcome with emotion. His entire life prior to this moment had been dedicated to the church and overcoming the suffering of the Greek people under Ottoman rule.

Born in the seaside village of Triglia on the southern coast of the Sea of Marmara, Chrysostomos was drawn to the church at an early age. He was educated at the Theological School of Halki, becoming the protégé of the Bishop Constantine who later was elevated to Ecumenical Patriarch of Constantinople.

Chrysostomos followed his mentor to Constantinople where he was ordained as a priest. His work in the church was rewarded in 1902 by his appointment as the Metropolitan Bishop of Drama in Macedonian Greece which had a predominantly Greek population. It was in Drama, seeing the persecution of his flock, that Chrysostomos under his priestly robes, became a spiritual leader of Greek bands of partisans who fought against his Turkish oppressors as well as Bulgarian revolutionaries.

Soon after arriving at his post, his nationalistic leanings and support of the partisan bands quickly earned him the ire of the ruling Ottomans. Faced with the obvious contradiction of his role as a bishop and the perception of being a partisan, his precarious situation required him to have a bodyguard. Considering the distance from his home and friends, the only person he could count on to protect him was a blood relative, his cousin Christos Papavasiliou. As a result, both were pursued by the Ottomans as well as the revolutionary Bulgarians.

In 1907, with the British Empire's renewed colonial interest in the Balkans, the newly-appointed British Consul General, Sir Harry Lamb, lobbied the Ottomans to remove the bishop's influence in Macedonia. Shortly afterward, Chrysostomos was exiled from Drama by the Turkish authorities.

Having spent the duration of the Great War in and around Constantinople, once the Armistice was signed, Chrysostomos was returned to prominence as the Archbishop of Smyrna, only this time, in the waning hours of Ottoman rule. His lifelong struggle against the oppressors of the Greek people was finally being rewarded as he knelt on the quay at Smyrna.

Reacting to the adoring crowd of cheering Greek Smyrniotes, some of the *Evzones*, the elite Greek mountain fighting forces, caught up in the monumental significance of the moment, formed a circle, placing their hands on each other's shoulders and spontaneously began a Greek circle dance. It was an expression of overwhelming joy.

Chrysostomos walked over to Colonel Stavrianopoulos. Out of respect and long-standing custom, the commander bowed and kissed the ring on the outstretched hand of the Archbishop and then crossed himself by joining his thumb, index and middle finger (a symbol of the trinity). Chrysostomos then blessed the commander with a gestured sign of the cross made in the air. He recited a blessing to the colonel and then gestured him to stand up straight.

In his native Greek the Archbishop said, "Colonel, the people of Smyrna are grateful for your sacrifice and protection. As you can see this is an important moment for them. I ask that you allow me to lead these brave men through the streets so that our people may cheer for them and show their appreciation for them. I want our people to embrace the fulfillment of their dreams."

3. *Archbishop Chrysostomos taken in 1920.*
Photo courtesy of C. Papavasiliou.

"It will be my honor!" the colonel said as he saluted the Archbishop.

While the moment was a powerful one for the Greek people of Smyrna, no one, especially the Archbishop or the Colonel even considered the unintended consequences of what they were about to do. For while the Greeks were celebrating the end to six-hundred years of subjugation, the Turkish Muslim population was watching the end of six-hundred years of lesser humans bowing to their superiority. People that prior to today, were not permitted to look at them directly as equals, were by virtue of four old men in Paris about to become their masters.

Oblivious to the likely visceral reaction of the Muslims at the south end of the quayside, Archbishop Chrysostomos began to lead the troops down the cobblestone street, lined with cheering Greeks who broke out and flanked the troops in a joyous grand parade.

As they passed the south end of the quay, which happened to be where the Turkish military barracks were located, a single shot was fired from the direction of the barracks into the formation of marching Greek soldiers. A single Greek soldier stumbled and fell to the ground. The shot triggered the pent-up emotions of centuries of silent humiliation and outrage. Pandemonium ensued. The armed Greek soldiers began a thirty-minute continuous barrage of gunfire into the Turkish barracks.

Finally, the Turkish officers waved a white handkerchief out the door of the barracks, while they shouted, "*Teslim ediyoruz. . .* We surrender!"

The colonel saw the handkerchief and yelled, "$Παύσατε$ $πυρ$... Cease fire!"

Slowly, the barrage of shots diminished and finally ended. After a moment of silence, the Turkish officers, still waving their handkerchiefs, walked out of the barracks followed by the soldiers with their hands raised above their heads.

The parade of triumphant Greek troops suddenly morphed into a different kind of parade. One where the armed Greek troops were leading the unarmed Turkish troops through the same street. While the Muslim population saw the event as a horrible overreaction to a single shot, the Greek population saw it as a lesson that centuries of maltreatment were no longer to be tolerated. Chrysostomos, was shattered by what he witnessed. He looked at the crowd and saw vengeance in their eyes. He was unable to quell the emotions of the crowd-turned-mob.

The Greek troops ordered their Turkish prisoners to hold their hands on their heads and walk in formation with Greek troops surrounding them. The colonel saw they had collected too many Turkish prisoners. He feared the worst was about to happen. He ordered the prisoners to be marched back up the quay to be loaded onto the *Patris* which would serve as a temporary prison ship, thereby reducing the chance of things getting worse.

The procession headed back up the quay, with Greek troops prodding their prisoners with their bayonets and the butts of their rifles. The Greek crowd that was moments ago, flanking their heroes in a parade, were now flanking the prisoners, taunting them with slurs and warnings of how they would pay for past ills.

As they walked back up the quay, a Turkish soldier, probably out of frustration, blurted out a remark in reaction to the butt of a rifle jammed into his back. Like a trigger, some Greek civilians jumped the soldier, knocked him to the ground and began to beat and kick him. As he begged for mercy, one of the civilians beating him became enraged. Perhaps he was one who had seen a daughter raped or mutilated by a Turk. Perhaps he was just a Greek who had been saving up his rage since childhood. He pulled a knife from his boot and stabbed the soldier.

The attack was a turning point. Suddenly, civilians were pulling knives. They cut and stabbed. It was a frenzy of mad men now intent on revenge for all of the humiliating experiences they had to endure their entire lives. Before the colonel could stop the madness, a few dozen unarmed Turkish soldiers were mutilated by the crowd. Greek soldiers, probably wanting to join in, were held back by their orders, but felt no inclination to stop the civilians. Finally, the madness subsided and the butchering ceased.

The procession of prisoners finally resumed as they marched toward the *Patris*. From other warships that had arrived at the quay, Allied officers now watched as the Greek soldiers prodded their prisoners with their rifles. In order to further humiliate the Turkish troops, at gunpoint, they were ordered to shout 'Long live Venizelos' and 'Long live Greece.'

Instead of a victorious moment of pride, the celebration became an example of Greek brutality that would be used against them. Not satisfied with a brief moment of revenge, bands of Greek civilians, took to the streets of the Turkish section and began to loot. With the prevailing disorder, now bands of thugs, both Turkish and Greek, took advantage of the moment to loot and plunder neighborhoods. These thugs were mostly the underbelly of every society who show no preference as to who will be their victim.

The disorder and madness continued into the next day. Americans and other European witnesses, unaccustomed to such brutality took away a view that Greeks were every bit as brutal as the Turks had been known to be throughout the centuries. What the Americans and Europeans saw as brutality, the Greeks viewed as long overdue equal justice. In the end, more than three hundred Muslims and one hundred Greeks were killed in the melee.

Colonel Stavrianopoulos was clearly overwhelmed by the events and unable to get control of the situation. It would be another six days before the Greek High Commissioner would arrive and begin to restore order.

Chapter 7.

The hasty decision to allow Greek forces to occupy Smyrna created a much larger problem than it solved. From its perch in Paris and based solely upon keeping Italy from acting unilaterally to occupy Smyrna, the Council had foolishly fueled the hatred and troubled history between Greeks and Turks. Perhaps they might have realized the foolishness of their decision, had they not been so preoccupied with punishing Germany.

Failing to secure Italy's interests as its representative in Paris, Vittorio Orlando resigned as Prime Minister just days before the much-heralded German Treaty was signed. Probably due to his inability to speak English, Orlando was never able to personally make a convincing argument for his country.

Six months after the opening of the Peace Conference, the Treaty of Versailles was signed in the Versailles Palace's Hall of Mirrors. Ironically, the Treaty was signed in the very same room where forty-five years earlier, the German Empire had come into existence. Although the terms for Germany would in hindsight, be as disastrous as the Council's decision on the Greek occupation of

4. *Georges Clemenceau signing the Treaty of Versailles in the Hall of Mirrors.*

Smyrna, at least for the moment it was done, and in the minds of most delegates, the most important work of the Conference was completed. With the signing of the Treaty, the Council could now concentrate on those pesky minor issues like the dismantling of the Ottoman Empire, the division of the Austro-Hungarian Empire, and most importantly, the newly enticing prospect of Mesopotamian oil.

Little more than two weeks after the signing at Versailles, now faced with a hostile Italy on the Council, Prime Minister Venizelos was summoned to Paris to respond to the Italian claim that his forces were violating the limits of the Greek occupation as specified by the Council. As the meeting was called to order, Lloyd George refused to make eye contact with Venizelos as he gave the opening statement.

"Mr. Prime Minister, thank you for appearing here today. I believe it is important that we get to the bottom of the allegations that have been brought forward by Minister Tittoni and the Italian delegation. I'm hopeful that we can clear this all up.

"In general, it has been alleged that your forces are routinely breaching the line we established as the Greek zone, and more specifically, that your artillery has been firing on Italian positions in the Meander Valley. I will ask you if this is in fact accurate, and more importantly, why you would engage in such a provocative activity?"

Venizelos, looking alternatively down at his notes and across at Lloyd George, presented his case.

"Esteemed members of the Council. Much has been made of the problems that occurred during the first days of our occupation. I have already apologized for the breakdown in our handling of the matter. But the criticism of our actions seems to ignore the fact that our troops were first fired upon by someone inside the Turkish barracks, and that this event occurred on the very first day our people were once again considered equals with their Muslim counterparts after hundreds of years of servitude. I suspect an objective observer would conclude that the provocative activity was in fact, the initial shot fired from the Turkish barracks.

"Minister Lloyd George, I ask you to consider how the people of the British colonies in the New World reacted to the yoke of a relatively tame British King George III.

"President Wilson, I'm sure you can appreciate the desire of your forefathers to be released from the yoke of the British monarchy. And that domination was from a monarch who shared the same culture.

"And you Minister Clemenceau, is it possible to ignore the violent creation of your own republic as a consequence of indifference and the decadence of your own aristocracy?

"Finally, Minister Nitti, how would the world look today, had Rome not descended into decadence? In this regard, I would point out that since our High Commissioner arrived in Smyrna, any violence against the Muslim population has been met with severe punishment.

"I would also state in my defense, that in his report last month, U. S. Consul Horton wrote that 'strong and well-armed Turkish forces had driven a Greek garrison of eleven thousand men from Bergama, about fifty-five miles from Smyrna, in attacks along the retreat route such that only six hundred Greek troops survived."

Venizelos paused for effect and scanned his accusers.

He continued, "Considering that the retreat route runs right through the Italian zone, and these heavily-armed Turks, are supposed to be a vanquished force in the process of destroying their weaponry, I would ask that Minister Nitti ask his Foreign Minister Tittoni, *who* is supplying this rebel force who seem to be operating in the Italian sector with perfect liberty?

"When the Council gave us their hasty approval to occupy Smyrna, it had not yet defined the Greek zone of occupation. And yes, in response to reports from towns and villages that were being attacked by Turkish *chettes*, we did respond by fanning out in three directions to protect the mostly-Greek populations. But then, when the Italian delegation returned from their earlier protest walkout, the Council finally set the limits of the Greek zone at three kilometers outside the city. That arbitrary decision instantly placed us in violation of a zone that didn't exist moments before.

"You will recall that last month, I had requested the Council to formally extend the Greek zone, so that our forces could repel these attacks. You will also recall that I signed the agreement with Italy-defined zones, under protest, because attacks were being launched by the Turks from the Italian zone with encouragement and supplies from Italy."

Clemenceau raised his gloved hand.

"Minister Venizelos, could you have not fallen back to within the Greek zone, before you approached the Council for a decision on extending the zone?"

Venizelos responded, "Minister Clemenceau, I suppose that from a vantage point overlooking the *Avenue des Champs-Élysées*, it seems a simple matter of moving our troops back from their positions in order to not violate the zone. But please do not minimize the fact that we are responding to people who are being mutilated and massacred by Turkish forces, with the connivance of the Italian authorities, and using the Italian zone as a base from which to execute sorties into the Greek zone.

"That is why I am asking . . . no begging, that the Council either provide a more realistic demarkation of the Greek zone, based upon the Turkish attacks, or give us the liberty of responding to these attacks wherever the Turks retreat to. Under the present condition, they have a nearby safe haven that allows them freedom to pick off innocents and then return to the Italian zone unmolested."

Clemenceau was unmoved by Venizelos' explanation. "Minister Venizelos, it appears the Greek view is quite different from the Italian view. Rather than this Council attempt to figure out whose version is more accurate, I'm going to request the Council to vote to require Minister Nitti and yourself to go off in some room and resolve your disputes between one another. I want you to come to an agreement on where the lines should be drawn and what the Greek occupation should be restricted to.

"But, aside from the two of you reaching a comprehensive understanding on the conflicting Greek and Italian territorial claims, I am still very troubled by the reported Greek atrocities committed during the occupation in May of this year. Therefore I am proposing the formation of an Interallied Commission of Enquiry to Smyrna. We need to determine if the Greek occupation forces are using their Allied mandate in order to commit atrocities on Muslim innocents."

Chapter 8.

The eighth of November 1919 proved to be a difficult day for the Greek Prime Minister. Entering the Quai d'Orsay, he alternated between worrying that the Council would be unified in their condemnation of Greece, and hoping Lloyd George would defend Greece's role in Asia Minor. Today, the Council was scheduled to take up the report submitted by the Interallied Commission of Enquiry on Smyrna.

Venizelos had been ordered to appear in front of the Commission mainly because the report was highly unfavorable to Greece. He feared the worst as the entire report was limited to the events of the Greek landing and the violence that it precipitated.

Venizelos was incensed that the tone of the entire report was critical of Greek actions, while dismissive of similar, but more frequent Turkish actions as isolated incidents. As he took his seat, he sensed the hearing was intended as theater for the world press. He feared that the motives of the Council had changed since he was first given the mandate to occupy Smyrna. Subsequent to the occupation, both Italy and France had switched their alliance to the Turkish cause, and he feared the Americans had joined the British in coveting the Turkish oil fields of Mesopotamia as fuel for their navies. He could only hope that his willingness to assist the British and French militarily when asked and their promises of loyalty would rescue him from the highly-biased report.

Clemenceau called the hearing to order.

"At my request, the Interallied Commission of Enquiry to Smyrna was formed to investigate the alleged atrocities perpetrated by the occupying Greek forces and Greek civilians under their protection against Muslim Turks. In that effort, the Commission held forty-six meetings, heard testimony from one-hundred-seventy-five witnesses from all nationalities and visited sites in and around Smyrna, including those in the Italian zone. The Commission was made up of one representative from each of the Council of Four and a non-voting observer from the Greek delegation. Rear Admiral

Bristol represented the United States. France was represented by General Bunoust. General Hare was the representative for Great Britain. Representing Italy was General Dall'olio and Colonel Mazarakis of Greece was a non-voting observer.

"Regarding witness testimony, when there was contradictory testimony between Greek and Turk, additional testimony was sought from French, English and Italian witnesses. In summary, the report concluded that:

> 1. If the military occupation was for the purpose of security and public welfare, then the occupation should not have been entrusted to Greece, but should have been the mandate of Allied troops.
>
> 2. The occupation should not continue by Greece alone, unless the Council decides that the country be annexed to Greece.
>
> 3. Said annexation is contradictory of Council's principles of protecting nationalities, because of Turkish majorities outside of the Smyrna zone.

"As a result of this inquiry, the Commission has recommended that termination of the Greek occupation was in order as well as the rejection of any Greek claims in Asia Minor."

For the first time since the Conference opened, Clemenceau used the report to openly question the Greek presence in Asia Minor.

"Minister Venizelos," Clemenceau said, "this report is highly critical of your efforts to keep order in Asia Minor. It appears that you would not be able to continue in that effort without the addition of Allied troops, command and control. Therefore, I ask you directly, does Greece have the ability to make the necessary military and financial efforts without any support of the Allies, until Turkey is completely pacified?"

The question put Venizelos in a corner. Clemenceau essentially went on the record eliminating the financial and military support that was promised to him and was looking for him to accept that condition going forward or evacuate all Greek troops from Asia Minor. By virtue of the Allied mandate to occupy Smyrna, Greece had totally over-committed herself to Asia Minor. He was left with only one option.

"Minister Clemenceau, Greece maintains an army of twelve divisions. We have no fear of Turkey's seventy-thousand-man army.

Greece fully intends to pacify Asia Minor with or without Allied military or financial support, and will justify your decision to choose Greece for this mission."

With that statement, Venizelos saw his financial support from the Allies evaporate and now wondered if that was the whole purpose of the exercise in the first place. Now Greece would have to win the peace on its own. Once the session adjourned, Venizelos walked over to where Lloyd George was standing. He asked, "David, may I speak with you for a moment?"

"Certainly, Lefty. I'm sorry that was such a difficult session for you, but the report was pretty critical of Greece."

"David, I was hoping you would have pointed out some of the problems with the Commission. Admiral Bristol is a known supporter of the new Turkish government, a supposedly vanquished enemy. Colonel Mazarakis was excluded from the Commission's meetings on the grounds that he would intimidate Turkish witnesses. How are we supposed to defend our actions when we have no access to our accusers? I certainly believed you would come to our rescue when the discussion about the shot fired from the Turkish barracks was dismissed as a valid provocation for my troops firing on the barracks. There was no such provocation when your General Dyer opened fire on innocent British subjects in Punjab killing hundreds and wounding thousands. Everything in the report seems to have been taken out of context and yet, you remained silent."

Lloyd George was visibly uncomfortable. "Lefty, I'm in a difficult position. I was hoping you would understand that we are walking a fine line here. Please, make what changes you must so that you can pacify the country. That is the only way, I can help you annex Asia Minor to Greece."

At that moment, Mr. Balfour from the British delegation, seeing his colleague in a difficult circumstance, approached them. "Minister Lloyd George, I apologize for the intrusion but I must remind you that you have a private meeting you must attend during the adjournment."

Lloyd George accepting the rescue, "I'm sorry Lefty, but I have to go. Let's talk later in the week and see if we can figure some way to make this better."

Later that month, President Wilson experienced his own equally bad day. For after fifty-five days of debate, the United States Senate voted down the resolution to approve the Treaty of Versailles.

By doing so, they also voted down the approval for joining the League of Nations. Thus, Wilson's transformational dream of world peace through his idyllic League simply disappeared.

Chapter 9.

General Mustapha Kemal had come a long way since his childhood in Thessaloniki (Salonica) in northern Greece. Born in 1881 to Turkish parents, ignoring his parents wishes for him to learn a trade, young Mustapha enrolled in the Monastir Military High School. Then he attended the Ottoman Military Academy. He clearly had military aspirations, in that by 1905, he had graduated from the Ottoman Military College.

Following graduation, he divided his time between his various military assignments and his membership in the radical Committee of Union and Progress. These activities would shape his future views about his country. He was clearly a savvy military tactician as his commands tended to produce victories. Beginning with the Italo-Turkish War, then the Balkan Wars and finally in the Great War as part of the Central Powers, he managed to prove himself as a capable and successful military commander.

Following the Armistice, Kemal was chosen to reorganize what was left of the Ottoman army and oversee the dismantling of the military weaponry. Based on his strong nationalist views, he instead used the assignment to organize a resistance movement that he called the Turkish War of Independence. Specifically, he advanced a philosophy that would become known as 'Turkey for the Turks.' Essentially, he concluded that the way to make Turkey independent was to rid itself of Christians who had dominated commerce within the Ottoman Empire for centuries.

By November 1919, Kemal became outraged by Clemenceau's ordering the French occupation of Cicilia in southern Asia Minor. French troops established a base in the Armenian city of Marash. The city, mostly populated by Armenians who had been deported by the Turks before and during the Great War, had returned home based upon the Allied assurances of safety from future Turkish atrocities.

Acting on Kemal's order, Turkish forces overwhelmed the small French presence, forcing them to evacuate Marash. The French defeat was a major embarrassment to Clemenceau in Paris, but proved significantly worse for the Armenian population whose only crime was their desire to return to their homeland.

From his field office, Kemal called for his lead captain, Kiliç Ali Bey, a Kurd he had recruited to organize the tribal *chettes* into an army. The captain entered his general's office and saluted his commander. Kemal returned the salute.

"Well, Captain, it looks as though the French have once again done what they do best. Surrender or retreat!"

The captain replied. "Yes General!"

"We now need to eliminate the vermin that the Allies convinced to return to our lands. I think they need some encouragement that will convince them to leave. Perhaps they need to believe that if they stay, they will not survive. Do you understand?"

"Yes sir!"

"Report to me, when Marash is free of Armenians."

"Yes sir!"

Upon hearing news of the French defeat in Cicilia by the Kemalist forces, a new report was released exposing the wholesale massacre of thousands of Armenians in the Marash area. The report was extremely disturbing to British General Lord George Milne who had been assigned to monitor the disarming and relocation of Turkish armies. Fearing the growing power of General Kemal, Milne decided Great Britain make a strong statement to discourage the fervor of Turkish nationalism that was now springing up. He understood that the Allies did not possess a force sufficient to control all of Asia Minor against the Turkish Nationalists, but he was confident they could at least occupy and control its capital.

In a pre-dawn coup, Milne marched his forces into Constantinople, taking over the public buildings and telegraph offices, and arresting Turkish Nationalists thereby preempting the Nationalist forces based in Ankara (Angora), from taking back Constantinople. The process was messy at best. Turkish forces and students resisted arrest. Students were killed by soldiers of the British Indian regiments. In the end however, the British now occupied and controlled the capital.

Three days after the British occupation of Constantinople, Secretary of War, Winston Churchill seeing that Great Britain was stretching its own military to the limit, realized that Britain did not have sufficient manpower to enforce the Turkish treaty if the Turks, in fact, were unwilling to accept it. Churchill also realized that the only major military force in Asia Minor belonged to Greece. With that reality, he felt compelled to confront Venizelos. Churchill asked General Sir Henry Wilson to summon Venizelos to a meeting. The request triggered a memory for the general reminding him of the moment at the Conference when he warned Lloyd George about the consequence of sending the Greek forces to occupy Smyrna. The moment was a silent affirmation of his own understanding of the game of peacemaking.

5. Winston Churchill speaking in 1916.

The meeting was arranged in such a way that Churchill and Wilson sat across a conference table from an isolated Venizelos. Truly understanding the significance of the British vulnerability, Churchill was characteristically resolute in his manner. He looked across the table at Venizelos, while his signature cigar bounced up and down between his teeth. Fostering a heightened drama, Churchill slowly removed the cigar before he spoke in his signature monotone.

"Minister Venizelos, I called you here today because I want you to be fully aware of Great Britain's position regarding your occupation of Asia Minor. I must caution you that Great Britain cannot, and will not help you with any British troops in either Thrace or in Asia Minor."

Following Churchill's lead, General Wilson decided to be even more direct.

"Minister Venizelos, you must understand that there will be *no* help! Neither men nor money, in the future. Our occupation of Constantinople and the deficiencies of the Greek efforts against the Turkish Nationalists have created this emergency. Do you fully understand that this is the position of the British government?"

Venizelos was stunned, but tried to keep his emotions hidden. "Mr. Secretary, have you spoken to Minister Lloyd George about this decision?"

"There is no need," Churchill replied. "M. Lloyd George does not have any oversight on our troop deployments or our purse strings. You may consider me as the authority on this issue."

Emboldened by his earlier warnings being proved correct, General Wilson interjected, "I don't want you to use any misunderstanding in the future as an explanation that you were unaware of this policy. Frankly, I think you are doing your country a great disservice by engaging in this war against the Turks. It appears this war with the Turks could last another ten years and cripple Greece in the process."

Churchill turned and looked daggers at Wilson. The purpose of the meeting was not to discourage Venizelos from fighting the Turks. He just wanted him to fight knowing that there would be no help from Great Britain. Churchill's stare caused the general to cower in his chair. Venizelos seeing the dynamic in front of him tried to appear calm. He attempted to give the impression of Greek strength without discussing numbers. "I must tell you General that I completely disagree with your every word. I believe Greece can overtake Thrace as well as Smyrna. . . by breeding alone. By the end of the century I believe our population will exceed that of the entire Turkish Empire."

The comment fell flat and produced no effect. The meeting seemed to go nowhere.

Then Churchill said, "I understand that David calls you 'Lefty'. . . is that right?"

Venizelos nodded.

"Well, Lefty, let me get down to the essence of why I called you here today. As the British Secretary of State for War, I was wondering . . . Given that Britain cannot provide any support to you, do *you* believe Greece can defeat the Turks if Kemal refuses to accept the treaty?"

Venizelos looked at Churchill and thought, *Oh! He's seeking my reassurance that we can win!* He replied, "Mr. Secretary, Greece's armies completely dwarf the Turkish forces. The reason for our difficulties has been the fact that the Turks find sanctuary in the Italian zone. As soon as we try to respond to their attacks, the Council informs us we are violating the Greek zone. If you will just take off our restrictions, untie our hands, we will deal with the Turks and the Treaty will pass with much more severe terms than are currently being discussed. We do not need British assistance. If the

British cannot afford to help us, we will do it ourselves. It is our people that they are killing and we will not stand for it."

Chapter 10.

In April 1920, almost a year after the Greek forces occupied Smyrna, delegates of the Allied Supreme Council with the exception of the United States, finally gathered in San Remo Italy to put finishing touches on the peace treaty with Turkey. While there, Great Britain and France used the opportunity to also sign the San Remo Oil Agreement, the result of several years of negotiation between the two Council members.

The treaty with Turkey was quite harsh for the Turks, which is why Winston Churchill had become nervous that the new Turkish nationalism would prompt a rejection of its terms. He was more disturbed by the fact that the new oil agreement publicly set out the lucrative terms of an earlier, *secret* agreement between Great Britain and France, negotiated during World War I. Clearly, its exposure to the light of day smelled as bad as it looked. Originally called the Sykes-Picot Agreement after the agents who negotiated it, the terms would secure a portion of the total oil production within the newly-created Iraq for France, and in return, give Britain permission for a British pipeline to cross French territory and control a port facility on the Mediterranean.

It was one thing to force harsh terms on the Turks. It was another for Allied powers to lock in future treasure from the spoils of war. The addition of the oil discussions came as no surprise to the U.S. delegation, in that six months earlier, the U.S. State Department had learned from its Ambassador John Davis in London, that secret discussions were being held. Washington was concerned that these discussions were being held in secret, preventing American diplomats from verifying their nature.

Earlier in April, when Hugh Wallace, Ambassador in Paris learned from a confidential source that the Anglo-French syndicate had been a reality for a year, the obvious conclusion was that Great Britain and France were attempting to keep America out of the middle eastern oil fields, and to divide up the oil assets between themselves. While incensed over the discovery, the Americans could not mention the knowledge of the deal, as it was still a secret and any mention would expose their sources.

Clearly, peace as a residue of the Peace Conference was welcomed as a side benefit, but the actions of the Council members exposed their true intentions. Aside from the lofty rhetoric, the entire board game of peacemaking showed itself to be little more than a clever disguise for France and England to grab and lock-in as much treasure as they could for their own future.

Before the ink was dry on the ill-conceived results of San Remo and in recognition of its supreme irony, Winston Churchill wrote, 'At last, peace with Turkey, and to ratify it, war with Turkey!' But neither Churchill, nor any of the old men on the Council had any intention of returning to war, and the Turks knew it.

Shortly after the Conference closed, its terms were made public. The terms confirmed that Smyrna would go to the Greeks; Armenia would become free and independent; Anatolia would be partitioned between France and Italy; the Turkish army would be reduced to a token force under Allied supervision; and the Dardanelles would come under international control.

Predictably, the Russian Bolsheviks seeing no benefit from San Remo, immediately came out in support of Kemal. The Italians, noting the difference between what they expected and what they received, were disenchanted seeing so much go to Greece. The French were displeased because what was solely theirs before, would now be shared with others.

It took only a month for General Kemal and the Turks to turn their outrage over the treaty's terms into action. Overnight, the Nationalists attacked a British battalion at the eastern tip of the Sea of Marmara. The attack was a conscious, provocative breach of the neutral zone created around the Dardanelles and the capital city, Constantinople. For the first time since the Armistice, the British army was directly threatened in a region where it only maintained a few battalions of soldiers.

The British immediately realized they would easily be overrun by the much larger Turkish force. Great Britain itself, did not have any available troops to reinforce the Straits. They couldn't very well ask the French or the Italians for help as they both had shown signs of aligning themselves with the Turkish Nationalists. The Americans having gone home after the war, had no available troops in Europe to support them either. And, just two months before San Remo, Churchill had warned Venizelos that Great Britain was reversing its promise to support Greece with 'neither men nor money.'

Lloyd George was trapped like a rat in a corner. How could he avoid losing face as he did when General Kemal defeated the British Navy at Gallipoli? This was an impossible blow to his reputation as a master of the universe.

Only someone with an ego that would rival Caesar, residing in the bubble known as the Paris Peace Conference, could rationalize an improbable solution to such an impossible circumstance. But Lloyd George knew that Venizelos was obsessed with recreating the Greek empire of ancient times. He also knew Venizelos was desperate to become a more important player on the world stage. And finally, he knew that the mutual hatred between Greeks and Turks had spanned centuries.

On a visit to London, Venizelos was summoned by Lloyd George to his office at Number 10 Downing Street. As he entered, the Greek tried to imagine the purpose of the meeting. He could only hope that there was a change of heart as far as supporting the Greek armies. Once seated, the two leaders exchanged small talk as a way of easing the tension in the room. Then Lloyd George employed his most gracious face. The face of a friend and supporter of the Greeks, but knowing he could not override Churchill's policy of 'neither men nor money.'

"Lefty, my friend! I have a *big* problem that I'm hoping you can figure a way to help me."

Venizelos replied, "You have always been able to count on Greece before."

"You understand more than anyone since our occupation of Constantinople, that we have over-committed our troops. That was the basis of your last meeting with Secretary Churchill, where we found ourselves unable to provide you with men or money in your occupation of Turkey.

"Last night, Kemal attacked our installation at Izmid. This was a conscious provocation on his part. Considering our paucity of troop levels in the region, Kemal will face no appreciable resistance if he proceeds to take over the Straits."

Venizelos' mind was racing. He could see where Lloyd George was going, but he needed something to combat the economic and political difficulties in Greece. The country was sliding toward insolvency. There was no prospect for monetary support to pay for the enormous troop levels he had fighting in Asia Minor. With no idea of how to respond, he simply asked, "Do you have something in mind?"

Lloyd George saw this as an opening.

"Now that the terms of the Treaty with Turkey are public, we are committed to them, but this attack on us demonstrates that the Nationalists will not accept those terms and they will fight rather than accept them.

"I am going to ask you, as a friend, and as a valued ally to Great Britain, to gather your own resources and impose the treaty on the Turks, yourself. Greece stands alone with the manpower to defeat the Turkish armies. Will you do it?"

Without any hesitation, Venizelos responded.

"Of course we will do it! No one knows better than Greece what an autonomous Turkey means. Even if it takes every last *drachma* in our treasury, we cannot allow the Turks to be left free to murder our people."

As insane as this promise was, all Venizelos could hope for was that something would change if they defeated the Turkish Nationalists. He realized there was no way a settlement would occur peacefully. While Greece still maintained a more powerful army than Turkey, with that single advantage he was committing that the Greek army would bring Turkey to her knees. With Venizelos' promise having been made, and the Greek reputation for dogged loyalty, Lloyd George breathed a sigh of relief that he had momentarily avoided another Gallipoli.

He took the opportunity to rationalize that the mighty British war machine, in this one solitary instance, would permit Greece to loan one of its army divisions to the British commander within the neutral zone, in order to engage the offending Turkish force.

With the uncomfortable prospect of having to reinforce British troops themselves, the other members of the Council voted in favor of the Greek troop loan to defeat the Turkish army. In consideration of the one-time manpower loan to defend Constantinople, the Allied powers were now forced to finally remove the restriction preventing Greece from pursuing Turkish Nationalists wherever they sought refuge.

It had been more than a year since the Treaty of Versailles memorialized the agreement with Germany. But, due to the bickering among the Council members, the amount of reparations was still yet to be determined. With discontent growing in vanquished Germany, not to mention the domestic discontent at home in Britain and France, a meeting of the Supreme Council was convened in Spa, Belgium in July 1920 to discuss Germany and the delicate subject of German reparations.

Befitting the stature of the individuals who would direct the fate of nations, the meeting was held in a city known for its healing springs since the 14th century. With the future of the world still in the balance, it was only fitting that the elite Council members should enjoy a change of scenery and perhaps a dip in the springs that might improve their health. Spa being the birthplace of Agatha Christie's newly-popular Belgian detective character, *Hercule Poirot*, a number of cynical journalists joked that perhaps the Big Four might absorb some of the detective's wisdom.

Aside from German military disarmament and reparations, another matter bubbled up to sufficient importance to warrant discussion by the Council. The matter involved the effects of the recent resoundingly successful Greek victory over the offending Turkish forces at Izmid. Clearly, the rescue of the British reputation from a Turkish force by placing Greek troops under British commanders improved Venizelos' plight. He believed Greece was now poised to occupy Thrace as well as Asia Minor.

This moment would be the closest Venizelos would come to his dream of the *Megali Idea*. He suggested to the Supreme Council that his forces should remain in the neutral zone until the Turks had signed the Treaty. Unlike his boss, General Paraskevopoulos, Commander in Chief of the Greek forces in Asia Minor, preferred to retrieve the forces from the neutral zone and stamp out the Turkish resistance completely.

Unfortunately for Venizelos, he had miscalculated the appreciation Lloyd George, and therefore Britain, would feel once the Turkish offensive was quashed and the threat removed. Rather than gaining more power and credibility from the Greek military successes, once the threat of a Turkish capture of Constantinople and the Dardanelles no longer existed, once again the British turned their backs on Greece and left them to deal with the Turks on their own. Jolly good!

Chapter 11.

On 10 August 1920 The Treaty with Turkey was finally signed at Sevres, France. Unfortunately for Greece, the Treaty was signed by the Sultan in Constantinople, the shaky head of the Ottoman Empire which by now, essentially existed in name only. The real power in Turkey was actually emerging in Ankara where the rebel general Mustafa Kemal, as head of the new revolutionary Nationalist government-in-waiting, rejected the treaty. The fragile treaty dictated by the old men in Paris, technically placed the Dardanelles under international control; France got Cicilia in the south; Italy got Adalia and the southwest; and the Greeks got Thrace. On paper it all tied up with a pretty bow.

Aside from his successes on the world stage, Greece's Venizelos faced a continuing but worsening crisis back at home. Competing political parties were blaming each other for the enduring economic crisis resulting from financing a large army on another continent. Being of the party in power, Venizelos became the obvious target for his opponents, the Royalists, who faired much better under the monarchy that existed before the Great War.

Just two days after the signing of the Sevres Treaty, as he arrived at *Gare de Lyon* railway station in Paris to board a train home to Athens, Venizelos was shot by two Royalist soldiers. He survived, but the attack provoked a rash of violence between the Venizelist and Royalist factions in Greece. Venizelos remained in Paris to convalesce.

Once recovered from his wounds, Venizelos did return to Athens. In spite of being welcomed back as a hero by his supporters, he now faced a much larger problem. Realizing that Kemal would never submit to the Treaty, the military wished to proceed toward Ankara and wipe out the Turkish Nationalist army before the harsh Anatolian winter shut down any effort to defeat them. Meanwhile, Athens was crying for demobilization of the armies to staunch the outflow of money necessary to support its offensive.

To make matters worse, at the end of September, King Alexander of Greece was injured while walking the grounds of an estate in Athens. Alexander had assumed the throne only three years before when his German-leaning father, Constantine abdicated. It was Constantine's departure that permitted Venizelos to be voted in and immediately join the Allied Powers in the Great War. Alexander's German Shepherd had been attacked by a pet monkey, and in trying to separate the animals, he was bitten by the monkey's mate.

6. King Alexander of Greece.

Within a month, Alexander died from blood poisoning, thrusting the country into a revived constitutional battle. This political battle became the essence of the election: whether to retain Venizelos and remain a republic, or return to a monarchy and bring back Constantine I.

On the second Sunday in November 1920, to the surprise of most people in Greece, as well as the dismay of the Allied Powers in Paris, Venizelos lost the election. Rather than drag out the process, he resigned as Prime Minister and watched as Dimitrios Rallis was sworn in. With the Royalists back in power, within a couple of weeks, a plebiscite decided that Constantine would be recalled and returned to his prior throne.

Taking his return to power as a mandate from the people, Constantine decided to continue Venizelos' push to defeat the Turkish Nationalists in Asia Minor. However, instead of retaining the battle-seasoned Venizelist commanders, Constantine replaced about fifteen-hundred senior army officers by reinstating his crony Royalists who had been dismissed by Venizelos. Critically, he replaced the Army Commander in Chief, General Paraskevopoulos, with General Papoulas, a conceited and gullible peacock. Moreover, having been out of the loop by living in exile in Switzerland, Constantine mistakenly underestimated the capability of the Turkish Nationalist forces. His most crucial blunder, however, was to misinterpret the economic reality for Greece of maintaining a large army on another continent.

Beyond his errors in judgement as to the cost and leadership of the Greek forces, the return of Constantine did not sit well with the Allied Powers. Having shown a loyalty to the German throne during the war now placed the Council in a position of supporting a supporter of the enemy. Overnight, with the exception of Lloyd George, the support for Greece from the Council as the occupying force in Asia Minor disappeared completely.

The unfortunate consequence of an ill-informed electorate returning the country to a monarchy at the end of 1920 was that the entire year of 1921 proved unkind to the Greek cause and the Greek people. Greece's fortunes spiraled downward as the four old men on the Supreme Council made decisions uniquely designed to improve their own selfish motives while creating intolerable consequences for everyone else. By returning Constantine to the throne, Greece transformed its military from the designated Allied freedom force to a disposable, and now unwelcome, foreign invasion force.

By the spring of 1921, Alexandre Millerand, who had replaced the ailing Georges Clemenceau as Prime Minister, used the return of the Greek king to enter into an agreement with the Turkish government. France would evacuate Cicilia in the south, in exchange for future oil concessions, exploitation rights, and investment priorities in sectors of banking, railroads, waterways and ports. France had already been secretly supplying arms to the Turks. Apparently, the concepts of hypocrisy and betrayal were lost on the French. For the Turks, it strategically freed up troops that were otherwise engaged against the French, to be added to the force fighting the Greeks.

On the very same day, Italy signed and ratified a treaty with the Turkish Government, leaving Great Britain as the only supporter for the Greek occupation. Even that support had been tepid since the Turkish threat on Constantinople was eliminated by the Greek forces.

Greece seeing no other alternative, commenced a second offensive to chase the Turkish armies toward Ankara. The only difference in this offensive from the last one, was that for the first time, Greek troops were mostly fighting against well-supplied Turkish regulars instead of the irregular *chettes*. With direct military aid now coming from Russia, France and Italy, prospects for the Turkish army had improved significantly. Within ten days of the Italian announcement of its support for the Turks, the much-weakened Greek forces, now under inept generals, were forced into a general retreat.

In what can only be a monumental denial of reality, the Greek forces were ordered by their incompetent Royalist generals to launch yet a third advance eastward toward Ankara, in hopes of a miraculous victory over the well-supplied and rested Turkish Nationalist army. Meanwhile, the Supreme Council in a demonstration of equally supreme hypocrisy, suddenly re-defined the Greek assault in Asia Minor from an Allied occupying force to a private war between Greece and Turkey. The new definition permitted the Supreme Council to now declare neutrality in the newly-defined Greco-Turkish War. It announced to the world that Greece and Turkey were engaging in a strictly private war, demonstrating a complete betrayal of the Greek forces that only months before, sacrificed its men and money to save Great Britain from a second embarrassing defeat at the hands of the Turks. From their elegant cocoon in Paris, the Council's declaration now permitted France and Italy to supply munitions to the Turkish Nationalists with impunity. It also ensured a death sentence for tens of thousands of desperate Greek soldiers who had been Great Britain's proxy army.

By September, the Greek army bereft of munitions and supplies and most importantly, the mandate of the Supreme Council, for a third time were forced to retreat back to the western shore of the Sakarya River.

By October, France's previously secret agreement was ratified into a formal Treaty with Nationalist Turkey. Now both France and Italy were openly lobbying for the removal of Greek troops from Asia Minor.

The ultimate betrayal of trust of the soldiers who spilled their blood on the promise of support from the Allied Powers, would also serve as the death knell for millions of Orthodox Christians whose only hope was Greek protection from Mustapha Kemal's mission, "Turkey for the Turks."

As 1922 began, 200,000 Greek soldiers were stranded in a severe winter season, without spare parts to maintain their decaying equipment, without ammunition, warm clothing, food or water in the wasteland of the Anatolian frontier. These soldiers, most of whom had been at war for more than a decade and now being led by maladroit generals, were completely spent. As if to accelerate the inconvenient truth of betrayal and the removal of Greek forces from Asia Minor, Greece was bankrupted by virtue of the sudden cancellation of Allied and American loans to Greece. Like the Christians of ancient Rome, the Greeks had just been fed to the lions.

Chapter 12.

In the past, the eighty-mile length of the Smyrna-Aydin Railway bustled with business between Smyrna, the main trading mecca for Europe and Asia, and Aydin (Aidin), center of the agricultural region of western Asia Minor. The railroad, originally built in 1856, was the main transportation link between the cities.

But on this spring day in April 1922, the first-class car of the train was only occupied by two passengers. The first was American author, foreign correspondent and occasional relief worker, Dr. Herbert Adams Gibbons, Ph.D., on assignment from the American newspaper, The *Christian Science Monitor*. The newspaper had been hearing reports of continued atrocities by the Turkish soldiers against Orthodox Christians in Asia Minor after the Supreme Council had declared neutrality in the Greco-Turkish War.

His companion was the Metropolitan Archbishop of Smyrna, Chrysostomos, who had agreed to accompany him on a tour of the city and to serve as Gibbons' guide to show evidence of the massacre of Christians in the area.

Looking out the window, Gibbons remarked, "Your Eminence, I thank you for accompanying me on this trip. So much has changed since we last met ten years ago. When we rode this train then, Aydin was a bustling city of 30,000. It was the center of trade for figs, oil, soap and licorice. Greeks made up twenty percent of the population and Greeks and Turks lived and worked together as they had done for hundreds of years. Now it is a ruin."

The Archbishop frowned, "Yes my friend, your report had a much different tone then. What you will see now, will destroy that memory and replace it with the horror we Greeks live with every day. When the Allies ordered our troops to occupy Asia Minor in 1919, the Young Turks had been murdering our people for years. In Paris, they danced at the promise of world peace, while the Young Turks were returning to the massacres they had committed before the Great War."

Gibbons nodded. "Yes! their brutality is burned into my memory. I was in Adana thirteen years ago. I saw what they did to the Armenians. Now it is the same to the Greeks. You know there has been a backlash against the Greeks ever since witnesses saw what happened when your troops landed in Smyrna."

Chrysostomos shook his head in shame, "Yes, and I am completely responsible for it. I thought only of the joy my people would feel for their liberation. I didn't think about what could happen if things turned bad. I pray each day for forgiveness for my stupidity.

7. *Turkish soldiers pose with beheaded, hanged Greek woman in Aydin.*

"But when we occupied Aydin that summer, we underestimated the *chettes* who escaped into the hills nearby, regrouped and ambushed our troops, forcing us to retreat for a few days. When we returned, our soldiers found that the Turks had gone house-to-house to hunt down our women and children. Anyone they found alive, they slaughtered by the gun, by the knife, or simply by throwing them off a cliff. The Turkish government had ordered soldiers and civilians to be issued government weapons and ammunition, and were provoked to pillage and burn the Greek quarter down to the ground. Nearly five-thousand Christians were murdered. And before those murders, came the rapes and mutilations. And they say they were reacting to the Greek brutality that I caused on that first day.

"Did we retaliate? Yes! We burned the Turkish quarter. We destroyed their mosques. We let them get a taste of their own medicine. But then, that British consultant came here. What was his name? Toynbee. . . Arnold Toynbee. He was pro-Greek all through the Great War as he wrote about the savagery of the Turk over centuries. Then, somehow, more recently, he has magically become pro-Turk and has now written about Greek brutality. But he didn't think it necessary to mention what our brutality was in response to. Now, all people look to, is his report and his reputation. No one asks about the basis of his complete change of heart. No one finds it worthy to print that most scholars criticize the validity of this work. Could it be his family's link to the British intellectual society pressuring him to mirror the government's about-face on their promise of Greek support?"

Gibbons thought the Archbishop was drifting away from the purpose of his visit and needed to be brought back to the present. He tried to coax the Archbishop back. "Your Eminence, I understand we will be escorted by two soldiers for our protection, and two civilians who are survivors of the recent massacre."

Chrysostomos smiled as he realized he had begun to rant.

"Yes, we will be escorted by two officers, but we will be protected by hundreds of soldiers. In fact, you will get to meet some of our soldiers. I need your reports to inform the world of what is really happening here."

Upon their arrival in Aydin, as they disembarked from the train, Chrysostomos noticed the assigned soldiers and civilians standing on the station platform. They approached the soldiers who, out of custom and respect, immediately bowed and kissed the Archbishop's ring. Then, they both stood at attention and saluted.

"Captain Apostolidis and Sergeant Papadimitriou reporting for duty, Your Eminence."

The Archbishop took the Captain's hand from his salute and guided it back to the officer's hip. "Captain, please do not salute me. I am not the partisan of my youth. I restrict my duties to that of guiding my people in the way of the Lord."

Chrysostomos turned to Gibbons. "Captain Apostolidis was chosen for this assignment because of his command of the English language. He is from the area, but I first met him many years ago in Macedonia when he was fighting against the Bulgarians."

Gibbons stepped forward and shook the Captain's hand. "It is a pleasure to meet you Captain Apostolidis." He nodded and then

8. *Captain Lazaros Apostolidis (3rd from left) and his partisan band in Macedonia in 1908.*

shook the Sergeant's hand. As they were standing off in the distance, Gibbons nodded and smiled at the two Greek survivors.

The Archbishop said, "Captain, take us to where we will spend the night. Dr. Gibbons is fatigued from his journey and we have much ground to cover tomorrow."

The next morning, the group met and Gibbons interviewed the two survivors of the massacre. Both survivors were in their eighties which was likely the reason they survived. For the next several hours, they walked through the charred rubble that was once the bustling Greek quarter of Aydin. They noticed a few survivors with rags over the faces, extracting charred bodies of family members from under collapsed buildings so that they could be buried. The faces on the survivors were more like zombies than people. From the stench that still pervaded the air, Gibbons was nauseated, immediately bringing him back to what he had witnessed in Armenian Adana thirteen years before.

He looked at the Prelate, "How can this sort of thing still be happening? You know, I was informed that Mr. Dulles, our division chief in the State Department was having difficulty keeping all this under wraps. He said it would be a simpler matter if these reports could be proven to be untrue. But with all the occurrences here and all along the Black Sea coast, the United States is trying to avoid giving the impression that we are only interested in protecting American interests while ignoring the plight of Christian minorities."

Gibbons continued, "An American relief worker I know, Dr. Mark Ward, had issued a report containing quotes from Turkish officials he had been in contact with. He quoted one of the officials who said, "We have been too easy in the past. We shall do a thorough job this time. Why do you Americans waste your time and money on these filthy Greeks and Armenians? We always thought that Americans knew how to get their money's worth. Any Greeks and Armenians who don't die here are sure to die when we send them on to Bitlis, as we always choose the worst weather in order to get rid of them quicker.

"My own view is quite different. I know prominent Turks who protest the unparalleled inhumanity. Greeks and Turks have been living and working side by side for hundreds of years. Massacres have *never* broken out spontaneously. I believe that these massacres are the result of government orders as part of a plan to rid Asia Minor of all Christians. That is why the paper sent me here."

As they continued through the rubble, Gibbons stumbled trying to step over what he thought was a roof beam from a burned-out house. He caught himself by grabbing the Captain's arm and then looked down to see the cause of his stumble. It turned out not to be a beam. It was the charred remains of a woman who was holding an infant to her breast. The fire had fused their bodies together. They obviously were burned alive.

Chrysostomos stopped in his tracks. He looked intently at Gibbons and then got on his knees to pray for the woman and her child. Then he stood up and waved his arm so they could continue their tour.

"Yes, my friend. I grew up in a village where Greeks and Turks lived and worked together. Your friends and neighbors were just that. Nothing else. But now these radicals are intent on getting rid of Christians by murdering them. It is far less expensive than feeding them as prisoners. My greatest fear is that the Allies, who sent our army here, are now demanding that our troops leave. The Allied Powers are willing to deal with the devil in order to satisfy their selfish interests.

"We do not show you these ruins and tell you these stories to excite your compassion or even your indignation. We only want you to realize that what happened at Aydin is our lesson and our warning. It will happen everywhere if we obey the Allies and evacuate our forces from Asia Minor. That is why we refuse to give up this country as long as any of us are alive."

After walking through rubble for several hours, having seen enough, the group mounted horses that would carry them to the southern outpost of the Greek forces along the Meander River. The road was wide enough for two horses to ride side by side. The procession was led by Captain Apostolidis and Sergeant Papadimitriou, followed by Gibbons and the Archbishop. The two survivors remained in Aydin. The horses headed south and settled into a slow walk on the dirt road. Gibbons spoke so that the soldiers could also hear what he had to say.

"Before coming to Aydin, I received word that the Italians are evacuating the regions we are riding through right now, and from Sokia to the south. I find it strange that as they evacuate, they are ordering Italian families, women and children, to move to behind the Greek lines. The report indicated that twenty families had arrived behind the Greek lines and when asked by the sentries why they were there, they said they were ordered to seek refuge from the Greek forces because they were apprehensive about what will happen when the Kemalists come. Apparently, the Italian commander at Sokia, is unwilling to leave their women and children to the mercies of the Turkish military. This clearly makes no logical sense to me."

The Captain turned in his saddle. "Dr. Gibbons, what do you find illogical? Politicians will always sacrifice their people for the sake of colonial aspirations. Surely you've heard that the Italians have negotiated a new agreement with the Turkish Nationalists. They declare neutrality in the ongoing conflict, while supplying the Turks with arms in exchange for oil and land after the war. But they also know what the Turks are capable of. So they tell their women and children to seek protection from the stupid Greeks- who will not refuse them. It makes perfect sense to me."

The group arrived at the Greek encampment at the Meander River after having ridden through fifteen miles of swamps. They could see a lot of movement and preparation under way. The Greeks were preparing to advance on Sokia as soon as the Italians evacuated.

As they arrived at the regiment's campsite, the group was greeted by a crowd of Greek soldiers who cheered for the new President Harding and the United States. As the group dismounted, soldiers came up to Gibbons, and recited names of a dozen American cities. He was surprised that forty percent of the soldiers were actually Greek-American citizens.

Gibbons was drawn to a particular soldier who spoke English with a rather strange sounding Italian-American accent.

"Where are you from, soldier?"

"My home is in Bridgeport Connecticut."

Gibbons chuckled, "You're a long way from home, soldier! Aren't you homesick?"

"Yes, I long to return home to Bridgeport, where nothing happens."

"Now?" Gibbons asked.

"Oh no! We must first save the bambinos." he answered.

Gibbons was struck by the spirit and splendid morale of these war-torn troops who would not give up the fight to save their compatriots. They possessed a dogged determination to see the mission through.

The group was led further through a swamp by following a telegraph wire erected along the river. They were escorted by a Sergeant and eight men, who, aside from their spirit, looked as though they were half-dead. They finally arrived at a crude, brush-lined dugout, where, along with their escort, were served their supper. As hungry as everyone was, no one thought to begin until Chrysostomos gave the blessing for the meal.

As they sat on rocks placed in the earthen dugout, Gibbons noticed the Sergeant seated to his right. "Where is your home?" Gibbons asked.

"Missalonghi!"

Gibbons recognized the name. "Have you ever heard of Lord Byron?"

The Sergeant smiled. "Yes, yes! I know all about this poet. . . and his house in Missalonghi. But his house does not put any food on my table."

Gibbons asked, "Are you eager to go home?"

"Yes! There, is the wife and babies, and I have been here two years, and she has to do all the work in the field."

Gibbons, like a reporter he was, followed up.

"Then you will be happy if there is peace?"

The farmer-turned-army-sergeant looked up from his metal dish, and then grabbed Gibbons' arm as he raised his fork to his mouth. The sergeant's grip felt like a vice.

"We cannot accept your peace, if it means letting the Turks come back here."

The sergeant went back to eating his dinner. Gibbons looked across the dugout only to see Chrysostomos staring back at him.

Chapter 13.

Shortly after the escorts accompanied Gibbons and the Archbishop back to Aydin, the Greek regiment had been ordered to enter Sokia, a town about twenty-six miles west of their position on the river. Captain Apostolidis and Sergeant Papadimitriou had just returned to the regiment in time to join the move on Sokia. The regiment was made up of seasoned soldiers, but moving men and equipment was still difficult as a result of the spring rains washing out many of the roads.

But by noon the following day, finding little resistance, Sokia was secured. Most of the Turkish troops were *chettes*, who tended to scatter at the first signs of an assault. Since Sokia was only six miles from the bay eliminating any escape to the west, the retreating Turks headed south in response to the Greek approach from the east.

Once in control of Sokia, the Greek commander heard from his advance patrol of the southward retreating *chettes* occupying the small villages in the Gheronda district about thirty five miles to the south of Sokia. At first, the *chettes* restricted their activities to looting the towns. Their typical method was to raid a home at gunpoint and demand food, money and family valuables that were small enough to carry off.

Seeing that the Greek forces had stopped at Sokia, and with Gheronda being well within what they thought to be the safety of the Italian zone, they remained there. Once stationary in Gheronda with lookouts posted, they confiscated the local supply of *raki* (a strong alcoholic anise-flavored Turkish spirit). Fortified by strong liquor, the *chettes*, who were essentially thugs with guns, chose to entertain their delusion of being conquering soldiers.

Imagining themselves like the conquering Turkish warriors of old, they felt entitled to the women and children to be used for their own amusement and satisfaction. The evenings turned into a drunken orgy of rape, mutilation and then murder. It was not uncommon for *chettes* to break into a home, and as the family watched at gunpoint, each drunken thug would rape a young girl or boy, or the wife of a villager.   After they were done, and probably depending on their alcohol level, they might enjoy watching the onlookers' helpless anguish as they cut off a young girl's breast, or perhaps sever a young boy's penis. The wanton brutality was unchecked as the villagers were unarmed and helpless. The thrill of total power over their victims, seemed to increase their bloodlust.

Word had filtered back to Sokia of the torture and murder occurring in Gheronda. Apparently, a boy who had watched his sister be raped and murdered, snuck out in the middle of the night, heading northward to find the Greek forces. Faced with another report of barbaric behavior the Greek commander was committed to intervening.

Logistically, moving the regiment south to Gheronda was difficult. A direct route to the district involved crossing two sets of mountains. The less direct route involved a single muddy dirt road, but the road wrapped around Lake Bafa, an unrealistic route considering the brutality being faced by the Greek villagers. The commander concluded that an assault by land would probably result in most if not all villagers being murdered before they could arrive.

The commander decided on an invasion by sea. Three Greek warships were dispatched to the port just west of Sokia. The invading force was loaded onto the light cruiser *Aktion*, escorted by the torpedo boat *Arethoussa*. The two warships were accompanied by the destroyer *Iphendoni*.

Under the cover of night, the *Aktion* and *Arethoussa* steamed along the coast for about fifteen miles, then passing through the strait that separates the mainland from the Greek island of Samos. Once through the strait, the ships steamed across the Aegean, wrapping around the peninsula to the south, before turning back north into the bay, five miles directly west of Gheronda. They arrived at the port of Taoushan-Bournou, which was not much more than a pier, but where the troops could be offloaded.

At 4:15 a.m., they were met with fire from the Turkish coast guards, but who were no match for the artillery onboard the warships.   The landing force, quickly defeated the small Turkish resistance and then tracked eastward toward Gheronda. The terrain was flat most of the way, but the invading force was given cover by the hills just outside Gheronda.

At 4:25 a.m. the destroyer *Iphendoni* arrived with its force at the coast of Karacolyoun, about six miles on the opposite side of Gheronda.

By first light, both invading forces attacked Gheronda from two sides. The Turks were completely surprised by the attack and were caught in a crossfire. After an initial fire fight, the Turks realizing the attack was from east and west, scattered again to the south.

Captain Apostolidis led a platoon of soldiers through the district to look for *chettes* who might have been hiding as many had been cut off from escape. They came across a home where a baby sat alone in the front yard, playing in the dirt. It seemed strange to him that a Greek mother would allow an infant to be unattended. The baby was playing with a stick. As he got closer, he stiffened as the stick turned into a Turkish bayonet. Apostolidis signaled his men to silently surround the house. Carefully, he stepped into the house and immediately saw an older woman sitting in the corner of the room mending some clothing. Alert to the oddity of the scene before him, he scolded the woman for leaving the baby outside alone. He noticed that she didn't respond by running outside. She just sat and mended.

One look at her face told him the story. He knew there was a Turk hidden somewhere in the home. He walked over and looked into the second room that made up the cottage and saw the empty pallets on the floor. He saw five pallets. Then, he looked around the room and noticed a table in the opposite corner that had been draped by a quilt with two olive vats standing in front of it. The look on the woman's face told him the *chette* was behind the quilt. But he guessed someone else was also under the table or he would have opened fire.

Apostolidis, ordered the old woman to go outside and get the baby, claiming he would take her with him to see the commander. The woman refused to move. He yelled at her forcing her to get up and walk out. Once she was outside, the Captain walked over to a chair and sat. His Sergeant walked in and saw him sitting by himself. A confused look on his face prompted Apostolidis to say to his friend in Greek, "Κάθησε φίλε μου! Νομίζω ότι τελειώσαμε. (Sit my friend! I think we're finished.)"

Papadimitriou knew something was wrong and kept his rifle aimed in front of him. Once he sat, Apostolidis said, "Now that we've rounded up the prisoners, we must escort them to the ship. Both civilians and prisoners will be taken to Samos for questioning. But let's sit for a while and rest."

After a few minutes of silence, he saw the quilt move slightly. Then Apostolidis spoke in Turkish, "*Beyefendi...* If you are alone under that table, I suggest you put your hands on your head and come out. If you are holding a girl or boy with you, I am willing to let you live as a prisoner. If, when we lift the quilt and the boy or girl is dead or dying, you will die the slowest and most painful death you can imagine. While I am in such a good mood, you should surrender."

After a minute of silence, A voice was heard from behind the quilt. "*Teslim ederim!...* I surrender! I am letting the girl go." Suddenly, a young girl of twelve or thirteen years stood up. Her face was bruised and swollen and her clothes were ripped and hanging. Apostolidis motioned her to leave. She silently ran outside.

Apostolidis was now relaxed. He now spoke more casually with his prisoner. "*Beyefendi...* I appreciate your letting the girl go. You are now my prisoner. If you will push your weapon out from under the quilt, I will tell my Sergeant here, not to shoot."

He waited. After a long moment, the rifle appeared from under the quilt. Apostolidis said, "Do you have any more weapons?"

He heard, "*Hayir...* No!"

"Then come out from there."

The quilt lifted and out from under it came a dirty, disheveled man, whose uniform consisted of military pants. Otherwise, he was dressed as any other civilian. His hands were held on his head as he rose to a standing position.

Apostolidis, got up from his chair and walked up to the *chette*. Coming from Asia Minor himself, Apostolidis spoke Turkish as well as Greek. With his face only inches from his prisoner, he asked in Turkish, "Where is the husband of this woman?"

"I don't know."

"So you didn't kill the husband?"

"No"

"Then if these women were alone," Apostolidis said, "what did you do to the girl?"

"I did nothing. I just took her prisoner because I was afraid you would kill me."

Apostolidis said, "But if you did nothing to her, why were her clothes ripped and why was her face beaten?"

"She was like that when I arrived."

"Okay! You are now a prisoner of the Hellenic Occupation Force. We will take you to our ship where you will be questioned."

The *chette* remained silent.

Then Apostolidis went to the door and called the young girl back into the house. By then she had covered herself up. Apostolidis crouched down near the girl and said, "This soldier said that he didn't rip your dress and he didn't hurt you. You were like that when he arrived. Is this true?"

The girl's face changed from fear to anger. She shook her head. "He ripped my dress and he hit me in the face. Kill him!"

Apostolidis looked at the prisoner. "The girl says you did hurt her. Who am I to believe?"

Now the face of the prisoner changed. He realized he would not be taken prisoner. He began to shake uncontrollably.

"So, now you shake with fear. When you had the gun you were a brave warrior and now you shake."

The Captain told the girl to go outside and tell her mother to come in. The woman creeped into the house and saw the prisoner standing there with his hands on his head. She walked up to him and spit in his face. "Στο διάβολο!"

Apostolidis asked the woman, "Είδες αυτόν τον άνθρωπο να βιάζει την κόρη σου? (Did you see this man rape your daughter?)" The woman nodded slowly. Apostolidis nodded as well. He reached down into his boot and pulled out his knife and handed it to her. "Before we send this pig to the devil, give your daughter some justice."

He fully expected the woman to stab the prisoner, but was surprised that she moved closer to the man and cut his belt. The Turk's baggy pants fell to the floor from the weight of the ammunition and valuables he had collected. To his surprise, Apostolidis watched the woman take the man's manhood in her hand and held it out. Then she looked up into his eyes. Now he was shaking so much that she lost her grip. But she grabbed it once again and stretched it out towards her. His eyes grew wide as he screamed for mercy. Without taking her eyes off his face, the knife came down and severed his manhood at the root. He screamed in agony as his hands reached down and grabbed his groin.

The woman held the bleeding pulsating member up to his face so he could look at it. Then she said in Turkish, "May all your daughters and their daughters pay for your sins." The man's mouth was open as he howled in agony and fell to the dirt floor. The woman now with a look of madness in her eyes, stuffed the man's member into his mouth. He reached up with one hand to remove it, but Apostolidis beat his arm with the butt of his rifle, breaking the bones in his forearm.

Then Apostolidis looked past the old woman and saw the young girl in the doorway looking at the bleeding *chette*. He saw the same look of madness on her face. Sergeant Papadimitriou asked, "Shall I put him out of his misery?"

The woman shouted in Greek, "Όχι, άφησε τον να επιθυμήσει τον θάνατο. (No! Let him wish for death.)"

The man squirmed for what seemed an eternity before he bled out. Once it was over, the soldiers dragged the body out and threw it in a ravine. Before they left, Apostolidis asked the woman, "Where is your husband?"

Still with the madness in her eyes, "They took him and my son and beheaded them for sport."

He said, "Take your daughter and come with us. We will take you to Samos with the others where you will find help. You cannot stay here anymore."

The invasion was successful in that they managed to capture many of the scum who had been terrorizing the district. The commander of the Turkish troops was captured in addition to a cache of ammunition. The entire operation was accomplished in just four hours.

Once Gheronda was secure and Turkish commander was taken prisoner, a platoon was sent up into the hills surrounding Gheronda to search for refugees who managed to escape. By noon, the search team rescued thirteen-hundred refugees.

Chapter 14.

The front entry doors of the exclusive Grand Hotel Kraemer Palace stood open so that the mild summer breeze could drift into its luxurious lobby, bathing patrons in the fragrance of the Aegean Sea whose waters lapped at the quay only a few steps opposite its entrance. The west-facing entry invited the descending sun's rays to reflect off the Kraemer Palace's white marble floor, further enhancing the warm summer glow in the city known to its visitors as the "Jewel of the Near East."

9. *The Grand Hotel Kraemer Palace as it looked in 1922.*

The arrival this afternoon of Dr. Herbert Adams Gibbons was not sufficient to cause any stir among the patrons in the lobby, who were accustomed to the Kraemer Palace's celebrated clientele. Long known to Europe as Asia's equivalent to Paris, the bustling city of Smyrna had also become a valued destination to American business, wealthy vacationers and most recently, American journalists.

Over the centuries, the city's diverse population of businessmen had created a unique blend of Europe and Asia, resulting in the city's component parts, exceeding its sum. Smyrna was comprised of a Greek quarter; a Turkish quarter; an Armenian quarter; a Jewish quarter; a European quarter; and the relatively recent appearance of an American enclave known as Paradise; all presided over by the equivalence of a ruling class known as the Levantines. The Levantines were actually descendants of Euro-Mediterranean traders and merchants, who settled in Asia Minor, and built fortunes on the commerce of trade between Europe and Asia.

Returning to Smyrna for the second time in three months, Dr. Gibbons was not one to engage in sociable mingling or dwell on frivolity, and thus wasted no time in getting down to the purpose of his visit. Once checked into his room, Gibbons unpacked, showered, shaved and dressed in a fresh suit. He returned to the lobby, walking past the crowd of hotel guests who were engrossed in social conversation. Then he walked out the front entrance onto the quayside.

He immediately could smell the sea that lapped the dock across the street. But the aroma of the salt air was mixed with other exotic smells and sounds. Only in Smyrna did a visitor inhale the aroma of roasting cinnamon, Greek olives, Turkish coffee, French pastries, and British sausage, while he could listen to the sounds of camels groaning to background sounds of Italian operettas, jazz musicians and praying holy men. Above all, Smyrna was a cornucopia of the exotic.

Gibbons began walking south along the mile-long cobbled quayside, until he was approached from the rear, by a horse-drawn trolley that traveled along the embedded rail. Few automobiles had

10. Horse drawn trolley travels along quayside in Smyrna before 1922.

11. View of the bustling quay in Smyrna.

found their way to Smyrna at this point in time, making them a rare mode of transportation next to the traditional horses, camels and oxen. A warm and sunny Friday afternoon had brought out Smyrna's European society, who often dressed up and strolled along the quayside, meeting friends and stopping to discuss the topic of the season.

In the summer of 1922, the topic on every Smyrniote's lips was the latest advance of Greek troops against the retreating Turkish Nationalist army to the east. But such conversation was in the context of intellectual gossip over the backdrop of sidewalk cafes, brasseries, bars and shops that lined the busy quayside.

Gibbons climbed aboard the trolley as the double-clank of the trademark trolley-bell was reminiscent of his last ride on a San Francisco cable car. His destination was the Governor-General's office in the *Konak,* a government building at the south end of the quay, nearest the Turkish quarter, and the site of the melee that occurred when the Greek forces first landed. Gibbons, once again on assignment for America's *Christian Science Monitor,* was in Smyrna to write a follow-up article about the Greek army's recent retaliation, in the face of continued Turkish massacres of Orthodox Christians in the towns south of Smyrna.

Fatigued after his very long journey from the United States however, Gibbons was now forced to cool his heels and wait in the Governor's reception area, before the Hellenic High Commissioner of

Asia Minor and Governor-General of Smyrna, Aristeidis Stergiadis, would see him.

His visit to the Governor-General was meant as a courtesy to inform the Governor of his intention to interview the same military officers who had escorted him last April. Having failed then to visit Stergiadis before heading south to tour Aydin, after his departure, determined he was expected to inform Stergiadis in advance of his mission. Now, he wondered how the man he was about to meet, would react to his prior diplomatic false step.

The lack of any reading material in the austere reception area caused his mind to wander. He noticed the spartan nature of his surroundings. Considering the wealth and importance of Smyrna, it seemed unusual that the office of the High Commissioner was not more elegant, or at least more fashionable. Instead, the furniture was simple and frugal.

He contemplated the information he had researched about Stergiadis. He knew that Prime Minister Venizelos skipped over the obvious choice to govern Smyrna and had picked an old friend from his revolutionary days on Crete. An acknowledged expert on Muslim law, as Governor General of *Epirus,* Stergiadis had earned a reputation for firm and impartial government. Apparently, he was chosen to quickly reimpose law and order in Smyrna and more importantly, erase the damaging effect on the Greek mission during the original landing of troops in May of 1919. If there was anyone who could turn that black eye around it was Stergiadis.

In fact, Gibbons was impressed to learn that Stergiadis' first order was to court-martial the main Greek offenders in the massacre, and to order compensation to the families of the Turkish victims. Reports indicated that Stergiadis wasn't liked by the Greeks in that he would favor the Turkish side of any dispute to demonstrate his absolute impartiality. He even censored newspapers that spoke disparagingly about Turks. On the negative side, Gibbons had heard that Stergiadis was high-strung, and possessed a harsh and explosive temper.

From behind him, he heard a Greek-accented voice, "Dr. Gibbons?"

"Yes?"

He stood and bowed, "Thank you for seeing me Your Excellency."

He saw a bespectacled man in an un-tailored, ill-fitting business suit standing in the doorway to the office. It was definitely

12. Aristeidis Stergiadis (2nd from left) stands with Greek military leadership of Asia Minor.

not what he had expected of the high commissioner for all of Asia Minor.

Stergiadis bowed ever so slightly, "Please join me in my office."

Gibbons walked toward his unkempt host. He noticed that the man had a walking stick and wondered if Stergiadis had an old war wound. The two men shook hands and then Gibbons followed Stergiadis into his office. Gibbons noticed that his host wasn't limping and thought, *So why do you need a walking stick?*

Stergiadis motioned to the simple wooden chair opposite his desk for his visitor to be seated. Gibbons noticed that the chair Stergiadis was using, was equally spartan. He sat. Stergiadis walked around the desk and sat down facing him.

"What can I do to help you Dr. Gibbons? I apologize, in that I do not get much free time to read the international papers that we receive here in Smyrna, but I have had the opportunity to read your book, and it is clear that you've communicated an excellent understanding of these rebel Turks and their brutality against our Armenian friends. Unfortunately, our own people, after so many years under the Ottoman boot, show they can be as barbaric as any Turk."

"I'm glad you enjoyed it." Gibbons said.

"You've traveled a very long way from your home. If I'm not mistaken, you will now miss the celebrations of your country's independence next week."

Gibbons smiled. "Journalists don't usually enjoy the luxury of scheduling their own travel."

Stergiadis decided to end the small talk.

"Newspapers have a great impact on how the world views us, as we liberate our people in Asia Minor. It is my responsibility to monitor who goes where and the accuracy of what they write. You are a journalist writing for foreign newspapers. You can understand why I have an interest in where you go and what you write."

Gibbons noticed the man was polite in his delivery, but his aura said something completely different. It was more dismissive, as though he was above whoever was sitting across from him, a sort of arrogance of gesture.

"Thank you, Your Excellency for seeing me on such short notice. My assignment for the *Christian Science Monitor* has been to visit sites where Turkish atrocities have occurred against Christians in Asia Minor and report those atrocities to our American readership. As you know, I was here two months ago and was invited to tour the city of Aydin and see for myself, the result of those atrocities. And, please understand my failure to meet with you in April was due to my ignorance of the protocol. I apologize for that."

Stergiadis nodded in acknowledgement.

"While I was here, I had a telegram from my home office suggesting that the Italians were evacuating Sokia, and that if the Greeks did not arrive in time, there would be another slaughter of thousands of Christians. Surely, you can understand a journalist's curiosity about one of the Allied Powers, entering into a separate treaty with the enemy, and as their last directive in theater, order their own countrymen to seek the safety of what amounted to an enemy. Archbishop Chrysostomos had assured me..."

Stergiadis slammed his walking stick on the desk making a sound as loud as a gunshot. "Achh!... Don't talk to me about that radical partisan. He is not a man of religion. He is a rogue nationalist who uses his position in the church to incite ignorant Greek peasants to carry out atrocities against their Turkish counterparts. You didn't believe anything he told you, did you?"

Gibbons was surprised. "I'm sorry Your Excellency, but I can assure you I am not a novice at this, and I can attest to the accuracy of the Archbishop's description of the massacre at Aydin. In fact, what I witnessed was almost identical to the Turkish atrocities that I personally witnessed thirteen years ago against the Armenians. You sound as though you are on the side of the Turks."

Stergiadis' face reddened. "I am not at all on the side of the Turks. But as you can see, I am not a military man. My background is the law. . . especially Muslim law. I was chosen by Prime Minister Venizelos for an almost impossible task, and I have taken that challenge as my mission. The Prime Minister, with the support of the British Prime Minister was to achieve for Greece, what had been taken away from us many centuries ago. If we are to rule over Asia Minor, we must show the rest of the world that we are able to be as fair to the Turks as we are to the Greeks and the Armenians. Smyrna has created a tremendous problem for me. These Greek Anatolians are backward and all they want to do is get revenge on the Turks for six hundred years of maltreatment. What I must do is show that we can govern without a hint of prejudice toward either Christian or Muslim. In fact, I choose to be more on the side of the Turk than the Greek for this very reason. So I rule with my knowledge of the law. . . not my patriotism."

Gibbons asked, "And what about the Archbishop? Are you being negative toward him in order to show your objectivity?"

"Not at all. I have attended his services. The man cannot give a sermon without breaking out into a frenzied nationalistic speech meant to incite patriotism and justice for injustices of the past. I do not view nationalism as something the religious leader of our people should be dealing with. He is supposed to preach about forgiveness, not vengeance."

Gibbons applied a little journalistic pressure, "I can assure you that in my conversation with him, the Archbishop stated the facts as the evidence confirmed. I for one, seeing what I have seen, would find it justified to bring nationalism into the conversation considering what the Greek people have endured for so long."

Stergiadis slammed his walking stick again. "Well, you don't have to govern these people. You sit thousands of miles away writing for a public that likes to read about torture and atrocity."

"Your Excellency, I don't want to minimize the difficulty of your task, but as far as the Archbishop is concerned, two years ago, my colleague, Sir Philip Gibbs, who served as one of the five official British reporters of the Great War, met with Archbishop Chrysostomos. At that meeting, Sir Philip inquired about the Turkish practice of forcing Greek Christians to convert to Islam, or be put to death. In that meeting, the Archbishop pointed out a picture on his wall of Saint Polycarp, who died for his faith in this very city, at the hands of the Romans in 155 A.D. The Archbishop told Sir Philip, 'Many of my people have suffered worse tortures during the last few years, and many Greek men and women have died, like Polycarp, rather than adopt the faith of their oppressors.' That may show elements of nationalism in his sermons, but this is a man who is deeply protective of his flock. I'm afraid, if I were in his shoes, I too, would have nationalistic tendencies. And you sir, are you not working here for the benefit of your country?"

Both men could see the meeting would go no further. Gibbons said, "I guess we'll have to agree to disagree on this point, Your Excellency. I appreciate your willingness to permit me to interview the two officers who were my escort last April. They speak English, they seem to know the area well and were familiar with the issue when the Italians decided to evacuate."

"I have no reason to forbid you to speak with these soldiers." Stergiadis straightened his back. "All I can do is warn you that if they are in the Greek army, they speak with a lifelong hatred for Turks and will likely exaggerate any truth."

Gibbons smiled. "I'm not exactly new to this. I don't take mere speculation as fact. I find corroboration before I print anything. You can rest assured, Your Excellency, that I am not here with any agenda other than the truth."

Stergiadis rose from his chair. The two men shook hands and walked out to the reception area. Stergiadis said, "Do you need me to contact these officers?"

Gibbons shook his head. "No, that won't be necessary. My aide has contacted their commander and I am supposed to meet them for dinner later this evening at the Greek Officer's Club in Bournabat."

Stergiadis rolled his eyes. "Make sure you keep your wits. That club is notorious for frivolous parties and who knows what else. I find it all a waste of time and money."

Gibbons remarked as he walked toward the door, "I will definitely heed your warning, Your Excellency!"

Chapter 15.

The horse-drawn taxi was waiting for Gibbons as he stepped out of the hotel. He didn't know where the officers club was in relation to the quay and he wasn't in the mood for this to be a search mission. He stepped into the carriage and received a giant smile from the driver whose mustache almost covered his face.

The driver immediately picked up on the fact that he was an American.

"Welcome!" he said in accented English.

"Greek Officer's Club in Bournabat, please!"

Without another sound, the driver snapped the reins and they were off. The hooves began clip-clapping on the cobble stones of the quay.

"How far is it to the Officer's Club?"

"*Δώδεκα*... Twelve kilometres... Not far!"

The driver obviously knew the route. Many of the streets were so narrow and crowded with people out for the evening, that the driver was only able to use the few wider, major streets. They started off from the European quarter where many restaurants and clubs reminded him of Europe. He could hear an Italian tenor singing to the patrons in a nearby restaurant. Then, he caught a strong whiff of garlic.

Once they crossed the famous *Rue de Franque,* the environment changed and he could sense they were now in the Armenian quarter. Clearly this was an affluent community. The brightly colored dresses of the women and the preponderance of business suits worn by the men matched the well-kept residences that all seemed to have flowers dangling from their balconies.

In a subtle change, Gibbons noticed the transition to the Greek quarter. Even more beautiful residences showed that the Greeks tended to display their affluence. Gibbons could hear a mother yelling out her balcony for her children to come home, probably for dinner. He passed a garden outside of a villa and heard a party from behind a wall, where the people were singing Greek songs, and laughing.

Once across the tracks of the railroad that stretched south to Aydin, they reached the Meles River and crossed it heading eastward toward the neighborhoods of Bournabat and Cordelio.

Gibbons' taxi arrived in Bournabat, the exclusive Levantine suburb, at 7:30 P.M. As the taxi approached the Greek Officer's Club, Gibbons could see a number of elegantly-dressed patrons arriving for an evening of food, drink and gaiety. He paid the fare and entered the club; a magnificent 18th century mansion, that had been converted to a dinner club as a result of the huge influx of Greek Army officers since the Greek occupation in 1919. Now, it was the place to socialize for both the Greek officers and the wealthy Levantines of the city.

He stepped into the main foyer and approached the *maître d'hôtel*. Once Gibbons caught his attention, he inquired as to the table previously set up for the interview. The ebullient, tuxedoed, *maître d'* made sweeping and grand gestures to lead Gibbons to a table at the back corner of the main dining hall. The table was ideal for an interview in that the corner provided a measure of privacy as well as a full view of the patrons and their activities.

Once seated, the *maître d'* immediately opened a bottle of *Vichy* water, turned over the stemmed glass and poured. Greeks, like the rest of the world, tended to see the French as fashionable and adopted many of the French phrases and customs as their own.

Gibbons looked up at the *maître d'*.

"Has Captain Apostolidis arrived yet?"

The *maître d'* again bowed and swept his arm in the direction of a table at the center of the dining hall, pointing toward a dozen people in animated discussion and laughter.

"Captain Apostolidis is visiting some friends at the center table. He asked that I collect him once you arrived."

The *maître d'* pranced over to the center table and bent over the shoulder of a man in uniform, whispering in his ear. The man reached into his pocket and handed the *maître d'* some bills. Another deep bow and he disappeared. The officer waved to his colleague seated across the table and then leaned over and whispered in the ear of an elegantly-dressed woman next to him. All three rose from their chairs and started walking toward Gibbons' table. Gibbons thought, *Why are you bringing that woman over here?*

As the trio approached, Gibbons stood and shook the man's hand.

"Captain, it is a pleasure to see you again."

Gibbons turned and took the other man's hand.

"It is also a pleasure to see you again, Sergeant. I see your leg has healed quite nicely."

Gibbons looked at the beautiful woman in front of him, prompting Apostolidis to speak in a heavy Greek accent.

"Dr. Gibbons, may I present to you, the most beautiful woman in all of Asia Minor, Miss Eleni Xenopoulou. I know you are here to interview us about Aydin, but Miss Xenopoulou is a member of one of the most important Greek families in Smyrna, and she has an interest in the political situation as well. I hope you won't mind if she joins us."

The woman performed the faintest suggestion of a curtsy as she took Gibbons hand. At 42 years old, Gibbons was not immune to the charms of an exotic, beautiful woman, and the fact that her ample bosom was prominently being displayed was distracting. Gibbons commented.

"It is indeed a pleasure to be in the company of prominence and beauty at the same time."

Eleni coyly displayed a demure smile. Gibbons, was familiar with the fact that the Greek girls of Smyrna were considerably better educated and more worldly than Greek girls from mainland Greece. Greek rules of propriety were far more conservative than most countries, thanks to a very strong influence of the Greek Orthodox Church. But in Smyrna with so many international influences, Greek girls learned early that with flirtatiousness, comes attention and access.

For the first time, she spoke in English with a slight British accent.

"Dr. Gibbons, I do hope you don't mind me sitting in. My family is very concerned about the political winds that have changed since our forces liberated us in 1919. I promise I will not interrupt in any way. You will not even notice that I am here."

Gibbons, although given to distraction as any man would be in the circumstance, knew full well what methods she was employing for access.

"Why Miss Xenopoulou, I appreciate your willingness to not interrupt, but I can assure you that it will be impossible not to notice that you are here. Perhaps we should all be seated and allow me to gather data for my report."

With everyone seated, Gibbons took out his notebook from his vest pocket, and opened it to a blank page. "Captain, do you still prefer to keep your given name a mystery?"

Apostolidis smiled as he poured a glass of water from the crystal pitcher.

"Greeks believe long names make them important. If you need my given name for your report, it is Lazaros. Considering my vocation as a soldier, I try to keep a distance from being associated with the notion of being raised from the dead."

"Well then Captain, do you mind if I call you by your rank?

Apostolidis smiled again, "Not at all Dr. Gibbons."

Gibbons looked over his spectacles at Apostolidis.

"The last time we were together Captain, you were preparing to head south from Aydin as soon as the Italian troops evacuated. I understand that after I left, your regiment did carry out an invasion of that city. Is that true?"

"Yes! Once we occupied Sokia last spring, the Turks reacted, as they have always reacted, by torturing and murdering the helpless civilian Greek population of the district of Gheronda, just 35 miles to the south."

Gibbons wrote feverishly to keep up with the Captain's testimony.

"We were supposed to capture the district by land. But, Gheronda is thirty-five miles from the front. The Turks could massacre the refugees before we ever reached them. So we decided to capture the town by way of the sea."

The Sergeant injected, "You see Dr. Gibbons, the town is only five miles inland from the sea."

Apostolidis continued.

"In essence, we managed a surprise attack and were able to rescue one-thousand-three-hundred refugees from being massacred. Here. . . I've written a report of the attack and the numbers of prisoners, captured arms, etc. This way you don't have to write so much."

Gibbons smiled as he accepted the report.

"And, can you tell me what the make up was. . . I mean numbers of men, women and children?

Apostolidis face showed his disgust.

"We talked of this before Dr. Gibbons. You already know the answer before you ask. In the thirteen hundred recovered, no male was found older than twelve years, except one man who was ninety-five years old."

Gibbons shook his head.

"And you personally were part of the invading force?"

"We both were there with our *komboloi* (worry beads) in our pocket."

Gibbons looked directly into the captain's eyes.

"Captain, I know this is a difficult subject. But in light of the furor resulting from the report on the Greek brutality during the occupation, can you tell me what transpired with your prisoners?

"Don't worry Dr. Gibbons. I have no problem telling you what we did. I am not worried what Monsieur Millerand thinks of us. Yes, we captured many soldiers. Most were *chettes*, but there were some regulars, and the commander was a regular. Obviously, we took the commander aboard the *Aktion*, along with the refugees that we transported to Samos. Then we brought this commander behind the Greek lines and I suspect he was interrogated to see if he had any useful knowledge. I do not know what finally became of him."

Gibbons stared at the Captain. After a long pause, "And what of the other prisoners? What happened to them?"

"Some of them were also put on the ships and taken prisoner. But I suppose you are interested in the others that we did not take as prisoners. I will tell you, but I am hoping you will not put this in your article."

Gibbons continued to stare at the Captain, but gave no answer. The Captain looked over at Eleni, then at his sergeant.

"We gathered the prisoners, most of whom were not feeling very well from the night before. We made them stand in a single line. Then we gathered the refugees and had them walk along the line of prisoners. We asked each refugee to pick out any soldier they had witnessed who raped, mutilated or murdered someone in their family."

Suddenly, in spite of the laughter, clanking dishes and conversations going on around them, nothing else was heard by those seated at the table.

"We gave these people a choice. They could provide their own justice for these monsters, or not. I saw a father, with wild eyes, take one of the captured sabers and behead the man that cut the breasts off his daughter. I saw a grandmother take a pistol and shoot into the eye of a man who killed her grandchildren. I saw a mother pull a knife from under her tunic and stab the man who killed her child. I don't know how many times . . . She just kept stabbing him until she had no strength left in her arms. Most wanted to kill one of these monsters, but some could not bring themselves to kill another person. In those cases, whether they wanted to watch or not, we used a firing squad. I can assure you, no trial was necessary in that the faces of these people told of the horror they had witnessed. If no one could testify to seeing them mutilate or murder someone, they were put on the ships. For those who were witnessed committing an atrocity, justice was done on that very day."

Apostolidis' face showed his outrage as there was another long silence at the table. Finally the Captain stirred.

"Dr. Gibbons. . . you have influence in your country. You are a famous newspaper man. You must tell your people what is happening here. These Turks are not men. They are animals and they are determined to kill every last Christian left in Asia Minor. My God, they are beheading innocent people and putting their heads on poles in the marketplace." They're savages! And now I hear our honorable Allies are demanding that we leave Asia Minor, and that we can trust the Turks to protect our people."

Gibbons could see the frustration in his eyes. "I believe the reason they've given Greece the cold shoulder has to do with this Interallied Commission of Enquiry that presented its report to the Supreme Council. It spoke mostly of Greek atrocities against the innocent Muslim Turks, especially on the first day of the occupation. But it also mentioned Aydin where we walked. "There have been many reports of Greek civilians and soldiers doing the same things you've been accusing the Turks of doing to your people. I'm certain that these reports of Greek brutality are the reason the Allies have turned against you. That, and the return of the king of course.

"Your Archbishop has confessed he feels he is responsible for the difficulties on the day of your occupation. And, that's why I'm here. I know you will be honest with me. I need to make sure I write an accurate report."

Apostolidis stared at Gibbons as tears welled up in his eyes. It was clear to Gibbons that behind his hard exterior, the Captain was emotionally fragile. Apostolidis said, "Dr. Gibbons, I know we had a connection in Aydin. I know you saw the truth there as we walked the streets. Now you talk about the Commission report about our atrocities. Yes, we stepped over the line when we landed. Everyone wants to ignore the six hundred years before that day. If I were there, when they shot at our troops, I would have done the same. If I were a civilian, I would have done the same.

"Did you happen to notice who was in charge of the Commission who wrote the report? Let me tell you who it was. The most powerful voice on the Commission was your Admiral Bristol. His attitude toward the Greeks is well known. He was both the Chairman and the author of the report. Six months before, he had written to a colleague and we have a copy of that letter, 'The Greek is about the worst race in the Near East.'

"So much for his objectivity. The next member of the Commission was General Dall'olio. Oh, I'm sure he was totally objective. What, with Italy's secret agreement to arm the Turks against us, I cannot imagine why he might go along with a report that blamed the Greeks. Remember these are the fellows that told their civilians to seek Greek protection from the *chettes*. Oh, and the Frenchman, General Bunoust. I suppose France's secret agreement with the Turks did not sway him either.

"I don't know what to make of General Hare, the Brit. I would have thought he would have objected to not letting our representative attend the interviews. How can you just accept whatever witnesses testify to, when you don't know who the witnesses are and will not allow the accused to defend himself. The whole charade was done to allow the Allies an excuse to reverse their promises and demand that we leave. They sang a different tune when the French asked for our help in Russia. We just went in and fought for them which is what real allies do.

"I will admit that our people and our soldiers did things that were just as bad as what the Turks did. That is the definition of vengeance. If you've seen your family be mutilated and murdered, you inflict that same justice. But to say there is no difference between a few days of occupation and six hundred years of those same excesses. If you see them as the same, I doubt you can help us with American public opinion."

Gibbons was moved. "Unfortunately, Captain, I am only one voice. But I will promise you that I will speak it as loudly and convincingly as I can. I've seen the brutality you speak of. I only hope that public opinion will force American politicians to do what is right."

With her eyes darting back and forth between Gibbons and Apostolidis, Eleni now wanted to make sure Gibbons had enough information to continue his supportive articles.

"Dr. Gibbons, please excuse my interruption, but no one seems to ever mention that under Mr. Stergiadis, Greece has built laboratories that have reduced the incidence of malaria, syphilis, rabies, smallpox and other diseases. And we distributed this medical relief to both Christian and Muslim. Before the Greeks arrived, the Turks did nothing. And when you talk about the attitude of all the Commission's witnesses against the Greeks, they fail to add that all these witnesses wanted the Turks to return because they could be dominated and taken advantage of. Because the Greeks have always been shrewd merchants, these European witnesses have lost their unfair advantage."

Apostolidis raised his index finger. "Dr. Gibbons, I have only one more thing to say about these reports of Greek atrocities. If you research it, you will find that after we landed in Smyrna, and yes after the problems we had before Stergiadis took over, we constantly received reports of atrocities being committed to our people by the *chettes*. The problem was that our troops had to remain within three kilometers of the Greek zone. So when the outlying villages would report that their women were being raped and mutilated, we would respond and be forced to violate the Greek zone. Unfortunately, the *chettes* would just commit their atrocities and then retreat to behind the Italian line. They were given safe haven there. How can you expect our people to endure these things and then have our hands tied by those peacocks who prance around Paris."

For the silence that followed, Eleni could see that useful testimony was essentially over. She asked, "Dr. Gibbons, so how long will you remain in our wonderful city?"

"Actually, I'm here for two weeks. I was supposed to meet with Rear Admiral Bristol, the fellow that the Captain just mentioned. I know how you feel about him, but I'm trying to get a spot as one of the American journalists assigned to report on the war in Asia Minor. Admiral Bristol is in charge of selecting who will be allowed in. I came here first, because, if I'm not chosen, I would not have been able to get this report at all."

Gibbons stood up prompting the others to follow. Eleni said, "Dr. Gibbons, will you join us at our table and perhaps be distracted from the reality of our difficult times?"

Gibbons smiled at the beautiful woman in front of him.

"Thank you my dear, but I have been traveling for many hours and I am completely exhausted. I hope you will excuse me from the distraction I would welcome any other time."

As Gibbons departed he looked back at the center table and saw everyone laughing, drinking and trying to forget whatever woes tomorrow might bring.

Chapter 16.

It was time for Gibbons to leave Smyrna for Constantinople. He had stayed long enough to acquire confirming eyewitness interviews for the Gheronda assault, as well as a second and equally unproductive meeting with Governor Stergiadis, who, while controversial, showed his fanatic obsession with fairness to be a genuine gift or curse, depending on which side of the war you were on.

Gibbons invited Captain Apostolidis over to the Kraemer Palace. He wanted to say goodbye, but also to get the Captain's view on a rumor that had been circulating around Smyrna since mid-June that appeared to run counter to reality and logic. The rumor was that even though the Greek forces had spent a year sitting in stalemate on the front, without enough food, water, or ammunition, apparently the Greeks were about to launch an invasion of Constantinople, and that they had been moving troops from the Anatolian theater toward the neutral zone around the capital city.

Sitting in the lobby, he looked up from his notes for a book he was planning, and saw the Captain enter the lobby of the hotel. He waved the Captain over to his area and they exchanged a handshake before they occupied the overstuffed lobby chairs. Gibbons poured out two glasses of chilled *retsina* (a Greek white wine that carries the aroma of pine resin) and toasted the Captain's health and fortune.

"Thank you Captain, for coming to see me before I left for Constantinople. I wanted your opinion on a rumor I've been hearing that makes no logical sense to me. Perhaps you can give me some clarification."

"My pleasure Dr. Gibbons. You keep supplying the *retsina* and we can talk all you like."

Gibbons nodded with a smile.

"Captain, what of the reports about Greek forces being moved from the front toward Constantinople? That movement would no doubt force the British and French to defend the neutral zone and resist the Greek forces. It just makes no sense to pick a fight with your ally."

Apostolidis took a sip of his wine and contemplated his answer.

"Dr. Gibbons, I guess I can see how the British and perhaps an American would view the action as illogical. I can tell you as a Greek, it makes perfect sense considering the status of the war, and the choices we are left with."

Gibbons was intrigued.

"My friend, please enlighten me. I'll no doubt be asked this very question when I arrive in Constantinople."

"In order to understand the Greek motive," Apostolidis said, "you must set aside your mentality as an ally of Great Britain. You must also set aside the notion that all Greeks are ignorant peasants that pick olives and cheat at cards. The Greeks have been building cities and engaging in commerce since your ancestors were still living in trees. Those in Greek society are as astute in politics as they are in commerce. We don't only follow what people say. We look at what they do.

"If you can at least do that, perhaps you can begin to understand. Remember, it was your own President Wilson who pushed us to invade Asia Minor. And he didn't do that because he wanted to help our people. He just wanted to stop the Italians from getting there first. He knew the British didn't have soldiers to stop the Italians from advancing on Smyrna. And that two-faced Lloyd George . . . he promised our Prime Minister, that if Greece occupied Asia Minor, Great Britain would support us and supply us. He betrayed us! Of course, Venizelos was foolish to believe the British would keep their promise. Yes, he was willing to invade because he wanted to free our people from the Turk. But, he was also to blame because of his crazy idea to make Greece the great empire it once was.

"And the Big Four. . . they were all fools to believe they could send in our armies and think we would not seek vengeance after centuries of watching Turks raping our women and children. We are a civilized people, but we can also be as uncivilized as our enemy. We believe in equal justice. Once we took over, the *chettes* never stopped killing and raping. You saw it yourself. They would just cross back over the line where Greeks were forbidden by the Allies to cross. You send us in, and then you tie our hands.

"Of course we are all not politically-savvy. We do have too many peasants who do not understand the subtleties of political power. That was obvious when Mr. Venizelos lost the election. The peasants wanted the return of the king they grew up with, even though he was linked to the Germans. As soon as Constantine was back in power, Monsieur Clemenceau started working against us and began sleeping with the Turks. That is when they began a campaign to revise the Sevres Treaty. There is an old Greek saying. . . 'Lie down with pigs and you wake up smelling like garbage.'

"Like the fool he is, Constantine replaced our war generals with his idiot friends. . . You can't print that. I'll be executed. Constantine, even though he hated Venizelos, liked the idea of bringing back the old Greek empire of ancient times. He liked the idea of being king over an empire rather than a small, poor country. But already the Allies were no longer enthusiastic about backing the Greeks. You saw our idiot king as an extension of the Germany you just defeated in the Great War.

"Lloyd George and the British Foreign Office who are still secretly telling us to eliminate the Turks, and the British War Office see it differently from each other. The British Secretary of War, Mr. Churchill, is the only one in London who can see what is happening. The Bolsheviks are making nice with the Turks. They are feeding the Turks with munitions as they split up Armenia between them. With the Russian alliance, the Greeks never will be able to defeat the Turks.

"So the Allies decide to just let things stay the way they are and see what happens. The key to the Allied motive is their notification to the Greek government that they were withdrawing their financial and moral support of the Greek occupation. They even introduced a financial blockade of Greece. That's the key!

"Now, it is clear that all of the Allied powers are claiming neutrality so that they can romance the Turks and get oil concessions to power their navies with oil. In order to show their neutrality, they are now supporting the idea that Greek forces should leave Asia Minor and leave our people at the mercy of our enemy who has shown he will massacre us for sport."

Gibbons could not look Apostolidis in the eye as his comments were ringing true, and not an example of the Allies' finest hour.

Apostolidis continued. "Look at it from our point of view. We did what the British asked. For the most part, we've improved the lives of everyone under our control for two years, and we've had to chase the Turkish murderers down, to keep them from massacring our people. But for a whole year now, you've cut off our supply lines. Our soldiers starve out in the desert while our enemy sleeps with the French, the Russians and the Italians.

"Did you know, the Greek and Turkish forces are separated by a river that is only fifty meters across and at this time of the year is only knee-deep? For a year these armies look at each other and do nothing. Greek soldiers and Turkish soldiers wash themselves in the river and even talk with one another. Our soldiers trade their cigarettes for eggs and pork that the Turks are forbidden to eat. They haven't fought in months. So, we ask ourselves, How are we going to end this? We are too poor a country to win the war on our own without British help."

Gibbons fully understood the Captain's points but it still made no sense to take forces from the main theater and move them to a secondary front they had no real desire to occupy. He asked, "Okay, I understand your dilemma, but how does invading Constantinople improve your position? You are taking aggressive action against the British, admittedly no longer a very strong ally, but certainly still your only ally."

Apostolidis refilled his own glass. "We Greeks are gamblers. We weigh the odds and then make our bet and live with the result. In this case, the last hand has been dealt, and we have a lousy hand. So our choice is either to take a long shot, or settle for no shot. The choice is a simple one. We must play our lousy hand. We send troops to Thrace. If we occupy Constantinople, the stalemate ends. Taking Constantinople is easy. But that is because no army is there to keep us from taking it. But we cannot survive over time, unless Great Britain takes our side. We cannot trust the French or the Italians. So we must take our one shot and hope the British will remember how they got us into this mess."

Gibbons could now see the logic. In some bizarre way it actually made sense. "Have the British given you any indication that they will take the initiative? Has your government secretly told the British why they're making this move?"

Apostolidis smiled. "I am only a soldier. I follow orders. I have no idea how it will end. I have only one hope. Look! The British position makes no logical sense. Let me ask you a question. Let us say it is a time when Scotland first became part of the British empire. If the British had suspected that France was using their ships to deliver arms and supplies to the Scots, do you agree that Great Britain was entitled to search French ships for contraband?"

Gibbons reluctantly nodded. "Why yes, if the Scots were planning a war, Great Britain would have the right as a combatant to blockade Scotland if necessary to protect itself."

The Captain nodded, "Now that we understand the stakes, do you not agree that upon determining that France and Italy were shipping war materials to the enemy in an acknowledged war, does Greece not have the right to search those ships for contraband?"

Gibbons was finally on the same page. "I guess so! And yes, the British upheld the French and Italian objection to Greece searching their ships on the basis that they were neutral countries. Britain is reacting solely to protect what she views as her own."

Apostolidis downed the rest of the wine in his glass. "So tell me. What do you suggest Greece do, holding the hand that she holds?"

As much as he didn't want to admit it, suddenly the insane Greek decision made all the sense in the world. Gibbons said, "They don't intend to occupy Constantinople. They're bluffing in the desperate hope that Britain will see that Asia Minor is better off in the hands of Greece than with the Kemalists."

Apostolidis raised his empty glass in a toast. They clinked glasses.

That evening, Gibbons accepted a dinner invitation from the wealthy Xenopoulos family, during which, the senior Xenopoulos thought it appropriate to provide his own unfiltered analysis of the Greco-Turkish conflict. Aside from the narrative, the dinner qualified in Gibbons' mind, as the most delicious and exotic meal he had ever consumed. The evening's end brought a whispered apology from the beautiful Eleni for her father's impassioned rant, in addition to a farewell glimpse of her glorious bosom. Gibbons concluded as he walked away that she would make an effective diplomat for any country.

Chapter 17.

    The next morning, there was only one other person Gibbons felt compelled to visit before his departure. He walked the five blocks from his hotel over to the Greek Orthodox Cathedral, Saint Fotini (Photini), where Archbishop Chrysostomos gave weekly sermons. Gibbons entered the church which, even though it was Saturday- had a number of worshippers occupying the nave. A deacon welcomed Gibbons and escorted him to the office of the Archbishop. Gibbons was seated and given a cup of *Tsai*. He glanced around the room and saw the picture of Saint Polycarp that Sir Philip had described in his own meeting with the Archbishop.

    Gibbons heard the door open behind him. He turned, glass teacup in hand, and saw his friend, Chrysostomos. He was struck by the sadness clearly visible in the man's eyes; a sadness that carried the additional weight of despair. Chrysostomos was adorned with his traditional black gown and *kalimavkion* (a black brimless cylindrical hat worn by Orthodox Christian priests). With the sun shining through the window, the Prelate's full beard seemed to take on an iridescent glow.

    Gibbons held out his hand and bowed his head out of respect.

    "Your Eminence, it is once again a great honor to be in your presence."

    Chrysostomos took Gibbons' hand and covered it with his other hand.

    "I am gratified you came to see me. I read your last article and I thought it worthy of our cause. Please sit. Tell me what is next for you."

    The two men sat across from one another.

    "Your Eminence, I sent off my last notes for an article that was printed in the *Monitor* shortly after. I have not seen the final printed version, but I tried to make the point without looking like a blind apologist. I've seen enough to convince me of both the validity of your concern and of the brutality of General Kemal and the rebel

Turkish nationalists. But what troubles me now is the sadness I see in your eyes. In our last meeting there was a passionate zeal and inspiration in them. Is there anything I can do to help?"

The Archbishop looked deeply into Gibbons' eyes.

"My friend, you must continue to tell the American people about our struggle. The Greek people have a special resonance with the American ideal. It is embedded deeply in our psyche. It is only a free people that will come to the aid of the enslaved. But do not tell them what I say. I am called a revolutionary that wears the priest's robes. But what I tell you now, you will find confirmation elsewhere. Let it be your own words, that will not be lost in the dismissal of a rogue priest."

Gibbons understood his friend. "Tell me what needs to be said."

"When our troops landed here in 1919, it was the result of a bargain between our Prime Ministers. We were the only nation that still had an army of two-hundred-thousand men after the Great War. That bargain gave us Thrace right up to the walls of Constantinople, and Smyrna with its hinterlands in Asia Minor. For our part, we would provide control over the Straits, a strategic Allied goal. This enabled Great Britain, with only nominal forces, to control Constantinople by themselves.

"The bargain, however, was not unilateral. If the Greeks were to supply the troops, considering how poor Greece is, it was understood that Britain would supply us with arms, munitions and support from her naval fleet. We all know Britain does not have the manpower as a result of the demands on her army from Ireland to India. Most of her soldiers went home after the Great War. Our soldiers could not! But now, any attempt by the British to support the Greeks, will provoke the French and the Italians. While they all agree the Greek army is the agent of the Allies in Asia Minor, already the newspapers talk of the deals made by the French and Italians to help the Turks.

"Two days ago your paper still talked of the imminent Turkish defeat, but the Turks now have the supplies to hold back the Greek advances. Our men have been at war for 12 years. They are tired and the only thing that keeps them standing is the hate they feel when they see their women and children raped and slaughtered by Turkish barbarians.

"Now the allies turn their backs on the Greek people and talk of revising the Treaty of Sevres and ordering the Greek soldiers to evacuate. You know this will mean the destruction and death of all Christians left in Asia Minor. And I will tell you today, as reluctant as I am to foresee the future, if the Allies agree to a Greek withdrawal without insuring protection for the Christians, we will all die, and you will see a repeat of this problem again in the future after we are gone. Just look at the past. History is a cruel but honest teacher."

Gibbons could see the cold reality of his friend's prophecy. "I'm familiar enough with history to see the wisdom in what you say. I promise you I will testify in my own words what that reality is, and I hope it will do some good. Please keep communications open to me at the *Monitor* and I will try to support your efforts and educate our people of how serious the situation is."

The two friends said their goodbyes. Chrysostomos walked Gibbons out to the street. Gibbons walked away from the cathedral and could tell the sadness of his friend had infected his own psyche. He committed himself to do whatever he could to be chosen as one of Bristol's embedded reporters covering the conflict.

Chapter 18.

The heavy rope was lifted off the iron mooring post that held the massive paddle steamboat's bow to the pier. The swift current of the Danube River at the port of Passau Germany, immediately caused the large ferry's bow, which was facing upstream, to edge away from the dockside. Once aimed toward the river's center, the rear mooring ropes were also released as the mighty paddle wheel began to rotate, followed by the loud ship's whistle sounding twice. The *Dampfschiff Schönbrunn* edged away from the Passau port pier.

13. The Schönbrunn continues to carry passengers in the 21st century.
Photo courtesy of Gordon Stewart.

First time passengers were surprised by the fact that the huge paddle wheel did not produce the expected cauldron of white foam, normally produced by sea-going vessels. Equally as surprising was the ferry's whistle which sounded more like a screeching train whistle than what one would expect from such a large ship. None of the passengers aboard had any clue that the commencement of this cruise down the Danube River, with its final port of call at Constantinople, would serve as the prelude to the end of five thousand years of Greek civilization in Asia Minor.

The *Schönbrunn* was a fine example of Austrian paddle-steamships built by *Erste Donau Dampfschiffahrts Gesellschaft* or as it was called *DDSG*, at their own Budapest shipyard in 1912. It was a substantial vessel displacing 565 tons of water and measuring 246 feet in length by 51 feet at its center-placed paddle wheel. It was outfitted for long distance services including overnight passenger accommodations and full dining capabilities, and was capable of carrying nine hundred passengers. However, this cruise would carry less than three hundred passengers.

The year of 1922 found Germany less concerned about its post-war disarmament and more concerned about its eroding economy. The trials of Germany's war criminals no longer populated the headlines, as the punitive nature of reparations had taken their place. The economy was teetering as the German Mark was in free fall, and it would be another six days before Germany would be relieved of making any cash reparation payments for the rest of the year.

Perhaps it was the general malaise about the German economy that produced a subdued departure for the *Schönbrunn*. In times past, passengers would be lined up at the rail waving to the onlookers as they prepared for a relaxing trip down the historic Danube. But this trip only produced a dozen or so passengers at the rail going through the motions of a less than convincing *bon voyage*.

Thirty minutes into the voyage, one of the *Schönbrunn*'s passengers, was already hugging the chamber pot in his second class cabin. Asa K. Jennings, a forty-five year old employee of the Young Men's Christian Association (YMCA), was blessed with an inner ear problem that produced severe and debilitating nausea whenever he found himself on board a vessel that produced even the slightest rocking motion.

Jennings' wife, Amy, twisted a towel to wring out excess water into a metal wash basin, so she could place it on the back of her husband's neck. Dealing with her husband's difficulties, had become more routine over their years of marriage. Their two sons, Asa W. (15) and Wilbur (13), and their daughter, Bertha (8) tried valiantly to ignore the condition of their father, as they played their own version of the charade guessing game.

Wilbur tried his absolute best to portray the actions of an American indian dancing a war dance. He stopped suddenly and looked at his siblings, as if the answer was obvious. Seeing only a blank stare on their faces, Wilbur began shooting an invisible bow and arrow as his older brother and younger sister looked-on waiting for the answer to materialize. Suddenly little Bertha shouted, "Sitting Bull!"

Amy instantly brought her index finger up to her mouth and whispered, "Shhhhhh! Your father is trying to fall asleep. Go up on deck and occupy yourselves."

Amy Jennings watched her children as they silently crept out of the cabin. She felt sorry that they had to sleep on pallets as the cabin only had enough room for one double bed. But the Jennings children were used to such inconveniences. The Jennings family was not a family of means. Their father had been an ordained Methodist minister back in upstate New York. Rural Methodist ministers were not paid to serve their flock on a full-time basis until the congregation had enough worshippers to be able to afford a minister's stipend. Consequently, Asa was a full-time farmer during the week and became his congregation's part-time minister on Sundays.

Amy couldn't help but think back to the crisis before Asa had joined the YMCA. In 1904, at the age of twenty-seven, Jennings had been stricken with Potts Disease, a form of tuberculosis that affects the spine by destroying the discs, leading to a collapse of the vertebra. In Jennings' case he was forced to wear a body-cast for two years. Finally out of frustration, Jennings impulsively cut the cast off himself, the resulting instability causing part of his spine to collapse. In one excruciating

14. *Asa K. Jennings.*
Photo courtesy of Roger L. Jennings (grandson).

moment Jennings lost five inches in height rendering him essentially a five-foot-three-inch hunchback.

During that difficult period, a string of physicians had all arrived at the same prognosis. Jennings would soon die as a result of his condition. Finally, during a conference of doctors at the hospital Amy was advised to prepare her husband for the fact that he was about to die. Amy had spent the entire night worrying over how she could be the bearer of such terrible news when she returned to the hospital in the morning.

As would be fitting of a minister's wife Amy sought comfort in the family bible. Probably a result of her distress as she reached for it, the bible slipped and fell open on the floor. She picked it up and through her tears, Amy read,

> JOHN 11:
> 4. When Jesus heard *that*, he said, This sickness is not unto death, but for the glory of God, that the Son of God might be glorified by it.

The words gave her comfort. In the morning she returned to her husband's hospital bed prepared to support him until the end. Strangely, Jennings was not at all concerned by the news. Instead, he smiled at her and said, "Amy, I can't die yet! I have a great work to do and I must go to see Jerusalem."

Amy wondered if her husband was now delusional. But then she looked deeply into his eyes that were as clear as she had ever seen them. He wore the same playfully sarcastic smile that seemed to always incense his more-devout parishioners. This was the same good-humored extrovert that she pledged to devote her life to. He was totally serious. At that moment, Amy was certain her husband would not die as the physicians had all predicted.

It had been eighteen years since he lay on his deathbed and defied the prognosis. Once out of the hospital however, no longer able to withstand the physical work of a farmer, Jennings had given up his ministry and instead took a job with the YMCA. Employment at the YMCA was a paid position allowing him to continue his personal ministry and also feed his growing family.

Amy had been pleased when they learned of Jennings' reassignment from the mission in Prague to the mission in Smyrna. For fifteen years, Amy had accompanied her husband who served as a YMCA secretary in both North America and in Europe. At the outbreak of the Great World War, he was sent to serve in France. After the war, he returned to the United States and served as the national boys' secretary, a post that had evolved to become a prominent position in the organization.

In the century before, the primary mission of the YMCA had been to convert Catholic and Orthodox Christians as well as non-Christians to the Protestant faith. But due to the strong ties inherent in the faiths of their prospective subjects, the organization was unable to convert many individuals. Over time, the YMCA's mission evolved from proselytism and conversion to more of a social gospel for good works. The change made the YMCA more palatable to Christians of other denominations, especially in their efforts to help boys develop an ethical sensibility.

Once again, Jennings was sent to Europe. This time he would go to the newly-created Czechoslovakia, as head of the YMCA mission at *Budějovice* in Bohemia. In October 1918, the country declared its independence from the Austro-Hungarian Empire with the blessing from the Allied powers. But post-war missions in Czechoslovakia were transitioning to using native secretaries, a prediction that Jennings' tenure was to be short-lived. Earlier that summer, he had been notified of his transfer to the mission in Smyrna, Asia Minor.

Amy was quite pleased because she had heard many stories about Smyrna. She'd heard Smyrna was a progressive, bustling city like Paris. It had a large European population with theaters, a vibrant economy, and all of the amenities of a world-class cultured city. That alone seemed like a welcome change from post-war Europe. But other than anecdotal hearsay, neither one of them had any idea of what Smyrna was like or what they were about to experience.

On the first day of its voyage, the *Schönbrunn* made short stops at Linz and then Melk Austria, arriving at its next major stop at Vienna. Having spent most of the first day's cruise lying on the floor of his cabin, Jennings managed to fall asleep sometime after midnight. He was finally awakened by the *Schönbrunn's* whistle warning that it was docking at the port of Vienna.

While the *Schönbrunn* was tied up, the river breeze had died down leaving the Danube to appear as if it were a plate of glass. Jennings felt well enough to park himself on a deck lounge chair and treasure the moments of not feeling the motion sickness. He was quite content to sit and stare at the city before him. The ferry remained at port most of the day allowing Amy to spend some time with the children. She managed to also arrange for Jennings to get a clear broth from the galley.

After sitting motionless for hours, Jennings stood for the first time at the rail and looked at the famous city. He wanted to be able to say he had seen Vienna and technically, that was now an accurate statement. But standing at the rail was about the most he could muster. He was extraordinarily fragile. He thought, *It took seven days on the voyage across the Atlantic before I was able to walk around. Surely, on a relatively calm river I can acclimate more quickly.*

By late afternoon, the *Schönbrunn* left Vienna and crossed borders once again, into Czechoslovak waters, stopping at Bratislava. Taking it as a step in the right direction, he consumed a small portion of dry toast, not willing to risk a relapse of his love affair with the chamber pot. With the next port at Budapest Hungary, the *Schönbrunn* would travel non-stop for fourteen hours.

Surprisingly, the extreme calm on this leg of the journey, allowed Jennings to recover sufficiently. When the paddle steamer docked in Budapest, Jennings was able to optimistically proclaim that he was almost back at 100% - almost being the least accurate portion of his proclamation. By mid morning, Jennings was resolute that he would leave the ferry and actually set foot on dry land in Budapest. The children were ecstatic that they too would leave the ferry.

Thankful of Jennings recovery, the Jennings family disembarked and all showed an appreciation for standing on solid ground. Once off the ship, Wilbur immediately began to whine, "What are we going to see? Are we going to have lunch here?

Jennings looked around. They had ventured only a few hundred feet from the *Schönbrunn* when he realized just how inaccurate the word 'almost' had been. Amy immediately saw he was in trouble. She began to talk of their returning to the steamer.

Asa felt bad enough and refused to make it worse by further disappointing his children.

"Amy, you take them on. I'll return to our cabin. I'm not that bad off. I'm just too weak to take a long walk. Don't worry! I'll be fine. I'll see you when you return."

Amy was tentative, but Asa's nod was enough for her. She watched as he turned and headed back to the *Schönbrunn*.

Once back on board, Amy realized that this would be the last place they would be able to disembark until Constantinople. Back in the cabin, she pulled out the boat's itinerary and stared at the list:

3 Aug	Mohács, Hungary
4 Aug	Novi Sad, Yugoslavia
5 Aug	Belgrade, Yugoslavia.
7 Aug	Rousse, Bulgaria
9 Aug	Constanta, Romania
11 Aug	Constantinople, Asia Minor

"Oh my gosh, this trip will be as long as the voyage over the Atlantic. I hope the water remains calm."

Amy Jennings was about to be disappointed.

Chapter 19.

The newly dominant House of Commons in the British Parliament was particularly contentious on the eve of adjourning for the next fourteen weeks, as the debate over the Greco-Turkish war continued to divide the government.

Sir Francis Lindley, the British ambassador to Athens, had just returned to London. His goal was to be sure that the British government understood the desperate conditions in which the Greeks found themselves.

The debate became contentious after a speech by Lieutenant Commander Joseph Kenworthy, MP, whose hostility toward Lloyd George was obvious to the entire House of Commons. It was Kenworthy's contention that a visibly-friendly Turkey had been severely alienated as a result of the British pro-Greece policy. His point was to show that a pro-Greek policy worked against the British changeover to oil as fuel for its navy, especially since its most likely

15. *The old House of Commons chamber circa 1921. It was bombed in World War II.*

source would be the oilfields of Mesopotamia (present-day Iraq). It was clear that his presentation was gaining favor with the majority of ministers.

Amidst the raucous remarks coming from the chamber, Lloyd George rose to respond to Kenworthy's attack. He set his note binder upon the table before him and stood quietly as he scanned the room. He refused to speak until the shouts from the chamber had subsided. Finally, there was silence.

"Mr. Speaker. . . my honorable colleague Baron Kenworthy speaks eloquently of the friendly government of Turkey. Perhaps his memory fails him. Must I remind him how during the Great War this friendly power slammed the gates of the Dardanelles in the face of Great Britain and France. . . without whose continuous assistance, the Turkish Empire would not have remained in existence? Must I remind the gentleman that the collapse of Russia and Romania was due almost entirely to Turkey's taking sides with Germany in the war? Must I remind him that the allocation to Greece of Smyrna and the surrounding area was the action of *all* the Allied powers at Versailles? That this area was handed over to Greece because it was predominantly Greek in population, wealth and historic association?"

The Prime Minister looked directly at Kenworthy and paused as the hall reacted with both cheers and jeers. "Mr. Speaker, this is not the isolated act of this country! But yet my honorable friend suggests that we evacuate this area and leave a half-million Greeks behind with no provision for their protection. He roils that Great Britain favors Greece in this war. Must I also remind him that it is the British, French and Italian forces who are preventing the Greeks from entering Constantinople?"

Kenworthy stood to protest the Prime Minister's comments, but Lloyd George stared him down displaying his annoyance. "The honorable gentleman makes much of the excesses committed by Greek soldiers. Must I remind him of what the Turks have done in Pontus. . . where hundreds of thousands have been deported or killed without provocation? Where a policy has been pursued, according to American observers of calm, deliberate extermination? Have I been mistaken that it was Britain's duty to see that these Christian populations were adequately protected from further outrage? Suppose, for example, the Armenians were in control of Asia Minor and that they had been guilty of the atrocities. Would this country not have been bound to intervene?"

Lloyd George relaxed his shoulders and leaned on the notebook in front of him. He scanned the chamber again. "Mr. Speaker, I forget who it was who said that we were not fair and impartial. I am not sure that we are. What has happened? Here is a war between Greece and Turkey. We are defending Constantinople, the capital city of one of the parties, against the other. If we were not there, there is absolutely no doubt that the Greeks would occupy that capital in a very few hours, and that would produce a decision. There is only one way now in which the Greeks can have a decision, and that is by marching through almost impenetrable passages for hundreds of miles into the country. I do not know of any army that would have gone as far as the Greeks have. It is a very daring and a very dangerous military enterprise. Mr. Speaker, there are even suggestions, not altogether perhaps without foundation, that the Kemalist forces are being re-equipped from Europe. The Greeks, under other conditions, would have been entitled to blockade the coast of Asia Minor. Peace! The Kemalists will not accept, because they say we will not give them satisfactory armistice terms. But yet we will not allow the Greeks to wage the war with their full strength. In conclusion, I earnestly hope that whatever happens, we shall see that the Christian populations of Asia Minor are adequately protected against repetition of such horrible incidents as have disgraced the annals of that land."

Lloyd George fell back into his seat. There was now an embarrassed hush in the hall. The Prime Minister looked around the chamber one more time as this would be the last time he could intervene in favor of Greece. He thought, *At least my comments might give the poor bastards enough hope to bolster their morale.*

Chapter 20.

The Hotel Commodore, originally built on New York City's famed 42nd Street as part of *Terminal City*, a complex of palatial hotels and offices connected to Grand Central Station, had opened its two thousand rooms in 1919 boasting the "most beautiful lobby in the world."

With tensions rising as a result of discussions amongst the Allies to force an evacuation of the Greek army from Asia Minor, the *New York Times* had arranged to meet with two delegates from Micrasiatic Defense League who had traveled from Smyrna to be interviewed by the prestigious newspaper. The interview was in response to a circulating rumor that the Greek government was establishing a new independent country in western Asia Minor.

The lobby of the Commodore was certainly living up to its reputation. The *New York Times* had cordoned off a lavish section of the lobby for a reporter and stenographer to meet with the two Greek envoys. Within the roped-off section, a table with coffee, tea and a

16. New York City's Hotel Commodore under construction in 1919.

mountain of pastries were set up for the interview, drawing onlookers to gather outside the ropes. Promptly at 10 a.m., the two delegates appeared in the lobby.

Mr. Stephanos Beinoglou, the official delegate for the Defense League was small in stature, probably from a food deficiency in his youth. Beinoglou was a native Greek from Smyrna whose English was marginal at best. Mr. Antonios Athinogenis, an attorney, was fluent in both Greek and English and was to serve as interpreter. Athinogenis, also a native of Smyrna, had been credited in 1919 with calming an uprising of Greek villagers in *Boudja*, a wealthy community on the outskirts of Smyrna.

The reporter greeted the two delegates and offered them refreshments. Once they were served coffee and cake, they sat across from each other in overstuffed lounge chairs in full view of the small crowd that had gathered in the Commodore lobby.

The reporter began, "Mr. Beinoglou, thank you for giving the *Times* this exclusive interview. There have been some rumors out of Athens that suggest the Greek government is looking to create a new, autonomous country with its capital at Smyrna. Can you comment on this rumor?"

Beinoglou understanding the question, began to answer in Greek. Obviously having interpreted before, Athinogenis began to translate simultaneously in English.

"The decision of the Allied ministers, places us in an impossible situation. Either we remain in our homes and be butchered by the Turks or we leave our homes to follow the Greek army and evacuate as refugees.

"We will choose neither course. We have decided that when the Greek army evacuates Asia Minor, we will remain to protect our homes and our families and die to the last man rather than surrender to the bloodthirsty Kemalists. We now have thirty-five thousand men in the army. We are recruiting our forces so that they will eventually reach one hundred thousand. We have organized a police force of twenty-five thousand officers."

The stenographer transcribed the statement as the translator spoke.

The reporter asked, "Are you saying the Greek army is in the process of evacuating or are they still engaging the enemy?"

The translator continued, "I am not here to discuss the actions of the Greek Army in Asia Minor. On our way to this country, word reached us that a more intensive mobilization of the population has begun. The Greek military authorities in Smyrna have mobilized Armenians and Circassians who have volunteered to join us. We know that even if the word is given to the Greek Army to evacuate the region, a large part of the army will never accept the order as long as the Christians of Asia Minor will have to fight for their lives."

"Under the Treaty of Sevres, the people of Asia Minor were freed from Turkish rule, but subsequent political conditions have caused the Allied foreign ministers at Paris to hand us back to the 'tender mercies' of Mustapha Kemal.

"The Allied decision became known to us last March so we began our defense then. You have probably read in this country that the Allies have promised the evacuated territory to the Turks, and supposedly, that the Turks would guarantee the safety of the Christians. We in Asia Minor have been here before. The real Turkish guarantee is death at the hands of the Turks or deportation from our homes. If our rights are to be ignored, if the sacrifices of our heroic struggles against ruthless barbarians must go unheeded, and if the Supreme Council acknowledges our sacred right to life is to be set aside, what alternative have we but to rise and die like men?"

The reporter leaned forward in his chair, "Are you asking that the Allies break their neutrality in order to fight for the Greek people of Asia Minor?"

"We do not ask the civilized world to go to western Asia Minor and fight our battles for us. We will do that! All we ask is the right to remain free. For we are free, and European diplomacy would take away our freedom. When we issue our call for volunteers, Greeks in America, Egypt, Constantinople and Europe will flock to our banners to put down the hand of the brutal Turk. Never again will we return to the state of slavery under which we were tyrannized for five centuries. We are here to inform the American people of what is going on in western Asia Minor and to ask the moral support of the United States, its people and its government. In that connection we will present a memorandum to your State Department.

"The Treaty of Sevres practically made us a part of Greece. Since that condition has been changed by the decision of the Allied ministers, we have decided to become an autonomous state, never again under Turkish rule. Many Turks in our territory, now able to compare life under their own officials with life under Greek rule, will fight with us. We will be joined in large numbers by Circassians who are Muslims.

"We have lost sixty thousand men on the battlefields of Asia Minor. Those men died to free western Asia Minor from the Turks. Many Turks have crept into the Greek lines and have begged permission for their families to come to Smyrna and other parts of western Asia Minor, away from Turkish misrule. We are not seeking to wage an imperialist war of aggression. but we will protect our homes."

Once the statement was completed, the reporter assured the envoys that his report would appear in the *New York Times*, so that America would at least hear his plea. In fact, an article about the interview appeared on page six of the *New York Times* on 6 August 1922.

The passionate plea had affected the crowd in the lobby. Now people were commenting making supportive remarks to the gentlemen who would now be faced with traveling to Washington, D.C. The interview was adjourned with the reporter commenting to his stenographer, "I doubt this will go any further than the calls of drowning men, facing imminent death.

Chapter 21.

The Black Sea has a perpetual stiff breeze and therefore choppy waters. The *Schönbrunn*'s paddle wheel was not the most efficient mode of power for this sort of water, as much of the forward motion is dissipated from the turbulence. For what seemed an eternity, Jennings was once again convinced he would never feel human again.

Once the *Schönbrunn* entered the Bosphorus, the strait that separates Europe from Asia, it meant they were only hours out of Constantinople. Jennings was looking forward to being on land again, even if only for a short while.

By the time the *Schönbrunn* docked at Constantinople, the strait's waters had calmed allowing Jennings to once again feel almost human. Surprisingly, shortly after docking, a porter showed up at the Jennings cabin, with instructions to cart their luggage off the boat. Jennings hadn't made any such arrangements, so he concluded these arrangements were made by his employer. With that challenge taken out of their hands, the family disembarked to stand on the dock and await the arrival of their luggage. Once on the dock they were met by a cacophony of strange sounds and fragrances. Mesmerized, the family just stood there staring at the city's edge. Then a voice called out to them.

"Mr. Jennings!. . . Asa Jennings?"

Startled by the fact that he knew no one in this part of the world, Jennings looked around. He saw emerging from the port waiting room a young, well-dressed man in a white seersucker suit waving at him as he approached. He thought, *Who in the world is this fellow?*

Amy looked at the approaching stranger. "Do you know this man, Asa?"

"Haven't a clue!"

Amy speculated, "At least he has a smile on his face. Could it be your new boss?"

The stranger extended his hand as he approached the family.

"Mr. Jennings, I presume!"

Jennings took the man's hand, "You're correct. I'm sorry, have we met before?"

The stranger laughed.

"No, I'm afraid we've never met, but I was given strict orders to meet you on your arrival and make sure you end up in Smyrna."

Seeing the confusion in Jennings' eyes, "My name is Edwyn Cecil Hole. But you can a call me Teddy. Apparently a close friend of mine is going to be your boss in Smyrna. Do you know E. O. Jacob?"

"No! I've never met him, but according to my papers, he will be my boss."

"Don't worry, he's a fine fellow. The E.O. stands for Ernst Otto, but no one calls him that. I like to call him Jake. He was worried that you might get lost and wanted to make sure you arrived before he left on his vacation. Sarah would kill him if he delayed their holiday again. I happened to be here on business, so we arranged that I would return to Smyrna on the same vessel."

Jennings was relieved. This was a very strange place. "I am very grateful for this consideration. We have no idea where to go next. In fact, a porter came to get our luggage, but I'm beginning to worry that he hasn't shown up. Is it possible he's stolen our things?"

Hole laughed again. "No, your things are just fine. I gave instructions that he take all your bags and place them in your cabin aboard the ship to Smyrna."

"Again, I am grateful for such wonderful consideration of my family. By the way, allow me to introduce you to my wife, Amy."

Hole tipped his bowler hat and bowed to Amy. "It is a pleasure to meet you madam."

Amy was flattered. "The pleasure is mine, sir."

Hole's smile turned serious. "Teddy! Please call me Teddy."

"Teddy" Amy said as her face flushed.

"and these three. . . Jennings waved his arm to announce, "are Wilbur, Bertha and Asa Jr."

Hole tipped his bowler again as the Jennings children stared in amazement.

Hole said, "It looks as though we're going to be here in Constantinople until later tonight. So we have the rest of the day until we have to be back here."

"So the ship leaves from this dock as well?

Hole pointed to the next ship over from the *Schönbrunn*. "It's right next to the one you came in on. The *Ionian Crusader*. It's a Greek ship."

Jennings asked tentatively, "Should we board and check to make sure they have all of our luggage?"

"Not to worry. You can be assured it is all there. I am an official of the British government and we control this city. If your luggage is missing, there will be hell to pay for everyone that works on this dock. If you feel you must, we can board, but I can assure you there is no need to check for your personal belongings."

"We are totally in your hands. . . Teddy!"

"Have you had lunch yet?" Hole inquired.

"No!" Jennings replied, "I've been a bit seasick and the children were too excited about getting back on solid ground."

"Well then, the first order of business is a good meal and some good conversation."

Hole directed the family to an official-looking car that was waiting at the curb. Once they all were seated, the driver inquired, "Where to, sir?"

"Pera House!"

Jennings eyes opened wide, "Isn't that the British Embassy?"

"Why, Yes it is. They serve an excellent British lunch there."

As they entered the Pera House, Jennings leaned over to Amy and whispered, "I've never seen so many seersucker suits in one place. It's like a uniform."

17. Pera House, Istanbul, Turkey.
Photo courtesy of John Elkington.

Once checked in, Hole arranged for them to be escorted to the patio facing the massive lawn overlooking a large garden. Cold drinks and snacks were brought to the table, and in a matter of minutes, the Jennings began to unwind from the difficult journey.

Jennings took a sip if his cold lemonade and raised the glass as if to toast Hole. "Teddy, from the way you arranged things, I suspect you wield some authority at the Embassy. Can you tell us what position you hold?"

Hole smiled at his guest. "Certainly, Mr. Jennings..."

Jennings interrupted, "Now if I'm going to call you Teddy, you must call me Asa."

"Okay, Asa, I have the pleasure of being a newly-minted British Vice-Consul. I'm stationed in Smyrna although my duties also include Mytilene (Mitilini), which is a port city on the island of Lesbos just off the mainland across from Smyrna. I say pleasure because it truly is a wonderful post. I find living in Smyrna is even better than living in Paris. It is a wonderful place and I hope I never have to leave."

Suddenly, Amy was interested. "Vice-Consul Hole... Teddy, can you tell us a little about Smyrna? I had never even heard about it until we were informed we would be moving there. This is all so new to us and I know the children are tentative about it as well."

Hole leaned forward in his seat. "I think I can help you there. I have a villa in Smyrna with my wife, Laura. You'll get to meet her soon. It's just a small villa but it does suit us perfectly."

Happy to have an audience, Hole spread his arms as if to take over the conversation. "Smyrna is like being in Paris, only more exotic. It is a wonderful life. You will think you are in paradise. Like I said, Jake Jacob your boss, is a good friend of mine. He lives in a little section of Smyrna that is coincidently known as Paradise. It is also called the 'little corner of America.' You will like living there. It has modern buildings built to American standards, beautiful gardens and even has its own electric plant. The power plant is very dependable, which is better than I can say for the rest of Smyrna. It also has a college and an elementary school with an American teacher. That is where you will send your children to school. Yes! You will never want to leave Smyrna."

Jennings got a curious look on his face. "So Smyrna hasn't been affected by the war between the Greeks and the Turks?"

"Oh no! Not at all. You really don't know anything about Smyrna, do you? Yes! The Greeks and the Turks are murdering each other out in the hinterlands, but none of that affects the city. Smyrna is an international city. It has many Europeans as well as Americans living there. French, Italian, British. It is truly international! Of course a big reason no one will ever try to break the peace in Smyrna is the fact that there is a fleet of Allied warships anchored in the harbor to protect European and American interests."

Jennings nodded in acknowledgement of this new information he found important to the welfare of his family. "Well, that certainly is a comforting thought. I was a bit concerned about that before we left Prague. But I would think, even if the city is protected by Allied warships, with a war going on, wouldn't the Greek population and the Turkish population have great animosity toward each other? I heard that there are more Greeks in Smyrna than there are Turks."

Hole shook his head. "You really are in the dark. May I offer you a cigar and a glass of wine?"

Jennings smiled back. "Why yes, thank you. That would be very enjoyable."

Hole ordered two glasses of wine and pulled two cigars from his jacket. He handed one to Jennings, "So have you always worked for the YMCA or were you ever in private industry?"

"Well, yes! I was a farmer back in New York State and I was also a Methodist minister. But my physical condition removed farming from what I could do to feed my family, which also had the effect of forcing me to retire from the church."

Hole was surprised. "A minister who drinks wine and smokes cigars?"

Jennings smiled in acknowledgement, "Did Jesus not drink wine?"

His smile grew with the silence that followed. Hole took a liking to the man seated in front of him. He leaned back in his chair and puffed his *Romeo y Julieta Perfecto.*

"You know, Greeks and Turks have been living side by side in Asia Minor at least since the Turks conquered it in 1299. This mess that we find ourselves in, is mostly the result of politicians who are rather ill-suited for their profession. Do you know any of the history of Asia Minor?"

Jennings shook his head.

"Well, what is called Asia Minor, used to be called Anatolia. . . and the city of Smyrna was first settled by Greeks back in 650 BC. But approximately one hundred years after they settled, Anatolia was conquered by the Persians, who reigned for approximately two hundred years. Then a young Greek warrior, later called Alexander the Great, took it back from the Persians while he was going around conquering the rest of the world. But soon after he conquered Anatolia, he died in Babylonia... probably poisoned by his own staff. Control of Anatolia was assumed by one of Alexander's generals, whose dynasty ruled until all of Anatolia was given over to the conquering Romans in about 150 BC.

"So the Greeks had it for a hundred years; then the Persians had it for two-hundred; then the Greeks had it again for two-hundred years before the Romans got it. And they held onto it for about five-hundred years before it became the Byzantine Empire which reigned for yet another nine-hundred years. The point being that the Greeks had been the native population in Asia Minor for around two-thousand-five-hundred years before it was conquered by the Turks in 1299."

Jennings took a puff on his cigar and sipped his wine. "But if the Turks conquered it in 1299, that would mean that they've been in control for six-hundred years. I don't think they would care if the Greeks were there longer than they were. They've been there long enough to think it's their homeland as well."

Hole smiled. "You're right of course, but it's not as simple as that. You have to understand the marked differences in the people. The Greeks have a completely different culture than the Turks. Rightly so, the ancestors of the Greeks, the Hellenes, completely changed human perception and thinking. They were the most advanced culture of the ancient world that is the basis for all of western civilization, and the reason we can sit around in this embassy and enjoy wine and cigars and discuss principles and ethical behavior. They were a culture that was based on a strong bond between the state, church and family.

The Turks on the other hand are direct descendants of the Hun hordes... nomadic tribes whose ruler Attila, led them to conquer the Romans. Since they were nomadic tribes, the Turks did not settle in any one place. They were a very militaristic race. It was perfectly acceptable for Turks to conquer villages after which, since they weren't paid very well, as conquerors, they were entitled to rape and pillage as a reward for their victory. So you have one side that is nomadic, militaristic and without roots, set against a people that had brought modern western thought to the world, and were industrious in building economic stability."

Jennings looked up at the bright blue sky and contemplated the differences that he had never considered before. "Well if you've got industrious homebodies pitted against bands of conquering militarists, it doesn't look very good for the homebodies."

Hole laughs. "You have a unique way of putting things Mr. Jennings. And you're right. That's why the Turks have ruled for more than six-hundred years. But that's not all of it. Because of those differences, when the Ottoman Turks became the most powerful empire in Europe and Asia, there wasn't much left to conquer and the Turks were not at all suited to business, economics and managing an empire. So they came up with this strange arrangement that actually worked for hundreds of years."

Jennings took another puff. "I presume it had something to do with Greeks working for Turks."

"In a way it did. The Ottomans declared that the Greeks, Armenians and everyone else, were inferior to Muslim Turks. So as long as everyone accepted the fact that Christians were inferior to Turks, they enjoyed relative autonomy within their religious communities and were allowed to prosper and develop in their communities. Another key to this strange arrangement was that Islamic law discourages Muslims from participating in commerce and banking. It was a vacuum that was going to be filled by Greeks, Armenians and Jews as they increasingly dominated the economic and industrial life of the country. It was this odd arrangement that allowed the Greeks and Armenians to become the wealthiest citizens in all of Asia Minor. So it is also under this odd setup that Orthodox Christians and Muslim Turks have coexisted for hundreds of years. The Greeks and Armenians evolved as they ran industry and the economy while the Turks remained in the 13th century."

Jennings tapped his cigar so as to drop the large ash that had formed. He said, "So this is what eventually led to the Greeks getting their independence. Didn't they get their independence back in the early 1800s?"

"Yes, The Greek Revolution from the Ottomans began in 1821. They were finally recognized as an independent state in 1832. But that was because at that time, it was quite fashionable in Europe to relate to the Greeks. After all, they were the basis of civilized society and modern thought. In the end, if the British, French and Russians hadn't intervened, I doubt whether Greece could have won its independence. But even after Greece was free, it didn't do much good for most Greeks living in Asia Minor. It made things worse for them."

Jennings nodded. "I can imagine."

"So do you know about the Young Turks or are you completely in the dark?"

Jennings shrugged his shoulders. "I've been in Czechoslovakia and the U.S. before that. I have no idea about what's going on in Asia Minor."

Hole took a sip of wine and set his cigar down in the large crystal ash tray between them.

"All right then. I need to give you a crash course so that you'll be able to understand all of the different forces acting on the city you'll be living in. As I was saying, the Ottomans had been running Asia Minor for hundreds of years, and by the 19th century, the Greeks dominated the coastal regions of the Aegean, the Armenians dominated the southern regions around Cicilia and the Sephardic Jews dominated Thessaloniki in Ottoman Macedonia. But the delicate balance between officially-sanctioned inequality and the relative tolerance allowing economic dominance to be taken by the minorities was upset by the Ottoman Empire's inability to keep pace with the other world powers in both economic and military power. The Ottomans would grant European powers more trade privileges, which served to create more interest in Asia Minor by those powers. It was inevitable that the minorities in Asia Minor would seek European influence in granting more freedom to their communities. With each new event, the Empire was losing its power and influence. As we sit here in Constantinople the once great Ottoman Empire is essentially dead and has been since the end of the war."

Jennings was confused. "So does that mean that the Greeks are going to beat the Turks?"

Hole placed his cigar between his teeth.

"It's not that easy. About 20 years ago, some medical students started up a secret society and called it the 'Committee of Union and Progress.' They were for a secular government and against the Ottoman theocracy. Then a group that became known as the "Young Turks" began in 1900. They too, were nationalistic and rejected the view of Ottoman religious precepts as a basis for government. These rabid nationalistic idealists originally came from the ranks of progressive junior officers in the army and medical corps, and evolved to include students, academics and professional elitists. They believed in a powerful nationalistic secular government that called for the union of all Turks in an empire that would recall the greatness of Genghis Khan.

"In 1906, these two groups merged and became a political party. As a party they became more powerful as they pushed for the idea of a country that was exclusively for Turks. They called it 'Turkey for the Turks.' I guess they looked around and saw that the industrial and economic sectors of Asia Minor were dominated by Christian minorities. Why not just get rid of them? You can see how this sort of thinking would hold up Genghis Khan as a model of behavior.

"By 1914, with brutal efficiency, the Young Turks deported hundreds of thousands of Greeks to either Greece or to the barren interior of Asia Minor. They planned the same fate for the Armenians and in 1915 began deporting them to the Turkish interior. Being deported to the Turkish interior is another way of saying 'walk until you expire.'

18. Greek Refugees being deported into the Turkish interior.

"But with the outbreak of the war, the idea of deporting minorities was no longer the primary goal of the Young Turks. They were concentrating more on their own survival. It was after the war, that they returned to thinking about removing minorities from what they viewed as the Turkish state. I'm afraid that this is where my own government is not without responsibility."

A waiter appeared at the table and handed the Jennings' children crayons and paper. Immediately all three began drawing.

Amy said, "Teddy? This history is fascinating, but can you tell me a little about life in the city? We have no idea about what to expect."

Hole smiled at the children. "You all will see things you cannot even imagine. Smyrna is a place where two completely different cultures met a very long time ago. Because it was a city that was useful to both Europe and Asia, the city prospered and the big differences between the cultures learned to live side by side. On the one hand, you will see the cream of European society enjoying Verdi's *Rigoletto* in a concert hall that will rival Carnegie Hall in New York City. But after the opera, they will walk along the harbor and see camels being unloaded after their long journey from the interior. Visitors will stay in hotels that will rival those in London and Paris and then they will shop at department stores that will rival anything they've seen anywhere in Europe. The private and sporting clubs are the same. But what makes it different from the top cities of Europe is that it is a mix of all of them. The natives have all grown up speaking multiple languages. Even the children will speak English, French, Italian, Greek and Turkish. I have never met anyone who didn't fall in love with Smyrna."

Asa W. raised his hand as if asking permission to speak. "Pardon me sir, but do you know anything about the school we will be attending?"

Hole reached over and patted his hand. "Do not worry! The American section of Smyrna is called 'Paradise' for a reason. There is an American school there for American families. You will even have an American teacher. But unlike the friends you had in America, you will learn to speak other languages like French, Italian and Greek. This way when you grow up, you will have friends all over the world."

Hole said, "We've been sitting here long enough. I think you should not leave this city without taking a little tour of it. I have a car outside waiting to show us Constantinople."

Hole rose and everyone followed. They walked out to the front drive where the car was waiting. The black Daimler Mercedes attached to the Embassy was equipped with two small Union Jack flags attached to the headlights. Once aboard, they were driven around Constantinople, or more accurately, they crawled trying to navigate around livestock, people and foodstuffs set up on the streets, and were struck by the merging of east and west; modernity and antiquity; all jumbled up in a pungent, undulating, exotic city. They drove along the Bosphorus for a few miles and then turn inland. Finally they stopped in front of a magnificent building.

Asa W. pointed at the domed roof. "Look, it's a church."

Hole said, "Behold! What you are looking at is Agia Sofia (Holy Wisdom) Cathedral. It was built back in the 4th century as the Greek Patriarchal Cathedral, considered the epitome of Byzantine architecture and was the largest cathedral for nearly a thousand years. But it was converted to a mosque in the 15th century by the Ottoman Turks. That was when they added the minarets and removed or plastered over the Christian icons and adornments."

19. Agia Sofia, Istanbul, Turkey. Currently serves as a museum for tourists.
Photo courtesy of C. Papavasiliou.

Next, they drove to a busy intersection and exited the automobile. They walked over to a small sidewalk cafe. Hole signaled to a waiter who immediately came to the table. Hole said to the waiter, "Çay ve üç lemonades Üç bardak, lütfen." The waiter immediately headed for the kitchen.

Jennings' eyes widened. "Was that Turkish you were just speaking?"

"Yes it was! I can order tea and lemonade in eight different languages and if pressed, I can write a note to the waiter asking for the same in another eight. It's one of the benefits of a classical English education."

Jennings looked at Hole in awe. "That's sixteen different languages. Suddenly I feel so inadequately qualified."

"Please, it's not due to high intelligence. I do have a knack for learning languages. They just come easily to me. It can be a burden in my line of work. I get involved in intelligence work that I would prefer to avoid. But since this is my first assignment as a British Vice-Consul, it's not like I can refuse."

As they sat and people-watched, Amy commented. "There sure are an awful lot of British soldiers walking around with weapons."

Hole nodded. "Yes, as I mentioned we. . . the English that is, now control Constantinople. Thanks to the Greek Army, who guard over the Straits for us, we are able to occupy the capital with a small force."

Jennings sipped his *tsai* as he looked at the action of the city around him.

"Okay then, Teddy, am I to conclude that it is these Turkish nationalists, or what you call Young Turks, that are the cause of the war between the Greeks and the Turks?"

Hole nodded, "Well, partially, but you'll recall I mentioned that my own government pushed for Greece to occupy Asia Minor to stop the deportations and murder of Christians inflicted by the Young Turks.

"For its participation in the war, Greece was promised Smyrna and the surrounding areas where the majority of the Greek population live. It made sense to the Allied Powers, and especially your President Wilson, that the area Greece wanted was populated by more Greeks than Turks. In reality, the Greek Prime Minister imagined Greece would once again become the empire it was in ancient times. He even coined a name for it, the *Megali Idea*.

"The problem was that Italy was also promised Smyrna, and she wasn't going to wait around for an auction. President Wilson warned that Italy was sending warships to Smyrna."

"And this is where we took our eye off the ball. Given the fact that Britain didn't have sufficient troop levels to stop the Italians, our Prime Minister, who was very pro-Greece, proposed that the Greeks should occupy Smyrna. You have to understand that most of Europe viewed the Turks as a savage and brutal race. He convinced the French and the Americans as well. So with the blessing of the Allies, Venizelos began his *Megali Idea* to recreate the Byzantine Empire. The animosity that the Young Turks had created by torture, rape and murder since before the war was a formula for destruction. Personally, I thought our decision to let the Greeks occupy Smyrna was a big mistake. Our leaders should have realized the Greeks would want to seek vengeance for the abuses they suffered under the Turks.

"Lloyd George was convinced that the Turks were savages. He wanted the Greeks to clean out the Turks, but he didn't want the Greeks to re-enter Constantinople which had been the capital of the Byzantine empire. His reasoning was simple. The British controlled Constantinople and he didn't want the Greeks messing with something he thought belonged to Great Britain."

Jennings said, "So I guess the Greeks weren't able to quell the violence as they are apparently out there killing each other right now."

"Well, again, it's complex. I am concerned. In fact, I just heard a rumor out of London that the French and the Italians have been supplying the Turks in Ankara with food, supplies and munitions. If this is true, they'll be rested, fed and ready to slaughter the spent Greek armies. I think we've abandoned the Greeks, and the Greeks are beginning to figure that out that they're on their own. I hope this is not true."

Jennings looked concerned. "So you think the Turks might defeat the Greeks?"

"I am concerned about that. There are millions of Greeks in Asia Minor and if the Turks once again get the the upper hand, I fear for the poor people that will be in their path."

Jennings, even more worried, asked, "Do you think they might break the truce in Smyrna?"

"Oh no! They'll stay out of Smyrna, because that would turn all of the Allies against them. There are too many Europeans and Americans living in Smyrna. Don't worry. You will be safe there."

After an hour of people and camel-watching, the children became restless. Hole pulled his stopwatch out of his vest pocket. "I think it's time for us to get back to the dock so we can board."

As they drove back to the port, they heard the Muslim call to prayer coming from one of the minarets.

Chapter 22.

The *Ionian Crusader* steamed across the Sea of Marmara toward Smyrna. Luckily, the water was quite calm. It did get a bit choppy when they entered the Aegean Sea, but thankfully, Jennings did not spend the journey hugging a chamber pot.

It was mid-afternoon when the *Ionian Crusader* approached the protected Smyrna harbor, causing everyone to come on deck. At a glance, Smyrna appeared to be everything Hole had told them. It was beautiful, exotic, and peaceful, except for the citizens strolling along the quayside enjoying the summer sunshine. Even before it docked the exotic aromas permeated the harbor. Jennings counted twenty-two warships flying the flags of the Allied powers. The site, as Hole had described, was very reassuring.

As they approached the dock, the ship turned completely around and then backed into dock at the quay. Once tied up, everyone disembarked and regrouped on the quayside. The sights and sounds of the harbor were an explosion to the senses. Hole looked over the crowd of well-dressed Smyrniotes strolling along the water's edge. Finally, he stopped and shouted, "Jake!. . . Jake!. . . E. O. Jacob!"

A face in the crowd recognized Hole and walked over. Hole said, "Jake, I'd like to introduce you to your new employee. These are Asa and Amy Jennings and their lovely children."

The director of the YMCA greeted everyone and quickly ordered their bags to be taken to their new home in Paradise. Jacob thanked his friend for meeting Jennings and his effort to make them comfortable. He proposed a celebratory dinner once everyone was settled. With that, Hole said his goodbyes and left quickly to return home.

Jacob led Jennings and his family across the quay to the adjacent street. "I have a car over here waiting to take us to your new home. Then tomorrow, you should take a day of rest. Perhaps attend one of the churches here. On Monday, I'll have someone pick you up in the morning and bring you to our mission office to get familiar with everything. I'm sure you'll transition easily as you've had more significant responsibilities in your past assignments."

The group approached a large blue 1920 Daimler Mercedes with two American flags attached to its trademark front flaring fenders. The Jennings children were duly impressed as the door was opened and they were invited to get in.

As they drove toward the American quarter, Jacob said, "You should know, in a few days, you'll be in charge. I have a vacation coming and I want to take it while there is still some summer left. But don't worry, this assignment will be a piece of cake, next to Prague. We have a great relationship with the people here and Greek Archbishop Chrysostomos, believes in our work and supports us. I expect you will have more boys to teach than you can handle. Can you speak Greek?"

Asa shook his head. Jacob laughed. "Don't worry! I'll be surprised if any boy you deal with will not know some English."

The car arrived at the Jennings house and all were impressed with how nice it was. Compared with their apartment in Prague, it was a palace. The house was outfitted with a garden overflowing with aromatic flowers. As Amy emerged from the car, she said, "Can you smell the jasmine? It's like the whole neighborhood has put on perfume."

Jacob unloaded a bag of groceries and small necessities for their dinner before he left them. Within an hour, the Jennings family was settled and smiling at their good fortune to have been given this assignment.

At 9:00 a.m., on Monday morning, the YMCA car was idling in front of the Jennings' new residence. Two short bursts on the car's horn was sufficient to bring Jennings to the front door. He motioned to the driver with a finger as if to say, 'hold on, I'll be there in a minute.'

A quick kiss to each of his children and Amy, and he was out the door and climbing into the front passenger seat of the Daimler-Mercedes. Less distracted than the day before, he took in the city as they drove over to the mission office. Already the street vendors were out and the city was bustling. When they arrived at the mission, Jennings noticed a dozen young boys standing around waiting for something to begin.

Jennings followed the driver into the mission, where Jacob was seated at a desk, working on a report. Jacob stood and shook his hand. "Did you get rested after your long journey?"

"As well as can be expected. I suppose it will take about a week to get back up to full strength. I don't handle travel on water very well. I developed an uncomfortably familiar relationship with the chamber pot in my cabin."

Jacob said, "I think you'll respond more quickly than you think. Smyrna is a fascinating city. It will fill your senses. Before I introduce you to the boys you'll be dealing with, you should know that my wife, Sarah, will be stopping by your home later this morning. She intends to take Amy and the children over to the American school and introduce them to the teacher and the other students. I think they'll be relieved about school, and I know Amy will embrace the Smyrna life."

Jennings smiled, "It will be a welcome change for me. Prague was a rather depressing place to be after the war. I know it was harder on Amy and the children."

Jacob spent the next thirty minutes explaining the setup and program in the mission. It was almost identical to the program he just left.

"Well, let's go out into the main classroom and meet the boys." Jacob said as he raised his arm pointing to the doorway.

He followed Jacob into the classroom and noticed fourteen young boys ranging from eight to fifteen years old. He commented, "These boys are all quite young. Are there no older boys that we can use to take the younger ones under their wing?"

"You won't find any boys over fifteen left in Smyrna. There has been a mobilization by the Greek army and most of them are now soldiers. The Greek army has occupied a few cities to the south, protecting the Christian population from the Turkish *chettes*, that are roaming bands of terrorists who feed off innocent civilians. But you'll immediately notice that the fifteen year olds are mature for their age. They've had to grow up quickly."

The two men stood in front of the boys. Jacob smiled at his audience. "Boys, I want to introduce you to the new Boys' Secretary for our mission. He has come a very long way to help you learn what you need to know to be able to work and provide for your families when you grow up. I want you to meet, Secretary Jennings."

A low rumble followed of a choir of boys saying almost in unison, "Good morning Secretary Jennings."

Asa was surprised that the boys were speaking English, albeit with a heavy accent.

Jacob then stepped forward. "Boys, I'm going to leave you now in the hands of Secretary Jennings. Don't worry, he is very familiar with our boys work program and he is familiar with how it works here in Smyrna. In short order he will learn all your names, and perhaps while you are already learning English here, he may learn some Greek and Armenian. Have a good day and God bless you all."

Jacob smiled as he left the area. Jennings stepped forward and smiled at the boys in front of him. They were much younger than the group he taught in Prague, but they also did look more enthusiastic.

"First of all, from this point forward, I don't want you to call me Secretary Jennings. Please just call me Mr. Jennings. As young boys it is more respectful to address adults as Mr., Mrs. or Miss, and since we will be working closely together there is no need to refer to me by my title. I hope to learn all of your names quickly, and I even hope to learn to speak in your languages as well. Since much of the commerce in and around Smyrna is agricultural, I will continue Mr. Jacob's emphasis on agricultural training for you so you can earn a living when you grow up. I also want to concentrate on Mr. Jacob's citizenship training. We will continue with the athletics program. And I understand the billiards table is a favorite. We will continue the movie night on Wednesdays and I intend to teach you all a little bit about music. But today, I want to talk about something related to agriculture, because I believe most of you will need to be good farmers when you grow up. So let's pull our chairs around so that we form a circle and can look at each other while we talk."

The boys scooted their chairs like it was a game until they somehow ended up in a circle with Asa not having to move his own chair. He thought, *Well, at least they're pretty bright!*

"Does anyone know the meaning of crop rotation?" Jennings looked around the circle as the boys also looked around to see if anyone raised their hands. No one raised their hands.

"Well, since I'm the only one here who knows about crop rotation, let me teach you. It is one of the most important lessons you can learn about farming."

Suddenly a boy about eight years old raised his hand. The boy's clothing was clearly worn to its end, but it was clean. In a heavy Greek accent, "Mr. Jenning. . . what means *ro-ta-shun*?"

Jennings immediately thought he was going to get great satisfaction from these boys. They actually had an interest in learning. He looked around for a prop, stood and walked over to one of the un-utilized chairs and brought it into the center of the circle. He tilted the chair up so that he held it steady leaning on one of its front legs. "This is a chair! Do you all agree?"

In unison all of the boys nodded. Using both hands, he began to spin the chair around its one leg. "This is chair rotation!"

The boys laughed as their individual lights went on.

He set the chair down on all fours and sat back down. "Boys, our Lord has given us a great gift. We can plant a seed in the ground, and with some water to feed it, it will grow to give us things to eat. When you eat fruits and vegetables, there are things inside them called nutrients. And they give your body what it needs to grow. Like us, when a plant is growing, it gets its nutrients from the soil. . . the ground. But it is like having a jar of sugar. If you keep eating a spoonful of sugar, eventually the jar is empty. If you keep planting the same crop every season, eventually, the soil becomes empty of the nutrients the plant needs to grow."

Jennings looked around at each face and it was clear they were with him. He thought, *Boy! This is going to be easy!*

He pointed to the chair. "Like the chair, if we plant something different for a few seasons, the soil will use different nutrients for a different crop. After a while, the soil will get back the nutrients it lost with the original crop. So let's say for this example, we take the land that we intend to grow crops on, and separate it into four sections. In each section, we plant something different. Then after each harvest, we rotate the crop for each section by moving it to the right. Then each season, the crop you grow is different in a single section. That means that if you plant cucumbers in one section, that section will not grow cucumbers again until the fifth season. Crop Rotation!"

He looked around and then waited. Some got it immediately. Others sat and thought about it for a moment and then, suddenly, the light would go on. You could see it in their faces. Suddenly everyone was smiling, including Jennings. He thought, *My God, we have arrived in Paradise. Will it be this easy with all we have to teach them?*

Jennings enjoyed the company of his boys for the rest of the day and felt completely refreshed by their willingness, brightness and immediate acceptance of him. He thought about bringing his own two sons after their school, to interact with these boys. If there was ever a time where he felt a sense of fulfillment, this was definitely it. He closed his eyes and thanked his God for the transformative moment.

As the Jennings family sat down for dinner that evening, each one had a story to tell about their first day. As families go, this was one memory that would remain with them. There was no tentativeness about their new home. Teddy was absolutely right. Smyrna was Paradise, and the little American community was aptly named.

The next day, Jennings met with Jacob before the boys arrived. He was animated in how rewarding his first day was, and how Jacob had made things easy for him.

Jacob said, "Asa, I would like to invite you and Amy to a dinner on Friday night. I intend to have you meet some new friends. They've been asking about you. This is for adults only, so let's make it for 7:30 p.m. We'll meet at the *Acropoli*. It's a Greek-owned establishment, but it is a favorite among the Americans and Europeans. The food is the best you'll find in Smyrna. Because it is a Greek place, there will be families that bring their children along. The Greeks bring their children wherever they go. But I'd like this dinner to be adults only, so that there are fewer distractions and everyone can get to know you better."

Jennings smiled. "Thank you so much. We will be there with bells on. I'm sure Amy would love some adult company after having only my children to talk to during our trip. I certainly wasn't much company for her while I was hugging the chamber pot."

The rest of the week was like the first day. Each day brought new experiences that were positive and rewarding. Smyrna was truly a magical city to be in. . . Paradise on earth!

Chapter 23.

The Friday evening of 18 August, 1922 on the *Rue de Franque* in Smyrna, looked like any other Friday evening in Smyrna. Since there were only a few automobiles in the city, walking, or more accurately, strolling was the most common form of transportation and part of the social order of things. The *Acropoli Restaurant* was no exception. The restaurant was packed with Greeks, Europeans and Americans who were there for a delicious dinner, but also to see and be seen. Outside the restaurant, strollers would peer in to see who was there.

The Jennings arrived promptly at 7:30 p.m. and were escorted by the ebullient proprietor over to Jacob's table which was actually three tables joined together to accommodate a large party. As they approached the table, Jacob rose from his seat and greeted the couple. Jennings was a bit surprised as all of the other guests were already seated. Jacob clinked a fork on his water glass to get the attention of his guests.

"Ladies and gentlemen. . . I want to introduce you to the latest addition to our mission. Asa and Amy Jennings. Asa and Amy, just arrived earlier this week from Prague, and before that were back in the U.S.A. Once they're seated, I'll go around the table and introduce you all to our new friends." Jacob gestured for the Jennings to be seated.

Jacob looked at Asa and Amy who were directly to his left.

"Immediately to your left, I want to introduce you to fellow North Americans. . . Reverend Alexander MacLachlan and his wife, Rose. Alex is the founder and President of our American International College here in Smyrna. Alex and Rose hail from Canada, but we don't hold that against them. And if your wondering. . . even though Alex is technically a clergyman, the College courses are completely secular. They're not here this evening, but Alex and Rose's daughter, Rosalind is married to Cass Reed, who is our dean of students at the College. They live on the campus as well. I'm sure you'll meet them very soon."

MacLachlan stood and bowed to the Jennings, "Welcome to Smyrna. We look forward to having you over for dinner soon so that we can become better acquainted."

Jacob continued, "Next, we are honored to have with us, the United States Consul-General George Horton and his dear wife, Catherine. Like you Asa, George hails from New York State. He is our resident expert on all things Greek, especially Classical Greece, and as you can imagine, George is our protector and advocate in this part of the world.

Horton smiled at Jennings, "It is a pleasure to welcome you to Paradise. So where in New York are you from?"

Jennings replied, "We're originally from the Utica area, upstate. And where do you call home, Mr. Consul General?"

"I'm less than a hundred miles to the west of you in a small town called Fairville that is just outside of Rochester, New York. I can assure you, the weather here will be a lot more hospitable than Utica, New York."

Extending his arm to the left of Horton, Jacob announced, "Next, I'd like to introduce you to Lieutenant Commander Aaron Stanton Merrill. Lieutenant Merrill is the chief intelligence officer for our United States High Commissioner, Rear Admiral Mark Bristol who represents our government in Constantinople. But since Aaron Stanton doesn't just roll off the tongue, everyone just calls him "Tip." Tip just got married earlier this year, but since sailors aren't allowed to bring their wives along when they sail the seven seas, he is accompanied tonight by the beautiful Eleni Xenopoulou, whose family operates the largest department store in Smyrna, and provides us with all of the things we eat, wear and treasure from all over the world. Tip is originally from Mississippi and of course, Eleni is a native of Smyrna, although from the number of languages she speaks, you would wonder where she calls home."

Merrill, in full military uniform adorned with braided epaulettes, stood at attention and bowed his head. "I hope you had a pleasant voyage to get here. If you like, I can arrange a tour of one of our warships that are docked in the harbor. I hear you have three young children. These tours always are popular with the kids."

Eleni, dressed to kill and smiling said, "Welcome to my home. Perhaps, if you let me, I can take your children to my family's store and get them something that will remind them of home."

Amy, graciously thanked her for her thoughtfulness.

Jacob once again extended his arm to the left of Merrill and Eleni, "Next, I'd like to introduce you to a member of Smyrna's most important Levantine families, Mr. Herbert Octavius Whittall, and his dear wife, Louisa. The Whittall family has been in Smyrna since we Americans were fighting for our independence from King George. I don't think that Herbert has any lingering hostilities because of that. By the way, you must take a tour of Herbert's home. It is aptly known in Smyrna as 'The Big House.' It is truly out of this world."

Whittall looked at Amy, "Yes, please allow Louisa to show you around the house. It is my family's tribute to our roots in Smyrna." Louisa attempted a friendly smile but fell short. She was dressed very conservatively looking like a frightened deer in the woods.

Jacob said, "And since we didn't want you to think that we Americans are off in a corner by ourselves, we thought we would have someone at the table that you already knew. Let me reintroduce you to British Vice-Consul Edwyn Hole and his lovely wife, Laura."

Hole smiled at his new friend, "Asa, my good man. . . It's good to see you wearing your true color. For a while, I thought you weren't going to make it here. When we met, you were an interesting shade of green."

Laura smiled at the couple. Hole offered for the table's amusement, "Ladies and gentlemen, I want to point out that Asa here, is the first Methodist minister I have ever met that enjoys cigars and wine after dinner. In fact, I've brought several of them so that you will attest to this."

The group laughed. Asa feeling it necessary to respond, "Amy and I thank you so much for your warm hospitality and this wonderful dinner party. We are not used to such elegant surroundings. I do appreciate the friendly nature of our company and I especially look forward to the warm climate as my bones no longer care for upstate New York. This is such a pleasant alternative to Prague, I think we will have to pinch ourselves each morning to confirm that this is not all a dream. And, yes, I do enjoy an occasional cigar and glass of wine, but I've always felt it would not offend Jesus to do so. I suspect he's more interested in my deeds than to obsess over my dinner habits."

Jacob held out his right hand palm-up, "And finally, of course, this is my dear wife, Sarah. She is my joy, especially since she has followed me around the world to be here in Paradise. Now you have met everyone. Of course, Sarah and I will be leaving you here in charge while we have a bit of a holiday. It's been a long time coming and we just need to get away. So you'll be in charge, Asa, until we get back."

Jacob raised his crystal water glass, "And now a toast. . ." everyone followed by raising their glasses, "Welcome Asa and Amy to Paradise, a place like no other in this world."

The group took a sip and laughter followed. Hole volunteered some advice. "May I suggest you try the *Moussaka*? It is a specialty here, and especially for an American palette, it will be an explosion of delicious and exotic tastes."

Asa frowned, "Considering my difficult journey, I suspect I should avoid spicy food for a while. Just what is *Moussaka*?"

Eleni laughed, "It's just ground lamb, eggplant and tomatoes topped with Greek white sauce, subtly spiced in a tasty way and then baked. I think they put some cinnamon in it. But please everything on the menu is the best you'll find anywhere in the city."

As the waiters took the orders, Jennings thought to inquire about the events going on outside the city. "If it is not too controversial for dinner discussion, Amy and I have been locked away on boats since we left Prague. Teddy has educated me somewhat about the war between the Greeks and the Turks, but is there anything that has happened recently that we should know about?"

Jacob decided to start off the discussion, "About the time you left Prague, Governor General Stergiadis announced to the people of Smyrna that there would be an organization formed to make Smyrna and all of western Asia Minor an autonomous region that would be self-governed. This was in response, I believe, to the recent turnabout of our British allies in asking the Greek army to evacuate Asia Minor. We knew the French and the Italians were backing the Turks, but now that Great Britain is cooling towards Greece, I don't see where this will lead. By the way, I of course, invited Commissioner Stergiadis to dine with us. Like all other invitations in the past, he declined. He doesn't believe in social gatherings and lives somewhat like a recluse."

Hole bristled a bit at the uncomfortable reference that the British had abandoned the Greeks, since he represented the British government.

"Jake, you don't seem to acknowledge the difficulty of the situation. When the Greeks threw out Venizelos and brought back the King, that placed us in a position of effectively supporting the enemy we had just defeated in the Great War. Heck, the Greek King is related to the German Chancellor. We really had no other choice."

Jennings looked over at Hole and thought, *That's the opposite of what he told me on the way over. He must be just stating the company policy.*

Lt. Merrill smirked, "They never should have pushed Greece to occupy Asia Minor in the first place. These Greeks have been under the Turkish thumb for hundreds of years. I could have told you the Turks would never stand for being under the thumb of the Greeks. I would much prefer Asia Minor was run by the Turks. We have something to get from the Turks. The United States can bring business and prosperity to Asia Minor."

MacLachlan joined in, "I agree with Tip. Before the Greeks took over, there was no trouble in Smyrna. The Ottomans left us alone and everyone prospered. Now that the Greeks are in control, they murder the Turks and jeopardize everything with this stupid war."

Horton shook his head. "Listen to all of you. You all look at this from your own selfish needs. Tip, you just glanced over something that is the whole point. The Greeks have been here since the Egyptians were building the pyramids at Giza. They gave the world our principles of freedom and justice. They are the reason we have western democracies. You glanced over the part where the Turks conquered Asia and half of Europe and made all Christians second-class citizens by law. You ignore the fact that the Turks have been slaughtering Christians for those same hundreds of years. As an American, what did we do when living under the yoke of King George became unbearable? That's right, we revolted and I can assure you some of our founding citizens took out their frustrations and anger on the British. You cannot fault the Greeks for their sporadic outrages.

"For it is this premise of the Young Turks to make 'Turkey for the Turks only' that foretells its plan to murder the Christians into extinction in this blood-soaked land. And, as a historian, I can provide you with examples of how this has been the general history of Mohammedan expansion in all the ancient homelands of Christianity."

MacLachlan interrupted. "George, you're a hopeless *Grecophile*!"

Horton replied, "I for one am proud to support the people who civilized the world. It makes me wonder that as the head of an

American institution of higher learning that you would support a people who rule by force instead of by law. I cannot understand your tendency to be a *Turkophile*."

Hole tried to rescue the discussion. "While you were on the Danube, my Prime Minister assured Britain's allies that the Greeks would not enter Constantinople as was announced in the press. If and when the Greek troops evacuate Asia Minor, we must ensure that the Christian populations are protected from the Turks. The Prime Minister had to remind the House of Commons, that this new friendly Turkish government, after we had supported their predecessors to keep the Turkish Empire in existence, shut down the Dardanelles preventing us from coming to the aid of our Russian and Romanian allies."

Finally, the beautiful, headstrong Eleni could not sit quietly any longer. "Teddy, Teddy. . . You lament how the Turks took your assistance, and then threw it in your face at their first opportunity. And you President MacLachlan, you chide us, the Greeks, for seeking vengeance on the barbarians who continue to rape and murder us. I don't hear the same outrage over the barbarism of the British. A month almost to the day, before a Turkish soldier fired his gun into the Greek column when our troops first arrived here, a British general ordered his troops to fire point-blank into a crowd of unarmed civilians. No, your good old boys in Paris said that was a panicked officer and the troops had no choice but to follow orders."

MacLachlan became stone-faced as he didn't care for being called out by a local Greek.

"And, what about Mesopotamia. In the summer of 1920, your British buddies were having a difficult time there. The Kurds kept demanding self-government, like your own President was calling for in his *Fourteen Points*. When they couldn't have their self-government, they blew up railroad tracks and even killed some British officers. What was the measured British response? They sent expeditions into the area and burned the Kurdish villages. Sound familiar? Isn't that what you're now reporting as barbarism when the Greeks refuse to let the Turks deport them and hand over their homes to other Turks? Soldiers burning villages isn't efficient enough for the British. They sent their airplanes over, strafing and bombing the Kurdish villages. It was quicker and less costly to send one pilot rather than sending a platoon of soldiers out to burn the villages.

"And, I apologize to my escort for the evening, Commander Merrill, for his preference for an ignorant, militant, race of thugs who are bent on the genocide of my people, as opposed to a people who honor the law, family and Christianity. Commander... I ask you, when your own navy was being assaulted by Ottoman pirates in the Mediterranean and you couldn't turn to England since you had just won your independence from her, who did you turn to? I can answer that for you. You turned to the Greek privateers to help you against the Ottomans, because your navy wasn't large or powerful enough to defeat the Ottomans on your own. Then, when the Greeks were fighting for their own independence from the Ottomans, and the Greek navy was overwhelmed by them, forcing Greek naval officers into piracy for their survival, you sent your new powerful navy to destroy the Greeks who helped you twenty years before.

"Teddy, did you forget who became your ally in the Great War once we got rid of our German King? Was it the Turks? No! It was the Greek people who fought the Germans and the Turks who were your enemy.

"And after the war... when your Prime Minister cajoled our Prime Minister to occupy Asia Minor on our own... Did you forget that the reason he did that was because Britain didn't have enough soldiers to do it herself? You had lost so many in the Great War and most of those that were left after the war went home. So what did you do? You convinced Venizelos that Greece should occupy Smyrna on its own, promising England's undying support. Then, because the gullible Greek people were fooled into voting to bring back our idiot king, you conveniently declared neutrality as you salivated over the oilfields of Mesopotamia. And now, we have to form a new country in order to protect ourselves from the murderous Turks.

"All of you, when you are in trouble, ask the Greek people to stand on the side of freedom and justice. Then, when greed and political expediency make you forget the difficult times, you turn your back on us. So tell me. If there is another war like the last Great War, will you ask the Turks to be your allies? Or will you smile once again at the Greek people, and tell them you will not abandon them? And afterward, when there is peace once again on your little island in the North Sea, will you turn your backs on us again? Clearly, we Greeks do not learn from our mistakes."

Hole, chuckled nervously. "My dear Eleni, I suspect if you were running the Greek government, you wouldn't let us get away with this sort of thing."

The tension at the table was broken and everyone laughed. At that moment, the food platters were brought to the table and everyone turned to the business of dinner. Mostly silent during dinner, it probably was a testament to the chef that everyone ate rather than talk. Jennings was offered wine and he graciously accepted. . . twice. Hole got a real kick out of that as everyone else turned the dinner conversation to lighter subjects.

After dinner, Hole pulled out a handful of *Romeo y Julieta Perfecto*s. He offered them around and managed a big smile when he offered one to Asa. As the men were about to light up, Eleni looked at Hole. "It's not polite to only offer your cigars to men. I'll have one! I've been to the continent many times. I'm not going to be dismissed to the kitchen."

The women were shocked but silent. The men were entertained, all except for Lt. Merrill who thought Eleni was out of place as his companion for the evening in not respecting his rank and stature. Actually, he was the very reason she asked for the cigar. She dismissed him as a pompous, arrogant ass that was not nearly as smart as he thought he was.

By the end of the evening, everyone had enjoyed the food, the wine, the animated conversation and the general gaiety that was Smyrna. It was a memorable evening.

Chapter 24.

On the Friday following the welcome dinner for Jennings and his family, the sky began to lighten at the approach of dawn in the hills outside of Afyon Kara Hissar, the capital of Afyon Province. The name Afyon Kara Hissar literally meant 'opium black castle' and had a history that dated back to Hittites in the 14th century BC. It was 25 August, but the chill marking an end of summer had already arrived on the Anatolian frontier.

Among the trees on a hill southwest of the city, hidden by a large boulder, stood the entrance to a bunker for the recently-appointed commander-in-chief of all Turkish Nationalist armies in Asia Minor. General Mustapha Kemal's military bunker was actually a deep hole dug out of a small clearing in the trees, with a tarp that stretched across the opening with tree branches covering it.

20. General Mustapha Kemal prepares for the Battle of Dumlupinar in 1922.

Inside the bunker, a soldier brought to his general, a cup of sweet Turkish coffee, as the seasoned general studied his map indicating the location of the long Greek front line that stretched north and south along the Sakarya River. He was confident of the Greek troop strength and location because he now had six French-made reconnaissance airplanes recently acquired from the Russian government in a swap agreement of foodstuffs, livestock and horses, for arms, munitions and equipment. General Mustapha Kemal was confident in his knowledge that he would finally defeat the Greek army that had chased him across most of Asia Minor over the last two years.

His banner of 'Turkey for the Turks' was the justification for the deliberate genocide of Orthodox Christians in Asia Minor. Incensed over Christians that were far superior in business, organization and administration, Kemal seized on the idea of eliminating the problem by simply eliminating the Christians.

So here he was, after an entire year of stalemate with the Greeks in no shape to fight, and the Turks rested, fed and energized. Kemal prepared for his long-awaited victory over the army he viewed as former servants of the Turkish people.

Kemal called in his staff officers. He sipped his sweet coffee as he stared at his men. "We have long waited for this moment. The infidel has defiled our women and our country. For this, no one is to show any mercy. Let *Dumlupinar* be remembered as the beginning of the end to our Greek rogue slaves. We will first cut off their meager supply lines and then cut off their heads."

Kemal paused and slowly scanned his officers for dramatic effect.

"It begins now! You have my order to attack!"

The Y.M.C.A. Mission office was quiet for a Saturday morning. Jennings had come into the office to take care of those responsibilities of his superiors who had left the day before for their long-awaited holiday. Both Jacob and Ed Fisher, his assistant, decided to take their vacations at the same time, knowing they had a competent secretary in Asa Jennings to take over in their absence.

Jennings was busy listing the new invoices on his report to the home office. He thought it a bit odd that he would be writing his own payroll check. That was a completely new experience for him. He heard the outer door creak open and then slam shut. He wondered who would have any business at the office on a Saturday. In a moment, he saw Hole standing in his doorway. Hole joked, "My my, it's a pity there's no one here to see just how conscientious you are in your new position."

Jennings chuckled. "I'm just worried that with three jobs to do, I'm going to fall behind and prove to my boss, that I need to be sent home. I still keep pinching myself that I've fallen into this wonderful job. Each new day is rewarding. My wife and children are happy. They even look forward to school. I need to make sure I do a good enough job so that they won't send me someplace else. What are you doing here anyway?"

Hole came over and sat down across from Jennings, slouching down in the chair. "Jake and I always get together on Saturday mornings. We trade intelligence. I tell him what's going on from my government, and he tells me what the Y.M.C.A. is telling him about what your government is up to. We have been in agreement that our governments are not always doing the best thing for themselves or anyone else. It's our way of keeping track of what is going on behind our backs."

Jennings put his pen down. "Well, Jake is not here. Would you like to trade information with his temporary replacement?"

Hole sat up. "Sure! What can you tell me about what the Yanks have messed up this week?"

Jennings shook his head. "Absolutely nothing! Either they didn't screw up or they're just not telling me. How about your bunch? What has Mr. Lloyd George done to us this week?"

Hole lit up one of his cigars. He offered one to Jennings, but he declined. "Well, Yank, it appears our Prime Minister's about-face on support of the Greeks is no longer the main gossip in parliament. The news took a while to get here, but it appears the gentleman from Wales has been venting his distaste for the aristocracy by selling knighthoods and peerages to traitors, tax evaders and fraudsters in order to finance a new political party in Britain. If it weren't a scandal of the government I've pledged my allegiance to, I would have thought it rather humorous. I suppose though that most Britons, who are <u>not</u> members of the aristocracy, do not believe this to be a terrible outrage. Lloyd George did appoint a Royal Commission to look into the scandal, but it appears that commission can only make recommendations as to the future of such behavior, but is barred from investigation any past behavior of this sort. It's unfortunate that it paints everyone with the brush of non-scrupulousness.

"There is also a complete about face in our government, now that the Greek army is run by idiots. With Venizelos gone, I'm sure the pressure is on the P.M. to do whatever he can to secure some of that oil in Mesopotamia. All of our ships are converting to oil, so we're going to need a secure source to run the navy. He keeps talking about demanding the Turks protect the Christians, but I suspect that's just lip service, as to keep from commenting on his own despicable behavior."

Jennings asked, "What about the new offensive? I heard that the Greeks have repelled the Turkish advance. What have you heard?"

Hole shook his head in disappointment. "That's just propaganda. The Greeks are in full retreat. They have nothing left to give. They're starving! They're out of ammunition, and they're leaders are complete idiots. I think things are going to get really bad for the Greeks now that their army will evacuate Asia Minor. They have no choice. The army is beaten. The allies are telling them to leave. I just pity the poor Greek people who will now pay the price. . . again. Oh! But I do have some humorous news to report. Have you ever heard of a fellow by the name of Sir Basil Zaharoff?"

Jennings' face went blank. "No! Never heard of him. Is he some British Lord?"

"Well, here is another example of the sort of behavior I just mentioned. I'm completely embarrassed over it. Sir Basil was knighted by King George. But if you dig a bit into it, since Sir Basil was not born in the kingdom, the title is honorary. He was born in Constantinople of a Russian father and a Greek mother. So, he isn't really a knight by birthright. It's like when a university bestows an honorary doctorate on a recipient who donates a pile of money. Sir Basil is reputed to be the wealthiest man in the world, outside of the United States. But the fellow is shrouded in secrecy. . . a complete mystery man. It's coming out of Rome dispatches that Sir Basil is branching out from his business as an arms dealer. While he may not yet be exposed as a traitor, tax evader or fraudster, it suggests that our monarch is no different than our Prime Minister when it comes to duplicitous behavior."

"It appears Sir Basil now wants to be a king, and Parliament is concerned that he has some sinister influence over our Prime Minister. You've heard how the Greek government has been pushing the idea of creating an autonomous Greek state in Asia Minor. Well, apparently, Sir Basil thinks he should be made the king of this new place. Apparently, he plans to finance this new baby with $15 million of his own money and has interested French and British bankers to loan the new baby state another $75 million. The scary thought is that this crazy idea is being discussed like it is a reasonable solution to the problem."

Jennings was curious. "How will this affect the Greek population here in Asia Minor if there's a new kingdom here?"

Hole laughs. "It won't make any difference at all. The Turks and the Greeks will still hate each other, and the Turks will just be at war with a new name. It's the same people they'd be fighting. All it will do is perhaps let Sir Basil play royalty when he visits the concessions he owns in Monte Carlo."

Jennings got serious. "Do you think a victory by the Turks will affect us here in Smyrna?"

Hole shook his head vigorously. "Not a chance! Haven't you been taking Amy for strolls on the quay? There must be two dozen warships sitting a few hundred feet from the *Rue de Franque*. If General Kemal enters Smyrna with anything but a police force, he'll have the entire Allied navy blow him to eternity. No, he'll just make sure the Greeks leave Asia Minor. He's not a foolish man. He'll do what everyone else before him has done. Smyrna will be Smyrna."

Chapter 25.

A long row of Greek soldiers staggered along a dusty road. In ranks of two, sometimes three, they walked. The men looked more like zombies than soldiers. Their uniforms were covered in dust from the desert they had just walked through.

It was only thirty miles to the east, where they had been overrun by Turkish regulars. But once routed by the well-supplied Turkish army, having essentially no ammunition left to defend themselves, the Greek troops ran in desperation to avoid certain death. But soon after they ran, it was clear the Turks weren't chasing them anymore. There wasn't any need to run. The running stopped and the soldiers began walking instead.

Soon, walking through the hot desert of Anatolia, with no water left, with no food left, the rifles and weapons became too heavy to carry. Without ammunition they were as good as boat anchors in the desert. So they began dropping weapons. They left artillery on the side of roads. They stripped down and dropped anything that was heavy to carry. They began dragging their feet trying to keep moving with as little effort as possible. They would have stopped, but they knew that inevitably, the Turks would catch up and murder them. So they kept walking.

Two of those in the desperate march were Captain Apostolidis and Sergeant Papadimitriou. They had been reassigned from the Gheronda offensive to the assault on Ankara. Their reassignment was ordered by General Hatzianestis from his residence on the quay in Smyrna. Apostolidis had heard that the general had been renovating a huge palatial home there. The rumors flying about were that the general was completely insane. After arriving on the eastern front, Apostolidis was certain that was true.

Now as he walked with his companion, he wondered if his end would come on the side of a dusty road from the lack of water instead of a soldier's death defending his countrymen. He thought back to his time as a proud Greek partisan fighting against the

Bulgarians in Macedonia. Would it all come down to expiring on a dirt road in the middle of nowhere?

As he walked, Apostolidis noticed a hint of green. There was actually some foliage. Could they be coming to the end of the desert? Then he smelled it. Somebody was cooking. It was faint but he could tell it was Greek cooking. An hour later, they staggered into a small Greek village. The tiny village of Louloudi was near the Turkish village of Küçükhüyük. The Greek people of the village were offering water to the soldiers up ahead. He desperately wanted to walk faster, but his body would not respond.

Eventually, he sat on a rock by the edge of the tiny village. An old woman dressed completely in black, handed him a cup of water. Then she handed one to Papadimitriou. As he drank, an old man came up to him. "You are an officer. A Captain. Please tell me, why are you walking? What of the battle? Where are your weapons?"

Apostolidis, finished his cup of water. He looked up at the man, whom he thought would have looked almost dead, if he hadn't been looking at something worse among his soldiers. "Our weapons are on the side of the road in the desert behind us. Without bullets, they are of no use to us. They are too heavy to carry. Soon, the Turks will be here. If you are here when they come, your women and children will be raped and murdered and you will be robbed of anything of value that you own. Tell your people to follow us to Smyrna. There are ships there that will take you to safety."

The man looked at him as if he were crazy. "Leave? How can I leave? This has been my family's home for hundreds of years. We cannot leave."

Apostolidis grunted in frustration. "You may have lived here for hundreds of years, but soon, if you are still here, you will be dead and some Turkish family will be given your home. That is what they did before the Great War. That is what they will do now. If you want to stay, stay. But you will meet your ancestors very soon if you do."

The man left him and began running through the street shouting that the Turks were coming to murder them. Apostolidis tried to slowly drink another cup of water. As he raised the cup to his mouth, he saw a young soldier sitting across from him with a desperate look on his face, staring into oblivion. With the cup inches from his face, he called out, "Στρατιώτη. . . Soldier, why do you look so desperate? You are still alive."

The young soldier awoke from his stupor. "Do you call this alive?"

Apostolidis laughed. "I'd say it is better than lying face down in the desert we just came from."

The soldier, nodded. "Not much better!"

"How old are you, soldier?"

"Twenty-two years, sir!"

"What's your name?" Apostolidis asked.

"Pavlos. . . Pavlos Papavasiliou!"

"Where is your home, Pavlos?"

"Triglia!"

Apostolidis' eyes widened. "Triglia. . . I know this village. This is the village that Chrysostomos comes from. Chrysostomos, the Archbishop was born in Triglia. I was with him back when we were fighting the Bulgarians in 1906. Back then he always talked about the school he was building. Do you know the school?"

"Yes, I went to that school."

"So you know of Chrysostomos?"

The soldier smiled for the first time. "Yes I know of Chrysostomos. He is my father's cousin. He came to our house many times. He gave my father his personal bible."

Apostolidis seemed to brighten talking about a subject that did not relate to his current circumstance. "So then, you know that he was our leader in Macedonia. . . in Drama!"

21. Ruin of Triglia school built by Archbishop Chrysostomos (1904-1909).
Photo courtesy of C. Papavasiliou.

The exhausted soldier nodded. "Yes, my father was with him in Drama. He was the only one Chrysostomos would trust to protect him."

"Christos? Your father was Christos?"

The soldier looked up at his Captain in disbelief. "You knew my father?"

Apostolidis laughed. "Yes we got drunk together. How is he?"

"Dead! The Turks beat him to death two years ago."

"Your father was a hero." Apostolidis looked for recognition from the young soldier.

"Funny! I didn't see a hero when I looked at him. I hated him. As the eldest, I had to become the father when he wasn't around. And he wasn't around very much. He was off either fighting the Turks, or getting drunk."

"But you are a soldier now. You've been doing the same thing."

"No I haven't killed any Turks. I am a medic."

Apostolidis couldn't believe it. "You are a doctor? You're too young."

"I'm not a doctor. I worked in the pharmacy in Triglia for one of Chrysostomos' relatives. Somehow that qualified me to put bandages on dying soldiers. I preferred that to doing what my father did."

Apostolidis came back to the present. "Well Pavlos, if we survive this walk to Smyrna and get on a Greek ship, you'll get to start a new life in Greece. Good luck!"

The soldier said, "I just hope I can find my family."

Apostolidis got up and walked over to where some villagers had gathered. They immediately began asking questions about what they should do. He wondered if he was the most senior officer in the line of soldiers. He thought, *Why are they looking to me for advice?*

The villager he spoke to, returned. Apparently he was one of the elders of the village. "What shall we do? Are there any reinforcements coming? Shall we hide among the rocks to the north? We cannot leave our homes. They are all we have in this life."

Apostolidis was frustrated beyond his patience. "I told you! You can stay and be dead. If you wish to stay alive, you must pack what you can carry and follow us to Smyrna. It is only two-hundred miles from here. There you will be able to board a ship to safety. The choice is yours."

Apostolidis looked into the eyes of the villager and saw the doom he felt himself. Within an hour, a handful of villagers had packed their family heirlooms, which were mostly comprised of a family rug, a Sunday church dress for the women and probably a cross made of gold. They gathered their sheep. Some had a cart that would be pulled by an ox. Within a few hours, most of the village was standing by the road looking at Apostolidis and their treasured homestead behind him. They were waiting, but didn't know what they waited for.

Apostolidis looked at them and then turned to look at the village. His face turned red. He fumed. He stood and faced his men. "Men. I am Captain Apostolidis. We have no guns. We have no bullets. We will walk two hundred miles to Smyrna. When we leave, this village will be given to Turks. I am not going to let them have it. If a Turk wants to live in this village, he'll have to build his own home."

Apostolidis walked to the first small excuse for a cottage. He took some hay from the animal pen and lit the place on fire. Soon others joined him. Within minutes the entire village was in flames.

Apostolidis looked at the villagers and then the soldiers who helped him. "We will not let them do this to us. We will burn every village between here and Smyrna. Get up and start walking! It will be your last order in Asia Minor... Burn them all!"

Chapter 26.
1 September

  General Trikoupis looked out over the troops under his command. It was the first of September and he could feel it in his bones. He knew this would be the worst day of his life. He thought about having begun battle with five divisions of committed, battle-tested men. Earlier this week, he had lost two of those divisions, and now his colonel had brought him news of a surprise attack for which he was totally unprepared. He had been concentrating on setting up a second line of defense northwest of Afyon and never thought the attack would come so soon after the last one. He no longer had a choice. His circumstance guaranteed that all of his men would be lost if he continued fighting. They were dying anyway from lack of water and nutrition.

  As the senior staff general, Trikoupis gave the order to raise the white flag. He would surrender, rather than watch his troops die by the Turkish bayonet. In doing so, he surrendered five thousand men and three hundred officers to the army of Mustapha Kemal. He knew the ultimate result would still be death once they surrendered, but he still held out the slim hope that the Allies might alter the death sentence.

  Once the shooting stopped, he ordered his men to put down their weapons and surrender. Soon after, the Turkish cavalry officers escorted Trikoupis and his senior staff to waiting horses. He rode under Turkish escort to the main field headquarters of the Turkish army. After some minor humiliation from the Turkish escorts, he was required to stand before the General Kemal's bunker.

  After standing for 30 minutes with his officers, he looked on as Kemal emerged from his bunker relaxed, confident and wearing a broad grin.

  "Welcome General Trikoupis! I apologize that I do not have any Turkish coffee to offer you at this time. I guess, I am required by protocol to declare that you are my prisoners of war. I will tell you that all of your officers and men, will be held as prisoners of war and

22. General Trikoupis (seated second from left) and his staff are forced to pose for a photo.

will perform work for our new Turkey as their punishment for attacking us. But I suppose hard work is less painful than death in battle."

Trikoupis looked at Kemal with hatred in his eyes. "I see you continue to lie, even in victory. My men will not ever get to work. You will march them into the desert and, when there are no witnesses, you will murder us all. We've seen your handiwork before. I only hope General Hatzianestis has mobilized reinforcements to change your plans."

Kemal broke out into exaggerated hearty laughter. "I guess you have not heard the good news. Apparently we know more about your army than you do. I'm sorry to inform you that General Hatzianestis has been relieved of his duty. He was more interested in what colors to paint the walls on his villa in Smyrna. Yes! He was relieved of his duty. If you didn't know that, you probably didn't know who has replaced him."

Trikoupis looked up at Kemal and stared blankly. Kemal put on a more conciliatory smile and said, "I am pleased to inform you that you have been promoted to fill General Hatzianestis' post as Commander-in-Chief of all the Greek Armies. I'm truly sorry that you didn't get to enjoy your new post before you surrendered those armies to me. Perhaps I can find a glass of *raki* so that we can celebrate your promotion."

"I will not drink with you!"

"Well then, that is your choice. Take him away!"

The sentries grabbed Trikoupis and dragged him away from their general.

Kemal turned on his heel to return to his bunker. Then he paused. He turned his head and looking back at his officer said, "Assemble the armies! Except for men to guard our prisoners. I want to make an announcement."

As the sun began to descend in the west, a sea of Turkish soldiers stood in an open field just west of Kemal's bunker. When they were all lined up, with cavalry on the left and infantry on the right, Kemal's staff colonel entered his bunker to inform him of the troops being ready to receive him.

Kemal looked in his field mirror, stroked his mustache, dusted off his uniform, placed his Cicillian black fez on his head, and marched out to greet his troops. He stood on a tall rock so that most could at least see his image. He shouted, "As your commander, I salute you for your victory." The crowd of soldiers cheered for their leader.

Again, he shouted, "I estimate that you have killed at least five thousand enemy troops in this offensive. I would have preferred you kill ten thousand but unfortunately, the other five thousand surrendered earlier today." Once again the cheers were deafening and now the raised their scimitars and rifles above their heads.

"I suppose their death will now come from the thousand cuts they will receive as our prisoners." He could hear the roar of laughter from troops nearest the front.

Finally, he produced a big smile. "Armies, your first goal now is the Mediterranean. Forward!" With his command, he raised his arm and pointed to the west. The crowd cheered their leader.

Kemal saluted his armies, performed a military about-face, and disappeared into his bunker. The cheers continued unabated for minutes.

Chapter 27.
6 September

The news that had been flowing into the American Consulate in Smyrna over the past few days was distressing to the U.S. Consul, George Horton. It was distressing to him because he was, in fact, in favor of Greek rule over Turkish rule. A student of history, Horton had studied the product of Turkish rule over the centuries and was confident, if the Greek army were forced to evacuate, it would mean certain death to the hundreds of thousands of Greek civilians.

Many of the wealthier Greek families, being intimately familiar with Turkish brutality, had the means to pick up and leave Smyrna. They were not about to wait around hoping that the wartorn Greek army would rally to win the day.

One of those Greek merchants, having become familiar with Asa Jennings' work at the YMCA, prior to boarding a ship that would take him to Mytilene, handed Jennings the keys to his home on the quay. Having heard about the coming stream of soldiers and refugees, Jennings accepted the home and immediately stocked it with provisions left by the wealthy Greeks, to serve as a supply center in case they would be needed for relief for the refugees.

Horton was on holiday in a tiny Greek village just south of Smyrna when he was brought the news of the first battalions of defeated troops being just a few hours outside of Smyrna. He rushed back to the city just in time to see the arrival of those first regiments. He was horrified to see the condition of these men. They looked more like walking ghosts, covered with dust. They dragged their feet and carried no weapons. Many were barefoot. It was truly like watching the walking dead, some giving up and collapsing right on the street.

Once back at the Consulate, the Reuters wire had just arrived prompting Horton to call a meeting of key Americans in Smyrna to discuss what was needed to protect both the Americans living in Smyrna and the Greek population that was about to find themselves at the mercy of their old masters. The meeting included Lieutenant

Merrill, Admiral Bristol's chief intelligence officer, Alex MacLachlan, President of the American College and with Jacobs and Fisher on holiday, Jennings, the temporary leader of the Y.M.C.A. mission in the city.

Horton called the meeting to order.

"Thank you for coming on such short notice. I've just received some very distressing news and I thought it imperative that we discuss how the news will affect the American involvement here in Smyrna. I've just learned that the Greek government in Athens has stated officially, it is resigned to a total evacuation of its forces from Asia Minor.

"Worse yet, as you may have seen on your way over here, thousands of defeated Greek troops are dragging themselves through the city on their way to the quay. Greek ships are arriving to transport them out of Asia Minor, probably to Mytilene. I'm afraid that I fear for the safety of our citizens here in Smyrna as well as for those hundreds of thousands of Orthodox Christians who have just become refugees in their own homeland."

To Jennings, the news seemed incongruous to everyone's position prior to today that in spite of whatever was happening in the outlying areas, there would be no problem in Smyrna. "Excuse me, Consul Horton, but I thought the presence of Allied warships was sufficient to deter any breach of the peace within the city."

Horton nodded. "Yes, and I still believe that to be true, but the wire also indicates that the British have dispatched the H.M.S. *Iron Duke* to Smyrna. In fact, British, French, Italian and American cruisers have received orders to leave for Smyrna immediately. As the American Consul, I have also made that request to our government. I'm confident the substantial show of force in the harbor will prevent any hostilities from occurring within the city, but I'm just as confident that there will be wholesale murder and destruction outside of the city.

"Mr. Morgenthau, our Ambassador in Constantinople, has warned that Kemal's nationalists will likely follow their military victory with a massacre. Unless Britain asserts herself by showing that she, and the others, have an interest in protecting these Christians, the Turks will be as merciless as they were with the Armenians.

"The Greek army has apparently been setting fire to many of the villages that they pass through in their retreat. This will no doubt result in Turks retaliating, as Mr. Morgenthau has warned. The people are without arms and cannot defend themselves. I think we need to decide what our American position should be and what our actions will be. The evacuation will probably be split between Constantinople and Smyrna. Those would be the only two ports of embarkation."

Merrill raised his hand to correct Horton. "George, I don't agree. If there is to be an evacuation it will not be through Constantinople. There's an agreed neutral zone set up. No one is permitted to cross the neutral zone. If they do, that will be a breach of the agreement. We'll have a full-scale war again and, this time, it will include the Allies. No, it's clear to me. All of the troops will be evacuated through Smyrna."

Horton shook his head. "That makes it even worse. The Greek army began with two hundred fifty thousand men in Asia Minor. I'm certain many of them are now lying dead on the ground, but there must be more than one hundred thousand left that will be arriving here shortly. I'm also sure that Mustapha Kemal and his army will be right behind them. That is the reason, I called for more ships to be stationed in the harbor. Whatever sympathy we feel for the refugees, I'm bound by orders to protect only the American citizens who are here."

MacLachlan decided to speak. "Well, I for one, think this is the best thing that could have happened. The Turks are not about to break the peace. They're getting exactly what they wanted. Greek rule in Asia Minor is over, and they'll finally be rid of the Greek army forever. Frankly, this is also the best thing that could happen for America and American business. I've spoken to many representatives in the clubs and restaurants and they agree with me. They all believe that the Turk is such a gentleman and the only one of his kind in Asia Minor. Everyone is pro-Turk."

Merrill nodded in agreement. "I agree. All foreigners in Smyrna would prefer the Turk to the Greek be in control. The Greeks have shown that they shouldn't be in control of anything. I think you should rescind that request for the cruisers. The only danger we have is the Greek army destroying anything in their path as they are forced to leave."

Horton became flushed. "You say the Turk is a gentleman as reports continue to come in about Turks murdering Armenian and Greek Christians. They continue to deport innocents, hoping they will die of starvation so they don't have to waste ammunition. There are even reports of entire villages where the Turks have hacked the population to death with axes in order to save ammunition."

MacLachlan replied. "There have been outrages committed on both sides. It's not just the Turks."

Horton interrupted. "Let's not lie to each other. Yes, foreigners have turned against the Greeks and for the Turks. That is true. But why is it true? It's *not* because the Turk is a gentleman. No! History tells us that the Turk rapes, murders and plunders for sport and profit. So why are foreigners pro-Turk? I'll tell you. The Governor-General, Mr. Stergiadis, has done all he could do to clean up Smyrna and rid it of yellow fever, smallpox and many other diseases which flourished under the old Turkish regime. It's been a much better-looking city in every way, but the Greeks place so many restrictions on imports and exports that the business of the port and the profits have dwindled. Those restrictions are contributing to getting rid of the disease. But now, even though the city is much better, we foreigners prefer to have the Turks, with their bribery and slothful methods of doing business, instead of the efficiency introduced by the Greeks. The Turk is ignorant in the affairs of business and therefore, we as foreigners, view him as an easy mark. We can take advantage of the ignorant Turk, where we cannot with a Greek. Only a fool or a liar would side with a Turk, unless he has an opportunistic motive. But that is not why we're here. I'm hoping you are correct and that we have nothing to fear from this circumstance, but I would like us to prepare in case you're mistaken."

Jennings raised his hand, "So, Consul Horton, if we have the Allied fleet in the harbor to discourage any violence, what else do we need to do?"

Horton thinks for a moment. "If we have one hundred thousand plus soldiers walking up to the quay, these men are probably starving. How do we feed them? What if some transport ships are delayed? Will they be desperate enough to try to get food and drink from Americans? How many American soldiers do we need here in the city to protect our people? What happens if the people who have been burned out of their homes. . . what happens if they follow the soldiers? There's no way the city has the available services to support that many desperate people. We can't handle that many vacationers, let alone refugees. Asa, I need you to begin to think in terms of relief. What places can we use to provide medical assistance?

"I'll try to get us more reinforcements and assistance. You folks go away and come up with plans to handle that many people coming into Smyrna. Not from a violence point of view, but more from just that much humanity in one place at one time. Then, we can re-convene and begin to prepare."

Horton stood and everyone followed suit. The meeting had ended. All were silent as they left the Consulate.

Reverend Charles Dobson, Smyrna's Anglican vicar, had seen the endless procession of weary Greek troops dragging themselves toward the quay. His alarm increased as he now saw, mixed among the line of soldiers, refugees carrying their few meager worldly possessions toward the same destination. Carts pulled by oxen, babies being carried by desperate mothers. He was certain this was going to get worse.

Rev. Dobson quickly walked over to the office of Archbishop Chrysostomos. Dobson was escorted into the Archbishop's office. He found his friend in a state of despair, concerned with the fate of his people. Dobson said, "My dear friend, what are we to do now?"

The Archbishop looked up. "We must find someone who will protect our people. This butcher Kemal will massacre all of us."

Dobson was surprised. "You think with all the warships in the harbor they'll murder innocents?"

The Archbishop's stare was resolute. "I have been fighting these beasts for twenty years. They do not value human life. Our women, our daughters. . . they will be raped, then butchered. All men will be murdered or deported. Do not be deceived into thinking that this barbarian cares about right or wrong."

Now the Archbishop's eyes were pleading. "My friend, you must send a telegram to your Archbishop of Canterbury. You must beg him to tell Lloyd George the gravity of our circumstance. Tell him we are about to face a calamity."

Dobson saw the certainty in his friend's eyes. "I will do my best to get his attention and intervention." He left quickly to send the telegram.

Chrysostomos left as well. He walked quickly to the office of the French Consul, Michel Grillet. Given immediate audience, Chrysostomos told the Consul his fears.

Grillet gave a reassuring smile.

"Your Eminence, please do not fear. I have ordered the immediate transfer of troops from France. I've been told they will be here within days. We have a fleet of warships in the harbor, and the French army is due momentarily. We have worked with the Turks for many years. They will not do anything to jeopardize that.

Chrysostomos felt somewhat relieved. "Are you certain it is only a matter of days?"

"Yes I am certain."

The Archbishop thanked Grillet and left.

Rather than returning to his office, he walked over to the Italian Consulate. Once again, Chrysostomos was given an immediate audience with the Italian Consul. Chrysostomos pleaded the same fears but was assured that with fifteen thousand Italian citizens living in Smyrna, Kemal is not about to cause any difficulties that might disrupt their treaty.

Chrysostomos had a slightly springier walk when he left the Italian Consulate. Both the French and Italians were confident that their new ally, Turkey, would not jeopardize its relationship with them. At least now, he had something positive to tell his parishioners.

Hoping for a similar response from the British, he next walked to the British Consulate. This time, the Prelate was forced to wait in the outer office. After thirty minutes, the Archbishop was escorted into the office of the British Consul General.

When the Archbishop came face to face with Consul-General Sir Harry Lamb, the troubled history that immediately followed their first meeting in Macedonia rushed back into his consciousness. He now stood in front of the very man who orchestrated his exile from Macedonia in 1907.

Sir Harry, clearly annoyed by the sudden appearance of the Greek Archbishop asked, "What on earth are you doing here?"

In spite of their past, Chrysostomos had only one goal which was the safety of innocent people.

"Your Excellency, I have come to beg your assistance for the innocent Greek people who have no protection against the Turkish armies that are following them to Smyrna. I am begging that the British military intervene to discourage any brutality by the Turks.

In spite of his blustering show of outrage, Lamb was actually enjoying the moment. He had considered his successful lobby to have this partisan priest exiled a victory of wills. Here, he was getting to enjoy it for a second time.

He asked incredulously, "Why have you come to ask me to defend you and to provide military intervention? . . . How can British soldiers be brought here for immediate defense when Greek soldiers are retreating?"

The Archbishop tried to remain calm. "I am not asking you to protect our soldiers. My concern is solely for our innocent refugees who have not been at war with the Turkish armies."

Lamb had unconsciously donned a smile of unfiltered egotism as he took great pleasure in destroying any hope in this rogue priest's eyes. "Unfortunately, in spite of my wish to help the innocents, my hands are completely tied. Great Britain has declared neutrality in this matter and I am prevented from violating that neutrality."

Chrysostomos left with a clear understanding that the British had completely abandoned Greece in its hour of need. Now, he could only hope the French and Italian consuls were honest in their assurances.

Curious, after the meeting in Horton's office, MacLachlan walked over to the quay before he returned to the college in Paradise. As he approached it, he was disturbed by the sight. It was late afternoon and he could still see an endless row of troops pouring onto the quay. Transport ships were already loading troops as others waited for a place to dock. He thought, *This is going to be worse than anyone thought!*

By the time he returned to Paradise, he could see the growing unease at the college. He was now thinking about how to protect the school. From the look of the Greek troops, he was no longer worried about them. He was more worried about the Turks that were behind them, especially the *chettes*. Teachers approached him for counsel. A few students brought to him a rumor they had heard about a band of *chettes,* five-thousand strong, approaching from the south. If that was true, they would have to pass the college on their way to the city.

Many of the students at the college were Greek and Armenian. McLachlan knew that putting Greek and Armenian students in the direct path of *chettes* was an explosive combination. He devised a plan to hopefully protect the American College by making certain there were American flags flying wherever possible. Then, he decided that he would go out and meet the *chettes* face-to-face, to warn them that the college was an American institution and that any interference with it would not only be resisted, but would create serious complications for the Turkish government and also for them.

As the sun set in the harbor west of Smyrna, Greek soldiers and refugees continued to pour into the city. A recent arrival to the bay of Smyrna, Charles Howes, a young British naval officer, was disturbed by the condition of the fifty thousand Greek troops that had now congregated on the quayside. He said to his fellow officer, "they're the most dilapidated, filthy, untidy, slouching lot of humans I have ever witnessed wearing uniforms."

He later learned from a patrol that had gone ashore that most Greek soldiers had received no supplies of food for twelve days and were "haggard looking, hungry, some barefoot, no officers, no regulations, no marching, just sloughing along in twos and threes as fast as their stumbling legs permitted."

Clearly, as the night advanced, there was a universal sense of doom that hung over the city. Considering the paltry number of Allied troops present, everyone felt that their world would end at any moment.

Chapter 28.
7 September

Grace Williamson looked out the second floor window of the English nursing home in Smyrna which she ran as a maternity home. Williamson, a Levantine of English descent, watched as the endless line of defeated Greek soldiers and refugees passed by on their way to the quay. One of the Greek expectant mothers from Aydin came up and stood next to her, watching the procession of refugees.

The pregnant mother asked, "Where will they all go? There are so many."

Williamson looked on, "Look! Mothers carrying their babies dressed in brightly-colored costumes. They provide the only cheerful sound. They must think this is a picnic or an adventure. They sing and shout because they don't realize what is happening to them and they're not hungry yet. Where will they sleep tonight and when will they get back to their homes and their vineyards that are full of grapes right now? What will it be in a day or two when they are out of food they've carried from home? Every place is packed with refugees. We have given all we can. The church garden and memorial hall are filled with respectable people. Some are the best class of Greek from your town of Aydin and Nazil. Well-to-do families who just got off with a bundle. It is pitiful and they will suffer more and more. It is awful! Our rooms are full of maternity cases. We cannot take anymore."

By mid morning, Consul Horton hurried over to see Lt. Merrill. He could see the stream of refugees had not abated and could see that this was fast turning into a humanitarian crisis. There wasn't enough food and water in Smyrna to care for all the refugees. He was hoping to get Merrill's help to secure military assistance. Horton found Merrill reading a *New York Times* reprint.

"Commander, we must do something for these poor people or a huge tragedy will soon befall them. . . a great wrong is about to occur."

Merrill didn't look up from his paper. "Listen to this, some elitist has written a sarcastic editorial. It says 'The Administration doubtless expects popular approval of the view, that Greek Christians may be shot down, so long as Americans are not knocked over by stray bullets.' Idiot bleeding heart. These idiots call me Pro-Turk. Yes, I am pro-Turk. . . not because I like the Turk, but because I love America. It's clear to me that American business interests are best served if we back the Turk and not the Greek. Admiral Bristol agrees with me."

Horton couldn't believe a U.S. Naval officer was saying this. "Commander, how can you take that position when we get daily reports that thousands of Greeks are being massacred in Trebizond by the Black Sea?"

"Oh Horton! You're a bleeding heart. All those eyewitness reports you're referring to are obviously propaganda from unreliable sources. Do you think America has any chance of getting any oil concessions from the Turks if we keep going on about the persecution of minorities? I can assure you that any American journalist who expects Admiral Bristol to allow them in Anatolia, has to assure him that none of this crap gets printed. If he has to censor what gets out, he assured me that he will."

Horton pressed him. "Look Tip, I'm not here to argue about your patriotism or your politics. We have a humanitarian crisis brewing outside your door and we need military assistance. Are you going to help me or not?"

Merrill was clearly annoyed. "Look George, Washington has already buckled to these liberals and are pressuring us. We've had to order the U.S.S. *Lawrence* to head for Smyrna. Hell, we already had the *Litchfield* and *Simpson* sitting in the harbor. But I'm not about to try to aid those one-hundred-fifty-thousand destitute and ignorant refugees sitting on the streets waiting for us to help them. My mission is to protect American lives and property. These refugees must look to their own government for help."

Horton was bursting with rage. "But their government is right at this moment in the process of abandoning them. I went by the *Konak* on my way over here. All of the Greek administrators are clearing out their offices. They're all leaving today. By tonight, there won't be any government or police to protect these people. We are the only ones left to help them."

Merrill raised his chin to show his inflexibility on this point. "I've told you what my mission is. I'm not prepared to do anything else. What I do is best for America. I have no other loyalty."

Horton stormed out of the office and hurried back toward his own office. His forward progress was greatly diminished by the wall of refugees hauling their meager worldly possessions toward the quay. When he finally arrived at his office, he found Hole waiting for him. "Where have you been? I was worried about you." Hole said.

"I was just over to see Tip. He's not about to help any of these people. He thinks if he sits back and does nothing, the Turks will give us oil concessions. I'm really worried about where this is going."

Hole's face showed more bad news. "I just saw General Hatzianestis, the ex-commander of all Greek forces, sneaking on to a ship that's carrying Greek city officials and workers. There are so many refugees on the streets, I could hardly move forward."

Horton said, "I just had the same problem."

Hole continued, "You don't understand. The entire Greek government is leaving the city today. I saw policemen climbing on the ship. I went over to ask Stergiadis what was going on. He's leaving today as well. Tonight there will be not one member of the Greek government left in Smyrna. Without any police, the city will fall into anarchy and chaos. Blood will run in the streets."

Horton desperate for a solution, "What about the Greek troops?"

Hole had a look of astonishment. "You know, when I was walking near the quay, I spotted the Greek troops being loaded onto the transport ships. I was surprised by their discipline. Everyone thought when they arrived, they would go out and do damage, like they've been burning villages on the way. But no! They're in such a state of exhaustion and depression. They just walk along like sheep being led. It is eerie to watch. These are soldiers hardened by twelve years of war, and they are like mindless sheep."

Jennings walked into the office. "Consul Horton, oh. . . Teddy you're here too! I just saw something strange. It looks like the entire Greek government is leaving on a ship."

Hole nodded. "That's what I came to tell him. Smyrna will be a city without a government tonight. This could be very bad."

Jennings' mind started racing. "We have to do something. Will the American soldiers help keep the peace?"

Horton said, "I just came from Merrill's office. He said his only mission is to protect the Americans here and their property. He has no intention of helping the refugees."

Chapter 29.
8 September

As the sun rose, everyone was relieved that the absence of any civil authority did not result in theft, vandalism, rape or any other kind of violence. Instead, there was a muted hush that lasted the entire night with just about everyone frozen in fear of what might happen the next moment. The morning sun actually brought about a city-wide sigh of relief.

The British Consul-General, Sir Harry Lamb fearing the worst, had worked with his consular staff through the night preparing the paperwork for British nationals to be able to leave the country. Horton was every bit as concerned as Sir Harry about the lack of any civil authority in the city in that there were still a large number of Americans living in Smyrna. More troubling was the equally large number of Greek-American and Armenian-American citizens who also were in the city.

Horton was torn between advising all Americans to leave or not to leave. On one hand, he didn't want to create a panic, but he also realized the heavy responsibility he bore if things went from bad to worse. He already had desperate refugees piling into the city looking for refuge. If he ordered an evacuation of Americans, surely it would incite a stampede of humanity looking to save themselves. Many American wives were already aboard ships in the harbor. Horton had advised his wife before he left for work this morning to do the same. But Catherine told him, "No George, I'll leave with you. Perhaps it might give some comfort to others who remained."

Still uneasy about the lack of any authority, Horton called a meeting of key people within the American colony in Paradise. Dr. Maclachlan from the college and E.O. Jacob, Ed Fisher and Asa Jennings from the YMCA were among those at the meeting.

"I called you here this morning because I remain concerned about our people today. I was relieved that we had no trouble overnight, and I continue to get assurances from the French and Italian consuls that Kemal's troops will behave if they decide to enter

Smyrna, but I want to take some precautionary measures in case their assessment is incorrect. I've chosen the American Theater to be the American central meeting point if things go bad. It's a large building right on the quay that will be convenient to boarding on transport ships."

Rufus Lane, a businessman and past Consul-General of Smyrna raised his hand to be noticed. "Consul Horton, I'm a businessman here in Smyrna. I think as Americans, we need to think more about how to help the refugees. There are thousands and thousands of them pouring into the city. They're dying of starvation and thirst and nobody is offering to help them. We didn't come here solely to save our own skins!"

Everyone at the meeting seemed to respond to his plea. They all joined and agreed that they had to do something for the refugees. The crisis appeared to change them all into a cohesive group preparing a plan. They established a Provisional Relief Committee. People donated money and equipment to the committee to provide services. The local American firms offered up their trucks and automobiles and individuals offered their personal services to help with the task.

The scene transformed into one of ordinary Americans doing what ordinary Americans do. If the government was ordering the military to stand down and not help the refugees, then American citizens would take up the slack on their own. Almost immediately, they donated money, purchased flour and hired bakers to make bread for the starving masses. Within hours they were feeding helpless refugees.

After the meeting adjourned, Horton contacted American authorities in both Constantinople and Washington DC, requesting additional warships be sent to protect American interests. He indicated that the ships already in the harbor were not nearly sufficient to stave off a catastrophe if things turned for the worse. Unfortunately, the request had to be made through Bristol in Constantinople, who had already decided that the Turks had the best of intentions and administrative abilities.

A short while later, Horton received a visit from his long-time friend, Archbishop Chrysostomos. The Archbishop was, as always, in his black gown priest's stove pipe cap. Horton gestured for him to be seated and offered him a glass of water. Chrysostomos looked terrible. He wiped his forehead and then spoke to his old friend.

"Yiorgo!" Chrysostomos always referred to the Consul by his name in Greek.

"I have been to the French and the Italians. They both claim that they will protect all of the Christians in the city. But they lie! They have betrayed us before and now are looking to be in the pocket of the Turks. I also went to see Sir Harry. He has abandoned us. Now there are only the Americans to save us. Can you do something to protect our people against these savages?"

Horton could not give him an answer. He knew that Bristol had already, in effect, abandoned the hundreds of thousands of Christians by refusing to help them. But there was no way he could tell his friend this. "Your Eminence, we have been friends for a long time. I understand that the French have offered you safe haven aboard a French vessel. You are an obvious target for the Turkish military. I implore you to accept the French offer of a marine escort and protection aboard a French warship."

Chrysostomos just sat silently and looked at his old friend. Horton looking back into the Archbishop's eyes, thought, *For the second time in my life, I'm looking at that shadow upon a human visage, knowing for certain that this person will soon die.*

23. *Archbishop Chrysostomos speaks for the youth programs he supported.*

As the day progressed, tens of thousands of Greek troops continued to be loaded on to transport ships, while refusing to allow any refugees to board. Seeing the dwindling crowd of Greek troops boarding the ships, as well as having been present for the meeting in Horton's office, MacLachlan's concern for his college intensified. He headed to the quay to request troops be dispatched from the

American destroyer to protect the college property. Captain Piper, commander of the American destroyer, USS *Litchfield* took twenty sailors with him, dispatching themselves to the college campus. Shortly thereafter, Lieutenant Commander Rhodes posted thirty-five men at the principle American institutions in Smyrna. In doing so, he warned his men against breaching Admiral Bristol's order that limited their actions to helping American citizens and American property.

The British also decided to land two hundred British marines to guard their Consulate and other key facilities. Unlike Admiral Bristol's warning, the British response to requests for protection of private property in Bournabat and Smyrna were rejected. He only would concern himself with British lives.

As the sun set on Smyrna for the second night in a row, the town was eerily silent as there was no longer any Greek civil or security authority, and the dwindling number of retreating unarmed Greek troops were solely focused on being evacuated in advance of the arrival of Turkish troops.

Chapter 30.
9 September

Captain Arthur J. Hepburn ('Japy' to his friends), was commander of the USS *Scorpion*, America's flagship of the naval fleet operating in Smyrna waters, as well as Chief of Staff to Rear Admiral Mark Bristol, who commanded the entire fleet.

Just after sunrise, Hepburn, was piped aboard the U. S. destroyer, USS *Lawrence,* his new flagship and stood on the bridge as it made its way into the Smyrna harbor. Through his field glasses, Hepburn could see the last Greek ship backed into the quay, awaiting to pick up the last remnants of Greek troops. He could also see a ragtag line of Greek cavalry troops, who would hold the unflattering distinction of being the last Greek troops to be evacuated from Asia Minor after their monumental defeat. As he scanned his surroundings, other than the twenty-one Allied warships anchored in the harbor, Hepburn could see an improbable fleet of tiny *caiques* (rowboats) filled to overcapacity, attempting to evacuate Christian refugees out of Smyrna.

24. *Desperate refugees board rowboats to escape the Turkish soldiers.*

From his vantage point on the *Lawrence,* Hepburn was relieved that, in spite of the horrific scene in front of him, the city was at least calm. He concluded once the last Greek ship had left the harbor, the expected arrival of Turkish troops would not carry the added risk of confrontation between Turkish and Greek troops.

Just before noon, Hepburn, through his field glasses, watched as the first of the Turkish troops trotted into the city. The mere sight of the Turkish troops caused a stampede of desperate Greek residents pushing and shoving to get out of their path. They rode slowly down the quayside as terrified Greek citizens look on, unable to control their shrieks of maddening fear. In contrast to the utter silence of the mounted soldiers, some of the riders with swords held high, called out, "*Korkma!...* Fear not!"

American sailors dispatched to what was known as 'The Point' at the north end of the quay, were surprised by the appearance of General Murcelle Pasha's cavalry force. At the front of the column, rode Captain Cherefeddin Bey. To the American sailors, the riders had the classic look of the Mongolian hordes that spawned the notorious Genghis Khan.

25. *Turkish cavalry enter Smyrna led by Captain Cherefeddin Bey.*

At the American Consulate, George Horton, Alex MacLachlan and Lieutenant Merrill, had been discussing the plan of relief for the refugees, and had just chosen the YMCA building as the headquarters of the effort. There was a mutual concern for the word 'Christian' being a part of the location, but its central location trumped the potentially explosive reference to religion. Suddenly, they heard horrific screams coming from just outside the American Consulate building. They all ran over to the window and could see a mob of women racing toward the front doors of the Consulate. Sailors guarding the entrance were almost overwhelmed by the rush of terror-stricken refugees. Merrill looked at the scene in amazement, "Look at their faces! They're insane with fear."

Horton looked up at the street along the quayside. He saw them! A column of impressive, mounted Turkish cavalry that Captain Hepburn had spotted with his field glasses, atop magnificent war horses, dressed in all-black uniforms and black *Circassian* fez caps moving southward down the quayside at a perfectly disciplined slow trot; each rider brandishing the trademark curved, gleaming *scimitar* sword held in the air. He commented to Merrill, "Anyone who knows anything about military matters can see that these are not just soldiers, but extremely well-trained soldiers who completely obey their officers. Look at that precision."

At a point in the procession when the cavalry reached the central section of the quay, a British officer, Captain Thesiger of the HMS *King George V*, stepped out into the middle of the street blocking the procession's path, and held up his hand as if to stop forward progress. From the deck of the *King George V*, the crew watched as the procession halted immediately to the mere raising of their commander's arm.

Captain Thesiger announced, "I am a captain in His Majesty's navy, and have been commissioned to assist in the surrender of this city to you. I can state that the city is calm and that no one has the slightest intention of resisting the victorious Turkish army. But if you enter yelling and brandishing your scimitars, you will undoubtedly be asking for trouble."

From their vantage point in the Consulate, Horton, Maclachlan and Merrill suddenly noticed a very troubling sight. While everyone had thought that the last Greek troops had been evacuated earlier on the Greek ships, they watched a row of disheveled and weary Greek troops just walking alongside the halted cavalry, as if their victors were invisible. It was clear the Greek troops were heading for Chesme, their port of embarkation to Greece. Suddenly, the defeated and the victor were within a few feet of each other.

From the row of Greek soldiers, someone hurled a hand grenade that hit Captain Cherefeddin on his cheek. The grenade failed to explode, but it did leave a gash on his cheek that bloodied his face. From behind the Turkish leader, some troops began firing into the crowd killing a half-dozen civilians. Instead of reacting, Cherefeddin simply dismounted, walked over to a Greek soldier who still carried a weapon, took his rifle and broke it across his knee. He then sent the defeated Greek along his way, untouched.

As the cavalry approached the *Konak,* at the south end of the quay, nearest the Turkish barracks, residents from the Turkish quarter came out to see their victorious soldiers. They cheered and yelped as the cavalry passed. Seeing the cavalry nearing the *Konack,* Lt. Comdr. Merrill decided to go and meet them. MacLachlan becoming concerned about there being so many Greeks at the college, decided to head back to the campus.

As a military representative of the American government, Merrill walked over to the *Konak* to congratulate the Turkish troops on their victory. He arrived at the *Konak* as the stoic Captain dismounted from his horse. Merrill approached him.

"As the representative of the U.S. government, I wish to congratulate you on your recent victory and as a personal note, Captain, your extreme self-control in not reacting to that grenade."

Cherefeddin looked at Merrill, "Thank you Commander! I did lose my temper when I saw a British patrol standing close by making no attempt to stop the assassin."

The triumphant arrival of the Turkish cavalry evoked a festival-like mood within the Turkish quarter of the city. Turkish music blaring, people singing in the narrow streets, hugging, kissing and the general euphoria that greets a military victory. During the Greek arrival, there had been no Greeks celebrating with weapons. Certainly no Turks had appeared with a weapon. But now that they were back in power, it seems that every Turk was armed and shooting celebratory rounds into the air.

What was missing was the victor. General Mustapha Kemal did not enter the city. Instead, he remained with his entourage in Nif, a village some miles outside of Smyrna. Kemal had agreed to meet with the French and Italian Consuls in his makeshift headquarters, but the streets were so filled with victorious troops and reveling Turkish residents, they could not get through. Having congratulated Captain Cherefeddin already, Commander Merrill decided it would be appropriate to congratulate General Kemal himself, as it was clear that Merrill was as pro-Turk as his commanding officer, Admiral

Bristol. He decided to take two American journalists with him as they attempted to reach Kemal.

Before they could get close, however, they were stopped by a Turkish officer, who ordered them to turn back. When Merrill suggested that they could provide publicity for the Turkish mission, the officer was unimpressed. They were forced to return to Smyrna. On the way back, they had to pass through the Jewish quarter of the city. They found that the Italians had taken a major presence there. In Italy's push to show she had more subjects under her control, many Jews were given immediate Italian citizenship. However, conditions were such that a Jewish militia had to be established to escort Jews from place to place, so that the Turks would not mistake them for Christians, and murder them on the spot.

When MacLachlan returned to the American campus he noticed that the marines had placed machine guns at the entrance. Immediately, he ordered that the American flag be raised over the building, so there would be no mistake by the Turks that the property was American. However, raising the flag resulted in hundreds of nearby Greek residents running to the campus for their own safety. Concerned about what he had just witnessed on the quayside, he ordered that sanctuary was conditional on all Greeks surrendering their weapons before they entered the campus. By 3 p.m., there were more than fifteen-hundred Greeks and Armenians who had entered the college. In that same hour, Sir Harry Lamb, ordered all British citizens to leave Smyrna, an action that caused even more panic among the residents.

By nightfall, following a long-standing tradition of the Turkish warriors of old, the Turkish *chettes*, decided it was time to enjoy the spoils of their victory. Spoils, in the mind of the *chette* included theft, rape, murder, dismemberment, and any other brutal act that would further strike fear into the hearts of his captives. In *his* mind, the *chette* was a victorious warrior, not an illiterate, savage thug.

At just before midnight, aboard the *Lawrence,* Captain Hepburn wrote out his report to Admiral Bristol, in a fashion his superior expected to hear. The report stated, "At this hour, 11:50 p.m., everything is quiet [and] peaceful. . . I must say that the Turks deserve a high mark for their efficiency, good discipline and high military standards.'

Chapter 31.
10 September

For the first time in centuries, Sunday morning arrived in Smyrna without the sound of Christian church bells. An ominous sign and obvious reaction to the presence of victorious Muslim Turkish troops in the predominantly Christian city.

Turkish *chettes* now without restrictions from their military authority, threatened any Christians they came across, firing their guns and relieving Christians of any money or valuables they might have had.

The first part of the city to be pillaged was the Armenian quarter. They broke into homes, took any valuables, and either removed daughters or raped them on the spot. If fancy happened to strike, they might just go ahead and kill the girl after their business was completed. Or, if they were feeling that their manhood needed bolstering, they might cut off her breasts as a souvenir and delight in her family's horror as they mutilated her.

Later that morning, amidst brilliant sunshine, General Mustapha Kemal Pasha entered Smyrna in an open touring car as he passed between lines of cavalrymen with their swords drawn and gleaming in the sun. He arrived at the *Konak* and appeared on the balcony of the government house the Greeks had just abandoned, allowing the cheering masses to savor his victory. Then, he left the balcony to formally assign his chosen officer, General Noureddin Pasha, to control the city as its military governor.

After appointing his military governor, Kemal was invited to the mansion of a wealthy Turkish merchant, Muammer Usakizade. Among the invited guests, was the celebrated Turkish activist, Halide Edib. As the party progressed with toasts celebrating the monumental victory, Usakizade's daughter, Latife, appeared at the party.

Latife, a law student in France, had returned to her father's home after Kemal's strategic victory at Sakarya, appearing with her grandmother as her chaperone. From her actions, Edib thought there was no hiding of Latife's affection for General Kemal. Later at the party, Kemal walked over to Edib. He leaned over and whispered, "She carries a locket around her neck with my picture in it. She came near me and showing the locket asked me, 'Do you mind?' 'Why should I mind?' he laughed with delight.

    Things were not so joyous, elsewhere in Smyrna. Greek parishioners had gathered for Sunday liturgical services at the Agia Sofia Cathedral seeking comfort from their shepherd, Archbishop Chrysostomos. The church was full as Chrysostomos tried to comfort them with the expected arrival of French and Italian troops to protect them. Having no confidence that any of it was actually true, the Prelate refused to tell them his true belief. He just continued to pray.

    After the service, a tall, young man who had been standing at the rear, came to the front of the church. He approached the Archbishop. Chrysostomos looked up at the man and forced a smile. "Yianni, What are you doing here?"

    The young man fell to his knees and kissed the Archbishop's hand. "My mother sent me to convince you to leave Smyrna. She had a dream. You must leave now."

    The Archbishop shook his head. "Your mother is a foolish woman to send you here. Without your father at home, you must protect your family. Leave immediately.

26. *General Kemal arrives in Smyrna in an open touring car.*

"She said I couldn't leave until I convinced you to leave." Yianni said, "At least go out to one of the ships. It is too dangerous for you and my father is not here to protect you anymore."

Chrysostomos took on a more serious tone. "Yianni, what are you now nineteen years?"

"Twenty!" Yianni replied.

"At twenty, you must now take the responsibility of only your family. There is no one else who can do it. You are my cousin and I love you dearly, but you know in your heart, I cannot leave these people to die here without me. If I did, I would probably kill myself afterward. You know this in your heart. Now listen to me. You must get out of this city. You cannot go back to Triglia by land. The Turks are arriving and you will be taken prisoner and killed. You must get on one of the boats and leave. Then you can try to get back to Triglia to save your family."

Yianni was conflicted. "But. . ."

Chrysostomos would not allow an answer. "Do it. Find a way to get out to a ship before the Turks find you and save your family. Go! Now!"

The Archbishop placed his hand on the head of his cousin's son and blessed him. With tears in his eyes, Yianni backed away from the Archbishop, turned and ran out of the cathedral.

In the afternoon, General Noureddin sent a patrol out to the Cathedral to bring Archbishop Chrysostomos to his office at the *Konak*. An officer and two soldiers entered the Archbishop's office and informed Chrysostomos that he was being summoned to a meeting with General Noureddin. Chrysostomos, was not troubled by this, for he was Smyrna's most senior religious leader and last remaining authority for the Greek population. The Archbishop followed the soldiers out to their waiting car.

By coincidence, a passing French patrol saw Chrysostomos enter the car with the Turkish escort. A civilian traveling with the French patrol, convinced them to follow the automobile with the Archbishop inside.

General Noureddin stood to the side of his balcony door. He gently moved the curtain slightly, giving him a glimpse of the Archbishop stepping from the car. Chrysostomos appeared somewhat lost as he looked around the Governor's office that was just across the street from the Turkish military barracks. To his left,

27. Pavlos Papavasiliou (standing) poses with his brother, Yianni and sister, Fofo. Photo courtesy of C. Papavasiliou.

a crowd of about fifty Turks stood behind several Turkish regulars who prevented the crowd from approaching the Governor's office building. They began to hiss, and call out obscenities in Turkish. Chrysostomos looked at the crowd and then up at the balcony. As he looked up, he noticed that the curtain had shifted a bit. He thought someone was watching what was going on. Suspecting the worst, a look of despair reappeared on his face, as he felt his end was near. General Noureddin, quickly moved from behind the balcony window to his desk and sat down. Momentarily, there was a soft knock at his door. Noureddin commanded, "Enter!"

The door opened and a Turkish regular hurried over to Noureddin's desk. Standing just outside the doorway, Chrysostomos stared at the General. The soldier whispered something in Noureddin's ear invoking a nod. Then the soldier gestured to his counterpart to enter. The guard standing behind Chrysostomos, pushed him with the butt of his rifle through the doorway, causing him to stumble. Chrysostomos regained his balance and slowly walked forward toward the desk. As he approached, General Noureddin, stood, straightened his uniform and came around his desk to face him.

Chrysostomos looked into the General's eyes and extended his hand as if to greet him. Noureddin slowly looked down at Chrysostomos' extended hand and spit at it. He grimaced as he spoke, "Filth!" Chrysostomos closed his eyes already aware of what was to follow, let his hand fall to his side.

Noureddin paced around the room with his hands clasped behind his back. He looked up at the ceiling as he spoke dismissively.

"So here we are outlaw priest. You have been inciting your people to sedition all of these years. You wear your robes of the priesthood and yet, we know you were with your terrorist cousin in the hills outside Drama, fighting against your Turkish masters. So, tell me. . . how does a man of God reconcile picking up a rifle to shoot his master? You can't! Therefore you are not a priest. You are merely a terrorist wearing a priest's clothing. We dealt with your cousin already and now we must deal with you. You are an enemy of the Turkish state and will be dealt with as such. Take him away!"

As Chrysostomos was led back out onto the street, Noureddin appeared at the balcony outside his window. He shouted, "My Turkish brothers, this terrorist posing as a priest, has been found guilty of crimes against his government. Treat him as he deserves!"

The Turkish regulars that had been holding back the crowd, stepped back and allowed what now was an angry mob, to grab Chrysostomos. As Noureddin watched silently above, the mob made guttural shrieks, as they dragged Chrysostomos down the street away from the *Konak*. Approaching the Jewish quarter, they reached a barber shop where its proprietor, known as Ismail, stood in the doorway, watching. Someone in the mob, pushed the barber to the side and yelled, "Let's give him a shave!"

He grabbed a white barber's cape and draping it over the Archbishop's body, tied it around his neck. Then, as mob psychology would take over, the closest enraged Turks began beating Chrysostomos with their fists, while some used sticks. Many spit in his face and shouted obscenities. One, driven to uncontrollable rage, pulled a knife from his belt and began stabbing the priest.

Chrysostomos, now lying on his back, raised his right hand with his three fingers joined. He made the sign of the cross with his fingers at those who were stabbing him and uttered,

"Please forgive them!"

This enraged the mob even more. Someone using a sword, slashed at the Prelate's raised hand, chopping it off at the wrist. Now, others grabbed at his long beard, pulling it out of his face by the roots. In a frenzy, the Turk with the knife, used it to gouge out his eye. Blood began to cover and turn the white cape bright red. He gouged out the second eye. Not being enough to satisfy their rage, another Turk pulled a knife from his belt and cut off Chrysostomos' ears. At this point Chrysostomos was delirious with pain. He tried to raise his handless arm, but was no longer able to. His utterances no longer intelligible. Still not satisfied, the knife wielder cut off the Archbishop's nose.

The French marines that followed the Archbishop to the *Konak*, upon seeing the uncontrolled attack on him, moved instinctively to help. Seeing this, their commanding officer, trembling himself, ordered them to stand down. One marine later recalled, 'They finished Chrysostomos there before our eyes.'

The priest was reduced to a bleeding mass of flesh on the ground outside the barber shop. He lapsed into unconsciousness as he bled out. With their enemy dead or dying on the street, the Turks decided to use a tradition that dated back to ancient times. An automobile was brought up to the barber shop and Chrysostomos' body was tied to the back bumper. For the next hour, the Archbishop's body was dragged around the Turkish quarter, as a declaration of Turkish victory over those who would oppose Turkish superiority.

News of the grizzly massacre reached Admiral Dumesmil, captain of the French flagship in the harbor. He commented upon hearing the news, "He got what was coming to him!"

Like a trigger, once news of the Archbishop's murder was out, the incidences of violence increased considerably. Clearly, every Greek and Armenian in the city had become a refugee. And with that, no place was safe. For the Christians, there was only one last hope. Either obtain shelter at an American building, or somehow get passage on a ship leaving the quay. Otherwise, the only future was death, or something worse.

Over night, the Archbishop's death turned Bournabat, the exclusive Levantine community, into an orgy of destruction. Turkish *chettes* took to ransacking the great villas of Bournabat. Items that could not be looted and carried off, were burned or destroyed. The mansions of Bournabat were torched. By the time the sun would rise tomorrow, Bournabat would be in ruins.

Chapter 32.
11 September

On Monday morning, MacLachan drove from the college in Paradise into Smyrna. Things clearly had deteriorated since the Greek Archbishop was savagely massacred. MacLachlan passed bodies on the roadside intermingled with loot too heavy to carry off.

MacLachlan's destination was the *Konak* to meet with General Noureddin. Considering the deterioration of order in the city, MacLachlan wanted to increase the level of protection for the college. Even if the school was serving mostly Greek and Armenian students, he reasoned it still was an American facility and the Turks would not deliberately attack an American institution.

MacLachlan was not given an immediate audience with the new military governor. While waiting in the reception area, he spoke with the General's adjutant.

"I noticed on my way over here, that there were many bodies along the way. Can you tell me anything about what happened

28. *Greek families grieve the loss of murdered family members*

overnight?" The adjutant officer didn't seem to have any problem telling what he had heard.

"Apparently our officers had uncovered an Armenian plot to terrorize General Kemal's victorious army."

MacLachlan, with close ties to the Armenian community, knew of no such plot.

"I'm surprised by this. There are a few fanatics out there, but the community does not support any of them. In fact, they denounce them as only making matters worse for the Armenian people."

Suddenly, the two men heard a commotion coming from the street. They went over to the window and watched as the Turkish troops escorted a group of Greek prisoners along the quayside. The commotion consisted of the Turkish troops forcing their Greek prisoners to shout, in Turkish, "Long Live Mustapha Kemal."

The adjutant explained, "You cannot blame our soldiers for this. After all, this is exactly what the Greeks made our soldiers do when they first occupied Smyrna."

The signal was given for MacLachlan to enter the general's office. When he entered, MacLachlan was immediately impressed with Noureddin's charm and cordiality. Noureddin said, "I understand that you would like us to allow for additional protection of your college. Is that correct?"

MacLachlan nodded.

Noureddin said, "We understand America's concern for its citizen's and its property, especially considering the lawless Greek soldiers that continue to roam through the city as well as Armenian terrorists who appear to be plotting attacks against our victorious army. But I think you will see there is no cause for concern. Please, you will need to contact my district commander for Paradise, and he will do what he can to help you."

MacLachlan smiled. "I will contact him as soon as I get back to the college. I appreciate your help in this matter. Thank you, General Noureddin."

Grace Williamson was disturbed and concerned for her patients as a result of the sound of gunfire over night. She heard about the destruction to Bournabat and the Armenian quarter, but her enthusiasm for the control of Smyrna now being back in the hands of the Turks was undiminished. She was pleased to see, as she walked to her British Consulate, that the streets were clear and she saw many patrolling Turkish police keeping the peace.

The purpose of her visit to the Consulate was to acquire additional provisions for her nursing home. The place was spilling over with residents and provisions were completely inadequate. After obtaining some emergency provisions, she quickly returned to the nursing home, somewhat tentative about her relative safety on the streets.

George Horton spent Monday morning gathering the witness reports from American workers in Smyrna. He believed these would be important in the aftermath of what was occurring in his beloved city. America's charitable institutions were operated by men and women who had mostly grown up in the light of the U.S. Constitution, and there was no cause to believe that these reports would not be truthful. Finally, he ventured out on his own to view the results of the previous night's violence.

Horton was shocked by the scene. Among the hordes of desperate refugees being pushed along toward the quayside, Horton witnessed an old woman stumbling to not fall as she was pushed. She was so weak, she wasn't able to keep up the pace required by the Turkish soldiers. Horton watched as a soldier poked her with the butt of his rifle in order to pick up her pace. But no poking was able to overcome her fatigue. Finally, the soldier struck between her shoulder blades with such force, that she left the ground and landed on her face on the cobblestone street.

He was outraged, but there was nothing he could do; he was under strict orders from Admiral Bristol that no American official could be seen helping the Greek or Armenian communities. As an official, his hands were tied, but the stand-down order did not extend to American citizens, not working for the government. American relief workers just could not stand by and let this brutal destruction of humanity continue without their intervention. After all, it was the American sense of justice and humanity that brought them to Smyrna in the first place. So while Horton's hands were personally tied, he openly encouraged the American workers to feed, shelter and give comfort to the afflicted refugees.

Horton would later write:

"Not one of them flinched or wobbled for an instant throughout a situation which had scarcely a parallel in the history of the world for hideousness and danger. They endured fatigue almost beyond endurance that they might do all in their power to save their charges and give comfort and courage to the frightened, hunted creatures who had thrown themselves on their protection."

MacLachlan returned to the college campus after his meeting with General Noureddin around noon. After lunch, he was informed that Turkish soldiers had entered one of the houses on the campus and were in the process of ransacking and looting it. This was especially disturbing considering the assurances he had just received from Noureddin and the fact that the property was flying an American flag.

Being squarely in the Turkish camp as far as who should be running the city, he was furious, and not about to let some foolish soldiers ruin his relationship with the new Turkish government. He immediately went over to the security officer, Navy Chief Crocker, and asked that he and several other sailors accompany him to the house in question to scare them away. Crocker left to round up a squad of sailors.

As the afternoon progressed, most of the shops, clubs and restaurants closed up shop as the entire city could feel the tension in the air. The larger establishments, like the Grand Hotel Kraemer Palace remained open as a function of its housing of foreign visitors.

Without any advance warning, the Kraemer Palace was visited by an important guest they did not recognize. The staff could tell he must have been a man of importance in that he came with an entourage. When he stepped into the foyer and asked to be seated, he was informed that the bars and restaurants were completely full. At that point, one of the man's entourage stepped up to the *maître d'* and whispered to him the stranger's identity. Instantly the *maître d'* snapped his fingers and a table was set up. A moment later, General Mustapha Kemal was seated.

The *maître d'* fearing an adverse opinion of him, approached General Kemal and inquired, "I apologize for the error. May I bring you a refreshment?"

Kemal replied, "Bring me *raki*!"

A bottle of *raki* was placed on the table along with a shot glass. The *maître d'* poured the clear liquid into the shot glass. Kemal reached for the glass and raised it to his mouth, but did not take a drink.

The *maître d'* said, "*chin chin.*"

Kemal smiled and set the glass down. He eyed a waiter standing off to his left and gestured with his finger for the waiter to approach him. When the waiter stood at attention to his side, Kemal asked, "Did King Constantine ever come here to drink a glass of *raki*?"

The waiter, not knowing the answer to the question ran off to inquire of the *maître d'*. In a moment he returned. "My employer has told me that the Greek King has never set foot in the hotel."

Kemal smiled at the waiter, "In that case, why did he bother to take Izmir?" (Turkish name for Smyrna).

Not expecting an answer, the General smiled, pushed the shot glass toward the center of the table, rose from his seat and left the hotel.

Reverend Abraham Hartunian, an Armenian priest, felt compelled to record in his diary, 'Today, 11 September, I saw with my own eyes, the Turks taking wagons loaded with bombs, gunpowder, kerosene, and everything necessary to start fires, here and there through the streets.'

At the American Institute, a young Armenian teacher, Anita Chakerian, saw Turkish guards dragging large sacks into the building, and depositing them in various corners. When asked, the Turks claimed that they were bringing rice and potatoes because they knew the people were hungry and would soon have nothing left to eat. They did warn that the bags should not be opened until there was no bread left to eat.

One of the American sailors stationed at the Institute thought this bold act of charity from the Turks seemed to be in complete contradiction of Turkish behavior since he had arrived. The sailor checked the bags and found them to be filled with decidedly inedible gunpowder and dynamite.

By late afternoon, with *chettes* brutalizing Greek and Armenian refugees in full view of, and with no concern of a reprimand by the Turkish military, the anarchy seemed to spread over to the regular troops. By now, the liquor was flowing as Turkish soldiers with no orders holding them back, were in full celebration of their victory. And like the hordes of old, celebration included plunder, rape and murder of unarmed civilians.

Confined to a war ship a few hundred yards from the quay, British sailor, Charles Howes used a pair of field glasses to monitor what was happening on shore. He was sickened as he watched two young women be seized by Turkish uniformed soldiers and, after watching them be raped, looked on as the Turks cut off their breasts and lay them on the ground outside one of the British headquarters.

At 4 p.m., Major Claflin Davis, a representative of the American Red Cross, accompanied by a few other officials from American charity organizations, secured an audience with General Noureddin, to discuss the spike in violence and deterioration of order in Smyrna, now under Turkish control. Unfortunately, General Noureddin's mood had changed considerably since his meeting with McLachlan earlier in the day.

As they were seated in the General's office, it was clear from Noureddin's body language that he was less than receptive. Davis began, "General Noureddin. . . We congratulate you on your decisive victory. However, since implementing your security over the city, there has been an enormous increase in theft, violence and murder. The streets are full of refugee carcasses. We are here to implore you to restore order and help us return the refugees to their homes in the interior of the country. This is the only way we can prevent a humanitarian disaster, the likes of which, the world has never witnessed. As we speak, there are thousands of refugees crushed together on the quay who are at the mercy of your irregular *chette* forces. I have heard that hundreds of thousands more refugees are en route. We do not have the resources or manpower to deal with so many refugees."

This was not what Noureddin wanted to hear. He was not about to sit here and let some mission worker dictate what he should or shouldn't do. Red in the face, Noureddin said, "Take them away!"

Davis looked bewildered.

"I'm sorry, what do you mean, take them away?"

Noureddin looked angrily into Davis' eyes.

"Bring ships and take them out of the country! That is the only solution."

Davis and his colleagues left the meeting with full knowledge that they were about to witness a catastrophe of monumental proportions. Each one realized that hundreds of thousands of human beings were about to die in the most grotesque fashion.

Once back in his office, he issued a memo to Admiral Bristol in Constantinople. In it, he warned that General Noureddin had refused to guarantee the safety of a single refugee. It read, '[I] believe this is a final decision [of the] Nationalist Government as [a] solution of [the] race problem.'

At dusk, George Horton was escorted aboard the USS *Litchfield* as a safety precaution. The day had proved dangerous enough and there wasn't adequate protection for the American Consul. He would be based on the ship until he was evacuated. The watch aboard the *Litchfield* had witnessed the violence edge ever closer to the European quarter of the city. Clearly, the Turkish government had abdicated their responsibility to control their soldiers. He was not going to take any chances.

Also aboard the *Litchfield* for their own safety were two American journalists, Constantine Brown and John Clayton, who were hand-picked by Admiral Bristol to document the events of the Turkish occupation of Smyrna. As Horton, Clayton and Brown sat in the officer's mess, the journalists recounted the horrors they had seen during the day. Clayton read back the page he had just typed and then, fell back in his chair, shrugged his shoulders and let out a long sigh. Then, he yanked the sheet out of the typewriter, crumpled the page and threw it in the waste bin, "I can't send this stuff! It'll queer me at Constantinople."

Brown nodded, "Bristol will be furious if he sees this. He was absolutely clear about what he wanted from us. The only way we got in was to promise the world would not hear anything that would hurt American interests here in Asia Minor. . . or I guess we're now supposed to call it Turkey."

Clayton shut his notebook. "Okay, let's just write about the Greek atrocities."

Horton was horrified by what he was hearing. He sipped his metal mug of coffee, "Gentlemen, I'm curious. As American journalists in the presence of one of the most spectacular dramas in history, how are you able to divorce yourselves from a story that will likely make you national heroes for reporting it, and instead, limit your reporting to events that will offset the very essence of it. I don't know what the game is or who is behind it."

Clayton and Brown looked at each other, then at Horton. Clayton said, "You don't understand what we had to agree to in order to be here."

Clayton put a new sheet of paper into the typewriter. He typed, 'The discipline and order of the Turkish troops have been excellent. When one considers they have just marched through a country laid waste by the Greek army, with thousands of Moslems slain, this is nothing short of remarkable. The apprehension of fear-ridden Smyrna has turned to amazement. After forty-eight hours of the Turkish occupation, the population has begun to realize there are not going to be any massacres.'

MacLachlan and the soldiers took one of the campus automobiles and drove over to the house that clearly showed *chettes* moving around inside. MacLachlan got out of the car and shouted in Turkish, "What are you doing here? This is an American house! This is American property! Get out of here!"

Instead of scattering, the *chettes* pointed their rifles at MacLachlan. When the *chettes* emerged from the house, they clearly outnumbered the American force. Chief Crocker, realizing the Americans were greatly outnumbered, drew his sidearm and placed it on the ground to show his intention was not to fight them.

As the standoff endured in silence, the American soldiers backed their way to a safe distance from the opposing force. While the soldiers were now a safe distance away, MacLachlan and Crocker were not, and they were now at the mercy of the *chettes*. One of them approached MacLachlan and demanded, "Give me that watch!"

MacLachlan started to hand it to him, but the soldier snatched it from his hand, tearing it from his suit coat. Seeing no resistance, the *chette* went through his pockets, removing all of his money, and then, taking the coat itself.

Then, MacLachlan noticed that a couple of other soldiers about four or five yards back, raised their rifles as if they were about to shoot him. In desperation, MacLachlan shouted, "This building belongs to the American college over there, and I am the head of that college. If you shoot me, there will be serious consequences and my government will respond."

But instead of fear, the *chettes* seemed to be spurred on. They removed more of his clothing, his shoes and socks, and then knocked him down several times and proceeded to kick and beat him with their rifles. One of the soldiers engaged his bayonet, lunging at MacLachlan. Instinctively, MacLachlan grabbed the rifle by the bayonet as he jumped forward, disengaging the bayonet, after which, the bayonet fell to the ground. Probably attempting to overcome the embarrassment of losing a bayonet, the soldier removed MacLachlan's trousers and snatched the gold ring from his finger. Then, they knocked him to the ground and severely beat him with their rifles.

Perhaps as a result of Noureddin giving some order after the meeting earlier in the day, a Turkish officer on horseback, suddenly appeared at the scene. "*Durdur*. . . Stop!" In an instant, the *chettes* backed off and stood aside. The officer rode over to MacLachlan. As the *chettes* backed away and then disappeared into the night, the Americans approached the officer and carried MacLachlan back to the campus.

Oddly enough, in spite of the beating and humiliation he took, as well as all the reports of inhumanity by the Turks, MacLachlan refused to alter his anti-Greek and pro-Turk view.

After dark, splashes could be heard on board the warships of people jumping off the quay into the water and swimming out to the Allied warships, but no one was picking them up. One of the jumpers, Marika Tsakirides, then, a thirteen year old Greek refugee later recalled, "I remember we were in a row boat. My mother and my brother and two other families. There were people in the water swimming out to the big ships and grabbing the tow lines. I remember one big ship with an English flag. The sailors were shouting 'No! No! No! No!'. I remember so well because it was the first time I heard 'No! No! No! like that in English. They were throwing water on the people and cutting the ropes."

The British chaplain, Reverend Charles Dobson, was in his home in Smyrna, when he observed a group of two-hundred people kneeling by the roadside. He watched as all two-hundred were butchered. As he later recounted in testimony, '[They were butchered] by steel to avoid rifle fire.' Apparently by official orders from the Turkish government, swords and daggers had replaced the noisier weapons on Monday evening.

In his report of the day, Lieutenant Commander Knauss, officer in charge of the guards at the American Sentry headquarters wrote, 'Pitiable objects, for two days, they have been huddled in small heaps, never stirring except when one of their number approaches with a gourd of fresh water. If the Turks come through, their faces express more than fear. They are terror-stricken. I feared a stampede would ensue in case of panic, so I made all preparations for running down the iron screen promptly. It was fortunate that we had done so, for at 2:00 a.m. several Turks rode into them and grabbed a man, and there was scarcely time to drop the door before the frantic mob tried to find their way in. Today I have seen during my rounds over a hundred dead and have watched four people killed in cold blood.'

Commander Merrill's report to Admiral Bristol described the scene in different terms. He wrote, 'The refugees are in a blue funk. No one can imagine without seeing them "under fire" what a chicken-livered lot the Christian minorities are.'

Chapter 33.
12 September 1922

By mid-morning, there were more than one-hundred-fifty-thousand refugees in Smyrna, and most of those had walked there from small villages in the countryside. Considering the fact that no Allied ships were willing to evacuate refugees, these desperate people were now in an impossible circumstance. From today onward, the only people with any chance of being evacuated were foreign nationals using their government's warships still sitting in the harbor.

The suspiciously wide discrepancy between the reports of his two assigned journalists and his officers, Merrill and Hepburn, when viewed alongside contradictory reports from unaffiliated American relief workers, forced Admiral Bristol to demand that Captain Hepburn only issue reports of atrocities for which his officers had personally witnessed with their own eyes. At least, with this restriction, any contradictory witness statement would never see the official light of day.

This morning, Captain Hepburn was driving around the city counting the bodies. Interested in keeping his reports accurate, Hepburn was having trouble determining the new bodies from those he had already counted. No one was removing bodies from the roadways, and in the heat of the day, the bodies swelled quickly, thereby rendering them indistinguishable from the older bodies.

Having driven to the Consulate, Hepburn first learned of the brutal attack on MacLachlan in Paradise, the night before. Determined to make sure the report was not exaggerated, he drove to the college campus. When he arrived, he saw that more than a thousand refugees had crowded themselves onto the campus.

Amy Jennings noted in her diary, 'They were not admitted at the gate beside our house as it would have directed the firing that way and over the campus. People were injured and killed, and later from our window we watched them buried. Asa going by auto into Smyrna-- shots flying around the car all the way.'

The YWCA was not exempted from horror. More than five-hundred women and children entered the mission seeking refuge. In another instance where ordinary American soldiers couldn't swallow the edict of their superiors, an American sentry, Melvin Johnson said, "They were jammed in there so tight there wasn't an inch to move, but then more of 'em would push up against the doors - crying - and, well, we weren't supposed to, but we'd let them in"

Later in the morning, clearly in defiance of his orders, Johnson and a colleague stepped outside in search of a bakery that might give a bit of bread to these starving women and children. "That's when we saw the victims. They were lying all over in the sun, swelling up with the heat. Two of 'em was women. We couldn't take but one look."

The journalist for British newspaper, *The Daily Mail,* George Ward Price, tried for most of the day, to seek an audience with Mustapha Kemal, under the guise of hearing from the Turkish leader, the terms he required for a lasting peace with the Allies. Finally given an audience, Price sat opposite the Turkish leader who was elegantly dressed in a plain tunic.

Price asked, "General Kemal, is the war with the Greeks over?"

Kemal wearing a smile, "There is nothing to fight about any more, and I earnestly desire peace. I did not want to launch this last offensive but there was no other way of persuading the Greeks to evacuate Asia Minor."

"Considering the presence of the Entente allies," Price pressed the General, "what do you see as your territorial demands?"

"My government claims all of the areas of our country that are principally populated by the Turkish race. Those areas would thus include all of Asia Minor, Constantinople and parts of Thrace."

Price was struck by Kemal's mention of Constantinople, in that there were still about seven thousand British troops controlling the capital city. As a British journalist, his next question was an obvious follow-up. "General Kemal, and what if the British refuse to leave Constantinople?"

Kemal's response was direct. "We must have our capital and if the western powers will not hand it over, I shall be obliged to march on Constantinople. I would rather obtain possession by negotiation though, naturally, I cannot wait indefinitely."

The Daily Mail ran the full interview giving its support to Kemal, with the argument that Britain would be wrong to oppose the new nationalist government.

Around midnight, the wind which typically blows southward, changed direction and began to blow northward from the foothills of Mount Pagus, over the city and out over the harbor. Shortly afterward, there were reports at the American Institute of several small fires that were extinguished by the local fire patrols. These small fires continued to pop up in neighborhoods that could be seen from the American campus.

Chapter 34.
13 September

The bright autumn sunshine on Wednesday morning was accompanied by the same south wind blowing northward toward the harbor. The quiet beauty of the morning belied the horrific orgy of bloodlust that lasted until the Turkish soldiers had exhausted themselves enough to fall asleep the night before. There was no reason to conclude that the unrestricted orgy of violence would not resume once they awoke.

The day before, the armies of General Kemal had spun out of control and were reduced to packs of mongrel dogs preying on weak and innocent refugees. Without a doubt, a single command from their revered leader, would have been enough to halt the savagery, but no such order was forthcoming. This wanton display of sub-human brutality had been the long-practiced tradition throughout Turkish history wherein, Turkish marauders would be rewarded for their victory by being allowed to terrorize, plunder, rape and murder as a testament to Turkish "manhood." But Kemal's silence was more calculated to accomplish his goal. . . "Turkey for the Turks." And, what better way to rid your new country of seven-hundred-thousand refugees than to keep killing until the remainder are gone, one way or the other.

Sir Harry Lamb had seen enough to be convinced that British nationals needed to be out of Smyrna. While most were already safe aboard British warships, there remained almost a thousand who had not heeded his earlier warning. Sir Harry met with Reverend Charles Dobson seeking his help to locate the remaining British nationals within the city. The unbridled violence of the day before made certain that no one was safe from Turkish bloodlust any longer.

Upon arrival at the YMCA Mission, Jennings found Ed Fisher standing by the window looking at the mob outside. He said to Fisher, "I was coming through the Armenian quarter, and as ill luck would have it, I fell in with a mob. There was firing from both sides, for of course, Turkish soldiers were everywhere. I now carry an

American flag with me wherever I go. That little bit of bunting is of more potential defense than any Colt automatic."

Jennings peered out the window with Fisher, "Finding myself in the middle of this pleasant little party, I pulled out my flag, pinned it on, and made for the nearest wall. I finally reached it and then walked sideways for quite a distance. I had always been told that if you must be shot by all means avoid being shot in the back."

Fisher said, "The Navy has issued orders that all Americans must leave within the hour."

As he said it, Arakel, a young Armenian boy who worked at the mission ran up to Jennings. "Please Mr. Jennings, if you leave they will kill me. Please, I beg you, save me."

Without a second thought, Jennings said to the boy, "Arakel, come with me."

Jennings knew that American families were permitted to take one household servant with them as they left Smyrna. He grabbed Arakel by the hand and left the office. He returned home using the Mission automobile to make sure Amy and the kids were safely evacuated. When he arrived back home, he helped Amy collect a few things and prepare to take them to the quay.

Jennings mentioned to Amy, "Amy, this is Arakel. He will be our one permitted household servant. Let him carry one of the bags. Without any further comment, the Jennings family climbed into the car, and drove to the quay.

29. *Turkish soldiers revel in their butchery.*

Once Jennings' family was safely aboard an American warship, he returned to the city with his elder son, Asa W. to do what he could for the thousands of refugees who faced imminent death or worse.

Since midnight, the fire brigade had responded to six major alarms. The brigade was manned by both Greek and Turkish firemen who were actually paid by the insurers of the buildings in Smyrna. The head of the fire brigade, Sergeant Tchorbadjis, noted that all of the fires had erupted in the Armenian quarter and that this many fires constituted an epidemic.

An alarm came into the fire station from Suyane Street reporting ten houses were already on fire. Tchorbadjis looked at his watch. It was 10:30 in the morning. He dispatched a fire team. They had barely brought those fires under control when another alarm came in from the Armenian church just a few blocks away. Then, a third alarm of yet another fire at a house on Tchoukour Street.

Tchorbadjis knew he didn't have the manpower to respond to all three alarms, so he sent off his men to the church fire and responded to the Tchoukour Street fire on his own. When he arrived at Tchoukour Street, he could see the fire was burning on the roof. He climbed up to the roof and found bedding on fire. He thought, *How did this get up here?* He quickly used his ax to push the bedding off the roof onto the street. He cut out a few planks that were smoldering until he was confident the fire would not restart. He then climbed back down and went into the house. When he stepped into the kitchen, he saw a well-armed Turkish soldier, setting fire to the interior of a drawer. The soldier turned and stared at Tchorbadjis, freezing him in his tracks. But then the soldier just left. Once his fear subsided, he immediately caught a strong smell of petroleum.

Tchorbadjis instinctively, put out the fire in the drawer. With the small fire out, he returned to the station and was met by Fire Chief Grescovitch who said, "You must try to keep the fire contained to the Armenian quarter."

Tchorbadjis replied "I will try my best, sir."

30. Children faced the same fate as adults.

But fires broke out so often and burned so fiercely that there was neither enough water nor enough manpower to contain them. As he responded to alarms, in every house, he saw dead bodies, mostly of people who had been cut with a knife or saber.

On his fifth response, he entered a house already partially consumed in flames. He noticed a trail of blood along the floor. He followed the trail that stopped in front of a cupboard. Curiosity got the better of him. He felt compelled to open this cupboard.

Suddenly, his hair stood on end. Stuffed inside the cupboard, was the naked body of a young girl with her breasts cut off. The sight made him retch and lose what little he had in his stomach.

After that, Tchorbadjis merely walked the streets, no longer bothering to put out fires. There were too many of them. He came across a house and as he walked past the garden, noticed a girl hanging from a lemon tree. He wondered, *Did the soldiers hang her or did she hang herself?*

At another house, he saw a group of armed soldiers milling about. Apparently there was an Armenian family hiding inside and the soldiers were deciding who would be the lucky one to go inside. The winner went in and moments later he heard screams coming from inside, and then nothing. Once it was quiet, the soldier came out the front door, his scimitar dripping with blood. He wiped it clean on his boots and leggings.

By now Tchorbadjis was numb from the horrors he was witnessing. On one of the roads as he walked, he saw a man about forty-five or fifty years old. The Turks had blinded him, cut off his nose and left him on the street. The man was crying out in Turkish, "Isn't there anyone here Christian enough to shoot me so that I will not get burned in the fire?"

Shaken, Tchorbadjis returned to the fire station. But he was forced to evacuate the station as the streets became too hot to work in and the crew wanted to get all the gear away before the station burned. But in the end, they had to leave the equipment behind."

Exhausted from their futile effort, Tchorbadjis sat with another fireman, Emmanuel Katsaros. Katsaros had to tell someone what he witnessed. He said, "I was hosing down the Armenian Club, to halt the advance of flames from next door to it, when two soldiers went into the club carrying tins of petroleum. I could see through the window that they were emptying some liquid on the piano. There was a soldier guarding the door. I told him 'On the one hand, we are trying to stop the fires, and on the other, you are setting them.' I couldn't believe it. The soldier told me, 'You have your orders and we have ours. This is Armenian property. Our orders are to set fire to it.'"

Tchorbadjis looked at his companion, "I cannot repeat what I saw. It is too horrible to think about."

Both firemen would eventually have to recount their experiences two years later when the American Tobacco Company brought suit in London at the High Court of Justice, against the Guardian Assurance Company, Ltd. for damages from the fire. Considering that over $100 million in claims would hinge on the decision of the case, it was no surprise that Justice Rowlett, the high court judge would find for the British insurer. Some interesting testimony came from Major Cherefeddin Bey who had led the first cavalry regiment into Smyrna. After describing how he had been struck by a hand grenade as he led his regiment down the quay two years before, proceeded to describe the man who threw the hand grenade as "a uniformed armed Greek soldier who threw the bomb." The major couldn't answer why when originally questioned after the incident, the thrower had been described as an Armenian terrorist. When questioned about what outrages occurred after his arrival, he stated he had seen no disorder because "nothing took place."

At noon, back in Paradise, where teachers spotted small fires the night before, Miss Minnie Mills, dean of the Inter-Collegiate Institute, was alerted by a teacher to the dining room window. Mabel Kalfa pointed out the window, "Look there! The Turks are setting the fires!"

Then, Miss Mills saw the silhouette of three Turkish officers in the window of a photographer's shop in the proximity of the school. Immediately after the Turks stepped outside the shop, she saw flames escaping through the roof of the building. Kalfa said, "Like all the other buildings this is burning from the inside."

Then they both watched as the soldiers approached a building known as the *Khan*. The building was comprised of a Turkish hotel upstairs with a number of small shops on the ground level. Once again as soon as the soldiers emerged from the building, another explosion, then flames coming from the windows. Miss Mills pointed, "Look Mabel, the Turks are carrying tins of petroleum into the houses. Look, like the others as soon as they go inside, in a few minutes a fire bursts forth. They're blaming these fires on the

Armenians but there's not an Armenian in sight. The only persons visible are the Turkish soldiers of the regular army, in smart uniforms."

By late afternoon, the fire near the American Institute was threatening all three sides of the U-shaped building. The two thousand refugees squeezed into the main building could smell the smoke outside and hear the explosions outside the walls. Petty Officer James Webster was standing all afternoon in front of the gate. He was forced to use the butt of his gun to keep the people away from the door, as the fire was getting closer all the time. But he knew that if he let them out, the Turks would kill them.

Miss Mills realized that the building was about to burn with people inside, and that there were only twelve sailors stationed there to protect them. She also realized that a frantic exodus by so many people would be disastrous. She decided, as much as she regretted her decision, to instruct her staff to separate the school family from the crowd of refugees so that a small contingent of sailors could possibly escort them to the quay.

Faced with being separated from their families the teachers, students and servants brought their families to the rear gate where they would leave from. It meant the group became several times the size she expected. Complicating things further, the more alert refugees who watched the actions of the Americans followed them to the rear gate as well.

Just as the shutters at the end of the building caught fire, Ensign Gaylord drove up to the rear gate in a truck. He was given a direct order from Captain Hepburn to evacuate only bona fide Americans. When Gaylord informed Miss Mills of his orders, she refused to leave without her students and staff. Bound by his orders, Gaylord ordered his own men to lift Miss Mills on to his truck. As they lifted her off the ground, she screamed out, "Girls, follow me!"

She was still struggling when the truck drove away.

Now Petty Officer James Webster was left with only six men to protect almost two thousand refugees. But staying in the building was no longer an option. Webster shouted, "We advise you all to leave together. Stay close together, as close as you can."

Webster then opened the gate to lead his two thousand odd refugees to the quay, not realizing what the state of affairs was. As the crowd followed Webster, Anita Chakerian, one of the students in the crowd trying to get outside, overwhelmed by the pushing, stumbled and fell by the exit. About to be trampled, she was lifted off the ground by an American sailor who carried her outside the gate, before he went back to help others. At that moment there still were over a thousand refuges trying to get out of the building. Chakerian, eventually finding it to safety would later say, "To this day, I still wonder who he was. God bless him for saving my life."

When they set out, neither Webster nor his men knew how to reach the quay. Some of the streets were blocked with rubble or were on fire, and as they walked, the Turks opened fire into the crowd behind him. In the end, two thousand women, children and old men, left the rear gate at the American Institute following Petty Officer James Webster the half-mile distance from the campus to the quay. An hour later, just forty refugees were still with him at the harbor. Most of the rest had provided live target practice for the Turkish soldiers.

By dinner time, almost a half-million refugees had made their way to the quayside. By now, however, the fire had also reached it. Fed by benzine and petroleum, the fire acted like a pulsating maelstrom. Flames reached hundreds of feet into the air. The crackling noises as buildings tumbled was almost deafening. The *Theatre de Smyrne* erupted into flames just after the Americans being sheltered there evacuated. Then, the American Consulate burned, minutes after Horton managed to escape with Consulate archives. The intense heat began to burn the mooring lines that held the ships to the harbor, forcing the ships' captains to move back almost a thousand feet from the harbor.

Oran Raber, a tourist who arrived a few days before recalled his experience as he sat aboard an American warship. "The flames leaped higher and higher. The screams of the frantic mob on the quay could easily be heard a mile's distance. There was a choice of three kinds of death: The fire behind, the Turks waiting and shooting from the streets on either side and the ocean in front."

That evening, aboard the British warship, HMS *Iron Duke*, Admiral Sir Osmond de Beauvoir Brock was insistent that ship's routine carry on as normal, in spite of the difficulties that were occurring on shore.

Also aboard the *Iron Duke* was the British journalist Ward Price. Price was shocked by the surreal nature of seeing British officers dressed in formal white mess jackets, partake in their dinner, while the horrific screams could be heard over the clanking of wine glasses and tinkling of silverware. The screams grew unbearably worse as humans were essentially being baked alive from the intense heat. The Admiral, seeing that the screams were becoming an annoyance at his officers' dinner table, ordered the ship's band to begin playing some lively tunes, to counter the disquieting noise from the quay. Once music could be heard emanating from the flagship *Iron Duke,* given that dinner hour is the same for the entire British fleet, companion ships ordered their own bands or phonographs to also play music to drown out the distracting screams of people burning to death.

Duncan Wallace, a veteran of the Royal Navy and long-time resident of Smyrna was also on board the *Iron Duke* for his safety. He marveled in disbelief at one of the strangest experiences of the night was to hear the band playing while the town was burning and cries and the roar of the fire filled the air. Another British national standing next to Wallace marveled to hear the ship's phonographs blasting the sweet strains of familiar records, like *Humoresque* and the swelling tone of Caruso in *Pagliacci* floating over the water. He lamented, "It's almost possible to lose oneself in the music, were it not for the fact that the quieter arias are suddenly drowned out by the frightful shrieks from the quay."

British Seaman Bunter aboard the *Iron Duke,* watched as hundreds of Greeks clung to the quayside trying to escape the intense heat of the fire. Stunned, he then watched Turkish soldiers appear and deliberately sever the victims' arms with their scimitars, resulting in hundreds of refugees falling to their deaths in the sea.

At the completion of dinner in the officers' mess aboard the *Iron Duke*, the officers scrambled on deck to survey what had been interrupting their dinner. One of the officers, Major Arthur Maxwell, through binoculars watched Turkish soldiers pour buckets of a liquid over the refugees. Initially, he thought they were pouring water over the victims. The truth became obvious as a wall of fire rose wherever they poured. He cried out to his fellow officers, "My God, they're burning the refugees." Screams from within the crowds could be heard, '*kemaste*' (we're burning)!

After joining the officers on deck, Ward Price wrote in his notes:

'What I see, as I stand on the deck of the HMS *Iron Duke*, is an unbroken wall of fire, two miles long, in which twenty distinct volcanoes of raging flame are throwing up jagged, writhing tongues to a height of a hundred feet.

All Smyrna's rich warehouses, business buildings and European residences were burning like furious torches. From this intensely glowing mass of yellow, orange and crimson fire poured up thick, clotted coils of oily black smoke that hid the moon at its zenith.'

Those Americans taking refuge aboard American warships could no longer stand by and do nothing about the conflagration in front of them. Claflin Davis of the American Red Cross, aboard the *Litchfield,* approached Captain Hepburn.

"Captain, there are two lighters (flat-bottomed barges) moored at the far end of the harbor. Can you see them?

Hepburn replied, "Yes, I can see them."

"Would it be possible for you to tow the lighters over to the quay? There are several thousand refugees about to burn to death. It would save their lives."

Hepburn said, "I understand your desire to help these poor people, but I can't help you here. The water in the harbor is too choppy for me to maneuver in close enough to do what you ask. I would be endangering the ship and its crew. The only way to move those lighters is by power launch and we don't have one. Here in Smyrna, only the British and the French have power launches at their disposal. The best I can do is to offer you a row boat to row over to the French and British vessels."

Davis took what he could get. He climbed into the row boat and rowed over to the French vessel, which was closest. Once on board, he was informed that the ship's captain had not returned from shore yet, and that they could not authorize anything until he returned.

Concluding there was no time to wait, Davis rowed over to the *Iron Duke.* Once aboard, he requested the officer on deck to take him to the commander of the British fleet, Admiral Brock. The officer of the deck escorted Davis to the Admiral's cabin and announced his presence. Davis stepped into the cabin and said, "Admiral Brock, I am here as a representative of the American Red Cross, to ask for your assistance in a matter we believe, is critical to our mission as well as our mutual efforts for the sake of humanity. Captain Hepburn, commander of the USS *Litchfield* has informed me that there is no American warship in this harbor equipped with a power launch. He has told me that the British Navy here is so equipped. I have requested of Captain Hepburn that he tow two empty lighters currently moored at the far end of the harbor, over to the quay so that some of the refugees could move to it and perhaps avoid the crush that exists now. They are literally burning alive. Unfortunately, Captain Hepburn indicates that the water is too choppy for the *Litchfield* to effect such a maneuver. I'm asking that as commander of the British fleet here, you utilize your power launch to effect the transfer of the lighters. We can give some relief to more than two thousand people."

Admiral Brock looked attentively at his unscheduled guest and clasped his hands in front of him. "Mr. Davis! I can appreciate your intentions to ease the suffering of people all over the world. The Red Cross is a magnificent organization. However, you don't understand the restrictions that I am bound by. I have repeatedly assured General Noureddin that Britain and more specifically, the British Navy, was absolutely neutral in this matter. Therefore, I cannot, and I will not allow British sailors to take part in the rescue of Greek and Armenian civilians. If I did, I would be breaking a promise made as the representative of His Majesty's Royal Navy. As much as I would like to ease the suffering of these people, the current circumstance is one of their own making."

Deeply disappointed, Davis rowed back to the *Litchfield* completely stunned. When he boarded the *Litchfield,* he found the crew to be very agitated by what they saw happening with the American flag flying a few hundred yards away. As the evening progressed, more and more comments bubbled up as the crew stood on the deck totally helpless.

Around midnight, however, Davis concluded that the same agitation must have been felt on the *Iron Duke.* That was the only explanation he could come up with to explain Admiral Brock's complete turnaround. For, suddenly there was activity on the *Iron Duke.* Orders were given that all launches be lowered into the water and be dispatched to the quay to pick up refugees.

Ward Price wrote in his notes for his report, 'The scene changed in an instant. A shrill piping; a shouting of orders; a trampling of feet. Half the mess-jacketed officers disappeared. In three minutes they were on deck again in blue uniforms, with mufflers around their necks and truncheons in their hands to beat back rushes for the boats. Within minutes, the launches, powered and unpowered, were heading toward shore.'

31. U.S.S. Litchfield anchored in Smyrna harbor.

What they saw once they arrived at the quay, however, was far worse than what they saw from the deck. More than a half million desperate souls crammed together with no possible route for escape. Machine guns at either end, eliminated any flight to either side, and the wall of fire prevented any retreat. The only way out left to them was to swim to safety, except that when the swimmers finally reached the warships, they were not permitted to board. So they were forced to tread water until fatigue forced them to surrender to a watery death.

Charles Howes an officer of the HMS *King George V* was one of the first to reach the quay. Another was Lieutenant Charles Drage of the HMS *Cardiff*. Their primary responsibility was to protect the launch from being swamped by the desperate refugees. Drage wrote in his diary after returning to his bunk, 'Prentice and some men jumped out and tried to clear a place [but] they were swept back into the boat and literally submerged in a pile of terrified people. I only got away by beating them on the head with a tiller.'

Ward Price joined one of the boats to witness the evacuation as a journalist. He wrote in his notes afterward, 'The bow touches the quay and a fighting, shrieking, terrified torrent of humanity pours over it. "Women and children only!" roared the officers, fighting with fists and sticks to keep back the men. It was unavailing as pushing back an avalanche. The only thing to do was to back out directly as the boat was full, literally to overflowing'.

Lieutenant Drage started rowing back toward the *Cardiff* with his own boat filled beyond capacity, when he came upon a baby among the thousands of corpses now floating in the harbor. The baby was floating upside down which he thought odd. Drage reached in and pulled the baby into the boat. Seeing what he thought was life, he slapped it on the back. Miraculously, the baby began breathing.

Charles Howes in the meanwhile loading his boat, found breathing difficult with such intense heat bearing down on him. He recounted later, 'Right along the sea front was a wall of unbroken fire with flames 100 feet high casting a lurid glow in the sky. The night was rendered at intervals by loud explosions and all the while the people in the rear were being massacred. The stench of burning human flesh was appalling, and the streets were stacked with dead. Men, women, children and dogs. . . the heavens were lit by the flames and myriads of sparks flew skyward, the crackling of the wood and the collapsing of the houses sounded like a salvo of guns. The whole of Smyrna, except the Turkish quarter, was now in the grip of the greedy fire. . . [and] as hard as our boats and sailors worked during the night, we did not seem to make much impression in diminishing the crowd.

'One of the saddest cases I met was that of a little girl of nine who, with her father and mother and baby in arms, were making their way to the boats when the parents were shot dead. This little girl picked the baby up off the ground and, dashing through the flames, reached the boat.

'I don't think the majority of English-reading people will believe this narrative and will say I exaggerate. Well, here is the truth. Think of the old-time tortures, add to them the modern appliances for the destruction of mankind, exaggerate it as much as you like and you will not realize half the horror of the evacuation of Smyrna.'

As the night wore on, more than two thousand Greeks and Armenians were brought aboard the *Iron Duke*. The American sailors rescued two thousand and brought them aboard the *Winona*. Like the others, the *Litchfield* was filled beyond capacity. Aboard the *Bavarian,* Rev. Charles Dobson comforted a mother and daughter, who had together been gang-raped by fifteen Turkish soldiers.

A prominent Dutch merchant of Smyrna, taking refuge on his yacht during the fire, later related that all through the night of the dreadful thirteenth he heard fearful screams from the shore, ending suddenly in a queer watery gurgle. He later learned the next morning that a lot of throats had been cut.

By the time the ships could take on no more refugees, Admiral Bristol's chosen journalist, John Clayton, could no longer keep his promise to refrain from writing reports that described any Turkish atrocities in exchange for access. In a break from his previous reports, Clayton wrote: 'The loss of life is impossible to compute. The streets are littered with dead. . . Except for the squalid Turkish quarter, Smyrna has ceased to exist. . . the problem of the minorities is here solved for all time. No doubt remains as to the origin of the fire. . . the torch was applied by Turkish regular soldiers.'

Ward Price went to his cabin after the ordeal to write his own report: 'Smyrna has been practically destroyed by a gigantic fire. . . without exaggeration, tonight's holocaust is one of the biggest fires in world history. The damage is incalculable and there has been great loss of life among the native population. . . many thousands of refugees [are] huddled on the narrow quay, between the advancing fiery death behind and the deep water in front, [and there] comes continuously such frantic screaming of sheer terror as can be heard miles away. . . picture a constant projection into a red-hot sky of gigantic incandescent balloons, burning oil spots in the Aegean, the air filled with nauseous smell, while parching clouds, cinders and sparks drift across us-- and you can but have a glimmering of the scene of appalling and majestic destruction which we are watching.'

From the safety of the USS *Simpson* as it steamed away from the harbor, George Horton tried to memorialize his thoughts: 'As the destroyer moved away from the fearful scene and darkness descended, the flames, raging now over a vast area, grew brighter and brighter, presenting a scene of awful and sinister beauty. . . nothing was lacking in the way of atrocity, lust, cruelty and all that fury of human passion which, given their full play, degrade the human race to a level lower than the vilest and cruelest of beasts. . . one of the keenest impressions which I brought away with me from Smyrna was the feeling of shame that I belonged to the human race.'

Chapter 35.
14 September

The fire burned all night. Until the ships were loaded to overcapacity with refugees, the unauthorized rescue continued as well. But the obvious grim reality was that once all the battleships were overflowing with refugees, they hadn't even made a dent in the crowd that was trapped on the quay. There were still a half million souls crammed together without any means of escape and the persistent gunfire as the Turkish soldiers continued to shoot into the crowd.

By daylight, the heat coming off the quay was so intense that the captain of the HMS *Serapis* was concerned that flammable materials on his deck would ignite, so he gave the order to lift the anchor and move the ship further out. The sailors assigned to the task were sickened once they realized that refugees were hanging on to the anchor chain for dear life. As the anchor was lifted, people were clinging until gravity won the war and they tumbled into the sea.

32. The U.S.S. Simpson anchored in Smyrna harbor.

But then the *Serapis* began to take on refugees until it could take on no more. After nine hundred refugees had been placed aboard the destroyer, Vice-Consul Hole went aboard to view the rescue operation. He was shaken by the revelation. Out of nine hundred women, children and old men already aboard the *Serapis*, less than a dozen were women between the ages of fifteen and thirty five. In Hole's mind there could be only one explanation. The Turks had taken most young women and either sold them, raped them, mutilated them, or murdered them. He was sick that his own government was culpable in causing such human destruction. The captain later reported, 'We had on board about as many as we could hold- the forecastle, upper deck and all the mess decks were full and there were also people in the boiler and engine rooms.'

Miss Emily McCallam had the misfortune of arriving in Smyrna on this morning. McCallam was the director of the Intercollegiate Institute of Smyrna. As her ship approached the harbor, she noticed scores of charred bodies bobbing up and down in the water. Clearly, she could see Smyrna burning and

33. View of Smyrna burning on the morning of Sep 14, 1922.

the throngs of desperate refugees on the quay, but could not understand why the bodies were charred. She soon learned from her American colleagues that many residents of Smyrna, including men, women and children, gathered on a lighter moored to the pier, hoping an American or Allied launch would tow them out to a ship. Instead, Turkish soldiers threw petroleum on them and burned them all to death.

Like his half-million co-refugees, Dr. Garabed Hatcherian, was faced with his impossible circumstance noticed that the fire had swallowed everything up to the Swedish Consulate. He found himself trapped between three deadly elements: fire, sword and water, a completely desperate situation.

The Hatcherians had fought their way to the sea wall, in hopes of climbing aboard an Italian lighter that was taking off refugees. He implored the seamen in French to accept his family as well. But they turned a deaf ear to his pleas and soldiers lined up in double rows to throw them off the lighter. Then Hatcherian looked out to one of the ships to see a film crew making a movie of the ship's crew refusing to help those who had swum out to the ship to be rescued.

That afternoon, most of the ships in harbor left in order to carry their human cargo to nearby islands or off to mainland Greece. A deep sense of foreboding was felt on the quay by those who were left behind, knowing that their last glimmer of hope for survival was steaming away from the harbor. Now, there was a general realization that they were completely at the mercy of the Turks. Not a good place to be.

A spark of hope bubbled up when a Japanese merchant ship chose to throw its cargo overboard in order to make room for refugees it would carry to safety. But this effort was nominal in the face of the breadth of humanity waiting for a miracle. There would eventually be a controversy over whether or not Japanese ships had evacuated refugees where the Allies wouldn't That controversy continues to remain unresolved today.

34. Refugees hoping to escape Smyrna collect on lighter moored to the quay.

Later that afternoon, U.S. Vice-Consul Maynard Barnes was making his way back to the safety of the *Litchfield*, when he witnessed five separate groups of Turks, armed with bloody clubs, circulating among the refugees on the quay, searching out victims. In one instance, he watched one of the groups club a defenseless man to death. The look of horror on Barnes' face must have been obvious to the assailants as one of them politely turned and explained to him that the victim was Armenian and shrugged his shoulders.

Once on board the *Litchfield,* Barnes related to a crew member, "The proceeding was brutal beyond belief. I was within ten feet of the assailants when the last blow was struck, and I doubt there was an unbroken bone left in the body when it was dropped over the edge of the quay and kicked into the sea. While walking from this scene to the point on the quay where the *Litchfield* was moored, a walk of not more than five minutes, uniformed soldiers and officers, and boys of twelve were taking part in the killings as heartily as their elders."

Later that night the fire was still raging, except there were now areas that had burned themselves out, leaving only rubble. But as if doubling down on a curse, the wind shifted and a new attack on those few outlying areas that had thus far escaped its wrath.

Chapter 36.
15 September

As the sun rose over the city, there were still areas burning intensely, a result of the wind shift the day before. But already, three quarters of the city had been reduced to rubble. The only part of Smyrna that remained untouched by fire was the Standard Oil complex at the north end of the city and the Turkish quarter to the south.

On one of his walks to view the status of the destruction, Jennings noticed the area by the Standard Oil complex, which had avoided the fire. He then noticed a home that had also remained intact, but had since been abandoned. Ignoring the navy's restrictions on American assistance for the Greeks and Armenians, without a second thought, he envisioned an immediate use for the building. The gathering of so much humanity in one place, presented the obvious problem that many of the women were pregnant. With no facility available to deal with pregnancies and inconveniently-timed births, Jennings immediately converted the house into an emergency hospital, where relief workers could bring expectant mothers or recently orphaned children. The newly-commissioned hospital was also the destination of a creative new practice spawned of necessity.

Since the Americans were claiming neutrality, Turkish soldiers tended to be less inclined to confront American sailors. Probably begun as a desperate measure in a high stress moment, American sailors found that if they came across Turkish soldiers about to have their way with a young Greek or Armenian girl, they could tell the Turks that the girl was their girlfriend. To which, the Turkish soldier would relinquish his prey. Now, the sailors had a place to bring these girls. The two houses that were converted by Jennings were now housing more than a thousand refugees.

While eyewitnesses estimated the number of homeless refugees on the quay at five hundred thousand, Admiral Bristol's report to his government indicated that there were fewer than three hundred thousand. Considering that there were more than three hundred thousand Christian residents of Smyrna before the arrival of Kemal, and estimates of about two hundred thousand Christians who walked into the city from the countryside, when taken in context, the five-hundred-thousand number was probably more reflective of reality. For three days, Turkish soldiers had been seen shooting into defenseless crowds for sport. For the same three days, Turks had been extracting any males between the ages of fifteen and forty-five, as prisoners of war, to be marched into the interior and either murdered or utilized as slave labor. It was reasonable to conclude that the actual number was somewhere between the two estimates, although reasonable may not be the appropriate term.

Yiorgos Tsoubariotis, an eleven year old Greek boy who spent the previous night hiding with his family in a cemetery grave, miraculously made it to the safety of a ship. But when he first

35. *Smyrna continues to burn.*

arrived at the quay, he was struck by the madness of the scene. The sea was full of bodies. There were so many that if you fell into the water you wouldn't sink because all the bodies would keep you on the surface. And you could see on every body the belly swollen, curving above the surface. Yiorgos was amazed that in the madness of this scene, there were young Turkish boys swimming amongst the bodies scavenging whatever valuables they could find. Their noses were covered by scarves tied on the back of their heads, so they would not breathe in the stench of rotting bodies. They held a sharp

36. In the aftermath of the fire, refugees were packed like sardines on Smyrna's quayside.

knife and skillfully cut from the bodies, the fingers that wore rings, and the ends of ears that wore earrings. They took bracelets and anything of worth they might find around people's necks.

Among thousands of young men extracted from the crowds as prisoners of war, Panayiotis Marselos, a Greek, was told he was being placed in a group of five thousand prisoners. Using a technique from seven years earlier with Armenian men, every few miles, the Turkish soldiers separated a group away from the road or path and then shot them. He later wrote, 'The slaughter didn't stop. We headed to Bournabasi, which we reach at night, and they put us in a barbed-wire enclosure. They start taking five at a time and killing them.'

While Marselos wasn't chosen for execution, after three days and nights with no food or water, they were allowed to drink from a river that featured a rotting corpse. 'I couldn't resist my thirst. I drank... and my brother drank too, and our lips were sticky from the fat secreted by the broken body.'

After a week, a guard noticed that Marselos had a gold filling. He was forced to knock the tooth out with a rock. For three months, he would walk with the five hundred Greeks that were still alive, from village to village, as members of their group were either sold off as slaves or murdered. Marselos wrote about one of those murders, '[They] cut off his nose, ears and other bits and then drove a sharp stick into the ground and forced him onto it. The stick went through him and then they set him on fire and burnt him.'

One of Smyrna's wealthiest Greek merchants, Socrates Onassis, lived on a hill overlooking the southern end of the harbor called Karatash. After the Turks defeated the Greek army, Onassis' friend Consul George Horton, warned him of the reprisals that might come from the Turks.

After Onassis sent his family off to Mytilene, he was arrested and placed in a prison in the Turkish quarter of the city. Socrates' eighteen year old son, Aristotle, was allowed to remain over the weekend in the Onassis home. No doubt, the gentler treatment of the Onassis family was a function of the possibility of collecting money and valuables before they would be murdered or ordered to march to the interior.

Young Aristotle proved useful to the Turkish officer who commandeered his home by providing him with liquor and tobacco. Now allowed to pass freely among the Turks, Aristotle managed to find passage out of Smyrna on the USS *Edsall*. This enterprising young man would go on to become one of the world's wealthiest entrepreneurs.

Asa Jennings' boss, E.O. Jacob, accompanied by his assistant Ed Fisher, in spite of their protests, were held up by a Turkish soldier and ordered to hand over £350 before telling them to run, firing a shot above their heads to speed up their departure. As they raced around the corner, they ran right into a Turkish officer leading a squadron of Turkish regulars. Jacob excitedly protested to the officer pointing in the direction of the fleeing soldier. Jacob said, "He can't have gone very far."

The officer asked, "Did he leave you anything at all?"

Jacob replied, "Yes, he left us about £50."

Using a less than sympathetic tone, the officer said, "Hand it over!"

Finally unable to ignore the mayhem any longer, consuls for Great Britain, France and Italy as well as Captain Hepburn, and Davis from the Red Cross held a meeting. Clearly, the bureaucrats on the ground in Smyrna were beginning to realize the less than attractive optics of Allied governments standing by while tens of thousands of innocent refugees were being butchered. Conspicuously missing from the meeting were Admiral Brock and the French Admiral Dumesmil who had no inclination to help Greeks or Armenians. With the exception of the French representative, all agreed that something should be done to reduce the casualties. Unable to come up with any ideas or reach a conclusion of this impossible situation, the meeting was adjourned.

Chapter 37.
16 September

This morning Turkish soldiers began concentrating on arresting all males between the ages of fifteen and fifty. The reason for the new initiative was the decree issued by Mustapha Kemal that any refugee still in Smyrna on October 1, just two weeks away, would be deported to the interior. While the decree allowed another two weeks to get out of Smyrna, the refugees already knew that deportation was a codeword for certain death. In truth, the two week grace period only applied to women, children and old men. Any Christian male of military age, was considered an enemy of the new Turkish government, and therefore was to be arrested as a prisoner of war.

Captain Hepburn finally managed to track down the French Admiral to convince him of the need for immediate action on the part of the Allies. But Admiral Dumesmil was preoccupied with more pressing issues. Not willing to mention it to Hepburn, Dumesmil was to immediately sail for Constantinople to confer with his superior about Kemal's recent threat to march on Constantinople. Considering the British objection to giving up Constantinople, to the point where they would defend it against the Turks, France would be placed in a difficult position. The French had been secretly helping the Turks for two years and could see all the work being blown up if they were forced to join the British in defending the city. Dumesmil concluded the best course was to merely delay.

What was unavoidable to anyone still in Smyrna today was the unmistakable odor of burned flesh permeating the entire city. Continuing to show the new Turkish government the appearance of their strict neutrality, Allied warships remained at anchor, awaiting instructions from their superiors in Constantinople.

In Bournabat, Levantine resident, Hortense Wood, had remained in her home throughout the difficulties. In fact, her beautiful villa had somehow remained intact, attracting the attention of General Kemal. He needed a place to hold his first military meeting and the Wood villa was irresistible.

Wood admired Kemal and his generals, even though most of Bournabat had been destroyed. She deluded herself into blaming the *chettes* for all of the destruction and violence, thereby holding Kemal above criticism. She later wrote in her diary, 'I so admire [him].' She graciously agreed to his request to utilize her residence as his temporary headquarters. She also wrote, 'The fate of the empire was being discussed just outside my bedroom door, near the piano.'

Meanwhile in Constantinople the British were now concerned Kemal would march on Constantinople. Lloyd George, supported by Winston Churchill, requested that reinforcements be sent to Constantinople. He then asked the Allies to send troops as well, but was met with a very tepid response. With the exception of New Zealand, Britain's request to the empire was also met with silence. With her own forces unsupported by others, Britain would not be able to stop Kemal's armies.

Knowing the British dilemma, Kemal continued his secret meetings with the French and Italians, allegedly seeking a diplomatic solution, while at the same time, threatening to march on Constantinople. Seeing problems arising for France, the French high commissioner urged Kemal to halt the Turkish advance. Instead, Kemal declared he was unable to stop his triumphant soldiers. He smiled as he stated, "Our victorious armies. . . I don't even know where they are. Who knows how long it would take us to reassemble them."

While playing his cat and mouse game with the Allies, he wrote to his generals, "We are pursuing a very calculating and moderate policy. We are trying to isolate the British."

With American public opinion turning against Admiral Bristol's pro-Turkish stance, and in the face of such openly barbaric cruelty, the American Secretary of State, Charles Evans Hughes received a telegram from Rear Admiral Bristol:

        767.68/321
        CONSTANTINOPLE
        DATED SEPTEMBER 15, 1922
        REC'D 3 PM

SECRETARY OF STATE,
WASHINGTON D.C.
185. SEPTEMBER 15, NOON.

FOLLOWING FROM SMYRNA: "FOURTEENTH. AM TURKS BURNED SMYRNA EXCEPT TURKISH SECTION CONFORMING WITH DEFINITE PLAN TO SOLVE CHRISTIAN MINORITY PROBLEM BY FORCING ALLIES EVACUATE CHRISTIAN MINORITIES. BELIEVE THAT THEY WILL NOW PREPARE FOR AN ATTACK ON CONSTANTINOPLE MERRILL."

BRISTOL

Back in Smyrna at dusk, the now familiar sound began to be heard on the decks of the ships at anchor. It was a haunting, strangely melodic, dirge sung in a minor key, like a choir of ghosts singing a Bach fugue. In actuality, it was the sound of hundreds of thousands of Orthodox Christians praying to their God for ships to arrive and save them.

As darkness obscured the horrific spectacle of death, the anchored ships began their nightly vigil to turn on their searchlights as a futile defense against the Turkish soldiers who waited for darkness to begin their nightly orgy of rape, mutilation and murder.

Chapter 38.
17 September

As the humanitarian crisis ballooned to historic proportions, American officials attempted to convince the Greek government to send mercy ships to rescue the refugees. But they were unsuccessful as the fragile Greek government did not relish placing their merchant fleet at the mercy of the Turks on Turkish soil. In order to proceed, the Greeks needed assurances from Kemal. Instead of assurances, Admiral Bristol received a telegram stating:

> 'KEMAL... SAID HE WOULD NOT TAKE RESPONSIBILITY TO ALLOW GREEK SHIPS TO ENTER THE HARBOR.'

Bristol now received increased pressure to send additional ships. While no warships arrived in Smyrna on this day, the freighter *Dotch*, did arrive with food and supplies bound for the American Relief Committee. On board the *Dotch*, passenger Dr. Esther Lovejoy, an American who had volunteered to travel to Smyrna, in order to assist the relief committee in its efforts.

Lovejoy had visited Smyrna before, but her fond memory of the beautiful city was destroyed by the images in front of her. Once on land, she estimated that there were still three hundred thousand refugees on the quayside, and all of them were in terrible condition. She would later write: 'The people squatting on the quay were filthy. They had no means of keeping clean. They dared not go back into the ruins of the city for any purpose lest they lost their lives. In less than two weeks, the quay had become a reeking sewer in which refugees sat and waited for deliverance. When the crowd stirred, the stench was beyond belief.

Lovejoy was fully aware of the crisis in front of her. In just thirteen days, any refugee still alive, would be deported into the interior. And she knew according to everyone involved, that this would be 'a short life sentence to slavery under brutal masters, ended by mysterious death.'

In a statement worthy of Admiral Bristol's supreme hypocrisy, General Mustafa Kemal transmitted a telegram to his Minister of Foreign Affairs, Yusuf Kemal, to supposedly confirm his written instruction carried by the French Admiral Dumesmil to Hamid Bey. In it, Kemal boldly stated the complete antithesis of what scores of eyewitnesses described. Clearly, an attempt to posture a push back for what would be viewed as the most savage genocide of humanity, he merely stated the opposite of what had transpired. By referencing fictitious testimonies and hijacking foreign correspondent reports, Kemal eliminated any possibility of a subsequent investigation.

FROM COMMANDER IN CHIEF GAZI MUSTAFA KEMAL
PASHA TO
THE MINISTER OF FOREIGN AFFAIRS YUSUF KEMAL BEY

TEL. 17.9.38 (1922) (ARRIVED 4.10.38)
TO BE TRANSMITTED WITH CARE IMPORTANT AND URGENT.
FIND HEREUNDER THE INSTRUCTION I SENT TO HAMID BEY WITH ADMIRAL DUMESMIL, WHO LEFT FOR ISTANBUL TODAY.
COMMANDER-IN-CHIEF MUSTAFA KEMAL
COPY TO HAMID BEY,

1. IT IS NECESSARY TO COMMENT ON THE FIRE IN IZMIR FOR FUTURE REFERENCE.
OUR ARMY TOOK ALL THE NECESSARY MEASURES TO PROTECT IZMIR FROM ACCIDENTS, BEFORE ENTERING THE CITY. HOWEVER, THE GREEKS AND THE ARMENIANS, WITH THEIR PRE-ARRANGED PLANS HAVE DECIDED TO DESTROY IZMIR. SPEECHES MADE BY CHRYSOSTOMOS AT THE CHURCHES HAVE BEEN HEARD BY THE MUSLIMS, THE BURNING OF IZMIR WAS DEFINED AS A RELIGIOUS DUTY. THE DESTRUCTION WAS ACCOMPLISHED BY THIS ORGANIZATION. TO CONFIRM THIS, THERE ARE MANY DOCUMENTS AND EYEWITNESS

ACCOUNTS. OUR SOLDIERS WORKED WITH EVERYTHING THAT THEY HAVE TO PUT OUT THE FIRES. THOSE WHO ATTRIBUTE THIS TO OUR SOLDIERS MAY COME TO IZMIR PERSONALLY AND SEE THE SITUATION. HOWEVER, FOR A JOB LIKE THIS, AN OFFICIAL INVESTIGATION IS OUT OF THE QUESTION. THE NEWSPAPER CORRESPONDENTS OF VARIOUS NATIONALITIES PRESENTLY IN IZMIR ARE ALREADY EXECUTING THIS DUTY. THE CHRISTIAN POPULATION IS TREATED WITH GOOD CARE AND THE REFUGEES ARE BEING RETURNED TO THEIR PLACES.

New Yorkers woke up to read their Sunday *New York Times* while they drank their coffee. When they reached page ten, they were confronted by the headline:

'U.S. TO AVOID NEAR EAST TANGLE
Seeks Only Protection Of Citizens And Interests In Mandate Area.
INTERESTED IN RELIEF
Washington Points Out America Had No Share In Treaty Of Sevres.'

While the article related the official U.S. stance on the Asia Minor problem, it was a carefully worded statement that maintained the U.S. policy to only protect American interests and citizens. However, in somewhat of a bombshell, the article boasted a second sub-headline:

Ex-Consul-General Calls Bristol "Pro-Turk"

The explosive article peeled back the 'American neutrality stance' to show the disturbing nature of America's involvement in the Smyrna disaster. The article stated:

> New York, Sept. 16.-- Gen. S. H. Topakyan, former Consul-General of Persia, in a statement to the press issued this evening, criticized Rear-Admiral Bristol for his conduct of American affairs in Constantinople, denouncing him as a "pro-Turk of the most rabid type and a hater of Greeks, Armenians and Jews."

The General, who has recently returned from Armenia, said that the word mercy is not in the Turkish lexicon and that, given a situation like the present in Smyrna and elsewhere, there is no unspeakable barbarity and villainy that the Turk will not commit, irrespective of the age or sex of his victims.

Calls Bristol "Pro-Turk"

"I regret to say, and I make the statement deliberately and solemnly, that the United States is today represented in this crisis by a man who is a pro-Turk of the most rabid type and a hater of Greeks, Armenians and Jews.

"The United States cannot afford to have its fair name besmirched and befouled by allowing such a man to speak for the American soul and conscience. To be quite frank, I refer to Rear-Admiral Bristol, who is now in Constantinople in charge of American affairs and of the American fleet.

Relates Alleged Conversation.

I do not make this serious charge without ample grounds. It was my privilege to be in Constantinople in the summer of 1920 after a tour of over a year of a large part of Europe, Asia and Africa on important business transactions. While in Constantinople I was often a visitor at the Constantinople Club, which is frequented by leading Europeans, allied officers and prominent Turks and other natives. While there I was known as a Persian representative, due to my connection with the Persian consular service. As such I came in contact with Rear-Admiral Bristol, who not suspecting my Armenian origin, but supposing me to be a Persian, deliberately told me once, 'I hate the Greeks. I hate the Armenians. I hate the Jews. The Turks are fine fellows.' This is the man representing America in the Near East at this crisis."

General Topakyan leaves for Washington tomorrow to repeat his statement to President Harding. He said that he had already personally stated these facts to Acting Secretary of the Navy, Theodore Roosevelt.

Responding to the growing public discontent with America's neutrality stance in Asia Minor, the *New York Times* added another sub-headline to the article:

> ### *Says U.S. Protest Would Stop Kemal*
> <u>Boston, Sept. 16 (Special)</u>. -- Protest from the United States Government would stop the onward sweep of the troops of Mustapha Kemal, the Turkish Nationalist leader, toward Constantinople, Dr. James L. Barton, chairman of the Near East Relief, declared in an interview here tonight.
>
> Dr. Barton, who spent years of work as a missionary in the Near East, is considered one of the foremost authorities on the problems of Asia Minor.
>
> "The only solution that I can see for the termination of the present state of affairs in Asia Minor today is for the United States to send Mustapha Kemal a strong note of protest against invading the neutral zone that surrounds the Dardanelles and Bosphorus," said Dr. Barton. "Mustapha Kemal has too great a respect for the United States to refuse such a proposal.
>
> ### Wants U.S. To Join Allies.
>
> "For the United States to join with England, France and Italy would bring an end to the present trouble."
>
> Had the United States continued her participation in European councils, the present grave situation in the Near East would not have arisen." Dr. Barton said.
>
> While Dr. Barton believes that Mustapha Kemal already has received aid from the Russian Soviet Government and that gold is being supplied the Turks, he said he knew Kemal well enough to feel sure the Turkish leader will take everything the Soviets offer so long as he does not have to sacrifice any of his power.

And so the U.S. government again resorted to kabuki theater with a dance for public consumption, while the agenda behind closed doors ran counter to the will of the American people. The U.S. government was neither prepared to officially stand behind the grass roots humanitarian effort of its people, nor was it prepared to help prevent a half-million innocent refugees of one of its World War I Allies perish at the hands of a supposedly vanquished enemy.

Chapter 39.
18 September

Monday morning brought no relief to the hundreds of thousands of pitifully desperate humans who squatted in the sewer that only recently served as a promenade for the social register. No food or water, no sanitation, the stench of death in every breath, with no answer from the God they prayed to last night for ships that would carry them away from this hell.

Asa Jennings' boss, E.O. Jacob was desperately trying to feed the multitudes of refugees caught between the high-stakes chess match being played by the Allies. With hundreds of thousands of starving Greeks and Armenians awaiting death to take them, Jacob managed to secure the use of military bakeries to supply bread, so his mission could distribute survival rations to the refugees.

By now, many refugees unable to stand the heat, filth, stench and threat while sitting on the quay, drifted back to their prior homes in the interior of Asia Minor. Even though there was no home to go to, they imagined they would find a way to stay alive. Jacob realized these returning refugees would find no food in addition to no home, and therefore traveled to the interior to provide bread rations.

But what he found was a circumstance equally as bad as being on the quay. In the interior, the men and boys were separated out, bound together and marched off, leaving the women and children housed in military barracks. On arrival at the barracks at Baldjova, Jacob found over eight thousand women and children with almost no water, having not eaten in five days. Jacob arranged for a shipment of bread, but somehow, the bread arrived having been soaked with gasoline, rendering it inedible. But now in addition to starving to death, women and young girls were at the mercy of the *chettes*.

As if to capitalize on the *New York Times* fanning the flame of public outrage over the treatment of Orthodox Christians in Asia

Minor, the *Washington Post* released an article that added fuel to the fire. The headline read:

> **Turks Threaten to Invade Neutral Straits Territory**
> **Ankara Warns Allies Greeks Must Not Be Given Sanctuary**
> **Kemal Pasha Makes Return of Thrace**
> **Condition for Resecting Neutral Zone**
> **Turkish Army Impatient**
> **Allies Need 33 Battalions for Defense of Constantinople**
> **and Have Only 20**

Whether or not the *Washington Post* wanted the U.S. to step in or not, the page one story sold many newspapers. Kemal claimed no threat against Great Britain, but in the same breath, conditioned his withdrawal on a British recognition of the Ankara government and its national pact returning Thrace to Turkey. Kemal declared his loathing of wars through his spokesman in Constantinople, Hamid Bey, but added his armies did not suffer from the less than serious battles fought by the Greeks.

Kemal was significantly more adept than the British High Commissioner, Sir Harry Lamb in the game of liar's poker. He knew the Allies did not have sufficient forces in place to defend against a Turkish invasion of the neutral territory, and probably would not be able to obtain reinforcements unless and until the United States committed its own forces. It was clear to him Britain would cave.

In the midst of the human catastrophe playing out on the quay in Smyrna, a manager of an American tobacco exporter fled to safety aboard the *Litchfield*, leaving behind twelve hundred bales of tobacco that were still intact. In his absence, some less-sensitive Americans somehow saw this as an opportunity. Finding others with similar intentions, they formed a partnership as shipping agents to contract with Turks securing freighters that would carry the abandoned bales to other markets.

Since the American Consulate had burned to the ground, a new temporary building in the industrial area was set up as a new Consulate. The building became both home and office to the American businessmen intent on taking advantage of the opportunity. Vice-Consul Maynard Barnes, who remained as the top U.S. official in Smyrna was, in his words, 'considerably inconvenienced' by those annoying relief workers who insisted on flooding the immediate area with penniless refugees as opposed to more business-oriented individuals.

Barnes was particularly upset that a nearby building was not available for use as an office, but was being hijacked to house refugees. Barnes filed a complaint with Rear-Admiral Bristol, who predictably replied with an order to 'get these people out of the Consulate.'

While Bristol was well aware of the mounting American public sentiment in opposition to his hands-off policy regarding the refugees, he took on the posture that he was not opposed to helping in the rescue. However, he and the State Department had no intention of taking the initiative to act. Bristol was of the opinion that the European powers got into this mess and were now trying to get the United States to bail them out of it.

Bristol was intent on discouraging the notion that the Turks intentionally would burn Smyrna to eliminate the existence of Christians in Asia Minor. This intention was not necessarily to insulate the Turkish government from international scorn. It was more to improve the prospects of American business investors who had invested in Turkish tobacco, and who would have millions of dollars in potential claims against predominantly British insurers. Yet another less-than-shining moment for Miss Liberty and the land of the free.

As dusk arrived, the haunting dirge began as the Christian prayers commenced. At darkness, once again the searchlights were lit to scan the quay to hopefully reduce the horrific acts of brutality and murder. Perhaps God would send ships tomorrow.

Chapter 40.
19 September

Tuesday morning arrived with no ships on the horizon. Instead, it would be another day of horror, stench, and starving. Relief workers clearly were battling against overwhelming odds and rapidly losing the battle. Many surrendered to despair. However, crisis affects everyone differently. Some people panic and become frozen in terror. Others simply are spurred into action. The two houses he converted into relief facilities were a testament to the fact that Asa Jennings was one of those people who are spurred into action.

Jennings and a handful of American relief workers continued to lose ground against the avalanche of death and destruction that was closing in. Jennings would later write: 'I have seen men, women and children whipped, robbed, shot, stabbed and drowned in the sea, and while I helped save some, it seemed like nothing as compared with the great need. It seemed as though the awful, agonizing, hopeless shrieks for help would forever haunt me.'

Captain Powell submitted reports to Admiral Bristol describing Jennings' activities as unauthorized and irresponsible. But unlike Commander Merrill, Powell turned his back in order not to see Jennings implement his relief measures. His only exceptions were to demand that Jennings remove the American flags he had placed on the two buildings and evicting any young men of military age from the property, as the discovery of same would be taken by the Turks as an action against them.

Jennings even ignored Powell's order that he live aboard the *Edsall*. With the task at hand being so much larger than any man, Jennings was now driven by the task and not the orders from the U.S. Navy. In fact, Jennings' overt humanitarian efforts were not only ignored by some Navy brass, ordinary sailors responded to his requests and became part of the humanitarian effort.

On one of Jennings' visits to the *Edsall*, he heard a cry for help coming from over the side of the ship. When he leaned over the edge, he saw a swimmer who was losing the battle to stay afloat. Without a second thought, he turned to a group of sailors and ordered them to drop a line to the swimmer. They immediately swept into action and recovered a young Greek boy. The boy was naked, shivering and frightened to death. Jennings wrapped him up, and upon being warned by the sailors, hid the boy.

Shortly afterward, another swimmer caught his attention. However, this swimmer was still a good distance from the destroyer. Clearly exhausted, the girl was not going to make it. Again without concern for Navy orders, Jennings shouted, "For pity's sake, why don't you lower a boat?"

The sailors wanted to lower a boat, but were frozen. Finally, they explained to Jennings that if an officer gave the order to lower a boat, it would have to be entered on the ship's log. And that would amount to clear and convincing evidence of a breach of the stated neutrality. Jennings shrugged his shoulders, "Then I'll give the order... Push off that boat!"

His orders were obeyed and the swimmer was brought on board. The sailors deposited the young girl at Jennings' feet, unconscious. At that moment an approaching officer made an immediate about-face and walked away without a word.

Once revived, the girl looked up with a wild expression in her eyes, seeing all those men standing about her. Finally, she realized she was with friends who would protect her, releasing a look of joy and thankfulness on her face. Then thoughts of what she had been through must have gripped her, for she began to cry, calling out some name in her grief. Everyone was helpless in that they could not understand a word that she was saying. Jennings then thought of the little fellow he had sequestered behind the boat and hurried back to his stowaway to see if he could help them with his few words of English.

Jennings brought the boy to where the girl was encircled by sailors. As they approached, the boy released his grip on Jennings and bounded from his side, throwing himself on the girl. Then from her lips there burst the name she had been moaning moments before. He was her brother, and there on the deck of the *Edsall*, they had been reunited.

Despite countless episodes of this sort, Jennings despaired because there were no ships to rescue any more refugees. Jennings said, "Everyone is praying for ships. I too, am praying for ships."

In spite of his nature to just do what was necessary, Jennings was at a loss. He was certain he was no more anxious for ships than others on the committee, and for that reason, he did nothing toward trying to secure ships. After all, that task had not been assigned to him nor was he asked to assist.

Another dusk signaled the resumption of the melodious chants of death - the unanswered prayers of the pitiful multitude. It foretold of yet another descent into an obscured spectacle of rape, mutilation and death. It was also a likely sign that many now viewed death as a welcome alternative to their suffering. Could they even survive one more day?

Chapter 41.
20 September

Jennings awoke suddenly. The utterly impossible circumstance without any conceivable solution must have worked itself out in his subconscious during sleep. Otherwise, there was no explanation for what would happen next. For Jennings was seized with what he would later describe as 'an uncontrollable urge' to somehow, at a minimum, save the people for whom he felt responsibility.

Jennings dressed quickly and rushed to board the *Edsall*. He was escorted straight to Captain Powell's cabin. The sailor knocked on the door three times. "Captain Powell Sir? Mr. Jennings is here sir to see you and he says it is urgent."

From behind the cabin door, they heard, "Jennings? Okay, enter!"

The sailor opened the door and Jennings stepped in.

"Good morning Captain! I need to borrow your launch."

Powell sitting at his desk looked up, "Mr. Jennings? May I ask why you'd like to borrow my launch?"

"Yes, sir. I need it to get over to the other ships to see if I can get them to take some of my people aboard. I know you are under orders and prevented from such an action and I wouldn't presume to ask."

"Oh, Give me a break, Asa! Quit working me! Check with the officer on deck and tell him you have my permission."

Jennings smiled at the Captain and turned to leave.

Powell called out, "Asa. . ."

Jennings turned his head to look back.

"Go and do your darndest!"

Minutes later, Jennings was in the launch with a sailor. "Where to sir?"

"Get me to the nearest ship. That one. Which one is that?"

"Sir? That's the French Liner *Pierre Lotti*. It's here to pick up French nationals."

The *Pierre Lotti* was actually built in Great Britain in 1913 for the Russian Company of Navigation and Commerce, and named *Emperor Nicholas I.* The ship had been seized by the French government after World War I and sold to a French Line that began operating it in the Mediterranean in November 1921.

Jennings boarded the ship and asked to be taken to the captain. He was escorted to the officers' mess. The captain enjoying a cup of French dark roast, obviously familiar with Jennings' activities asked, "How may I help you Monsieur Jennings?"

"Captain. . . I am personally responsible for almost two thousand people who are stranded here with no possible way of leaving. Can you help me by taking on these people and bringing them to safety?"

The Captain stiffened. "Monsieur Jennings. . . I presume the people you speak of are refugees you are keeping in your buildings. I am afraid I cannot honor your request."

Jennings pressed. "Captain. . . these are human beings. They are certainly going to die if we cannot save them. Is there any way you can help me?"

The captain shook his head. "Monsieur Jennings. Your own American navy will not take refugees. If you have Americans in your building your navy will take them. If you have any French citizens, yes, I will take them. But, like your own ships, I cannot take refugees. My government is neutral in this matter and I am bound by that neutrality. I am sorry!"

Jennings just walked out and returned to the launch. "Drive me to the next ship. Which one is that?"

The sailor was prepared. "Sir, that is the Italian cargo ship, *Constantinapoli.*" The sailor headed for the Italian ship.

As the launch approached the huge liner it appeared to be empty. Jennings saw an officer on deck and based upon the decorations on his shoulders, he concluded it was the captain of the ship. It was already 4 p.m. With no time to waste, Jennings stood up in the launch and yelled out to the captain,

"Does the captain have refugees aboard?"

From the deck he heard the captain' response. "No!"

"Would the captain take refugees aboard?"

"I'm sorry Mr. Jennings. My orders are to take cargo to Constantinople. I am not authorized to transport refugees."

Jennings thought, *This obviously isn't working! What do I do now?*

Desperation being the true mother of invention, Jennings just blurted out, "Can the Italian Consul here change such an order?"

The captain shrugged his shoulders.

Jennings persisted, "Has he the authority to change those orders?"

The captain again shrugged his shoulders again. "Well, yes he does. . . but will he?"

Jennings viewed this as an opening. He scrambled aboard the ship and was escorted over to the captain standing by the rail.

"Captain, I have no time to waste. If the Italian Consul overrules the order and will allow it, will you take £5,000 to transfer my cargo of two thousand refugees to Mytilene?"

The captain was hesitant. Jennings had no idea where he would obtain the money to pay for the passage, but he was already in unchartered territory. Seeing the captain's hesitation, "And I'll add another £1,000 straight to you for your trouble."

Apparently, the sweetener was enough to win the day. With the captain's nod, Jennings ran back to the launch.

"Where to now sir?"

"Take me ashore! I need to see the Italian Consul."

Once ashore, Jennings asked around to determine where Consul Miazzi was. Like other consulates, the Italian Consulate was now a pile of rubble. He determined from crew members on shore that Consul Miazzi was in the Jewish quarter where he was visiting a wealthy, but newly authorized Italian citizen trying to arrange for his family to be extricated from their predicament. Jennings drove the YMCA vehicle over to the neighborhood and determined where the Consul was by the Italian troop escort standing outside the residence. Jennings approached the troops and requested an audience with Consul Miazzi.

The head of the guard, entered the residence and returned with the Consul.

Jennings was energized. "Consul Miazzi, I have just been aboard the *Constantinapoli* and spoken to the captain. He has indicated that you have the authority to change his orders from carrying cargo to Constantinople to transporting refugees out of Smyrna. I have two thousand women and children in my hospitals who are facing imminent death. I ask you to please use your authority to change those orders. By doing so, you will be responsible for personally saving the lives of thousands of human beings. Something that will go down as a historical event."

Miazzi was tied to the Turkish authorities by virtue of Italy's treaties. But, with the Turkish government's desire to remove Greeks from Turkish soil, he realized that no one had ever suggested the importance that would be associated with saving so many lives with one decision.

Miazzi stiffened. "Mr. Jennings, I can appreciate your position as a relief worker. You have no political agenda and are only interested in saving lives. . . with no regard to their origins, and I respect that. I hope you can see that my position as the representative of the Italian government in Asia Minor, that I must also consider the political considerations of Italy's neutrality. However, in this one instance, because like you, I value human life more than anything else, I will grant a change in the order so you may transport women and children only, out of Smyrna. The only condition you must now fulfill, is that you must receive permission from the Turkish authorities to carry out this evacuation. Without their agreement, I will not change the order."

Aside from all the posturing, Jennings thought he had just heard what was permission to use the *Constantinapoli* to evacuate refugees. Now if he could only convince the military governor he would be able to save his charges. He climbed back into his vehicle and headed for the *Konak.*

A short while later, Jennings was at the office of General Noureddin Pasha. He asked the desk officer for an audience with the general. The officer looked at this frail little man in wonderment and smiled. "And who shall I say would like to speak with him?"

"My name is Asa Jennings and I am the head of the American Relief Operation here in Smyrna."

The officer was dubious, but not prepared to make a decision that might risk his future. He stood and disappeared into the general's office. A moment later he returned. "You may go in now!"

Jennings walked past the officer and stepped into the general's office. Noureddin was seated at his desk. He looked up at the little man in front of him. "You are the head of the American Relief Operation?"

"Yes sir. When my superior left Smyrna, I became the highest ranking official of the operation."

Noureddin was amused. "And what is it that you would like from me?"

"General Noureddin, in speaking with several of my associates who had met with you before, they indicated that you personally suggested we bring ships to Smyrna in order to evacuate the refugees from the city. I have managed to secure the services of the Italian ship *Constantinapoli* to transport two thousand women and children out of the city. The cost will be covered by the American Relief Operation. The only thing left for me to do in order to accomplish this evacuation is to obtain your permission as military governor and perhaps some oversight by some of your soldiers to ensure all goes well in the evacuation."

Jennings hoped that by reminding Noureddin of his own words, he might appeal to Noureddin's pride. He fully expected resistance, but was prepared to push the point as far as he could. He was shocked by the response.

"If I said it, it is law! I remember the meeting. I will grant you permission to evacuate only women and children. You understand that no man of military age, that is between fifteen and fifty years, is permitted to leave as they are all our prisoners of war. I will provide sufficient soldiers to ensure that my orders are followed. You may evacuate your refugees immediately."

Jennings bowed to the general. "Thank you General Noureddin. I appreciate your willingness to help us. I will do my best to make sure your orders are not disobeyed."

Jennings turned and left the office. He was momentarily ecstatic. He was no longer thinking about the hundreds of thousands he couldn't save. He was only thinking about the two thousand he could save.

Chapter 42.
21 September

On the quay, it was another day like the days before. Hopelessness beyond comprehension. Having arranged for the passage money from the American Relief emergency fund, Jennings completed all of the preparations so that his evacuation could begin this morning. Upon rising, he headed straight for his two houses that comprised the YMCA makeshift hospital. He gave instructions that all of the women and children gather in front of the building so that he could personally lead them to the quay to board the ship. He warned that the workers must prevent any men of military age of being part of the group as it would only infuriate the Turkish authorities who might even cancel the evacuation.

When he arrived at his safe house, he saw hundreds of Turkish soldiers standing in two rows starting from the front door. It was clear, Noureddin wanted to make sure this order was carried out without any subterfuge. A large line of refugees stood quietly waiting to be led. Jennings looked at the line. For a moment his thoughts drifted to those already on the quay who he imagined would not react well if they saw this line being evacuated. But he shook it off. He forced himself to think only of this group. Jennings stepped up to the head of the line and waved his arm so that the refugees would follow him.

The procession walked single file behind him toward the jetty that would serve as the debarkation point. As it turned out, the double row of Turkish soldiers went right up to the pier. Jennings walked past them where four power launches were staged to carry refugees out to the *Constantinapoli*. There was no discussion from the soldiers. They merely stood watching. Jennings turned to look down the line of refugees and already saw Turkish regulars walking up to the women demanding any valuables they might have under threat of being prevented from leaving. He looked for an officer in charge to prevent the ongoing extortion, but no officer was visible.

Jennings watched as the first group of women and children were loaded onto the launch. He watched as the launch pulled away from the jetty toward the ship. Suddenly, about fifty feet down the line, he heard a commotion. He heard Turkish soldiers yelling and women screaming in agony. He watched the soldiers pull a woman carrying a baby from the line and throw her down on the ground. Jennings walked toward the confrontation.

As he approached, he saw the soldier pull the shawl from the woman. But it wasn't a woman. It was a man who obviously had shaven his mustache off as it was not tanned from the sun like the rest of his face. The woman in line, grabbed the baby as the soldier slammed the butt of his rifle into the man's gut. Two other soldiers stepped up and started kicking the man silly. Jennings feared they would cancel the evacuation, but he understood the desperation of trying to keep a family together.

Seeing no officer yet, Jennings found a crate nearby and climbed on it. He shouted out as loudly as he could, "This line is for women and children only. If any man attempts to hide in the line to gain passage, the trip will be canceled and your families will remain here."

Jennings was making his speech for the benefit of any officer who might be in earshot. He was determined to see these refugees to safety. He noticed a few people down the line were pulling away with their families tugging at them to remain. He shook his head to deny the distress in his gut.

As the women and children were being loaded on the *Constantinapoli,* unknown to Jennings, at the ship's destination in Mytilene, two senior Greek army colonels had staged a coup and declared a revolutionary anti-royalist government. One of them, Colonel Gonatas, rallied the captive audience of eighty thousand troops to support the new government, as it needed military support if they hoped to win over Athens.

Having endured his own private hell on the quay for almost two weeks, Yianni Papavasiliou could think of nothing besides his last meeting with his father's cousin Archbishop Chrysostomos. An hour before daybreak, Yianni watched as a bullet pierced the head of the woman squatting next to him on the quay. He could take it no longer. He was intent on saving his mother and siblings. Having become a strong swimmer by virtue of living in a seaside village,

Yianni leapt into the water and started to swim out to the ships. He couldn't tell where he was swimming other than seeing the remnants of the fires behind him.

Yianni kept swimming from ship to ship, in each case finding no way to board. Each ship with a stairway, was manned by an armed sailor. Yianni kept swimming from ship to ship, finding a brief rest by holding on to a ship's anchor chain or another refugee who was already hanging on.

By mid-morning Yianni came close to an Italian ship that was obviously loading women and children refugees from a launch on to the metal staircase hanging from its side. Seeing his opportunity, Yianni swam over to the outside of the launch that was still half-filled with refugees. He climbed over the side and then stood by a woman with a small child and an infant. Without asking, Yianni picked up the small child and looked into the eyes of the mother. She remained silent. Then, she removed her shawl and handed it to Yianni. When they got to the stairway, Yianni climbed out with the woman and only got a look from the sailor who was surprised to see a man aboard the launch. Yianni didn't fool anyone, but he was safe aboard ship.

For most of the day the evacuation continued with a few instances of men posing as women to escape deportation and death. By late afternoon, the number of refugees agreed upon by the Italian captain had been ferried to the *Constantinapoli*. Jennings, intent on making certain that the transport was carried out as agreed, boarded the last launch and joined his group on the ship. As he looked back at the quay, he realized that the hundreds of thousands did not panic and race to the jetty. He surmised that the line of armed Turkish soldiers standing guard along the pier was a major factor. But he also concluded that these people were in shock. They were no longer functioning humans but the living dead waiting to see what would befall them next.

Once under steam, the *Constantinapoli* headed for Mytilene about seventy miles away. What Jennings could not know was that an anti-royalist coup had already taken place as his rescue ship steamed toward safety.

Once the ship passed outside of the protected harbor, a strange phenomenon occurred on the deck where most of the refugees now stood. The flood of emotion of those who were mostly mothers with their children, realizing they had just been snatched from the jaws of death, was overwhelming. Those nearest where Jennings was standing, cried out words of gratitude for his managing the impossible.

Jennings was also unable to maintain his composure. The scene was a genuine outpouring of love and gratitude to this improbable hero. He broke down and cried along with everyone else. Later, Jennings would write: 'I could scarcely get through the mass of people that crowded around me. They fell at my feet in gratitude. They kissed me. Old men got on their knees, kissing my hands and feet, tears streaming down their faces. They did everything they could to show their thanks. It was one of the hardest experiences I ever went through. When I finally reached the cabin assigned me, I dropped on the berth and burst out crying. It was nerve-wracking and yet I think my tears were tears of joy as well, that God had enabled me to bring safety to those two thousand unfortunates.'

37. Refugees board the Italian Constantinapoli.

Once the heightened emotion subsided, Jennings began to think about the task before him once they landed. Even though they would dock in friendly country, dropping two thousand people into an unknown destination would create confusion and disruption. He went to work by having the refugees organize two relief committees to lead their people. With language and culture as the determinant, he established one Greek and one Armenian committee. Next, he went to the ship's radio room and wired the Red Cross chapter in Constantinople, informing them of the refugees about to land at Mytilene. He requested that the landing fall under the auspices of the Red Cross and that he be given the authority to make all decisions in his own discretion. Both requests were approved immediately.

The *Constantinapoli* arrived in the harbor at Mytilene after dark. Jennings concluded they were arriving because he heard the sound of the ship's horn announcing itself. Suddenly he realized that he had not required the services of the chamber pot. Pleased at the thought of avoiding that extra complication, he left the cabin and walked up to the rail on deck. It was completely dark outside, but he could see the lights peppering the black backdrop, signifying the town of Mytilene. He stood at the rail marveling that the rescue actually happened without catastrophe. As he stared into the darkness, he could see that the lights appeared and disappeared as the ship progressed toward the shore. He wondered what trick of his mind would cause the on again/off again nature of lights as they proceeded.

Once the ship was close enough to shore for the town lights to reveal what caused the phenomenon, he was dumbstruck by what now was visible. He counted no fewer than twenty large ships at anchor in the harbor. He could not believe his eyes. He ran up to the bridge and confronted the captain. "Captain, there must be twenty ships anchored here. Whose ships are they?"

The Captain laughed. "They are the Greek fleet. They are the ships used to evacuate the Greek armies from Smyrna."

Jennings was confused. "Don't they realize we can use these ships to save all the Greek refugees on the quay?"

The captain shrugged his shoulders.

Once the *Constantinapoli* was docked and the process to offload passengers began, Jennings went ashore to find the Greek authorities. To his shock, he learned that earlier in the day, the government in Mytilene had changed and was now controlled by the army. Jennings demanded that the Governor-General of Mytilene summon all of the Greek commanders who operated the fleet in order to confer with them. He added he would like to see the British Consul and any other Allied Consul currently in town.

Within the hour, the group was convened in what amounted to the town hall. The Governor-General stepped to the front of the hall. "*Κύριοι!*. . . Gentlemen! I would like to take this opportunity to thank Mr. Jennings for his heroic efforts to rescue our people from the Turks. He has informed me that the two thousand refugees are under the care of the Red Cross. I am taking this opportunity to pledge to Mr. Jennings that we happily accept these people into our care and as many others as he can rescue. As long as we can feed them, we will welcome them. Now, Mr. Jennings would like to speak to you."

Jennings now acting with the persona of a man in charge, stepped up to the front of the hall. "Gentlemen! As you can see I just managed to evacuate two thousand Greek women and children from a fate worse than death. It was not a function of my actions but more an improbable string of fortunate accidents. As far as their care is concerned, I appreciate the Governor's welcome, but I realize how each additional refugee will place burdens on the food supply of those already here. In that regard, I have requested and received authorization that food currently stored in the Near East Relief warehouses will be shipped as soon as possible to feed those now in Mytilene.

"Let me now say, as we arrived here tonight, I see that in addition to a new government here in Mytilene, the entire Greek fleet sits at anchor, while hundreds of thousands of your countrymen await death on the quay at Smyrna. The Turkish government has ordered that all Greek refugees must be evacuated in the next ten days. Anyone still in Smyrna on October 1st, will be deported into the Turkish interior. . . and you all know what that means. I've gathered you here, because I want your permission to order these vessels back to Smyrna to save your people. This is the miracle that they all have been praying for since the fires began."

A man seated in the front row of seats rose from his chair and spoke in a heavy Greek accent. "Excuse me, Mr. Jennings. The miracle of which you speak is not as simple as you suggest. We all desire the rescue of our people from under the boot of our enemy. But there are other serious considerations that you have not thought about."

"I'm sorry sir, but we have never met. Can you identify yourself?"

Yes! My name is Frankos. Brigadier General Frankos. The fleet you mention happens to be under my personal command. What you haven't considered is that with no forces in Smyrna to protect our fleet, there is nothing preventing the Turks from seizing our vessels and declaring they now have a navy. If that should occur, our mainland and the surrounding islands would be vulnerable to a

Turkish invasion. As much as we regret the effect on our countrymen, we cannot allow our fleet to be risked in this manner."

Jennings hadn't even considered that but he didn't really believe it was a logical argument. "General Frankos, we have already received a show by the Turkish authority that they welcome us bringing ships to evacuate your people. They are more interested in getting rid of the Christian population than they are in amassing a navy."

Frankos smirked. "Mr. Jennings, I admire your enthusiasm, but we have been intimately familiar with Turkish tactics for hundreds of years. Please excuse me if I question the validity of your assurances."

"General, I'm sure you are familiar with the U.S. Commander Powell. Commander Powell has assured me that he has secured permission from the Turkish authorities to allow Greek ships to enter Smyrna harbor as long as they are not flying the Greek flag when they do so, and they do not tie up at the wharf. Considering the human treasure at risk, I would say that is a small risk to be able to rescue hundreds of thousands of people."

Frankos became conciliatory. "Please understand I mean no disrespect, but I am afraid I will require a written guarantee from the United States, and even with that guarantee, I can only spare six ships from the fleet."

Out of desperation, Jennings viewed this too, as a tiny opening. Six ships was certainly better than no ships. His only course of action was to obtain that written guarantee. Jennings realized he needed to speak with the new head of the army as his new mission was quite fragile. He walked over to the Greek military command post that was in charge of the eighty thousand Greek soldiers. He entered the post and was greeted by the officers who all knew him by now. He asked, "Is there any way I can speak with your Colonel Gonatas?"

A captain responded, "Please wait here, Mr. Jennings, I will see if he can see you now."

A few moments later, Jennings was escorted into the Colonel's office.

The uniformed colonel greeted him. "Good evening, Mr. Jennings, how goes the rescue?"

"Slower than I'd like!"

"Is there anything I can do to help?"

No, you have your own things to worry about. I'm here, to find out if you have any news from Athens. I have heard some disturbing rumors about King Constantine and the war that continues in Thrace."

The colonel shook his head in disgust. "I don't know what you've heard, but for things that couldn't get worse, it seems they are."

Jennings now showing the posture of a leader rather than a YMCA worker, "Forget about the rumors, please tell me what is really happening and will it have an effect on what I am doing to rescue your countrymen?"

"Our government is crumbling. Our excuse for a king replaced our general staff with his cronies, which resulted in our defeat. Our men have been fighting for more than ten years now. Yes, they were devastated in Asia Minor, but now they sit here seeing the country they fought for die in front of their eyes. If we told them to board those ships tomorrow for Thrace to support their comrades, they would all be waiting on the pier to board. As we speak, there are pamphlets being printed that will be dropped in Athens tomorrow demanding the abdication of the King."

Jennings looked troubled. "And you don't think this will have any effect on my authority to oversee the evacuation of the refugees?"

"Do not worry Mr. Jennings. Our country and its people stand behind you for doing what no other man could do. Whatever government we have after tomorrow, you will still have its full support. Do not even think about it. You have enough things to worry about."

Anchored at Mytilene, Jennings boarded the American destroyer, *Litchfield,* under the command of Lt. Commander Rhodes. As the *Litchfield* left Mytilene harbor, he wired ahead to Commander Powell that he was on his way to Smyrna to get the written guarantee that Frankos needed to release the ships.

Jennings stood on the bridge of the *Litchfield* as it plowed through the waves, heading back to Smyrna. Deep in thought, his mind raced to think about what else he might obtain from Powell to make the task easier. His mind drifted back to his conversation with Frankos. He went over the exchange in his mind. Suddenly he thought, *Why only six ships?* There are at least twenty ships in the harbor. There's no other battle that would require the Greek navy.

Six ships would hardly make a dent in the numbers stranded on the quay. But he dared not radio Frankos to find out. He decided to cross that bridge when he returned with the guarantee.

A sudden wind caused the ocean to spray as the bow cut a path through the waves. The spray splashed on Jennings' face. He smiled as he again realized he was not seasick. He'd been so focused on the problem, that his inner ear problem couldn't get any time in his consciousness. Now his eyes were fixed on the horizon, in an attempt to will the Smyrna harbor to come into view.

Chapter 43.
22 September

The *Litchfield* raced back to Mytilene arriving after midnight. Having thrown caution to the wind, Jennings was not about to wait around for morning. He rushed over to General Frankos' quarters and had him awakened. The General, still not fully awake, entered his sitting room in less than a cheerful mood.

"This had better be an emergency! Do you think there are no limits on what you can do, Mr. Jennings?"

Jennings had been sitting in a chair as the orderly went in to wake the general. He stood. "My apologies General Frankos, but I can think of no greater emergency than the one with which we are faced with."

The general rubbed his eyes to get fully awake, "So, what is it that couldn't wait until morning?"

"I have returned from Smyrna with your written guarantee from the U.S. Navy. I need to borrow all twenty of your transport ships that are harbored here in Mytilene."

Frankos fully awakened by Jennings' statement, "I told you I could only release six ships to you, if you got the guarantee. . . not twenty."

Jennings was no longer conscious of the fact that his tone was no longer one of requesting permission. It sounded more like he was issuing orders. "General Frankos, I understand your reasons for holding back most of the ships. It is natural for the leader of the Greek naval forces to be reluctant to commit his entire fleet to this rescue. But six ships cannot hold enough refugees to make a difference. We have a major catastrophe facing us. I need all of the ships."

Jennings handed Frankos the letter from Powell. Frankos walked over to his desk and got his reading glasses. He read the letter from the perspective of how this could hurt him. It would be his decision and there would be consequences if it all went bad.

"Mr. Jennings, do you think I am a fool? This letter says that the U.S. Navy will escort us in and out of Smyrna. It says nothing about protecting our fleet. The Turks have many troops in Smyrna. The United States has no troops in Smyrna. Do you think a few guns on the *Litchfield* will stop an outlaw country from obtaining an entire navy, when there are no forces there to stop them?"

Jennings could immediately see that the general actually had a point. Considering the history with the Turks, realistically the American guarantee was actually not very reassuring. Jennings was not about to stop dancing though. "General, I am prepared to accompany the fleet myself!"

The general looked surprised. "Does that mean you will protect the ships?"

Jennings was amused as he thought, *Does this guy really think that my presence in some way is more reassuring than a few American warships sailing alongside?* It was clear the general was expecting an answer, and in his new mode he was perfectly willing to give one.

"It means, General, that we believe the Turks to be sincere and we will not break confidence with them. We Americans have assumed full responsibility for the evacuation of that quay, provided we can get the ships. Will you, or won't you, give us these ships?"

Frankos was clearly intimidated, but his instinct for survival was far more powerful than the assurances from the diminutive and frail man that was speaking to him. Looking at the general's face, Jennings realized that his bluff, while actually convincing, would not produce any results soon enough to do any good. He was already silently praying that some new idea would appear to him.

"Mr. Jennings, I will consider what you have just told me. I will consult with my superiors and get you my answer later this morning. Beyond that, I can do nothing for you at this moment."

Jennings stood looking out over the harbor. The gray mist of early morning was filtering the first light coming from the east. As he stared out at the twenty ships, he thought of the irony that one man's concern for his career was preventing the rescue of hundreds of thousands of innocents. He thought *"What kind of world have we become?"*

From some obscure part of his brain, Jennings became fixated on a particular ship in the harbor. There was something different about this ship. It looked quite a bit larger than most of the other ships. Somehow, it looked even familiar. Actually, it looked like an American battleship. Jennings now curious, walked over to a Greek sailor who sat on a bale of cargo. "Excuse me. Do you speak English?"

"*Ναι*! . . . Yes, little bit!"

"What is the name of that ship out there? The big one!"

The sailor squinted as he looked. "That is Greek battleship *Kilkis.*"

As if his mind was working behind the scenes, Jennings somehow remembered that prior to the Great War, The United States had sold the old battleship, USS *Mississippi* to the Greek government. *Could that be the Mississippi?* For no logical reason, Jennings took this as a sign that he could somehow get something done. The ship had a new name and was flying a new flag, but it began as an American battleship.

He looked back at the sailor again who was now studying him intently. He held out his hand and said, "My name is Jennings, Asa Jennings!"

"I know who you are Mr. Jennings. Every Greek knows who you are. I am Petros. Petros Papadopoulos. How can I help you?"

Jennings said, "Where can I find a row boat?"

The Petros said, "Rowboats on beach. . .there!"

Jennings now showing the demeanor of a leader, "I need your help. I have to go out to that ship. Will you take me? There are hundreds of thousands of your countrymen who wait for us to save them."

The sailor smiled, "*Παμε*! . . .We go! I am tired of sitting doing nothing."

As they approached the *Kilkis*, the sailor yelled to the officer on deck. "*Ο κ. Jennings, αιτείται αδείας επιβιβάσεως επι του πλοίου.*" ("Mr. Jennings, seeking permission to come aboard.")

The officer waved his permission, and Jennings climbed the stairs up to the main deck.

"My name is Asa Jennings. . ."

"I know who you are Mr. Jennings. Welcome aboard!"

Jennings was surprised the fellow knew of him. "I need to see your captain immediately. It is extremely urgent!"

The officer saluted. "Please follow me, sir!"

Jennings followed the officer up to the bridge, where he saw the back of an officer drinking an early morning cup of coffee.

The officer approached the captain and whispered in his ear. The captain turned in his seat. He stood up and walked over to Jennings. "Mr. Jennings. We are grateful for your efforts to save our people. What can I do to help?"

Jennings smiled at the warm reception. "Captain, I apologize, but I do not know your name."

38. The Greek battleship Kilkis steaming in Aegean waters.

The captain saluted him. "I am Ioannis Theophonitis, and I am at your service!"

Clearly, this man was looking to help him. "Captain, I met with General Frankos earlier this morning and I provided him with a written guarantee from the U.S. Navy to escort the Greek ships in and out of Smyrna, so we can rescue the refugees on the quay. General Frankos seems tentative and refuses to do anything until he asks for advice from his superiors. We don't have time to wait for that conversation. I need to go over his head and contact the Greek government in Athens directly. Can you help me do this?"

Theophonitis said, "It is four o'clock in the morning. Do you think anyone is up at this hour?"

Jennings sported a big smile. "There's only one way to find out!"

"We will have to send the message out in code. If you will write it down on paper, I will have it coded so we can send it on to Athens."

A sailor handed Jennings a note pad. Jennings thought for a moment and then began to write. A few moments later he handed the note to the Captain. Theophonitis gestured to Jennings with the note. "May I?"

"Of course, Captain, be my guest!"

He read the message...

> PRIME MINISTER WAR & MARINE DEPT. MILITARY GOVERNOR OF MITYLENE BOCAS & AMERICAN PRES. OF REFUGEE RELIEF NEAR EAST ACKNOWLEDGE THAT 150,000 REFUGEES ARE PRISONERS ON THE QUAY SMYRNA. STOP.
>
> TURKISH TERMS FOR THEIR DEPARTURE ARE SEVEN DAYS FROM TODAY. AMERICAN DESTROYERS ACCORDING TO ORDER OF THE HIGH COMMISSIONER & ADMIRAL BRISTOL WILL GIVE PROTECTION OF THE GREEK STEAMERS WITHOUT FLAG ENTERING SMYRNA TAKING REFUGEES ON BOARD. STOP.
>
> AMERICAN COM[MITTEE] WILL ALSO CARE FOR FOOD SHELTER. MEMBER OF AMERICAN COM[MITTEE] NOW ON BOARD SHIP AND AWAITS ANSWER STOP.

Theofonitis looked up at Jennings. "Mr. Jennings, you don't have very much experience in dealing with Greeks, do you?"

"Not before last month!"

The Captain looked directly into Jennings' eyes. "Please let me make a few changes that will say the same thing, but be a bit more forceful to get their attention."

Jennings responded with a warm smile. "By all means, Captain."

Theophonitis rewrote the message and gave it to his radioman to encode and send.

Within minutes of sending the message, a message was received back from Athens. it read:

> WHO IS ASA JENNINGS? -STOP-
> ON WHOSE BEHALF IS HE ACTING -STOP-

Jennings, normally prone to give honest answers, was completely out of character at this point. He drafted a reply:

CHAIRMAN OF THE AMERICAN RELIEF COMMITTEE IN
MYTILENE -STOP-

As far as Jennings knew, he was the only American in Mytilene. He was, after all, in the middle of a relief effort. And as the only American in the relief effort, he had declared himself the chairman of it. Technically, in the strange world he was now operating in, this was an accurate statement. But his reply did not generate a quick response this time. Jennings and Theophonitis stared at each other waiting for a response. Finally it came.

REQUEST REQUIRES CABINET ACTION -STOP-
CABINET CURRENTLY NOT IN SESSION -STOP-
REQUEST FORWARDED TO PRIME MINISTER -STOP-
WILL CALL CABINET MEETING ASAP -STOP-

Now that the request was in play, the Greek bureaucracy began to churn. Messages looking to establish who Jennings and the American Relief Committee were, and what influence they had, began to flow. The entire day was wasted on bureaucrats doing what bureaucrats do. As Jennings and Theophonitis continued their game of radio liar's poker from Mytilene, precious hours were lost.

As another night began on the quay, the haunting melody of group prayer again carried over the Bay of Smyrna. Refugees clutching what meager possessions they still had, were by now accepting the fact they would likely meet their end on the quay at Smyrna, but continued to chant their prayers.

Chapter 44.
23 September

Yet another day, and the Smyrna quay continued to host the end of hundreds of refugee lives through exhaustion, starvation, and murder. As the morning sun shined its light on the devastation, the bodies continued to mount, as more in the crowd were now accepting their fate. No one was coming to save them.

In Mytilene, Saturday morning became a repeat of Friday's duel of radio messages. In each case, Jennings provided a carefully worded answer, in the hope it would be sufficient to somehow get the ships released. Then, a message came through:

> WILL AMERICAN DESTROYERS PROTECT SHIPS IF TURKS
> ATTEMPT SEIZURE -STOP-

Obviously, this was a question that required only a single word answer, yes or no! And, by virtue of the authority given him, he was not able to give an accurate answer. So, he evaded it:

> NO TIME TO DISCUSS DETAILS HOW SHIPS WILL BE
> PROTECTED -STOP-
> STATED GUARANTEES SHOULD BE ENTIRELY
> SATISFACTORY -STOP-

By four in the afternoon, it became clear they were deadlocked. The Greek cabinet was close to toppling, and was not about to make a decision that would accelerate its demise. In Jennings' mind, another day was gone and he was beyond desperate. He was about to 'throw caution to the wind.' He looked at Theophonitis with new resolve. "I need to send one more message. If this doesn't work, nothing will."

Jennings wrote it out and Theophonitis handed it to the radio operator. It read:

> IF I DO NOT RECEIVE A FAVORABLE REPLY BY SIX O'CLOCK P.M. -STOP-
>
> I WILL WIRE OPENLY, WITHOUT CODE, SO THAT MESSAGE WILL BE PICKED UP BY ANY WIRELESS STATION -STOP-
>
> THAT TURKISH AUTHORITY GAVE PERMISSION FOR GREEK SHIPS TO EVACUATE REFUGEES FROM SMYRNA -STOP-
>
> THAT AMERICAN NAVY GUARANTEED PROTECTION TO GREEK SHIPS -STOP-
>
> THAT I ASSUMED RESPONSIBILITY FOR DIRECTING SHIPS SAFELY TO GREEK SOIL -STOP-
>
> THAT WE ONLY LACK SHIPS -STOP-
>
> THAT GREEK GOVERNMENT REFUSED GREEK SHIPS TO SAVE GREEK AND ARMENIAN REFUGEES AWAITING CERTAIN DEATH OR WORSE -STOP-

Clearly, to both Jennings and Theophonitis, the next message would likely seal the fate of the entire Christian population on the quay in Smyrna. But, the next reply was not at all what they expected:

> WOULD JENNINGS AGREE TO BE ABOARD LEAD GREEK VESSEL -STOP-

He had no idea where this is going, but Jennings sent a response:

> YES BY ALL MEANS -STOP-

Jennings looked at Theophonitis. There was confusion in his eyes.

Theophonitis nodded, "This is most interesting. The only reason they would ask you to be on the first Greek ship is that if the Turks capture it or sink it, they can say it was the ship the American was on, that the Americans led Greece into the trap, and that the Americans are responsible for the entire affair. I think you are going to get your ships, but you are their scapegoat. Would you expect anything else from politicians?"

Just before six p.m., a radio message was received aboard the *Kilkis*:

> ALL SHIPS IN AEGEAN PLACED UNDER YOUR COMMAND TO REMOVE REFUGEES FROM SMYRNA -STOP-
>
> ASA JENNINGS BY ORDER OF CABINET HEREBY NAMED ADMIRAL OF ENTIRE GREEK FLEET FOR PURPOSES OF RESCUE -STOP-

Jennings grew a broad smile as he handed the message over to Theophonitis, who stood and saluted Jennings. "Admiral sir! What are my orders?"

"Orders? The only thing I know about ships is how to be sick on them."

Theophonitis desperately tried to keep from laughing.

"No sir! You are the commander of our fleet. You must give the orders that we will execute."

Jennings was light-headed. "Well, I guess we should inform all the captains of the fleet to get ready to sail to Smyrna."

The captain saluted his new, slightly shaky admiral. He ordered messages be sent to all twenty ships ordering their captains to a meeting aboard the *Kilkis* within the hour.

The meeting took place in the mess hall of the *Kilkis*. It was large enough to accommodate the ships' captains and their executive officers. Since it was Captain Theophonitis who called the meeting, he stepped up to the front of the hall to call the meeting to order.

"You all know why we are here. In the last twenty-four hours, my friend, Mr. Asa Jennings called on me here on the *Kilkis* to facilitate his communication with Athens regarding our countrymen who are trapped on the quay at Smyrna. After a number of coded messages between us and the cabinet in Athens, the Prime Minister and his cabinet voted on our request and I will now inform you of their decisions and orders.

"The cabinet has officially elevated Mr. Jennings to the post of Admiral of the Greek Navy for the specific purpose of rescuing the refugees from destruction in Smyrna. He has been given full authority to command our fleet in this regard. Admiral Jennings has secured the services of the United States Navy to escort our fleet with

American destroyers into and out of the Smyrna harbor. He has also received official permission from the Turkish Nationalist Government to enter the harbor of Smyrna with Greek ships to effect the evacuation. The only condition to the fleet is that we cannot fly the Greek flag when entering the harbor and the Greek ships cannot physically tie up to the dock. But we can rescue all of those poor people who did nothing but try to live their lives in their homeland.

We are all under Admiral Jennings' command, so I would like to let him speak to you directly."

Jennings was tentative as he walked up to the front of the hall. "Thank you for being so prompt in attending. Captain Theophonitis has informed me that all of our ships can be up to steam before midnight so I ask that you all return to your ships and prepare them for our first voyage."

The captain of the *Propondis* stood, "Admiral Jennings, will you be accompanying us to Smyrna or will you be directing the effort from here?"

"I have assured the cabinet in Athens that I will be aboard the first Greek ship. In fact, you've shown me that you can speak English, which qualifies you to be the lead ship in this instance. I will be aboard your ship leading the fleet."

In spite of his reluctance to make the journey, the fact that his ship was to be the lead ship sparked a new interest in helping the refugees. It was clear to Jennings that most of these Greek captains were not enthusiastic to return to Smyrna. One of the captains stood, "Admiral sir, my ship will not be seaworthy in time for your departure. So I will not be able to join the fleet."

As soon as he said it, another captain repeated the same refrain. One after the other, most claimed problems in becoming seaworthy in time to carry out the rescue. But Jennings was not about to see his plan destroyed by cowards. He decided to try another bluff.

"All those captains that have mentioned their ships not capable of being seaworthy, by midnight need to add their ships' names to this list. I will be ordering one of my naval engineers to board each and every vessel to determine if the statement is true or if for some reason, the statement is not true. Any ship found to be capable of becoming seaworthy by midnight, will result in an immediate court-martial of that captain. I will then determine from the cabinet whether I also have the authority to have the offending captain executed at dawn tomorrow."

After the meeting, Jennings shared a cup of coffee with Captain Theophonitis. "I'm glad you will be with us tomorrow when we steam toward Smyrna. I need someone who understands the mission."

Theophonitis shook his head. "I'm sorry Admiral Jennings, I would love to be with you. But I am unable to honor your wish. I have other orders that will require me to leave here tomorrow in another direction."

Jennings was confused. "What could be more important than rescuing hundreds of thousands of Greeks?"

"The survival of my country is more important. You've met Col. Gonatas. I can only tell you that I am following his orders. If you think you can dissuade him, then be my guest, but I'm certain he will not release me. You'll know soon enough the result of my new orders."

Jennings realized there was something big about to happen. He wished Theophonitis well, and decided that his mission could not get bogged down in another affair of state.

Chapter 45.
24 September

Remarkably, by midnight, all twenty ships were up to steam and ready to begin the journey to Smyrna. With Jennings now on the bridge of the *Propondis*, he gave his first order. "Captain, run down the Greek flag and replace it with an American flag. Then please run up a signal flag aft, that signifies 'Follow Me.' Once this is done, the order is 'full steam ahead.' Let's go save some lives."

Once again, Jennings smiled at his lack of any need for a chamber pot. He had apparently developed sea legs.

About halfway through the four hour journey, the U.S.S. *Lawrence* pulled up alongside the *Propondis*. Commander Wolleson knew Jennings. Thinking he would be more comfortable on a U.S. warship, Wolleson wired the *Propondis*:

> ADMIRAL JENNINGS -STOP-
>
> WOLLESON OFFERS THE HOSPITALITY OF A RIDE ON USS LAWRENCE. -STOP-
>
> CAN MAKE ARRANGEMENTS TO HAVE YOU BROUGHT ABOARD -STOP-

On the bridge of the *Propondis*, a radio operator handed the message to Jennings. He appeared to be caught up in the excitement of leading a fleet of ships. He read the message, and then wrote out his own response:

> COMMANDER WOLLESON -STOP-
>
> GREAT TO HAVE YOU ALONG -STOP-
>
> WOULD LOVE TO RIDE WITH YOU BUT HAVE PROMISED ATHENS I WOULD REMAIN ON LEAD SHIP -STOP-
>
> PERHAPS NEXT TIME -STOP-

As the flotilla of ships steamed toward Smyrna in single file, Jennings could hardly hide his excitement. He would look back on this moment as the most exciting experience of his life. But as the *Propondis* closed in on her destination, Jennings could see the plume of smoking ruins that were once the "Jewel of the Near East." As they drew nearer, Jennings could make out the skeletons of the once bustling quayside. In a moment, as he could now clearly see the charred remains of the city, his excitement turned to sadness. The sight would be far more desolate than anything he saw during the Great War. The black line that stretched more than a mile along the coast was lifeless.

He would later recall: 'Yet I knew it was a border not of life, but of living sufferers waiting, hoping, praying, as they had been doing every moment for days- waiting, hoping, praying, for ships, ships, ships. As we approached, and the shore [spread] out before us, it seemed as if every face on the quay was turned toward us, and every arm outstretched to bring us in. Indeed I thought the whole shore moved out to grasp us. The air was filled with the cries of thousands, cries of such transcendent joy that the sound pierced to the very marrow of my bones.

'No need for us to tell them what these ships were for! Those who had scanned that watery horizon for days looking wistfully for ships, did not have to be told that here was help, here indeed was life and safety! Never had I been so thankful, so truly happy, as I was that early morning as I realized that at last, but thank God in time, I had been able to bring to these despairing legions a new hope, yes, a new life.'

Finally, Jennings was no longer trying to accomplish the impossible all by himself. While Jennings was playing liar's poker with the Greek cabinet in Athens, Captain Powell was notifying the Turkish officials of what Jennings was up to, trying to coordinate the effort.

Dr. Esther Lovejoy, the American doctor that had arrived on the seventeenth, and in the face of the looming crisis, had begun working to hold back the ongoing humanitarian disaster. Now she worked to figure out how to get the refugees out of Smyrna. The logistics were frightening. By her count, more than three hundred thousand refugees on the quay had to be evacuated in the space of six days. That meant fifty thousand per day, an impossible task.

Technically speaking, the Turkish authorities had agreed to allow all women, children and men too old for the military, to be evacuated. However, here again, reality was quite different from what was promised. Seeing the complications inherent in not allowing a Greek ship to tie up, the Turkish authorities, decided to allow the ships to tie up at the very end of the railroad pier. The aim of their accommodation was soon made clear.

The railroad pier was equipped with a narrow walkway that was enclosed by metal fences. It was further divided into three long distinct sections, each of which had its own gate. Each gate was guarded by double lines of Turkish soldiers. while the entrance to the pier was occupied by a crowd of senior Turkish officers.

Lovejoy attempting to prepare the process on the railroad pier, realized what was afoot. The purpose of the fences was to force the refugees to pass through the narrow gates, where they could be carefully scrutinized and all men who appeared to be of military age detained for deportation into the interior.

Clearly, the sight of the Greek fleet brought relief and exhilaration to the desperate souls squatting on the quay. But the sheer numbers also sparked the dread of not being one of the first to board and being left behind- again. Once the *Propondis* tied up at the railroad pier, a wave of terrified refugees pushed forward to avoid being left behind.

There is perhaps no better way to describe this bizarre scene than to use Dr. Lovejoy's own words as she would later write: 'The description of that frantic rush to reach the ships is beyond the possibility of language. Pain, anguish, fear, fright, despair and that dumb endurance beyond despair, cannot be expressed in words. . . Fortunately, there seems to be a point at which human beings become incapable of further suffering. A point where reason and sensation fail, and faith cooperating with the instincts of self-preservation and race preservation take control, releasing sub-human and super-human reservoirs of strength and endurance which are not called upon under civilized conditions of life.

'Thousands and thousands of refugees, with heavy bundles upon their backs, pressed forward along the quay, struggling to reach and pass through the first gate. The Turkish soldiers beat them back with the butts of their guns to make them come more slowly, but they seemed insensible to pain and their greatest fear in the daylight was the fear of not reaching the ships.

'Many of the women . . . were pushed off the quay into the shallow water, near that floating mass of carrion which washed against the stonework. No effort was made to help them out of the water. Such an effort would have necessitated the putting down of bundles, or children, and every person in the crowd strong enough to carry anything was carrying a pack or a child, or helping the sick and old of his own family. So these women stood in the water waist deep, holding up their little ones, until they were able to scramble out and join the crowd, with nothing in the world left to them but the wet rags on their backs.

'The mother's instinct is hard to control. With a wild expression of countenance she turned, dropped her bundle and went over that iron picket fence, which was at least seven feet high, like an orangoutang.

'A soldier was ordered to stop her, and he cornered her between the fence and a small building on the inside, beat her with the butt of his gun, and finally pinned her against the building with the muzzle of it, in an effort to make her listen to reason and obey orders. But that poor mother had reverted to the lower animals and was acting on instinct. She couldn't be controlled by a gun unless it was fired. With her eyes on her child, who was being pushed along with the crowd in the distance, she broke away and the soldier shrugged his shoulders impotently as much as to say: 'What is the use of trying to manage such a crazy creature.'

'Individual soldiers would seize the more prosperous-appearing women, drag them out of the line and rob them in broad daylight. Any men of military age who attempted to escape with their families were given even rougher treatment. They were severely beaten, then officially arrested and placed with the group of prisoners awaiting deportation to the interior.

'As family after family passed through those gates, the father of perhaps forty-two years of age, carrying a sick child or other burden, or a young son, and sometimes both father and son, would be seized.

'In a frenzy of grief, the mother and children would cling to this father and son, weeping, begging and praying for mercy, but there was no mercy. With the butts of their guns, the Turkish soldiers beat these men backward into the prison groups and drove the women toward the ships, pushing them with their guns, striking them with straps or canes, and urging them forward like a herd of animals, with the expression, *'Haide! Haide!'* which means 'Begone! Begone!'

'In a city with so large a population, there were of course, a great many expectant mothers and these terrible experiences precipitated their labors in many instances. Children were born upon the quay and upon the pier, and one woman who had been in the crush at the first gate for hours, finally staggered through holding her just-born child in her hands.

'Children fell off the pier and were drowned, young men committed suicide, old people died of exhaustion and, at the end of the pier, when two or three ships were loading at the same time, children were lost and their mothers ran to and fro frantically calling for their little ones, and great was the joy if the lost were found.'

Powell as part of his duty, wired Rear Admiral Bristol in Constantinople, informing him of Jennings' accomplishment. Bristol concluded since the evacuation was already under way with agreement from the Turkish authority, he and the other High Commissioners finally agreed that the navies of the Allied powers would now work together in Smyrna to assist the refugees.

In the evening, as Jennings oversaw the first evacuation of the Greek fleet, General Mustafa Kemal was celebrating his victory with members of his senior staff at a party at the mansion of wealthy Turkish merchant, Muammer Usakizade, the father of Kemal's paramour, Latife. Obviously, Kemal was in great humor as the breadth of his victory began to set in. In one month, he had gone from the brink of defeat to complete victory. There is little doubt he believed his accomplishment was completely his own and not the duplicity and greed of the Allied powers.

By the close of the first day, the Greek fleet rescued fifteen thousand Greek and Armenian Christians from the jaws of death known as the quay at Smyrna.

Meanwhile, under the cover of darkness, the battleships *Lemnos* and *Kilkis,* formerly the United States dreadnoughts *Idaho* and *Mississippi,* and a fleet of Greek destroyers, serving as troop transports carried the Greek army out of Mytilene, en route to mainland Greece.

Chapter 46.
25 September

The morning sun brought new relief to the still hundreds of thousands of pathetic refugees gathered on the quay. But today was somewhat different than yesterday. Yesterday, they stared westward at an empty bay that boasted the hopelessness of a razor thin straight line that was the horizon. The prayers of many nights still unanswered. Today, there was the real hope of escape from the hell of the last three weeks. There were ships. Ships that would carry them away from this madness, this stench, this horror. For those who still had their husbands and sons with them, there was the less certain hope that some miracle would help them disguise the men in their lives so their families could build a new life in a new world.

They dared not think that such a hope of keeping their family together was merely a fantasy. They dared not think that the narrow path guarded by Turkish soldiers with three checkpoints would not expose their disguises and haul away their men, never to be seen again. They would not think of this reality because their prayers had been answered. They had prayed that God would send ships and God had sent them ships.

But the morning brought another twist. It had turned cold in Smyrna. In many cases, the heavier clothing carried by refugees had been left on the road getting to Smyrna, or perhaps burned in the fire that ravaged them, or perhaps pushed into the sea by people who needed the room otherwise taken up by clothing. There no longer was the intense heat that would slow-cook them alive. Now there was the wet-cold that would set them to shiver.

This morning's world outside Smyrna seemed to be upside down. A few years ago, the Greek forces answered the call of the Allies to occupy Asia Minor and stop the Young Turks from slaughtering Christians. Now they talked of the Greek soldier as the invader, who had to leave so that the honorable and just government of Mustapha Kemal could rebuild his country. Newspapers now sung the praises of the civilized Kemal who overcame the scorn of Europeans to become the great Conqueror for Islam.

As the orderly evacuation of Greek and Armenian Christians entered its second day, General Kemal had turned his attention to another part of the country he had lost in the Great War. In an eerily familiar instance of history repeating itself, General Kemal's government today officially announced that two Kemalist cavalry divisions, totaling three thousand men, had occupied Eren-Keui, which happened to be within ten miles south of the British positions at Çanakalle (Chanak).

Clearly, a breach of the neutral zone, the Turkish cavalry, armed with machine guns, placed themselves provocatively close to the small British force at Çanakalle. General Harrington, the British High Commissioner, instructed the Nationalist representative to 'request' that General Kemal order their withdrawal. He didn't demand it. He requested it. The instructions given the representative boasted that the consequences of failure to comply with the 'request' after a reasonable time, would fall upon the heads of the Kemalists.

The Allied High Commissioners met to discuss the violation by the Turks of the neutral zone. The French Commissioner, went so far as to telegraph General Kemal, urging him to immediately withdraw his troops.

Strangely, even though the Allies decided that the Turks should be completely removed from the European side, the Kemalists unofficially asked for permission to transport troops from the Asiatic banks of the Dardanelles to the European side by means of pontoon bridges. The Kemalists pointed out that by using this method, since the two shores are less than a mile across, they could avoid violating the neutral zone. Sources in the Allied camp suggested they would not object to the passage of a small military and administrative force into Thrace since it would avoid a breach of the neutral zone.

Even more strangely, although such permission had yet to be granted, a force of ten thousand Turks stood organized to take over the administration of Thrace, with large trucks transporting three hundred men daily to Thrace. And what was the purpose of the escalation of Turkish men and equipment in Thrace? The object of the movement was to cut off the retreat of Greek troops who remained in Thrace. Could it be that the Allies were allowing the Turks to do exactly what they accused the Greeks of planning just months before?

The difference of course was that Greece was a western culture that not only created the rule of law but actually believed in it, while the Turk viewed the rule of law to be whatever the ruler dictated it to be. In another strange behavior by a recently vanquished- then reborn army, the British High Commissioner received word that the Turkish steamer, *Karabiga*, yesterday, while transporting troops and munitions across the Sea of Marmara, under the cover of night, rammed and sank the British torpedo boat *Speedy*. The report indicated that the British vessel was cut almost in two, killing ten British soldiers. Upon receiving word of the unauthorized transfer of men and munitions, the British high command ordered the seizure of the *Karabiga* by the British navy.

Meanwhile, Jennings stood on the shore in Mytilene. He managed to bring fifteen thousand refugees out of Smyrna, but they were almost as crowded in the refugee camp in Mytilene as they were on the quay. But there was not one word of complaint.

He was troubled by the delays in off-loading and organizing the refugees here on Mytilene. They should have already been back at Smyrna. As it stood, they wouldn't be able to leave again until tomorrow morning.

Chapter 47.
26 September

As Jennings stood on the bridge of the *Propondis*, he could see the first light coming up behind Mount Pagus and the rubble that was once a bustling cosmopolitan city. He was determined to get many more refugees onto his fleet of mercy ships today. His armada was now only seventeen ships, but he'd already received word that the Allies would now join the bandwagon and assist in the evacuation.

Once again as the lead ship entered the harbor, he could see the outstretched hands of the refugees, hoping to be one of today's lucky ones. He had just received a cable indicating that a British cargo fleet was steaming toward Smyrna to join in the rescue. But he wondered what would be the result of Colonel Gonatas' ultimatum of the Greek government. He wondered about the war in Thrace and how it might affect the attitude of the Turkish government in Smyrna and their willingness to continue the evacuation. Jennings silently prayed as the *Propondis* entered the harbor.

On shore in Smyrna, Dr. Lovejoy continued her effort to organize and facilitate the evacuation of refugees. She concentrated her efforts on the women, many of which were either pregnant or brand new mothers. She suspected delirium to be setting in, because even though at this moment less than five percent of the refugees had been evacuated, she had a sense that in their race against the clock, they were beginning to turn the tide.

Constantine I of Greece, King of the Hellenes, sat in his study on the second floor of the Royal Palace. This was the palace that was originally commissioned for his birth as the Crown Prince of Greece in 1868. He sipped his afternoon coffee as he stared out the window overlooking the royal gardens. He was troubled by his devastating loss in Asia Minor and wondered how it was possible. In the deep recesses of his mind, he dared not allow the thought to surface that the horrific defeat was somehow tied to his replacing the army's general staff appointed by Venizelos. If the thought did surface, he would have to admit that his generals were cronies, not seasoned warriors.

After meeting with his crown council earlier in the afternoon, Constantine's staff held a press conference to announce he would depart Athens immediately to personally command the Greek army in Thrace. The announcement also declared that as of later tonight, martial law would be imposed in Athens.

He thought back to his original departure from Greece in June 1917, forced into exile in Switzerland. He smiled as he remembered his return after his son's death, and the plebiscite that returned 99% of the votes in favor of his return. But here he sat, once again facing a hostile public as a result of the Asia Minor catastrophe. He thought, *Will I have to leave again? What if I order a new offensive in Thrace. . . Will the armies support me?*

As he took another sip of coffee, he became confused. He squinted as he focused outside of the window. *Is it snowing? Snow in September?* Then he looked more closely. *It's not snow. It's paper.* There was paper falling from the sky like snow. In a moment, one of the pages was blown up against the window and he could tell there was printing on one side.

Constantine commanded his manservant to fetch one of the papers from the royal garden. Momentarily, the servant returned and handed his king the leaflet. The despairing monarch read the leaflet:

> *To the King, Crown Prince and Premier:*
> *The army of Mitylene and Chios charge me to inform you that these claims which are in accord with the desires of all but an insignificant minority of the people are necessary for the safety of the people:*
>
> ONE--   *Abdication of the king in favor of the crown prince.*
>
> TWO--   *Dissolution of the assembly.*
>
> THREE--   *The formation of a new cabinet.*
>
> FOUR--   *The calling of new elections.*
>
> FIVE--   *Reinforcing the troops on the Thracian front.*

> May patriotism prevail in the present crisis to prevent civil strife. This is the only way a complete catastrophe can be averted.
>
> [Signed]
> COL. GONATAS

Constantine stared at the leaflet. No longer could he avoid the obvious. The military was dropping leaflets on his city declaring that he must abdicate for the good of the people. Instead, he would leave tomorrow for Thrace.

In Thessaloniki, the Greek fleet carrying half the new Greek revolutionary forces under the command of Colonel Gonatas, landed along the coast. The forces managed to capture Thessaloniki without firing a shot. Likewise, the other half of the force landed at Port Laurium, thirty miles south of Athens and accomplished the same .

Commander Powell, now armed with Admiral Bristol's reluctant new position of joining Jennings' humanitarian effort to evacuate refugees, studied the process from a logistics point of view. In spite of the heroic effort, there was no way that they could evacuate between two-hundred-fifty-thousand and three-hundred-thousand people by the October 1st deadline.

He requested and received permission to meet with General Noureddin Pasha to discuss the deadline. He walked over to

39. *King Constantine I of Greece in a German*

Noureddin's office and was escorted in.

"General Noureddin, Thank you for seeing me on such short notice."

Noureddin, seated at his desk, extended his hand. "Please sit down Commander. And what may I do for you today."

"General, we are grateful for your cooperation in helping us to evacuate the refugees that remained on the quay. I know you've given us until October 1st to complete the evacuation, and that after that, all those remaining on the quay, would be deported into the interior."

"That is correct, Commander!"

"I can understand the logic in creating an arbitrary deadline, as it relates to your government's mission to achieve a 'Turkey for the Turks.' Considering your government's ultimate mission, I have done some research into the number of ships available to accomplish the mission and the time left to the deadline. I am here, because it is clear to me that we will not be able to accomplish the goal as long as the deadline remains as October 1st."

Noureddin truly enjoyed seeing an American naval officer groveling. "And how many extra days would it take to accomplish the mission, Commander Powell?"

"We need at least another week to get it done."

Noureddin smiled. "Commander, I am a reasonable man. You have asked for a week. A week is seven days. To show you I am a reasonable man, I will give you eight additional days to accomplish the mission. In fact, my sources tell me that a British fleet is also on its way to help with the mission. I will allow these ships to land at Urla, Chesme and Ayvalik to evacuate refugees gathered at those ports. Would that help you?"

"Absolutely, General Noureddin. I appreciate this accommodation and I will do all I can to complete the mission to your satisfaction."

Noureddin looked down at the papers in front of him as if to dismiss the American. Without looking up at him, he said dismissively, "Good day, Captain!"

Powell stood, saluted, turned and left quietly. As he walked back to the quay, Powell thought to himself, *The American navy is now the tool of the Turkish government to rid itself of those inconvenient Christians. The world is upside down!*

Darkness hid the rubble once again as those remaining on the quay prayed for more ships tomorrow. Of those women, children and old men who managed to board one of the fleet, tonight's prayers were prayers of thanks. By tonight another forty-three-thousand refugees were on their way to safety. By tomorrow, everyone would know that the deadline was 8 October and anyone who could survive without food and barely a taste of water, and who was lucky enough to avoid being shot by the Turkish soldiers, would finally emerge from hell on earth.

At 11 p.m. in Athens, King Constantine I, abdicated his throne for the second time, in favor of his son, Crown Prince George.

At midnight, there were big demonstrations on the streets of Athens. Cheering crowds filled the streets as the 'new' Greek army moved among the crowds to maintain order.

Chapter 48.
27 September

In the early morning hours, the citizens of Athens were first moving about the center of the city. Under the watchful eye of revolutionary army officers, members of the Greek cabinet all resigned their posts. As the absence of any ministers began to settle in on the consciousness of those who paid attention to the political life in Athens, an anonymous group threw out the name of General Nider, a Venizelist, mentioned as a possible choice for heading up the new ministry and cabinet.

News of the mass resignations found its way to the streets in central Athens. Suddenly, there was intense excitement. Crowds began to form on the streets. Parades and demonstrations spontaneously formed and local shops were closed for the day, but there were no indications of violence or disorder. It was clear the insurrection was popular with most Athenians and no resistance was expected from the Royalists.

A report surfaced that an advance guard of fifteen-hundred insurgents was on its way to Athens from Laurium by train and expected to arrive by the afternoon. Another report suggested that transports landing at the port of Piraeus, as well as other detachments marching across the mountains to the north of Athens would be arriving today as well. For all practical purposes, a bloodless coup had been accomplished.

Prince George remained at the Royal Palace awaiting the troops and their leaders. He stood ready to assume the throne being vacated by his father. The king and queen oddly had yet to leave the city. In fact, throughout the day, Constantine who was already packed to leave for Thrace, frantically met with members of the cabinet that had already resigned, to discuss the alternative of his remaining in Athens to defend the city against the insurgents. The cabinet members, mostly friends of Constantine, advised against remaining in the city. Constantine ordered his remaining core of loyal cavalry to leave for the passes in the hills north of the city to defend against what he still viewed, in spited of the cheering public, as advancing rebels.

Cheering crowds now lined the streets of Athens as the newly arrived troops moved through the city to keep order. A large part of the Greek army and navy, revolted and joined the rebel forces that had arrived from Mytilene. Before the day was over, the entire military was on the side of the revolution.

News reached Constantinople that Turkish cavalry from Eren-Keui with reinforcements, was advancing to the northeast toward Asmali-Tepe, apparently to cut off the British advanced post at Kephex. It was clear the Turkish forces continued to ignore the prohibition of entering the neutral zone. A British column supported by artillery was leaving Çanakalle to counter the threat.

Meanwhile, in response to the British protest of the advancing Turkish forces, the Kemalist representative declared that Turkey would respect the neutrality of the straits, pending an armistice conference between British and Kemalist Generals. Although the British generals knew that the situation was critical, they were grateful that, at least for the moment, a new war between Britain and Turkey was averted.

General Harrington sent what seemed to be a most conciliatory message to Mustapha Kemal at Smyrna. He urged that an early meeting of the British and Kemalist generals at Moudania or Ismid was the most effective way of reaching an amicable understanding of the present difficult situation created by the Kemalist advance in the Dardanelles. Harrington went on to declare it would be a pity at the present juncture to allow local occupations of the Straits to jeopardize peace.

In a seemingly bold response for a participant on the losing side of the Great War, Hamid Bey the Ankara representative stated: "The Kemalists naturally will come across the so-called neutral zones, but they have not the slightest intention of firing upon the British occupying these zones. If however, the British move against us, we will be forced to reply."

Also in Constantinople, Rear Admiral Bristol, claimed to be doing his utmost to hasten the departure of refugees on the quay at Smyrna but the fact that the Turks insisted upon examining passports before permitting refugees to leave was creating significant delays.

In Smyrna, acting as a special correspondent for the *New York Times*, Mark Prentiss interviewed Fethi Bey, the Kemalist representative. In the interview, Fethi Bey specifically offered "to freely exchange all the Christian population in Asia Minor for the Moslems of Western Thrace." This offer would eventually become the agreement known as the 'Great Population Exchange.'

It was 6 p.m. at Port Laurium where Colonels Gonatas, Plastirac and Phocas, the leaders of the revolt, telegraphed an ultimatum to the government saying that a refusal to grant their demands would result in civil war. Since there was essentially no government left to act on the ultimatum besides the king, the colonels marched on Athens.

Constantine responded to the ultimatum by sending the following message. "I will sign this decree only on the understanding that Crown Prince George succeeds me." The noise from the streets floated into the palace through the windows. It was clear it was over.

General Papoulas, the newly appointed governor of Thrace, was sent out to meet the column of revolutionary troops marching toward Athens to inform them that Constantine had abdicated and that the cabinet had resigned. Before returning to Athens, he handed the leader of the column the formal abdication statement:

'By the wish of the people I returned in December, 1920, and assumed royal power. I made a declaration that I would guard our constitution and conform to the wishes of the people and the interests of the nation. I have done all that was possible to guard those interests, but regrettable events brought the country to a critical position.

I am sure that the country will conquer all its obstacles and continue its brilliant and glorious career if the people are united and if the nation is aided by powerful friends.

It is not my desire to leave the slightest doubt that my presence is an obstacle to this sacred unity. I abdicate in favor of my son George and I hope that the people will support and help him.

I am happy that an occasion has been given me to sacrifice myself again and I will be happier still to see my people in full accord with their new king.

Constantine.

By nightfall, there were now less than two-hundred thousand refugees remaining on the quay at Smyrna. The rescue operation continued under the oversight of Asa Jennings, assisted by Dr. Lovejoy.

Chapter 49.
28 September

News reached Constantinople that Kemalist forces had occupied, without opposition, positions in the regions of Dumbrek, Lampsaki, Yaghjihar and Sangakeli, all inside the neutral zone of the Dardanelles. This marked the fifth violation of the zone by Turkish forces. Protests issued by British officers within the neutral zone failed to stay the advance of the Turks. The British protested that British flags were posted throughout the invaded territory and were therefore regarded as a provocative act.

The British continued to reinforce their troop positions at Çanak, a sign that hostilities might once again resume. They went so far as to convert Moudros Bay on the Greek island of Lemnos, into a subsidiary naval base for the fleet operating in Turkish waters. Moudros had been the site of the 'Armistice of Moudros,' which ended the hostilities between the Allied forces and the Ottoman Empire after the World War. Clearly the Allies, and the British in particular, chose once again to ignore the dripping irony of the circumstance.

The French and Italian generals stationed in Ankara had a different view. They expressed the opinion that the British ought to withdraw from Çanak and confine themselves to the European side of the Straits. Clearly, this opposing view was the product of a recent meeting between French envoy, Henry Gandhillon and General Kemal, in which France had undertaken not to engage in military operations against the Turks in Asia Minor. More broadly, it would be in line with the secret agreements negotiated between the Kemalist government and separately with France and Italy, during the Allied-sanctioned Greek advance on the Kemalist forces.

Meanwhile, on the quay in Smyrna, the evacuation was now progressing with greatly increased efficiency. In addition to the Greek fleet of freighters and passenger ships, the British and

American navies had joined the evacuation effort. By the end of the day nearly half of all refugees had been rescued out of the Smyrna harbor.

Chapter 50.
29 September

Great anxiety persisted in Paris over the stalemate of British troops being in close proximity with Turkish troops in the neutral zone. Clearly, by not responding to the British note over the terms of peace, Mustapha Kemal was trying to change the terms of the agreement. The French government was nervous that the delay could have devastating effects on the people of France. They feared that if Kemal asked for changes in the terms, the British would likewise seek changes in the other direction. The changes would be predicated on the demand that the Turks not invade the neutral zone. Except that the Turks had already invaded the neutral zone. This scenario would likely erode to a new posture toward conflict.

If the talks did take a bad turn, the British had already promised to get the Greeks out of Thrace. If that failed because of the past alliance, the Turks might decide to force the Greeks out on their own. That placed them in a direct clash with the British. If the British and the Turks went to war, the British would likely ask France to help. If France helped the British, they would lose all of their efforts over the last few years to obtain the fruits of their secret alliance with Turkey. If they sided with the Turks, they would end up fighting along side an enemy against an ally. If they claimed neutrality, they would lose any gains they had made over the years and be locked out of any future gains if the British won the war. No matter how they looked at it, it was not good for France.

In Boston, the Near East Relief organization called a mass meeting at Symphony Hall. One of the guest speakers was revered Massachusetts Senator, Henry Cabot Lodge. In his comments to the riveted audience, Senator Lodge spoke of the Turk in Europe:

"It is a horrible condition. The destruction of Smyrna is one of the greatest tragedies of our time. One cannot escape the vision of those people fleeing before the Turks and not shudder to think that such things can happen in our day. Nowhere else in the world except Turkey could such things happen.

"The inhumanity of the Turk goes beyond belief. It is founded on a religious hatred and its object is to exterminate Christianity. The responsibility of the nations that have kept Turkey alive, owing to their own jealousies, is very great. The Armenians have fought the battle for fourteen hundred years because they would not give up their faith. . . Sixty thousand Greeks had fought under the American flag in the World War.

"The Ottoman Turks have been in Europe since the 15th century. In the days of their success they were a scourge to Europe, the source of innumerable wars, the executioners in countless massacres. The Turks are brave soldiers and good fighting men, but there the praise must stop.

"There is not one good word to be said in defense of the Turks as governors or rulers. When they came into the region that is now called the Balkans, they found there large and prosperous cities, built up during the early middle ages on the ruins of the Roman civilization. They found a fertile and cultivated country. The cities which they captured sank into deserted villages.

"Wherever they have trodden, trade, industry, commerce, the arts and civilization have withered away. They have preyed upon the jealousies and controversy of the other nations of Europe, and in this way have sustained themselves at Constantinople. They have been the cause of many wars. The massacres of which they have been guilty, which stretch back to the day of their arrival and which have never been worse than during the entire 19th century, almost surpass belief and imagination. At least half of the Armenian people have been slaughtered in cold blood, and the remnant is only preserved now because a large part of Armenia has fallen under Russian control and the other Armenians have taken refuge there.

"Such a nation as this, such a government, I should say as this, is a curse to modern civilization. Like a pestilence, it breathes forth contagion upon the innocent air. My earnest hope is that among the results of the war, which I firmly believe will be a complete victory for the cause of right and freedom, one of the great results I pray for will be the final extinction of the Turkish Empire in Europe.

"I fervently hope that the great city of the Eastern Roman Empire may be so controlled that the Straits will be free to all nations of the earth and no longer be used for corrupt bargains in order that the trade may be held up or allowed to pass at the will of tyrants who, under one name or another, rule over Turkey.

"I hope and trust that we shall see the holy places which are sacred to all Christianity, as well as those which are sacred to the Jewish people, pass forever out of Turkish hands, and that we may no longer behold the Mosque of Omar dominating the city of Jerusalem. I should be sorry indeed, as an American, as a lover of freedom, if when this war closed and the United States comes with commanding voice to the settlement of the terms of peace, we should appear at the great council of the nations as still the friend of Turkey."

The audience stood to applaud the Senator as average Americans heard about the catastrophe. At the close of the Senator's comments, a professor at the International College in Smyrna, Prof. S. Ralph Harlow, who had left Smyrna the day before the fires were set, spoke in terms that Bostonians could relate to. He said:

"I seem to recall that Boston at one time had a tea party. It had thrown tea into the harbor rather than pay what it believed to be unjust taxation. At Smyrna, they were throwing children into the harbor to save them from the Turks. Bostonians had objected to a tax on tea. The Armenians of Asia Minor for centuries had to pay a tax *in* women and children."

Harlow added, "The Greeks have fought with the Allies. It is their families who are the victims of these massacres. America owes a debt to those who have laid down their most precious possessions to wipe tyranny off the face of the earth."

The meeting ended with an audience outraged to learn that Orthodox Christians were brutally massacred while the most powerful navies in the free world stood by and did nothing. Clearly the American public was finding out what was happening in their name. Only it was too late.

After another full day of evacuations, less than one hundred thousand refugees remained on the quay at Smyrna. Accompanying them, were tens of thousands of bloated, decaying Christian carcasses, and the associated stench, set among the backdrop of charred remains of one of the most vibrant cities in the history of the world.

Chapter 51.
30 September

In Athens, members of the new Greek revolutionary committee and the provisional cabinet decided that general elections for a new national assembly should be held in early November.

In Constantinople, rumors were circulating that Turkish residents of the city were assisting in the killing of remaining Christians. The Kemalist representative was denying the veracity of those rumors. However, tensions had been high since Mustapha Kemal's refusal to withdraw from the neutral zone and his demand that the British evacuate their position on the Asiatic side of the neutral zone.

In Washington DC, a report was received at the State Department from Rear Admiral Mark Bristol, the American High Commissioner at Constantinople, stating that more than seventy four thousand refugees had been evacuated from Smyrna over the last few days. With almost fifty thousand remaining, a request was made for additional flour and clothing to fill the need. In accordance with previous instructions, Bristol was ordering the evacuation of all Americans from Constantinople, indicating that the process had already begun.

In Paris, the French government announced its refusal to intervene in a military way in the event a conflict broke out between the British and the Turks. Their intention was to declare neutrality should a conflict begin.

In Moscow, Acting Foreign Minister Karachan was departing for Ankara to commence negotiations with the Turkish Nationalist government. The discussion would include the possibility of mobilizing its forces to assist the Kemalist regime. Reports indicated that Russian submarines were already maneuvering in the Black Sea as well as its Black Sea fleet showing increased signs for activity.

In Mytilene, reports of Turkish airplanes dropping bombs on Greek ships anchored in harbor were communicated to Athens and the Allied Powers.

In London, the Italian embassy was denying that Rome was withdrawing all troops and all civilians from Constantinople. It was known, however, that all Allied civilians and probably all Allied troops, with the exception of the British, would depart from Constantinople immediately if an outbreak occurred.

As a result of today's events, British Prime Minister, Lloyd George had called a late night emergency war council meeting of the cabinet, to discuss the reports issued by General Charles Harrington, British Commander-in-Chief. As a result, Great Britain had completed its final plans for war against Turkey in Asia Minor, including the immediate transfer of troops and artillery to reinforce the forty thousand men already guarding the Turkish straits. Additionally, final plans were in place to reinforce the fleet of forty man-of-war ships lining the Dardanelles.

With the country once again on a war footing, at midnight, the Prime Minister adjourned the war council, with a plan to reconvene in hopes that more favorable news would be forthcoming from Harrington on the war front.

What began as a collective sigh of relief from most people on the earth for the end of hostilities of the Great War, brought together the great leaders of the victorious allies in Paris to decide on what world peace would look like going forward. No one bothered to ask if these four old, vain liberal elitists had the knowledge, experience, ethics and resolve to make the world a better place. Instead, ordinary people cheered as the Big Four dictated decisions that would ultimately plague the earth for the next hundred years.

Aside from their disastrous redrawing of the world's borders, these self-absorbed narcissists sent the armies of a poor nation, to fight a war for which they were unprepared and too weary to fight themselves. Then, in midstream, they betrayed their most loyal ally by turning against the Christian armies of Greece, in favor of their new pal, Mustapha Kemal, and his oil-soaked territories.

After all, in the grand scheme of things, what difference does it make if this barren wasteland is run by Greeks or Turks anyway?

On 30 September 1922, The *New York Times* provided us with the profound answer to that question in its published translation, of a French translation, of an article in the Turkish Nationalist Journal:

> 'By our victory we have acquired a situation which permits us to dominate the events of the world.
>
> Events of the last three years had lined up all the big nations and all the little nations, but this array has broken against the resistance of the Turkish nation on our front. We are today masters of the world situation. We are no longer at the mercy of events. It is we who direct events. We have brought beneath our will the policy of the entire world. History tells of no people, at no period, who like the Turks are today such masters of their destinies.
>
> "Might makes right" has always been our national motto. Present and past civilizations have recognized as an absolute rule that "conquerors have the last word." Since we are victorious, since we have won the greatest victory in history, it is we who, in spite of all the world, will say the last word. We are going to dictate peace as we like.

As the sun began to dip into the Bay of Smyrna as seen from the quay, there was a continued chill in the air signaling that the fall season was definitely here. After another heroic effort to load the line of now stoic refugees onto the transport ships, those odd fifty-thousand remaining, huddled together, had no sense that there was any danger of them being deported into the interior and certain death. Now, the only hazard was that a Turkish soldier's bullet would end their struggle, or their body would finally give in to the lack of nutrition or cold. However, with the British and Turkish forces standing once again, on the edge of another war, Mustapha Kemal could easily withdraw his eight day extension, and thereby sentence those who patiently awaited a new day of rescue, to a walking death. British and American forces now fully engaged in the rescue, worried that this was still a real possibility.

In spite of her desire to see the evacuation through to the end, Dr. Lovejoy realized the humanitarian crisis was not over. The crisis had been moved to Mytilene on the island of Lesbos. Without a major movement of food and medical supplies to Mytilene, or wherever they might ship these homeless and destitute people, their death would be different, but it would still be death. Instead, she was hitching a ride on the U.S.S. *Litchfield,* to begin her return to America. There she could begin a new mission to raise awareness and capital to save these helpless victims obtain a chance of a new life.

She stood at the aft rail of the *Litchfield* as it pulled away from the quay. It was already dark and she could no longer see the faces of those left, but she knew exactly what they looked like. Like all of the prior nights since she arrived, soon the shrieks would once again begin pleading for the searchlights to be turned on, in hopes of dissuading Turkish soldiers, who had already begun their nightly consumption of *raki.* Soon it would once again seem like a good idea, to snuff out the life of a Christian infidel for the glory of Allah. After the shrieks would come the dirge of prayer, perhaps softer by virtue of the reduced numbers, but there still.

Lovejoy would love to have been on that last ship to see the faces of relief, that would appear as a consequence of their departure from hell. Hopefully, she would be able to raise enough donations to prevent their next hell. With the quay slowly becoming a barely visible line on the horizon, her thoughts drifted to the man who single-handedly moved this hellish mountain. Asa K. Jennings would remain in her mind, the American hero of the century. Quietly, but forcefully, Jennings did what no other man would or could do. Yet she had not seen any articles in major newspapers telling of his miraculous feat. Instead, the news would now talk of the great Allied military machine that saved humanity from the jaws of a fiery death in Smyrna.

Epilogue.

In spite of his Herculean accomplishment to evacuate 350,000 refugees from the quay at Smyrna, Asa Jennings' work was not completed. His feat had inspired the Allied powers to further assist his effort by providing military vessels that would increase his fleet of mercy ships to fifty-five. By year end, Jennings had led the evacuation of an additional 150,000 refugees from Asia Minor. By the time he was done, Jennings was responsible for the evacuation of almost 1.5 million Christians from Asia Minor.

Not burdened by narcissism, Jennings just humbly went about the business of saving refugees, while the Allied governments went on a public relations campaign to take credit for rescuing Christian minorities. Having earned the respect of Mustapha Kemal, Jennings was asked by Turkey's founding President, to establish Turkish social organizations on the model of the YMCA. . . but without any reference to Christianity, as the term was felt to be offensive to Muslims. He continued this work until his death in 1933.

After his defeat in the 1920 elections, Venizelos went into a self-imposed exile, but surfaced after the destruction of Smyrna to represent Greece in the negotiated Treaty of Lausanne in January 1923. He returned to government by being elected Premiere in 1928 and served until his party was defeated in 1932. The Great Depression of the early 1930s was probably a factor in a second but unsuccessful assassination attempt in 1933. In 1936, Venizelos left Greece for the last time to settle in Paris, but shortly after his arrival suffered a stroke and died.

Constantine I, having abdicated the Greek throne a second time, this time chose Italy as his country of exile. It was a short-lived exile in that he died four months later in Palermo Sicily.

As the world tried to swallow the changes that Georges Clemenceau and his counterparts had designed for them, and in a classic misreading of one's own inflated ego, in 1920, he agreed to serve as France's president if the people chose him, but he refused to campaign for the post. When the party chose someone else as their candidate, Clemenceau waited until after the election to resign as Prime Minister and then retired from politics completely. He traveled, took potshots at the governments he no longer dealt with and wrote his memoirs in response to Ferdinand Foch's memoirs that were highly critical of him. He did manage to complete a first draft before he died. His memoirs were later published posthumously.

As the fires swept through Smyrna, Lloyd George was quite absent from the tragedy in that he was being attacked by a coalition of British political parties. In the aftermath of being exposed for selling knighthoods, he was forced to resign as Prime Minister in October 1922. But his disgrace wasn't sufficient to run him out of politics in that in 1929 he was declared British parliament's longest-serving member. He spent the 1930s as a marginal political figure as he wrote his memoirs. He died in 1945.

Archbishop Chrysostomos' sacrifice for his people was revered by Orthodox Greeks worldwide, especially on mainland Greece, where statues were erected to commemorate his devotion to his church and his people. In 1992, he was declared a martyr and Saint of the Eastern Orthodox Church and to this day continues to be venerated by millions of Orthodox Christians.

While his story is lost to history, Captain Lazaros Apostolidis, likely was evacuated to Mytilene with the Greek army. If that did occur, he would have likely been part of the Thessaloniki or the Athens invasion forces that would depose the monarchy and establish the Second Hellenic Republic in 1924.

Pavlos Papavasiliou, one of the soldiers evacuated to Mytilene, was part of the Greek force that invaded Thessaloniki in the coup which paralleled the evacuation of refugees from Smyrna. Pavlos did find his younger brother Yianni on Mytilene, and both were reunited with their mother and four siblings who were saved by the Greek shipowner, Philipos Kavounidis who sent a ship back to his birthplace, to evacuate all of the remaining residents of Triglia, Asia Minor.

Like most of the Asia Minor refugees newly settled in Thessaloniki, the Papavasiliou family was starving. With few options for survival, Pavlos' mother, Sofia, dispatched her son to travel to America, where the streets were paved with gold. His instruction was simple. Send money from America so that the family wouldn't starve. Out of desperation, she later gave the same instruction to her second son, Yianni. Eventually, Pavlos' and Yianni's younger brother Nick would follow his brothers to America.

The three brothers, like so many other Greek immigrants in America, worked at menial jobs through the Great Depression, but continued sending money to support their family in Greece. Eventually, all three married and raised their own families. In Pavlos' case, his son eventually became curious enough to research what he had refused to ever discuss. That son became one of the authors of this book.

The three siblings left in Greece, also married and raised their individual families. Today there are six distinct branches of the family that continue the family legacy.

Obviously, the real story doesn't end here. In fact, it continues to this day as the passage of time allows historians to be more objective in their conclusion about this part of the historical record. They have begun to wake up to the fact that the Paris Peace Conference is the primary root cause of the savage conflict and inhumanity that continues into the new millennium.

To some, this interpretation of the events resulting in the burning of Smyrna will appear as an attempt to lay blame at the feet of Turkey and the Turks. That, however, is *not* the intent. The methods and actions of militant Turks are cultural characteristics that go back thousands of years. Their brutality is merely a symptom; a symptom that modern Turks refuse to acknowledge as many have been raised in a modern society influenced by western civilization. That refusal to acknowledge the sins of their ancestors is a problem that will certainly not be solved by this author.

Yes, there remains an element within Turkish culture that continues to embrace its militant roots. Nomadic warriors have conquered civilizations throughout history. But, if one looks at modern Turkey objectively - with much of its population embracing the pursuits of modern western civilization and seeking out a rewarding and peaceful existence - these are not people who should be blamed for the sins of their fathers. They are not the problem. It is the minority who still believe they will conquer and rule. It is the ignorant militant who is brainwashed by fundamentalist zealots who hearken back to the conquerors of old, who had no respect for human rights or dignity. These archetypical individuals reside in Istanbul; as well as in Athens or Yerevan or the plains of Montana.

The mission of this work is to place the cause of this ongoing catastrophe at the feet of four narcissistic, arrogant, and corrupt old men who, without careful understanding or study, decided they could conjure up and demand a new world order. Four old men who naively thought their creation would provide lasting peace, with them at the top of this new world order relishing the power that ruling the world might bring them. It blames the sycophants who thought that by standing close enough to these celebrated fools, they might enjoy some of that power.

This is a wake up call to those who think that ends always justify means. It is a demonstration of how corruption, arrogance and greed have flourished in spite of the fact that everyone can acknowledge intellectually that these characteristics are the source of all destruction in our world.

To those apologists for the Republic of Turkey who will decry this story as a lie, it is an understandable attempt at 'Say it isn't so!' They will be outraged by the defamation of the "father of modern Turkey." Above all, they will claim as loudly as they can, that the holocaust portrayed here never happened, and, in fact, that the fire of Smyrna was set either by Armenian terrorists or Greek soldiers. Instead of facing the glaring contradictory points that most Armenian and Greek men had been taken prisoner by then, and the Greek military had already been evacuated to Mytilene. They, like Americans who still believe that George Washington came clean about chopping down the cherry tree, will never give up their idol.

Those innocent refugees who perished on the quay cannot be returned to their families. The innocent Muslim families that were forced to be victim to the rage of abused Christians as a consequence of their leader's brutal bloodlust, also cannot be undone.

When ordinary people live their lives as families who raise their children and visit with their neighbors, no matter what their religion, there is no possibility of a spontaneous holocaust. It is only when the lust for power, coupled with ignorance, and a deep-seated self loathing, push them to take by force what they cannot achieve by deed.

We stand beyond the 90th anniversary of the burning of Smyrna, and as you already know, things are no better. In fact, things are worse. The killing of innocents continues as the sick psychopaths who lead nations by the sword, intimidate and abuse others in order to elevate themselves.

A modern Greek or Armenian, cannot blame their Turkish counterpart for the sins of their fathers. Neither can the modern Turk blame the Greek or the Armenian. They must all set down their country's flag long enough to see the inhumanity that had drawn our fathers to the dark side. Once admitted, there is no lie to defend. Turk, Greek and Armenian can move forward to see it does not happen again.

We are closing in on a century since the total destruction of 'Jewel of the Near East.' What have we learned since then?
Yes! That's the point. We've learned nothing, because instead of looking to what we've done before, we just keeping repeating those sins of our fathers.
- The peace that followed the '*war to end all wars*,' only lasted seventeen days before Russia invaded Estonia.
- The peace dictated by the Paris Peace Conference and the League of Nations to make sure a Great War of nations would never reoccur, only had to wait two decades before they would have to start numbering the World Wars.

And where are we today? Rogue states feverishly develop nuclear weapons, so that they can intimidate their way to world power. Dictators mask their low self-esteem by abusing their own countrymen. Leaders of the supposed civilized countries keep spending money they don't have to garner enough votes to stay in power. The world keeps turning end over end as it is being flushed down hell's toilet.

And yet the example of Asa K. Jennings, where there was no hope, he found hope and overcame the impossibility of his situation to accomplish the impossible. So it is what faces all those who despair at the current state of our world. The hope of our salvation will come from ordinary people who will overcome extraordinary circumstances.

Cast of Characters
(alphabetical)

The use of silhouettes instead of photos in some instances was due to the fact that either a photo could not be found or permission/license was unavailable at the time of publication.

ALEXANDER, KING OF GREECE
(Aug 1, 1893 - Oct 25, 1920)
The second son of Constantine I, King of Greece, Alexander succeeded his father in 1917 by virtue of Constantine's forced abdication. Alexander had no political experience and was rendered powerless by his Prime Minister, Eleftherios Venizelos. After receiving a monkey bite, Alexander's death caused a political upheaval that eventually brought back his father as King of Greece and the resignation of Venizelos as Prime Minister.

APOSTOLIDIS (APOSTOLIDES) LAZAROS, CAPTAIN GREEK ARMY
(c. 1880- after1922)
The captain's last name suggests that he was originally from Asia Minor. Historical texts place him in Kastoria, a city in northern Greece in the region of Western Macedonia where Apostolides led a band of partisans that fought against the Internal Macedonian Revolutionary Organization (IMRO) a Bulgarian revolutionary group. Later, Apostolides' band moved to an area outside Drama, where he first met the Metropolitan Bishop of Drama, Chrysostomos. He entered the Greek army during World War I, and reached the rank of Captain. He then was part of the occupation forces that landed in Smyrna in 1919. It was likely his earlier relationship with Chrysostomos that resulted in General Papoulas assigning him to accompany foreign correspondent, Dr. Herbert Adams Gibbons, to the city of Aidin, so that Gibbons could report on the massacre of 5,000 Christians, by the Muslim population. Apostolides is later used as a character to be interviewed by Gibbons, and also as a retreating soldier driven to burn Greek villages on their trek to Smyrna. It is likely he was part of the evacuated Greek forces from Smyrna, and subsequently, was likely part of the Greek coup invasion forces that occupied Thessaloniki or Athens.

Athinogenis, Antonios Esq.
Attorney
(1874-1963)
One of two official delegates of the Christian Micrasiatic Defense (aka Micrasiatic Army) that was formed to resist the efforts of the Allied Ministers proposing that the Greek army evacuate the territory, thereby permitting the country to come under the rule of Mustapha Kemal. The delegates traveled to New York City to raise awareness of their plan to defend the Christian minorities in Asia Minor with a new independent native force. Athinogenis, fluent in Greek and English, acted as the translator for the interview held at New York's Commodore Hotel.

Balfour, Arthur James, 1st Earl of Balfour,
Prime Minister of Great Britain
(Jul 25 1848 - Dec 5, 1930)
Born in Scotland, Balfour was a British Conservative politician and statesman who served as Prime Minister from 1902 - 1905. He served as First Lord of the Admiralty before joining Lloyd George's coalition government as Foreign Secretary. In the context of the Paris Peace Conference, he was credited promising the Jews a homeland in Palestine.

Barnes, Maynard Bertram
U.S. Vice-Consul in Smyrna
(Jun 28, 1897- Aug 2, 1970)
Born in Minnesota, Barnes was appointed the U.S. Vice-Consul in Patras Greece in 1919 and then as Vice-Consul in Smyrna from 1921 to 1922. After the Smyrna disaster, he then became U.S. Consul in Constantinople in 1923 to 1924.

Beinoglou, Stephanos
Delegate CMD
One of two official delegates of the Christian Micrasiatic Defense (aka Micrasiatic Army) that was formed to resist the efforts of the Allied Ministers proposing that the Greek army evacuate the territory, thereby permitting the country to come under the rule of Mustapha Kemal. The delegates traveled to New York City to raise awareness of their plan to defend the Christian minorities in Asia Minor with a new independent native force. Beinoglou, as spokesman for the mission, utilized Athinogenis as the translator for the Interview held at New York's Commodore Hotel.

BLISS, TASKER H.
GENERAL U.S. ARMY
(Dec 31, 1853 - Nov 9, 1930)
Born in Pennsylvania, Bliss entered West Point. He served at the rank of Major in the Spanish-American War and later became Collector of Customs in Cuba. He was promoted to brigadier general under Teddy Roosevelt. He was promoted to chief of general staff during World War I and after retirement, was recalled to serve as Plenipotentiary at the Paris Peace Conference.

BRISTOL, MARK LAMBERT
REAR ADMIRAL U.S. NAVY
(Apr 17, 1868 - May 13, 1939)
Born in New Jersey, Bristol graduated from the United States Naval Academy and served in the Spanish-American War. He commanded the USS *Oklahoma* during World War I and was promoted to Rear-Admiral in the United States Navy, where he served as the United States' High Commissioner in Asia Minor (Turkey). Based in Constantinople (Istanbul), he was in charge of all U.S. Navy operations in Asia Minor and Mediterranean waters. Bristol ordered that no navy personnel could assist any Christian refugee, and that they were there to protect American citizens and assets only. As the American delegate, he led the Interallied Commission of Enquiry to Smyrna investigating alleged Greek atrocities perpetrated against innocent Muslim Turks after the occupation of Smyrna by Greek forces in May 1919. Bristol was the author of most of the report.

BROCK, SIR OSMOND DE BEAUVOIR
ADMIRAL BRITISH FLEET
(1869 - Oct 15, 1947)
Born on the British island of Guernsey, Brock joined the British Navy in 1882. He was engaged in naval engagements in the North Sea during World War I thereafter becoming a Deputy Chief of Naval Staff. As a British Admiral, he was Commander-in-Chief of the Mediterranean Fleet. During the Smyrna crisis he served as the commander of the HMS *Iron Duke* that was stationed in the Bay of Smyrna. He is credited with ordering music to be played during dinner aboard ship in order to drown out the screams of minority Christians who were burning alive on the quay.

Brown, Constantine
Journalist
(1890 - Feb 24, 1966)
Brown was an American journalist in both Washington D.C. and abroad. After obtaining a Ph.D. in political science at the University of Berlin, Brown was in Cambridge England doing post-graduate work when WWI began. He covered the Russian revolution for the London Times and was the first newspaperman ever to interview Lenin. During the Greco-Turkish War, he was one of the journalists chosen by Admiral Bristol to report on only Greek atrocities.

Bunter, Benjamin
Seaman British Navy
Bunter was serving as a British seaman aboard the Iron Duke, under Admiral Brock during the burning of Smyrna. While standing on deck, Bunter witnessed Christian refugees hanging from the quay in Smyrna in order to escape the intense heat of the fire. He then saw Turkish soldiers using their scimitars to sever the victims' arms so that they would fall into the sea. He watched hundreds die in front of his eyes.

Bunoust, Gen.
General French Army
A general in the French army, Bunoust was appointed as the French delegate to the Inter-Allied Commission of Enquiry ordered by Prime Minister Georges Clemenceau, to investigate alleged Greek atrocities perpetrated against innocent Muslim Turks after the occupation of Smyrna by Greek forces in May 1919.

Chakerian, Anita
Teacher
(Jul 4, 1898 - Nov 14, 1993)
Anita Chakerian, a young teacher at the American Collegiate Institute, saw the Turkish guards dragging large sacks into the building, which they deposited in various corners. The soldiers said they were bringing rice and potatoes because they knew the people were hungry and would soon have nothing left to eat. They warned sacks were not to be opened until the bread was exhausted. Such unexpected generosity led one of the sailors to investigate; the bags held gunpowder and dynamite.

CHEREFEDDIN BEY,
CAPTAIN, TURKISH NATIONALIST CAVALRY
As an officer in Turkish Nationalist Cavalry, Cherefeddin led the first cavalry troops into Smyrna after the evacuation by Greek troops the day before. The mounted troops rode in a column of two, with some troops holding their swords held over their heads. Cherefeddin suffered a gash to his face as he was hit by a grenade that was thrown from the crowd. The grenade failed to explode. Instead of reacting, Cherefeddin dismounted and broke the soldier's rifle across his knee before remounting and continuing the procession.

CHURCHILL, SIR WINSTON
SECRETARY OF STATE FOR WAR
(Oct 26, 1874 - Apr 7, 1965)
Born into British aristocracy, Churchill served in British politics for more than 50 years and is regarded as one of the greatest wartime leaders of the 20th century. He was best known for his leadership of the United Kingdom during World War II. He became Secretary of State for War in 1919 and thus participated in the Paris Peace Conference. In 1921 he became Secretary of State for the Colonies and had input into the British efforts in Asia Minor.

CLAYTON, JOHN
JOURNALIST
Clayton was an American journalist. During the Greco-Turkish War, he was one of the two journalists chosen by Admiral Bristol to report on only Greek atrocities. While watching Christians being burned, shot or drowned to death, Clayton sat aboard the USS *Litchfield* and typed out an erroneous report ignoring the holocaust going on in front of him. Later, after the ships had taken on as many refugees as would fit, Clayton could no longer write erroneous reports in exchange for access. He began to tell what he saw.

CLEMENCEAU, GEORGES
PRIME MINISTER OF FRANCE
(Sep 28, 1841 - Nov 24, 1929)
Clemenceau was a French statesman who began his career as a writer and political activist became Prime Minister of France during World War I, and was one of the principal architects of the Treaty of Versailles at the Paris Peace Conference of 1919. Although he was a trained doctor, he never practiced medicine. Fluent in English as well as French, and since the Conference was to be held in Paris, he was deemed the President of the Conference. During the Conference he was almost assassinated when a gunman shot him as he left his house en-route to a meeting for the Conference. He was recognized because he always wore a pair of gloves to hide a severe case of eczema.

Constantine I,
King of Greece
(Aug 2, 1868 - Jan 11, 1923)
Constantine I was the King of Greece from 1913 to 1917 and then from 1920 to 1922. He was the only monarch to abdicate the throne twice. Because of family ties to the Central Powers, and his refusal to support the Allied Powers, he was forced to resign as King by Venizelos who then had Greece enter the war on the side of the England and France. After his son Alexander, now king, died of a monkey bite, Constantine returned to the throne, but once again was forced to abdicate after the humiliating defeat of the Greco-Turkish War.

Cottin, Louis Emile
Carpenter
(Mar 14, 1896 - Sep 8, 1937)
Born into a working class family, he became a carpenter. By 1915, he met several anarchists and maintained close friendships with them. After witnessing municipals guards fire on strikers at a munitions factory, he became profoundly disgusted with Clemenceau and decided to kill him. On Feb 19, 1919, Cottin fired 7 shots at Clemenceau who was in his car. Six of the seven shots missed and Clemenceau survived the attempt.

Crocker, Louis E.
Chief Warrant Officer, U.S. Marines
Crocker was a Marine Chief Warrant Officer aboard the destroyer U.S.S. *Litchfield,* who commanded a naval guard of 17 sailors, assigned to protect the staff of the American International College at Smyrna. During this assignment, as Turkish troops were seen looting a campus property, Crocker and a small group of sailors, accompanied College President MacLachlan to confront the offending Turkish soldiers. As a result MacLachlan and Crocker were both stripped and beaten.

Dall'Olio, A.
Lieutenant General, Italian Army
A lieutenant general in the Italian army, Dall'Olio was appointed as the Italian delegate to the Inter-Allied Commission of Enquiry ordered by Prime Minister Georges Clemenceau, to investigate alleged Greek atrocities perpetrated against innocent Muslim Turks after the occupation of Smyrna by Greek forces in May 1919.

Davis, Charles Claflin
Director, Red Cross South Eastern Base
(Aug 11, 1873 -   )
A graduate of Harvard Law School, Davis served as the Director of the South Eastern Base of the American Red Cross, headquartered in Constantinople. He led the relief efforts during the catastrophe in Smyrna. Davis personally witnessed and testified to the fact that he saw Turkish military torching buildings in Smyrna which led to the fire that destroyed the city. He also led a group of officials from American charity organizations to meet with General Noreddin Pasha and discuss his intervention to quell the spike in violence and deterioration in order in Smyrna on September 11, 1922.

Davis, John W.
U.S. Ambassador to the United Kingdom
(Apr 13, 1873 - Mar 24, 1955)
Davis was an American politician, diplomat and lawyer. He served as a Congressman from West Virginia, Solicitor General and later as Ambassador to the United Kingdom under President Woodrow Wilson. He was best known as the Democratic candidate for President during the 1924 presidential election, but lost to Calvin Coolidge. In the context of this story, Davis was the Ambassador in London when he discovered that England and France were having secret negotiations to keep American out of the middle eastern oil fields.

d'Espèrey, Louis Franchet
General French Army
(May 25, 1856 - Jul 8, 1942)
Born in French Algeria, d'Espèrey was given command of the French Fifth Army during World War I. Then he was badly defeated by the Germans in 1918, from which he was removed from the Western Front and appointed commander of the Allied armies at Thessaloniki. In Macedonia he was successful in knocking Bulgaria out of the war, but his accomplishment was only possible after Greece sent a three-hundred-thousand man force to support the French in the Battle of Skra fi Legen. It was the Greek force that determined the outcome which resulted in Germany signing the Armistice.

Dobson, Charles
Chaplain, Anglican Church in Smyrna
(Nov 25, 1886 - May 6, 1930)

A New Zealander, Dobson joined the Anglican Church, later becoming a Chaplain-Captain in the New Zealand Expeditionary Forces. He became Chaplain for the Anglican Church of St. John in Smyrna in 1922. Dobson risked his own life to help the refugees during the crisis, He escaped with his family to Malta with 800 other refugees aboard the SS *Bavarian*. Dobson subsequently wrote a report chronicling the Turkish atrocities entitled 'The Smyrna Holocaust' in 1923.

Drage, Charles Harding
Lt. Commander British Navy
(Mar 1897 - 1983)

Drage served as a British Lieutenant aboard the HMS *Cardiff*, during the burning of Smyrna. According to his diary, Drage was responsible for protecting the launch he was in while trying to evacuate people off the quay from being swamped by the rush of desperate refugees. He admitted in his diary that at one point he was forced to beat someone over the head with a tiller in order to save the launch from capsizing. A tiller is a horizontal bar fitted to the head of a boat's rudder post and used as a lever for steering.

Dulles, John Foster
Legal Counsel to American Delegation
(Feb 25, 1888 - May 24, 1959)

Born in Washington DC, Dulles entered politics in 1918 when he was appointed by President Woodrow Wilson as legal counsel to the U.S. delegation of the Paris Peace Conference, where he served under his uncle Secretary of State, Robert Lansing. He later served a Secretary of State under President Dwight D. Eisenhower. In the context of this story, Dr. Gibbons on assignment with the *Christian Science Monitor* admitted to Archbishop Chrysostomos that Dulles informed him he was having difficulty with all the reports of Turkish atrocities, avoiding giving the impression America was only interested in protecting American interests as opposed to helping defenseless Christian minorities.

Dumesmil, Adm.
Admiral, French Navy

French Admiral Dumesmil was the commander of the French fleet stationed in Smyrna Harbor during the crisis. He was stationed aboard the French Navy's armored cruiser *Edgar Quinet*. While Dumesmil was credited with taking part in the evacuation of Christian refugees, in actuality, the *Edgar Quinet* only ferried 75 refugees to Marseilles.

DYER, EDWARD HARRY
BRIGADIER GENERAL, BRITISH INDIAN ARMY
(Oct 9, 1864 - Jul 23, 1927)
Born in the Punjab region of India, Dyer was a temporary brigadier general in the British Indian Army who was responsible for the Jalianwala Bagh massacre in Amritsar. In fact, he was nicknamed the *Butcher of Amritsar*. After ordering his troops to fire on unarmed people, killing hundreds and wounding thousands, Dyer was removed from duty. Oddly enough, he was considered a hero to many pro-imperialistic Britons.

EDIB, HALIDE
TURKISH NOVELIST, ACTIVIST
(1884 - Jan 9, 1964)
Born in Constantinople, Edib was a Turkish novelist and feminist political activist. She was best known for criticizing the social status of Turkish women. Aside from speaking Turkish, Arabic, French, English and Greek, she graduated from an American College. Although labeled by the British as an agitator, she joined Mustapha Kemal's resistance movement and later became a confident of his.

FERDINAND, FRANZ
ARCHDUKE OF AUSTRIA.
(Dec 18, 1863 - Jun 24, 1914)
Born is Austria, Ferdinand was the eldest son of Archduke Karl Ludwig of Austria, who was the younger brother of the Emperor Franz Joseph. When his cousin committed suicide in 1889, Ferdinand became the heir apparent because his father renounced the throne. On Jun 24, 1914, he was assassinated, along with his wife in Sarajevo. This event was considered by many as the trigger in a line of events that led to World War I.

FISHER, EDWARD M.
ASSISTANT DIRECTOR, Y.M.C.A., SMYRNA
Fisher was the physical director for the Smyrna Y.M.C.A. He was the assistant to E.O. Jacobs. Both Fisher and Jacobs went on a vacation shortly after Asa Jennings arrived in Smyrna, leaving Jennings in charge just prior to the destruction of the city. After returning to Constantinople, Fisher would provide a powerful description of the holocaust for the Associated Press, which would be printed in national American newspapers.

Foch, Ferdinand
Field Marshall, French Ninth Army
(Oct 2, 1851 - Mar 20, 1929)
A Frenchman, Foch was a French soldier, military theorist and considered an Allied military hero of World War I. It was Foch who accepted the German request for an armistice. Considered a prophet by some, Foch declared after the Treaty of Versailles, "This is not a peace. It is an armistice for twenty years." World War II began twenty years later. At the end of the Great War, he was promoted to Marshal of France. In the context of this story, Foch was sent to meet President Woodrow Wilson when he returned to France, in order to deliver Clemenceau's demands.

Franklin-Bouillon, Henry
French Socialist Politician
(Sep 3, 1870 - Sep 12, 1937)
A French politician and member of the radical socialist party, was the propaganda minister for the French government. In the context of this story, although Turkey was a supposedly defeated enemy, toward the end of 1921, Franklin-Bouillon showed up in Ankara to sign a treaty with the Turkish government calling for the evacuation of French troops from Cicilia in exchange for future economic concessions. By doing so, France was in effect betraying its ally, Greece.

Frankou (Frankos), Gen.
Brigadier General, Greek South Army
Frankou was the Commandant of Greece's South Army. Later after Greek forces were evacuated to Mytilene, he was placed in charge of all Greek vessels used in the evacuation, that were anchored in Mytilene harbor. In the context of this story, after offering Jennings only six ships for the evacuation and stalling in order to speak to his superiors, Jennings boldly went over his head to deal with the Greek government in Athens.

Gandhi, Mohandas (Mahatma) Karamchand
Indian Political Activist
(Oct 2, 1869 - Jan 30, 1948)
Born in Bombay India, Gandhi traveled to London to study law. Once accepted by the bar, he moved back to India. Unsuccessful due to shyness, he traveled to South Africa and became a civil rights activist. This was a turning point in his life and he returned to India in 1915 to become an activist for Indians. In the context of this story, Gandhi is mentioned as an activist that campaigned for passive resistance and non-cooperation. Subsequent to this campaign, the story relates the Jalianwala Bagh massacre in Amritsar.

Gaylord, Ens.
Ensign, United States Navy
American Ensign Gaylord was given an order by Captain Hepburn to drive to the to the American College and order the sailors to abandon the building. His orders included gathering all Americans and escorting them to the docks. When too many people showed up and Miss Mills refused to leave her staff, three sailors lifter her onto the truck so that Gaylord could drive her away.

George II,
King of Greece
(Jul 20, 1890 - Apr 1, 1947)
Born in the royal villa outside Athens, George was the eldest son of Constantine I of Greece. George pursued a military career with the Prussian Guard, serving in the Balkan War. When Constantine I was exiled the first time, George followed him into exile in 1917. He finally was elevated to the throne when his father was forced into exile a second time in 1922. In the context of this story, Crown Prince George is mentioned as taking the throne when Constantine I abdicates a second time.

Gibbons, Dr. Herbert Adams Ph.D.
American Author/Journalist
(1880-1934)
Gibbons was an author, journalist and served as a foreign correspondent in Asia Minor during the Greco-Turkish War. Aside from his later work writing books and for magazines, Gibbons traveled to Asia Minor for the Christian Science Monitor to chronicle the atrocities of the Turkish soldiers on Greek Christians. In the context of this story, Gibbons tour the city of Aydin with Archbishop Chrysostomos and Captain Apostolides.

Gibbs, Sir Philip
English Journalist/Novelist
(May 1, 1877 - Mar 10, 1962)
An English journalist and novelist who served as one of the five official British reporters during World War I. In the context of this story, Gibbs is mentioned in a conversation between Dr. Gibbons, and the Governor-General of Smyrna Stergiadis, relating his own experience with Archbishop Chrysostomos.

GONATAS, STYLIANOS
COLONEL, GREEK REVOLUTIONARY LEADER
(1876-1966)
Gonatas was a Greek military leader and Venizelist politician, who eventually became Prime Minister of Greece, after a coup forcing Constantine I to abdicate his throne. In the context of this story, Gonatas took over the government of Mytilene while Asa Jennings was ferrying his first refugees from Smyrna. Gonatas led invasion forces to enter Athens. Eventually became Prime Minister of Greece.

GRESCOVITCH, PAUL
COMMANDER, SMYRNA FIRE BRIGADE
As commander of the Smyrna Insurance Company Fire Brigade, Grescovitch wrote a report claiming the fires were being started by Armenians disguised as women or as Turkish soldiers. His report is in complete contradiction with the overwhelming number of witnesses who maintained the fires were a planned and executed operation of the Turkish military to eliminate the minority Christian population in Smyrna.

GRILLET, MICHEL
FRENCH CONSUL SMYRNA
Grillet was the French representative in Smyrna during the crisis of September 1922. In the context of this story, Archbishop Chrysostomos, fearing for the safety of his people, he went to see Grillet, who assured the Prelate he had nothing to worry about, as the French army was due in a mater of days and would protect the population.

HADJINIAN, ARAKEL
STUDENT AT Y.M.C.A MISSION IN SMYRNA
Arakel is a fictitious Armenian name given to the boy who was at the YMCA mission when Asa Jennings designated him as his one permitted servant, so that he could accompany his family to safety. At printing the actual name still had yet to be discovered.

HAMID BEY,
TURKISH ENVOY
Hamid Bey was General Mustapha Kemal's envoy who was used to communicate and disclosure the positions of the Turkish Nationalist Government in Ankara. In the context of the story, Hamid Bey was nothing more than a propagandist for Kemal.

Hamid II, Abdul
Sultan, Ottoman Empire
(Sep 22, 1842 - Feb 10, 1918)
Abdul Hamid II was the 99th caliph and the 34th sultan of the Ottoman Empire. During his reign the Empire suffered a continuous decline in power from 1876 until he was deposed in 1909. He was responsible for the modernization of the Empire. In the context of this story, he is only mentioned in passing referring to his overthrow.

Hare, R. B.
General, British Army
A general in the British army, Hare was appointed as the British delegate to the Inter-Allied Commission of Enquiry ordered by Prime Minister Georges Clemenceau, to investigate alleged Greek atrocities perpetrated against innocent Muslim Turks after the occupation of Smyrna by Greek forces in May 1919.

Harlow, Samuel Ralph
American Clergyman and Missionary
(1885-1972)
Samuel Ralph Harlow was a clergyman and Christian missionary to the Near East with the American Board of Commissioners for Foreign Missions. He also served as professor of religion and Biblical literature at Smith College in Northampton, Massachusetts. Harlow's life and career were characterized by his work as a pacifist, civil rights activist, Zionist, international lecturer, and author of A Life After Death and several other books on religion, social action, and paranormal phenomena. He was a professor at International College in Smyrna from 1912 to 1922. In the context of this story, he is mentioned as speaking after Senator Henry Cabot Lodge in Boston, in an effort to raise awareness and support for the Greek refugees.

Harington, Sir Charles Harington
General, British Army
(May 31, 1872 - Oct 22, 1940)
Harrington was a British army officer during World War I. Between 1918 and 1920, he commanded the occupation forces in the Black Sea and Turkey. In the context of this story, General Harrington put Britain on a war footing after Turkish forces invaded the neutral zone and Britain was preparing to return to war against Turkey for a second time.

Harding, Warren G.
29th President of the United States
(Nov 2, 1865 - Aug 2, 1923)
Mentioned once in the cheers of Greek soldiers greeting Archbishop.

HARTUNIAN, REV. ABRAHAM
ARMENIAN EVANGELICAL CLERGYMAN
Hartunian was an Armenian clergyman who was from the city of Marash, where Mustapha Kemal, eliminated thousands of Armenian refugees. In the context of this story, Hartunian records in his diary, how he witnessed Turkish soldiers lighting the fires that destroyed Smyrna.

HATCHERIAN, DR. GARABED
ARMENIAN PHYSICIAN
(1876-1952)
Having lived through the horror of the burning of Smyrna, Hatcherian an Armenian physician wrote a journal about his experiences that was published under the title 'An Armenian Doctor in Turkey.' In the context of this story, some of Hatcherian's eye-witness testimony is described.

HATZIANESTIS, GEORGE
COMMANDER IN CHIEF, GREEK ARMIES
(1863-1922)
General Hatzianestis was in command of the Greek army in Thrace, when he was asked to become the Commander in Chief of the Asia Minor army. Thought to fluctuate between unbalanced and completely mad, he was thought to be incapable of leading an army. After disastrous handling of the Turkish offensive, he was later accused of high treason and executed as one of the *'Trial of Six'.*

HEPBURN, ARTHUR "JAPY"
CHIEF OF STAFF, U.S. NAVAL DETACHMENT-TURKEY
(Oct 15, 1877 - May 31, 1964)
A graduate of the U.S. Naval Academy, Hepburn served during the Spanish-American War. He was Rear-Admiral Bristol's Chief of Staff in Constantinople and served aboard the U.S.S. *Lawrence* when it was stationed in the Bay of Smyrna. He was responsible for the evacuation of thousands of refugees from the quay. He would later become Commander in Chief of the U.S. Atlantic Fleet.

HOLE, EDWYN CECIL
BRITISH VICE-CONSUL IN SMYRNA
(1889-1976)
Known as 'Teddy' to his friends, Hole was a young British Vice-Consul in Smyrna and Mytilene. He had studied Oriental languages at Pembroke College, Cambridge before entering the Levant Consular service. In addition to working for the protection of British nationals in Smyrna, Hole also worked to assist the refugees in leaving the city. Hole plays a much larger part in the story, in that he is used to educate Jennings (and therefore provide exposition of background to the reader) about the history of Asia Minor, the Greeks, the Armenians and the Turks.

HOLE, LAURA
WIFE OF EDWYN CECIL HOLE
(1899-1988)
Born in Smyrna of Prussian, French and Italian descent, Laura's family had lived in Asia Minor since the 18th century. She married Edwyn Hole in Smyrna in 1919, after she left school in Paris to return to Smyrna. She was an accomplished pianist. Laura and Edwyn were active socially until the fire that destroyed the city. She is used as a character in the story at a social dinner to introduce certain characters and exposition of certain known positions on the prevailing issues in Smyrna at the time.

HORTON, CATHERINE
WIFE OF U.S. GENERAL CONSUL, GEORGE HORTON
Born Catherine Sakopoulos, she married Horton in 1909. She is used as a character in the story at a social dinner to introduce certain characters and exposition of certain known positions on the prevailing issues in Smyrna at the time.

HORTON, GEORGE
U.S. GENERAL CONSUL IN SMYRNA
(1859-1942)
Horton had served as U.S. General Consul in Athens and Thessaloniki prior to becoming General Consul at Smyrna. During the destruction of the city, Horton was responsible for protecting Americans and their assets. But being a Grecophile, he also tried to help the refugees to the extent he could under his standing orders to only help Americans.

House, Edward M.
Advisor to President Woodrow Wilson
(Jul 26, 1858 - Mar 28, 1938)

A Texas born American diplomat, politician and presidential advisor, House inherited a fictitious rank of Colonel although he had no military experience. He served as an advisor to President Woodrow Wilson. In the context of this story, House accompanies President Wilson to the Paris Peace Conference and serves as his liaison with the other delegates.

Howes, Charles
Lieutenant, British Royal Navy

Howe was a young British Lieutenant assigned to the H.M.S. *King George V* anchored in the Bay of Smyrna. Howes kept a diary of the events he saw unfolding in front of him. His recollections are used in the story to relate what he personally witnessed.

Hughes, Charles Evans
U.S. Secretary of State
(Apr 11, 1862 - Aug 27, 1948)

Born in New York State, Hughes worked as a lawyer and a professor at Cornell University before becoming Governor of New York. He was later appointed as an associate justice of the U.S. Supreme Court. He resigned from the Supreme Court to run for President in 1916. After losing the election, in 1921 he was appointed as Secretary of State under President Harding. He would later be appointed as Chief Justice. In the context of this story, Hughes receives a telegram from Admiral Bristol indicating the Turks had burned Smyrna except for the Turkish quarter.

Jacob, Ernst Otto "Jake"
Traveling Secretary, Y.M.C.A. Mission
(1886 - 1966)

Jacob was the traveling secretary for the YMCA stationed in Smyrna at the time of its destruction. He was Asa Jennings' boss at the mission in Smyrna and his diaries are used to relate events occurring at the time. In the context of this story, Jennings arrived in Smyrna just in time so that Jacob could go on vacation, leaving Jennings in charge. Both experienced the destruction of Smyrna.

Jacob, Sarah
Wife of E.O. Jacob

The wife of E.O. Jacob, in the context of this story she is used as a character at a social dinner to introduce certain characters and exposition of certain known positions on the prevailing issues in Smyrna at the time.

Jennings, Amy W.
Wife of Asa K. Jennings
(Nov 4, 1876 - May 19, 1970)
The wife of Asa K. Jennings, Amy accompanied Asa on his overseas assignments and until she was placed aboard an evacuation ship was in Smyrna at the time of its destruction. She is used to relate early experiences of the family, the trip to Smyrna and at a dinner of characters for exposition of issues and positions on the events.

Jennings, Asa K.
Boys' Secretary, Y.M.C.A.
(Sep 20, 1877 - Jan 27, 1933)
The improbable hero of this story, Jennings retired as a farmer and Methodist minister from upstate New York, to become an employee of the International YMCA. Transferred to the YMCA mission in Smyrna, Asia Minor in August, 1922, he almost single-handedly was responsible for the rescue of hundreds of thousands of minority Christians, facing imminent death. He later went on to oversee the rescue of millions of minority Christians from Asia Minor in what was called the 'Great Population Exchange.'

Jennings, Asa W.
Elder Son of Asa K. Jennings
(Jun 26, 1907 - Jun 15, 1972)
At fifteen years old, the eldest son of Asa K. Jennings, he accompanied his family to Smyrna and remained with his father to assist him in his efforts to save the refugees. He later went on to perform government work and relief efforts to assist Turkey during World War II and afterwards. He is used as a character in the story to relate the family trip to Smyrna.

Jennings, Bertha
Daughter of Asa K. Jennings
(May 10, 1914 - Dec 11, 1977)
At eight years old, Bertha was the only daughter of the Jennings. She accompanied her parents on their overseas assignments. She is used as a character in the story to relate the family trip to Smyrna.

Jennings, Wilbur
Younger Son of Asa K. Jennings
(Jul 18, 1909 - Nov 1, 1995)
At thirteen years old, Wilbur was the younger son of the Jennings. He accompanied his parents on their overseas assignments. He is used as a character in the story to relate the family trip to Smyrna.

JOHNSON, MELVIN
SAILOR, U.S. NAVY
An American sentry guarding the college in Paradise, Johnson could not continue to stand down and defied his orders not to assist the refugees. In the context of this story, Johnson's quotes are used to express his reactions to the horror of the events around him.

JOSEPH I, FRANZ
EMPEROR OF AUSTRIA
(Aug 18, 1830 - Nov 21, 1916)
Emperor Franz Joseph I, was the Emperor of Austria, Apostolic King of Hungary, King of Bohemia, King of Croatia, King of Galicia and Lodomeria and the Grand Duke of Cracow. When his nephew Ferdinand was assassinated, he responded by invading Serbia, and beginning the chain of events that would become known as World War I.

KALAFATIS, CHRYSOSTOMOS
MARTYRED ARCHBISHOP OF SMYRNA
(1867- Sep 10, 1922)
The Greek Archbishop of Smyrna, an outspoken shepherd of his people, was known to have been a partisan in Macedonia in his earlier years, refused to flee Smyrna, knowing he would be sacrificed. He died at the hands of a Turkish mob, becoming a martyr, later elevated to sainthood in the Greek Orthodox Church. In the context of this story, the Archbishop was a major character in the events that preceded the destruction of the city. His path crossed many of those who met with him as the leader of the Greek population in the city.

KALFA, MABEL
TEACHER, INTER-COLLEGIATE INSTITUTE IN SMYRNA
A teacher at the Institute in Smyrna, Kalfa worked under the supervision of Ms. Minnie Mills. In the context of the story, Kalfa witnesses Turkish soldiers lighting fires in nearby buildings.

KARACHAN, MINISTER
ACTING FOREIGN MINISTER OF RUSSIA
Karachan is mentioned at the end of the book as being the acting Russian Foreign Minister who travels to Ankara to offer Russia's support against Great Britain in controlling the Black Sea and the Dardanelles.

KATSAROS, EMMANUEL
FIREMAN, SMYRNA FIRE BRIGADE
Katsaros was one of the Greek fireman in Smyrna later called to be a witness in a lawsuit against the insurers of the warehouses in Smyrna that were destroyed. In the context of the story, Katsaros must tell someone of the atrocities he's just witnesses while carrying out his duties.

KEMAL, MUSTAPHA "ATATÜRK"
GENERAL TURKISH NATIONALIST FORCES
(May 19, 1881 - Nov 10, 1938)
The revolutionary general of the Turkish Nationalist rebel force, later to become known by the Turks as the 'Father of Modern Turkey.' With the secret alliances formed with France and Italy, he defeated the Greek armies who were over extended in their pursuit of Turkish forces, became easy prey for the well-supplied well-trained regular Turkish armies fighting in the Anatolian interior. Kemal engineered the humiliating Greek defeat resulting in the mass retreat in Smyrna. Kemal appears as a major character in the story.

KEMAL BEY, YUSUF
TURKISH MINISTER OF FOREIGN AFFAIRS
(1878 - Apr 15, 1938)
Yusuf is mentioned in the story as the recipient of a telegram from Mustapha Kemal in which the Turkish leader provides a view of the fire in Smyrna that completely contradicts the witness testimony. The telegram purports to suggest that the Turkish forces did everything in their power to put out the fires and protect the population of Smyrna.

KENWORTHY, JOSEPH, LT. COMMANDER
MP, HOUSE OF COMMONS
(1886-1953)
Baron Kenworthy was a minister of Parliament during the time of the Smyrna tragedy. In the context of the story, Kenworthy openly opposes Lloyd Gorge in Parliament regarding his support for the Greek government in the war with Turkey.

KILIÇ ALI BEY,
CAPTAIN, TURKISH NATIONALIST ARMY
Kiliç Ali Bey is a fictitious Turkish name given to a Kurd officer under General Mustapha Kemal, who was responsible for the deportation and murder of Armenian civilians in Marash, after the defeat of French troops occupying the city. At printing the actual name still had yet to be discovered.

KNAUSS, HARRISON E.
LIEUTENANT COMMANDER, U.S. NAVY
Lieutenant Commander Knauss, the officer in charge of the guards at the American Sentry headquarters is mentioned in the story for filing a report regarding what he saw during the Smyrna tragedy.

LAMB, SIR HARRY HARLING
BRITISH CONSUL-GENERAL AT SMYRNA
(Sep 15, 1857 - 1948)
Sir Harry was the British General Consul at Smyrna, who was charged with the protection of British citizens and interests in Asia Minor. He ordered the evacuation of British citizens from Smyrna on to British warships anchored in the harbor. Lamb is a minor character in this story. He also was a British official working with the Ottoman Empire in Macedonia and was instrumental in having Archbishop Chrysostomos exiled from Drama, Macedonia.

LANE, RUFUS W.
SMYRNA BUSINESSMAN
A Smyrna businessman and former Consul-General of Smyrna (1898-1905) rallied others to begin a relief effort for the refugees once he saw the U.S. government ordered the U.S. Navy to stand down. In the context of the story, Lane attends a meeting of concerned citizens and inspires the group to begin feeding the starving masses.

LINDLEY, SIR FRANCIS OSWALD
BRITISH AMBASSADOR TO GREECE
(Jun 12, 1872 - Aug 17, 1950)
Sir Francis Lindley was the British Ambassador to Greece between 1922 and 1923. In the story, he is mentioned to have discovered the secret agreement between Great Britain and France to share the oilfields of Mesopotamia.

LLOYD-GEORGE, DAVID
PRIME MINISTER OF GREAT BRITAIN
(Jan 17, 1863 - Mar 26, 1945)
Lloyd-George was a British liberal politician and statesman. He ultimately became Prime Minister of the United Kingdom leading a wartime coalition government between 1916 and 1922. At the end of World War I, Lloyd-George became one of the *'Big Four'* ministers at the Paris Peace Conference and the main promoter of Greece occupying Asia Minor. He is a minor character in the story based upon his participation in the Paris Peace Conference.

LODGE, HENRY CABOT, JR.
U.S. REPUBLICAN SENATOR FROM MASSACHUSETTS
(May 12, 1850 - Nov 9, 1924)
Lodge was a leader the U.S. Senate, known for his positions on foreign policy. He was openly opposed to the Treaty of Versailles because it didn't call for an unconditional surrender. In the context of the story, when President Wilson returns to the U.S. to promote his League of Nations, Lodge releases a round-robin statement showing that the push to agree to a treaty will not pass the Senate.

LOVEJOY, DR. ESTHER
AMERICAN DOCTOR
(Nov 16, 1869 - Aug 31, 1967)
Lovejoy was an American doctor who volunteered to come to Smyrna to assist in the relief effort, arriving after the fire, she immediately understood the magnitude of crisis. She worked tirelessly to ease the plight of refugee women and children in the midst of no sanitation, and brutality inflicted by Turkish soldiers.

MACLACHLAN, DR. ALEXANDER
FOUNDER & PRESIDENT, AMERICAN INT'L COLLEGE
(1859 - Sep 9, 1940)
Reverend MacLachlan, a Canadian, was the founder and President of the American International College in Smyrna. From his later writings, it is clear that MacLachlan was staunchly pro-Turkish and consequently anti-Greek. His writings, even suggest his one-time close friend, Archbishop Chrysostomos, became an abuser of Turkish citizens in Smyrna, even though it is contradicted by the overwhelming testimony ascribing to Chrysostomos' nature. Even though MacLachlan is stripped and beaten unconscious by the Turkish chettes found looting a campus property, he continued to maintain his pro-Turkish stance.

MACLACHLAN, ROSALIND "ROSE" (BLACKLER)
WIFE OF DR. MACLACHLAN
(Mar 23, 1866 - 1940)
The wife of Alexander MacLachlan, Rose is a minor character that appears at a dinner party for the purpose of welcoming Asa Jennings to the American community in Smyrna. The dinner party used as exposition of background of events and issues in Smyrna at the time.

MALLET, SIR LOUIS DU PAN
BRITISH AMBASSADOR AT CONSTANTINOPLE
(Jul 10, 1864 - Aug 8, 1936)
Mallet is mentioned in the story as one of the men looking over the shoulder of the Big Four, while they carve out borders for the new world.

MARSELOS, PANAYIOTIS
GREEK REFUGEE SURVIVOR OF SMYRNA
Greek survivor. Panayiotis Marselos was a soldier. He had been serving in Thrace but was sent to Smyrna in August 1922 to accompany and deliver a group of soldiers who had been tried in a military court and found guilty. He was in Smyrna when the Turkish army entered the city and the fires began, starting with the Armenian neighborhood.

MARESCOTTI, COUNT LUIGI ALDOVANDI
SENATOR, KINGDOM OF ITALY
(Oct 5, 1876 - Jul 9, 1945)
Maresctti is briefly mentioned early in the story as he was chosen to call the first plenary session of the Paris Peace Conference to order.

MAXWELL, ARTHUR
MAJOR, BRITISH ROYAL NAVY
An officer aboard the HMS Iron Duke, Maxwell is used in the story to relate his eyewitness account. While watching through binoculars aboard the *Iron Duke*, Maxwell observes Turkish soldiers pouring water over a crowd of refugees, only to be horrified as the water bursts into flames as it touches the victims.

MAZARAKIS (-AINIAN), ALEXANDROS
COLONEL, GREEK ARMY, SMYRNA DIVISION
(1874-1943)
Mazarakis is mentioned as being the non-voting Greek observer for the Interallied Commission of Enquiry on Smyrna. rIn the context of the story, Mazarakis was not allowed to be present when Turkish witnesses testified, essentially proving the commission was essentially a kangaroo court.

McCALLAM, EMILY
DIR, INTERCOLLEGIATE INSTITUTE IN SMYRNA.
Ms. McCallam, is briefly mentioned in the story when she arrives in Smyrna on the day after the fire began. She describes the horror of charred bodies filling the bay.

MEHMED, VI
36TH AND LAST SULTAN OF THE OTTOMAN EMPIRE
(Jan 14, 1861 - May 16, 1926)
The Sultan is briefly mentioned in the story as he who signed the Treaty of Sevres freeing Greek and Armenian Christians from Ottoman rule. Because the Treaty was signed by someone not recognized by Kemal, he was able to ignore the terms of the treaty.

MERRILL, AARON STANTON
(1890-1961)
Lieutenant Commander Merrill was the Intelligence Officer on the staff of Rear-Admiral Bristol. Merrill tended to parrot Bristol's pro-Turkish leaning based upon what was best for America in Asia Minor. He is a character in the story, because he is appealed to by other major characters in their efforts to avoid a humanitarian disaster.

MIAZZI, CONSUL
ITALIAN CONSUL AT SMYRNA
Miazzi is mentioned in the story when Jennings is faced with a perceived opportunity to utilize an Italian ship to rescue refugees. He confronts Miazzi at the home of an Italian citizen in Smyrna.

MILLERAND, ALEXANDRE
PRIME MINISTER OF FRANCE
(Feb 10, 1859 - Apr 7, 1943)
Having replaced Clemenceau as Prime Minister, Millerand used the return of the Greek king to justify his secret support and supply of the Turkish armies.

MILLS, MISS MINNIE
DEAN, COLLEGIATE INSTITUTE FOR GIRLS
(Jan 17, 1888 - Feb 26, 1952
An American teacher, Mills was in charge of the Shool for Girls when the fire broke out and was responsible for getting her American staff to safety. She is used in the story to describe her witnessing Turkish soldiers lighting the fires that destroyed the city.

MILNE, GEORGE
FIELD MARSHAL BRITISH ROYAL ARMY
(1866-1948)
Field Marshall Milne, also the 1st Baron Milne, was a British military commander. In march 1920, Milne led the British forces to occupy Constantinople, in order to discourage Kemalist forces from doing the same.

MILNER, ALFRED
1ST VISCOUNT MILNER
(Mar 23, 1854 - May 13, 1925)
Milner was a British statesman who was one of the most important members of Lloyd George's War Cabinet in World War I. In the context of this story, Milner was at the Paris Peace Conference, assisting Lloyd George and a part of the various meetings of the Supreme Council..

Morganthau, Henry Sr.
U. S. Ambassador to the Ottoman Empire
(1856-1946)
Morganthau was the United States Ambassador to the Ottoman Empire during World War I. He was identified as the most prominent American to speak out against Turkish atrocities of minority Christians in Asia Minor. He is a minor character mentioned in the story in that he took part in the American efforts to help the refugees.

Murcelle Pasha,
Cavalry General Turkish Army
(1873- Feb 18, 1932)
Mentioned once as it was his cavalry that marched into Smyrna behind the retreating Greek troops.

Nicolson, Sir Arthur
1st Baron Carnok, British Politician
(Sep 19, 1849 - Nov 5, 1928)
Nicholson is briefly mentioned as the father of Harold Nicholson, who plays an important role in the presentment of the early days of the Paris Peace Conference.

Nicolson, Sir Harold George
British Diplomat
(Nov 21, 1886 - May 1, 1968)
A British diplomat, author and politician. Born in Tehran, Persia the son of a Baron. Nicholson was a young diplomat working for the British delegation at the Paris Peace Conference. In the context of the story, he plays a role in advising the Greek Prime Minister and points to the irony of the Big Four without any knowledge or expertise, carving up continents for their own benefit.

Nider, Konstantinos
Lieutenant General, Greek Army
(1865 - 1942)
There is a brief mention of Nider as a possible choice for heading up the new revolutionary Greek cabinet after the coup in 1922. He was a long-serving, battle-seasoned officer. He is listed here for reference.

Nitti, Francesco Saverio
Prime Minister of Italy
(Jul 19, 1868 - Feb 20, 1953)
Nitti was an Italian economist and radical political figure. He served as the Prime Minister of Italy between 1919 - 1920. He replaced Vittorio Orlando at the Paris Peace Conference. In the context of the story, Nitti, takes Orlando's place and plays an integral part of the disaster.

Noureddin Pasha, Ibrahim
Military Governor of Smyrna
(1873- Feb 18, 1932)
Noureddin Pasha was the commander of the Turkish National Central Army in the Pontus. Known to have brutal leanings, he is credited with the order to deport all Greek males between 16 and 50 years old. He was infamous among Greeks and Armenians for his advocacy of extermination of the Greek and Armenian races. He was later appointed the Military Governor of Smyrna, and is credited with ordering the mutilation and murder of Greek Archbishop Chrysostomos.

Onassis, Aristotle
Businessman
(Jan 20 1906 - Mar 15, 1975)
A native of Smyrna, Onassis, a shrewd sixteen year old of a wealthy Greek family, managed to bribe Turkish officials and somehow obtain passage out of the city. Onassis would later become one of the world's most celebrated shipowners and members of the international jet set, culminating in this marriage to Jacqueline Kennedy. He is a minor character in this story by virtue of having lived through the incident.

Onassis, Socrates
Father of Aristotle Onassis
The senior Onassis is briefly mentioned as one of the wealthier Smyrniotes who are imprisoned. In the context of the story, it is his son who outsmarts his Turkish oppressors and manages to secure his rescue out of imminent disaster.

ORLANDO, VITTORIO EMANUELE
PRIME MINISTER OF ITALY
(May 19, 1860 - Dec 1, 1952)
Orlando served as Prime Minister of Italy from 1917 through the close of the Paris Peace Conference in 1919. He resigned due to his failure to secure Italian interests at the Conference. Orlando is a minor character in the story based upon his participation in the Paris Peace Conference.

PAPADIMITRIOU, SERGEANT
SOLDIER, GREEK ARMY
One of two Greek officers assigned to accompany foreign correspondent, Dr. Herbert Adams Gibbons, by General Papoulas, to the city of Aidin, so that Gibbons could report on the massacre of 5,000 Christians, by the Muslin population. The perpetrators were being directed by officials of the Turkish government, military and civilian, to plunder and burn the Christian sections of the city. Papadimitriou is later used as a character to be interviewed by Gibbons, and also as a retreating soldier driven to burn Greek villages on their trek to Smyrna.

PAPADOPOULOS, PETROS
GREEK SAILOR
Fictitious name for a Greek sailer who escorted Jennings to Greek battleship Kilkis in Mytilene harbor.

PAPAVASILIOU, CHRISTOS
COUSIN OF ARCHBISHOP CHRYSOSTOMOS
(c.1860 - 1920)
Grandfather of co-author, and cousin of Archbishop Chrysostomos, Christos became the personal bodyguard to his cousin during the Greek Struggle in Macedonia. As Metropolitan Bishop of Drama, Chrysostomos had no one he could trust so far from home, it fell to Christos to serve his cousin. Both were deemed to be enemies of the Ottoman government. Christos died after being beaten by Turks in his home town of Triglia, Asia Minor. He is briefly mentioned in the story.

PAPAVASILIOU, PAVLOS
SOLDIER, GREEK ARMY IN ASIA MINOR
(Nov 21, 1900 - Nov 24, 1973)
Father of co-author, Pavlos birth records were altered so that he wouldn't be called to serve in the Turkish army. After the Greek occupation of Asia Minor, Pavlos became a medic in the Greek army, probably as a reaction to his father's partisan activities. His qualification for being a medic was the dubious experience of having worked in a pharmacy in Triglia, that was owned my another relative of Archbishop Chrysostomos. He is used as a character- a retreating soldier in the run up to the disaster in Smyrna who speaks with Captain Apostolidis, a major character.

PAPAVASILIOU, YIANNI
REFUGEE, AND RELATIVE OF CHRYSOSTOMOS
(Apr 9, 1902 - Apr 24, 1986)
Uncle of co-author, Yiannis was sent to Smyrna by his mother to warn his father's cousin, Chrysostomos to leave before he was murdered. She had a dream. Instead Chrysostomos ordered young Yiannis to get to a ship and save his family. After 6 hours in the water, Yiannis somehow boarded an Italian ship that carried his to Mytilene. These facts are dramatized in the story.

PAPOULAS, ANASTASIOS
COMMANDER IN CHIEF OF GREEK FORCES
(1859 - Mar 1935)
General Papoulas, a close friend of King Constantine was appointed commander of the Greek forces in Anatolia, replacing General Paraskevopoulos. The Greek army was defeated under his command. Eventually he attempted a coup and was convicted of treason and executed. He is a minor character in this story, mentioned as a result of his position in the events.

PARASKEVOPOULOS, LEONIDAS
COMMANDER IN CHIEF OF GREEK FORCES
(1860 - May 16, 1936)
General Paraskevopoulos led the Greek forces to many victories. He was appointed by Venizelos and was a seasoned wartime general. He is mentioned in the story by virtue of his position and the Greek army advances.

PHOCAS COL.
COLONEL, GREEK REVOLUTIONARY LEADER
Mentioned once as one of the three revolutionary colonels that carried out the coup of the Greek government from Mytilene.

Pichon, Stéphen
French Minister of Foreign Affairs
(Aug 10, 1857 - Sep 18, 1933)
Pichon served as the French Minister of Foreign Affairs under Prime Minister Clemenceau. He is a minor character in this by virtue of his participation in the Paris Peace Conference. It is Pichon's office that serves as the main meeting place for the Big Four.

Piper, Captain
Commander of the USS Litchfield
Piper is mentioned in the story as a result of his leading a group of 20 U.S. sailors to guard the American College in Smyrna. The actions of Piper and his soldiers is part of the story of destruction.

Plastirac Col.
Colonel, Greek Revolutionary Leader
Mentioned once as one of the three revolutionary colonels that carried out the coup of the Greek government from Mytilene.

Politis, Nikolaos
Foreign Minister of Greece
(1872-1942)
Politis was a Greek diplomat of the early 20th century. He was a professor of law by training, and prior to World War I taught law at Paris University and the University of Aix. A supporter of Eleftherios Venizelos, he served alongside Venizelos as delegate to the London Conference in 1912-13, and as his Minister of Foreign Affairs in 1916-1920 and again in 1922. He also served as the Greek representative to the League of Nations. He is mentioned as a participant in the Paris Peace Conference.

Powell, Halsey "Harry"
Captain, U.S. Navy
(Aug 3, 1883 - Dec 24, 1936)
Captain Powell was a U.S. Naval officer commanding the USS Parker during World War I. He received the Navy Distinguished Service Medal. During the Smyrna affair, Powell worked for Rear Admiral Bristol, which was mirrored in his rhetoric. But he tended to ignore or look the other way during Jennings' and others' efforts to help the refugees. He is a minor character in this story that is mentioned as a function of his involvement.

Price, George Ward
British Journalist
Price was a British journalist who wrote about the horror he witnessed in Smyrna. He managed to get an interview with Mustapha Kemal, but his most moving articles concern the inhumanity of the Turkish soldiers.

Prentiss, Mark
NY Times Journalist
Prentiss was an American journalist that wrote for the New York Times. He is a minor character in the story but is mentioned for the events he was a part of.

Prinzip, (Princip) Gavrilo
Assassin
(Jul 25, 1894 - Apr 28, 1918)
In his assassination of the heir to the Austro-Hungarian throne, his action became known as the trigger for the start of World War I (The Great War). He is a minor character in that he is mentioned in the lead up to the Paris Peace Conference within this story.

Raber, Oran
Tourist
Raber is mentioned in the story as relating his experience of having been in Smyrna at the time of the disaster.

Rallis, Demetrios
Prime Minister of Greece
(1844-1921)
Rallis is mentioned in the story as replacing Venizelos in 1920 as Prime Minister. Rallis would not survive long enough to see the destruction at Smyrna.

Reed, Cass Arthur
Dean of Students
(1884-1933)
Reed was the Dean of the American International College in Smyrna. He was likely placed in that role by his marriage to the daughter of Alexander MacLachlan, the found of the College. Reed is a minor character in this story in that he is mentioned during the events containing the College.

Reed, Rosalind (MacLachlan)
Wife of Cass Reed
(Dec 17, 1891 - Apr 28, 1918)
Wife of Cass Arthur Reed, dean of students at the American International College in Smyrna, and daughter of Alexander MacLachlan, she is mentioned in this story by virtue of her family relationships.

Rhodes, J. B.
Lieutenant Commander, U. S. Navy
Commander of the USS *Litchfield*, was given strict orders from Admiral Bristol, not to do anything except help American citizens to a zone of safety and not to allow any Christian natives to force their way into American buildings. He is mentioned in the story to reflect that point.

Sherwood, Miss Marcella
School Supervisor
Ms. Sherwood served as the supervisor to the Mission Day School for Girls in Punjab. While bicycling around the city, she was assaulted by a mob that was also responsible for murdering three British bank employees. This attack angered General Dyer to instruct his infantry brigade to fire on an innocent crowd of Indians.

Sonnino, Sidney
Italian Minister of Foreign Affairs
(Mar 11, 1847 - Nov 24, 1922)
Sonnino was a liberal Italian politician, who served as a translator for Vittorio Orlando, Prime Minister during the Paris Peace Conference. He is a character early on in the story to reflect the diverging agendas of the Paris Peace Conference.

Stavrianopoulos, Dionysios
Commander of Greek 12th Div.
(Jan 1, 1875 - 1972)
Stavrianopoulos is the regiment commander of the first Greek troops to set foot in Smyrna as part of the Allied occupation. He is the unlucky leader who, under his command, precipitated the the first outburst of hostility of the occupation and the associated Greek vengeance aimed at the closest Turk.

STERGIADIS, ARISTEIDIS
GOVERNOR GENERAL OF SMYRNA
(1861- Jun 22, 1949)
Stergiadis was the High Commissioner and Governor General of Smyrna, after the unfortunate melee that occurred on the day of the Greek occupation of Smyrna. Hated by the Greek population, he tried to show his impartiality by favoring the cause of the Muslim population whether or not that position was appropriate. He is a character in this story until he leaves Smyrna during the evacuation of troops.

TCHORBADJIS, SERGEANT
LEADER, SMYRNA FIRE BRIGADE
Tchorbadis' testimony at a later trial against the insurers of Smyrna warehouses, is used to describe the concerted effort of Turkish soldiers to burn down the Armenian and Greek quarters of the city.

THEOPHONITIS, IOANNIS
CAPTAIN OF THE GREEK BATTLESHIP KILKIS
Captain of the Greek Battleship *Kilkis*, Theophonitis was critical to Jennings' duel of wits with the Greek parliament, by changing Jennings' hand-written messages in translation to be more aggressive.

THESIGER, CAPTAIN
BRITISH ROYAL NAVY
Thesiger was on the quay at the moment the first Turkish cavalry rode into Smyrna. He is mentioned at the critical point of stopping the cavalry's forward motion to welcome the victorious Turkish army and that he was delivering the city to the victors.

TITTONI, TOMMASO
FOREIGN MINISTER OF ITALY
(Nov 16, 1855 - Feb 7, 1931)
Tittoni was an Italian diplomat and politician. He became the 17th Prime Minister of Italy and later became Italy's Foreign Minister at the Paris Peace Conference

TOPAKYAN, S. H.
FORMER U.S. CONSUL-GENERAL TO PERSIA
Topakyan is mentioned through a newspaper article that exposes Admiral Bristol's pro-Turk leanings and his dislike for Greeks and Armenians.

Toynbee, Arnold Joseph
BRITISH HISTORIAN
(Apr 14, 1889 - Oct 22, 1975)
Toynbee was a British historian who wrote a 12-volume analysis of the rise and fall of civilizations. He was very pro-Greek during World War I but then became pro-Turk in his writings after the war. He is mentioned in passing during a conversation in the story.

Trikoupis, Nikolaos
GENERAL, GREEK ARMY IN ASIA MINOR
(1869-1956)
A senior Greek commander in the August 1922 assault, Trikoupis was was forced to surrender to Kemalist forces after ordering a retreat. He was later captured by the Turks and brought to the camp of General Mustapha Kemal. While being interviewed by Kemal, he learned that he had been elevated to commander-in-chief of all Greek forces. He is a character in this story by his involvement in the Greek offensive/retreat.

Tsakirides, Marika
GREEK REFUGEE & SURVIVOR
Mentioned in the story as a 13 year-old survivor describing her ordeal in the water trying to be saved by Allied Naval ships.

Tsoubariotis, Yiorgos
GREEK REFUGEE & SURVIVOR
11 year old Smyrna Fire survivor describes his personal ordeal hiding from Turkish soldiers and his flight to safety.

Usakizade, Latife
PARAMOUR OF GENERAL MUSTAPHA KEMAL
(Jun 17, 1898 - Jul 12, 1975)
Infatuated with General Mustapha Kemal, she married him in 1923. They divorced in 1925. In the context of this story, Latife first meets Kemal in September 1922, when she returns to her father's mansion in Smyrna and meets the General.

Usakizade, Muammer
WEALTHY TURKISH CITIZEN OF SMYRNA
Father of Latife Usakizade, he was a wealthy Turk, who, in the context of the book entertained General Mustapha Kemal after the Turkish victory. It was at this party that Kemal met his future wife.

(VALIADIS), CONSTANTINE V
PATRIARCH, GREEK ORTHODOX CHURCH
(Nov 1833 - Feb 27, 1914)
He was the Ecumenical Patriarch of Constantinople and mentor of Archbishop Chrysostomos. He is mentioned in the story when describing Chrysostomos' history.

VENIZELOS, ELEFTHERIOS
PRIME MINISTER OF GREECE
(Aug 23, 1864 - Mar 18, 1936)
Venizelos served as Prime Minister of Greece from 1910 to 1920 and then again from 1928 to 1932. He is primarily responsible for the abdication of King Constantine I. He is a character in this story because he was a major figure in the events as they happened from the Paris Peace Conference to the burning of Smyrna.

(VON CHOTKOW), SOPHIE
DUCHESS OF HOHENBERG
(Mar 1, 1868 - Jun 28, 1914)
Sophie was the wife of Archduke Franz Ferdinand who was heir presumptive to the Austro-Hungarian throne. She was assassinated, along with her husband in Sarajevo.

WALLACE, DUNCAN
BRITISH RESIDENT OF SMYRNA
(1882 - Sep 1939)
Smyrna Resident and veteran of the Royal Navy was aboard the HMS *Iron Duke* during the fire. His description is mentioned as part of the eyewitness accounts in the story.

WALLACE, HUGH CAMPBELL
U.S. AMBASSADOR TO FRANCE
(Feb 10, 1864 - Jan 1, 1931)
Wallace was an American businessman, political activist and diplomat. He served U.S. Ambassador in Paris from 1919 to 1921.

WARD, DR. MARK
AMERICAN RELIEF WORKER
Ward is referred to in a conversation, mentioning his report of Turks complaining of being to lenient with Greeks, and the suggestion that such leniency would end.

WEBSTER, JAMES
PETTY OFFICER, U.S. NAVY
Webster is mentioned as a character who recounts his experience while guarding the door at the American Institute and then leading 2,000 refugees towards the quay, losing most of them to being shot by Turkish soldiers along the way.

WHITTALL, HERBERT OCTAVIUS
HEAD OF PROMINENT LEVANTINE DYNASTY
(1858 - 1929)
One of the celebrated Levantine families in Smyrna, Octavius was the head of the family business and prominent citizen of Smyrna. He is used in a dinner engagement to introduce characters and events before the Smyrna disaster.

WHITTALL, LOUISA JANE (MALTASS)
WIFE OF HERBERT OCTAVIUS WHITTALL
(Apr 25, 1875 - Jun 22, 1942)
The wife of Herbert Whittall, in the context of this story she is used as a character at a social dinner to introduce certain characters and exposition of certain known positions on the prevailing issues in Smyrna at the time.

WILLIAMSON, GRACE
PROPRIETOR OF BRITISH NURSING HOME
(1865-1945)
Ms. Williamson, a Levantine of English descent, ran an English nursing home in Smyrna. The story describes her pro-Turkish attitude in the face of contradictory behavior.

WILSON, SIR HENRY
FIELD MARSHAL, BRITISH ROYAL ARMY
(May 5, 1864 - Jun 22, 1922)
Field Marshall Wilson was a British Army officer and Irish Unionist. He served in the British Parliament briefly and was assassinated by IRA gunmen in 1922. He is mentioned in the latter British efforts against the Turks.

WILSON, WOODROW
28TH PRESIDENT OF THE UNITED STATES
(Dec 28, 1856 - Feb 3, 1924)
Wilson served from 1913 to 1921. A leader of the Progressive Movement in the United States, he served during World War I, after which he was one of the 'Big Four' leaders of the Paris Peace Conference in 1919, held at Versailles, France. Wilson is a minor character in the story based upon his participation in the Paris Peace Conference.

WOLLESON, EDWIN ARMIN
COMMANDER, U.S. NAVY
(Dec 28, 1856 - Sep 19, 1960)
Captain of the USS Lawrence during the Smyrna catastrophe. He is mentioned while escorting Jennings and his flotilla of Greek ships to rescue refugees.

WOOD, HORTENSE
LEVANTINE RESIDENT OF SMYRNA
Resident of Bournabat who was star struck by General Mutapha Kemal. She opened her home to be used as the general's headquarters.

XENOPOULOU, ELENI
GREEK SOCIALITE OF SMYRNA
The daughter of the owner of the most exclusive department store in Smyrna. The store, named Xenopoulo was located on La Rue Franque, was said to compete with any Paris store. Based upon her family's status in the community, Eleni was a much desired and eligible socialite.

ZAHAROFF, SIR ZACHARIAS BASILEIOS
ARMS DEALER
(Oct 6, 1849 - Nov 27, 1936)
Born in Asia Minor, Zacharoff became an arms dealer and financier, eventually becoming one of the world's most wealthy men outside the United States. During the Smyrna catastrophe, Zacharoff attempted to finance and thereby become King of a new independent country to be formed once the Allied powers decided that the Greek forces should evacuate Asia Minor. He is a minor character in this story by virtue of his place in the Greek effort to protect Asia Minor Greeks from the return of Turkish rule.

Illustrations

Illustration	Page
1. The Big Four posing for a photo. 5	
2. Greek Smyrniotes celebrate occupation force arrival. 40	
3. Portrait of Archbishop Chrysostomos of Smyrna. 42	
4. Georges Clemenceau signing Treaty of Versailles. 46	
5. Portrait of young Winston Churchill. 56	
6. Portrait of King Alexander of Greece. 65	
7. Turkish soldiers pose with beheaded, hanged Greek woman. 69	
8. Captain Lazaros Apostolidis and his band of partisans. 72	
9. The GrandHotel Kraemer Palace as it looked in 1922. 83	
10. Horse-drawn trolley travels along quayside. 84	
11. View of the quay in Smyrna. 85	
12. Aristeidis Stergiadis & Greek military leaders of Asia Minor. 87	
13. The paddle-steamer *Schönbrunn* docked at a Danube port. 108	
14. Portrait of Asa K. Jennings	110
15. House of Commons chamber in British Parliament.	115
16. New York City's Hotel Commodore under construction.	118
17. Pera House, the British embassy in Istanbul, Turkey. 124	
18. Greek refugees being deported into the Turkish interior. 130	
19. Saint Sofia, 4th century Greek cathedral in Istanbul, Turkey. 132	
20. General Mustapha Kemal prepares for Battle of Dumlupinar. 149	
21. Ruin of Triglia school built by Archbishop Chrysostomos 156	
22. General Trikoupis and his officers are forced to pose for a photo. 160	
23. Archbishop Chrysostomos speaks for the youth. 176	
24. Desperate refugees board rowboats. 178	
25. Turkish cavalry enter Smyrna led by Captain Cherefeddin Bey. 179	
26. General Kemal arrives in Smyrna in an open touring car. 184	
27. Pavlos Papavasiliou poses with brother Yiannis. 186	
28. Greek families grieve the loss of murdered family members. 189	
29. Turkish soldiers revel in their butchery. 203	
30. Children faced the same fate as adults. 204	
31. The U.S.S. *Litchfield* anchored in Smyrna harbor. 212	
32. The U.S.S. *Simpson* anchored in Smyrna harbor. 215	
33. View of Smyrna burning on the morning of Sep 14, 1922. 216	
34. Refugees collect on lighter moored to the quay. 217	
35. Smyrna continues to burn. 220	
36. Refugees packed like sardines on Smyrna's quayside. 221	
37. Refugees board the Italian Constantinapoli. 247	
38. The Greek battleship *Kilkis* steaming in Aegean waters. 256	
39. King Constantine I of Greece in a German uniform.	274

Bibliography

Published Sources

Arlen, Michael J. *Passage to Ararat*. New York: Farrar, Straus & Giroux, 1975. Print.

Dakin, Douglas, M.A., PhD. *The Greek Struggle in Macedonia 1897 - 1913*. Thessaloniki: Institute For Balkan Studies, 1966. Print.

Davis, William Stearns, Ph.D. *A Short History of The Near East: From the Founding of Constantinople*. New York: MacMillan, 1922. *Print*.

Dobkin, Marjorie Housepian. *Smyrna 1922: The Destruction of a City*. 1971; New York: Newmark Press, 1998. Print.

Gage, Nicholas. *Greek Fire*. New York: Alfred A. Knopf, 2000. Print.

Greene, Frederick Davis, M.A. *Armenian Massacres and Turkish Tyranny*. Astoria: J.S. & A.L. Fawcett, 1990. Print.

Halo, Thea. *Not Even My Name*. New York: Picador, 2000. Print.

Horton, George. *The Blight of Asia*. 1926; ??? Print.

Lewis, Bernard. *The Emergence of Modern Turkey*. 3rd ed. New York: Oxford University Press, 2002. Print.

Milton, Giles. *Paradise Lost; Smyrna, 1922. The Destruction of a Christian City in the Islamic World*. New York: Basic Books, 2008. Print.

Mohr, Anton. *The Oil War*. New York: Harcourt, Brace an Co, 1926. Print.

Murat, John. *The Great Extirpation of Hellenism & Christianity in Asia Minor: The Historic and Systematic Deception of World Opinion Concerning The Hideous Christianity's Uprooting of 1922*. 1992; Miami: Jean de Murat, 1999. Print.

Naimark, Norman M. *Fires of Hatred: Ethnic Cleansing in Twentieth-Century Europe*. Cambridge: Harvard University Press, 2001. Print.

Papoutsy, Christos. *Ships of Mercy: The True Story of the Rescue of the Greeks, Smyrna, September 1922*. Portsmouth: Peter E. Randall, 2008. Print.

Pears, Edwin, LL.B. *The Destruction of the Greek Empire and the Story of the Capture of Constantinople by the Turks*. *New York:* Greenwood Press, 1968. Print.

Shea, Nina. *In The Lion's Den: A Shocking Account of Persecution and Martyrdom of Christians Today and How We Should Respond*. Nashville: Broadman & Holman, 1997. Print.

Toynbee, Arnold J. *The Murderous Tyranny of the Turks*. Astoria: J.S. & A.L. Fawcett, 1917. Print.

Unofficial - Articles

Abdullah, Achmed; Anavi, Leo. "Mustapha Kemal Represented As Military Genius and Patriot" *The Sun* 26 September 1922: Pg. 9. Print.

Associated Press. "180,000 Are Homeless In Asia Minor Regions" *The Sun* 21 December 1922: Pg. 2. Print.

Associated Press. "200,000 In Smyrna Hopeless of Rescue: Three Destroyers in Harbor, but Their Crews Must Do Guard Duty Shore." *The New York Times* 19 September 1922: Pg. 1. Print.

Associated Press. "Allies Will Battle: Fear Greek Troops Will Attack Turks Despite Orders" *The Washington Post* 1 August 1922. Print.

Associated Press. "Constantine Party Wins In Greece Over Venizelos: Election Returns Not Complete, but Government Virtually Concedes Its Defeat." *The New York Times* 16 November 1920: Pg. 1. Print.

Associated Press. "Expect Coup D'Etat By The Greek King: Naming of General Metaxas as a Kind of Dictator Is Said to Be Constantine's Plan: May Lead To An Outbreak." *The New York Times* 25 November 1922: Pg. 2. Print.

Associated Press. "GreekGenerals Held; Prince To Be Tried: Brother of Constantine Is Charged With Having Disregarded Orders in Field." *St. Louis Post-Dispatch 1* December 1922: Pg. 35. Print.

Associated Press. "Greeks Hand Over Smyrna To Allies; Looting Reported: Greek Soldiers, Armenians and Turks Committing Acts of Murder and Incendiarism. American Forces Landed." *The New York Times* 9 September 1922: Pg. 1. Print.

Associated Press. "Greeks Reported Ready To Get Out of Asia Minor: French, British and Italian Dragomen State Plan Based on Immediate Armistice." *St. Louis Post-Dispatch* 7 September 1922: Pg. 1. Print.

Associated Press. "Hundreds Caught In Flames" *The New York Times* 15 September 1922. Print.

Associated Press. "Kemal Brings Nations Close to 'Zero Hour': London Cabinet Holds Midnight Meeting to Consider Peace or War." *Detroit Free Press* 1 October 1922: Pg. 1. Print.

Associated Press. "Kemalists Seize Erenkeui: Main Body of Nationalists Only 15 Miles From Chanak." *The New York Times* 26 September 1922: Pg. 1. Print.

Associated Press. "King Constantine Welcomed by Mighty Throng on His Return To Athens After Long Exile: His Arrival Was Compared by His Admirers to Napoleon's Return From Elba, and Tears of Joy Flowed Freely Down Cheeks of Cheering Horde." *San Francisco Chronicle* 26 December 1920: Pg. W1. Print.

Associated Press. "Lloyd George Urged To Save Christians: Alleged Massacres By Turks in Asia Minor Brought Up in Commons" *The Sun* 16 June 1922. Print.

Associated Press. "Lloyd George Tells Why British Yield To Turk" *Chicago Daily Tribune* 24 September 1922: Pg. 2. Print.

Associated Press. "Massacres Up In Commons" *The New York Times* 15 June 1922. Print.

Associated Press. "Names Conditions Of Turkish Peace: Lloyd George Says Allies Will No Abandon Helpless To Massacre." *The Sun* 5 August 1922. Print.

Associated Press. "New Raids In Straits Zone" *The New York Times* 28 September 1922. Print.

Associated Press. "Premieres To Discuss Near East Problem: British Fleet Gathers in Turkish Waters" *Boston Daily Globe* 1 August 1922. Print.

Associated Press. "Smyrna Burning, 14 Americans Missing; 1,000 Massacred as Turks Fire City; Kemal Threatens March On Capital: Our Consulate Destroyed" *The New York Times* 15 September 1922: Pg. 1. Print.

Associated Press. "Turks Defy British, Seize Dardanelles Neutral Zones: Also Want Fortifying of Strategic Points Stopped." *Detroit Free Press* 28 September 1922: Pg. 1. Print.

Associated Press. "Turks Launch Drive Against greek Front: Headquarters of Nationalists Is Moved to Ismid- Wires to Constantinople Cut." *The Washington Post* 29 August 1922: Pg. 1. Print.

Associated Press. "Turks Threaten to Invade Neutral Straits Territory: Angora Warns Allies Greeks Must Not Be Given Sanctuary- Kemal Pasha Makes Return of Thrace Condition for Resecting Neutral Zone- Turkish Army Impatient. Allies Need 33 Battalions for Defense of Constantinople and have Only 20." *The Washington Post* 18 September 1922: Pg. 1. Print.

Associated Press. "U. S. Sailors Rescue Many in Smyrna Fire: Brave Lads Risk Lives in Holocaust to Aid Women and Children." *The San Francisco Chronicle* 19 September 1922: Pg. 6. Print.

Associated Press. "U. S. To Avoid Near East Tangle: Seeks Only Protection of Citizens and Interests in Mandate Area." *The Sun* 17 September 1922: Pg. 10. Print.

Clayton, John. "Kemal Declares His Terms: Ready For Conference With Allies and Russia." *The Manchester Guardian* 27 September 1922: Pg. 7. Print.

Correspondent. "Armenians Believe Turks May Thwart Allied Inquiry: Little Evidence of Atrocities Would Remain, It Is Asserted, If Nationalists Have Forewarning." *The Christian Science Monitor* 11 July 1922: Pg. 1. Print.

Correspondent. "Asia Minor Peoples Plan To Defy Turks: Envoys Say 1,000,000 Menaced Inhabitants Will Fight to Death." *The New York Times* 6 August 1922.

Correspondent. "Asks For Help, In Near East: Professor Thinks Isolation Dangerous Policy." *The Los Angeles Times* 10 August 1922.

Correspondent. "Complete Correspondence That Led Up To England's Declaration of War Against Germany: Full Text of the Famous "White Paper" of the British Foreign Office Containing 159 Documents Giving Diplomatic Correspondence That Preceded the Outbreak of Hostilities" *The New York Times* 23 August 1914: Pg. WP1.

Correspondent. "Constantine Abdicates: Political Revolution With Military Revolt." *The Manchester Guardian* 28 September 1922: Pg. 9. Print.

Correspondent. "Constantine Is Planning Return to Greece, Swiss Reports Say; King Makes Gain" *The New York Times* 18 October 1920: Pg. 1. Print.

Correspondent. "Crown Awaits Prince George As King Constantine Quits" *San Francisco Chronicle* 28 September 1922: Pg. 5. Print.

Correspondent. "Declare Kemalists Must Abandon Zone: British Cabinet Gives Harrington Free Hand to Enforce an Ultimatum" *The New York Times* 30 September 1922: Pg. 3. Print.

Correspondent. "Events Which Ended George's Ministry: Correspondent Analyzes Sequence of British Blunders In Near East Which Came Near To Provoking General Moslem War." *The Sun* 22 October 1922: Pg. B14. Print.

Correspondent. "Franz Josef In Manifesto States Case: Had Hoped to Finish Reign in Peace, but Honor Prevents" *The Chicago Daily Tribune* 29 July 1914: Pg. 1. Print.

Correspondent. "French Opinion On The Near East: Greek Revolution Too Late." *The Manchester Guardian* 29 September 1922: Pg. 8. Print.

Correspondent. "Germans Rejoicing In Venizelos's Fall: Junkers and Socialists Alike Acclaim It- Former Enthusiastic Over Constantine's Chances." *The New York Times* 23 November 1920: Pg. 14.

Correspondent. "Greek General Reveals Source of Asia Disaster: Gounaris Men Ordered Angora Drive." *Chicago Daily Tribune* 16 November 1922: Pg. 15. Print.

Correspondent. "Greeks Are Beheaded In Asia Minor" *The Washington Post* 1 August 1922.

Correspondent. "Greeks Are Beheaded In Asia Minor" *The Washington Post* 1 August 1922.

Correspondent. "Heir To Austrian Throne, Archduke Ferdinand, and Wife Slain By Assassin: Escape Bomb; Die By Pistol" *The Washington Post* 29 June 1914: Pg. 1.

Correspondent. "Kaiser Invades France; Czar Enters Germany: Uncle Sam Promptly Extends Helping Hand to 150,000 Subjects Abroad" *The San Francisco Chronicle* 3 August 1914: p. 1.

Correspondent. "Kemalist Power Relies On Intimidation And Violence: Turks Are Nearing End of Their Rope and Greeks Need Only Patience to Win" *The Christian Science Monitor* 13 July 1922: p. 5. Print.

Correspondent. "Lodge Calls Turks Blight: Senator Speaks At Near East Relief Meeting." *Boston Daily Globe* 30 September 1922: p. 1. Print.

Correspondent. "Mustapha Kemal's Coup" *The Washington Post* 2 September 1922: Pg. 6. Print.

Correspondent. "No Easy Thing to "Kick the Turk Out of Europe, Bag and Baggage"" *The Boston Daily Globe* 11 April 1920: p. E8.

Correspondent. "Papal Secretary Receives Americans" *The New York Times* 27 July 1922.

Correspondent. "Refugees In Need Of Help In Orient" *The Christian Science Monitor* 30 September 1922: Pg. 2. Print.

Correspondent. "Reports Smyrna Quiet: Greek Headquarters Says Stories of Disorders Were Exaggerated." *The New York Times* 4 June 1919: Pg. 23.

Correspondent. "Russia Invades Germany; Germany Invades France, But Does Not Declare War; England's Decision Today; Belgium Menaced, Luxembourg and Switzerland Invaded; German Marksmen Shoot Down a French Aeroplane" *The New York Times* 3 August 1914: Pg. 1. Print.

Correspondent. "Says Asia Minor People Welcome Rule by Greeks" *The Sheboygan Press Telegram* 21 June 1922: p. 9. Print.

Correspondent. "Slain Archbishop Foresaw Massacre: Chrysostomos Sent Letters to Foreign Officials Predicting Smyrna Disaster." *The New York Times* 23 August 1914: Pg. WP1.

Correspondent. "Smyrna's Last Days: A Manchester Man's Experiences." *The Manchester Guardian* 28 September 1922: p. 16. Print.

Correspondent. "Smyrna Almost Completely Destroyed: Allied Warning To Kemal. Any Attempt to Cross the Straits Will be Resisted." *The Manchester Guardian* 24 September 1922: p. 35. Print.

Correspondent. "The Near East Situation: The Greek Evacuation." *The Independent* 30 September 1922: Print.

Correspondent. "The Greek Revolution." *The Washington Post* 29 September 1922: p. 6. Print.

Correspondent. "The Struggle in Asia Minor: British Position- Intervention By Group of Powers" *The Guardian* 5 September 1922: p. 7. Print.

Correspondent. "The Two Kemals: The Polished Aristocrat of European Circles in Contrast With the Ruthless Commander of Fanatical Turks." *The New York Times* 1 October 1922: p. 106. Print.

Correspondent. "The War In Asia Minor: Allied Responsibility Urgency of Venice Conference." *The Observer* 3 September 1922. p. 10. Print.

Correspondent. "Turkish Forces Falling Back: Eren Keui is Evacuated By Mohammedans." *San Francisco Chronicle* 1 October 1922. p. E1. Print.

Correspondent. "Turks Torture Greek Refugees: Frightful Situation Faced by Deportees" *Los Angeles Times* 31 December 1922. pg. 119. Print.

Correspondent. "Unredeemed Hellenes Issue Appeal To World: Turkish Massacre in Asia Minor Declared to be Aimed At All Christians." *The Sun* 25 September 1922. p. 7. Print.

Correspondent. "Woes Of Smyrna Described At Boston Mass Meeting: Senator Lodge Says Diplomatic Aid Would Be Given If Possible- Large Subscriptions Received." *The Christian Science Monitor* 30 September 1922. p. 2. Print.

de Fontenoy, Marquise. "Kemalist Envoy At Rome In Disfavor At Washington" *The Washington Post* 27 September 1922: Pg. 6. Print.

Dunn, Robert. "The Big Idea for Turkey: How the Problem that Confronts the World in the Near East Must Be Solved." *McClure's Magazine* December 1922, Vol. 54, Number 10, Pg. 22. Print.

Gibbons, Floyd. -No Headline- *The Chicago Daily Tribune* 31 July 1922: p. 5. Print.

Gibbons, Floyd. "Greeks and Turks Clash in Constantinople Drive: Smyrna Made Free State in Athens Coup." *The San Francisco Chronicle* 31 July 1922: p. 1. Print.

Gibbons, Herbert Adams, Ph.D. "Greeks Firm For Anatolia Campaign: Mr. Gibbons Says Determination to Protect Christians Promises Well for Army's Success." *The Christian Science Monitor* 16 May 1922: pg. 3. Print.

Gibbs, Sir Philip. ""Chaos Increases While Leaders Talk: Plenty of Sympathy, But Little Action By European Nations, While Turks Gain Power and Soviet Russia Spreads Its Control." *The Sun* 17 September 1922: Pg. 14. Print.

Gibbs, Sir Philip. "'Mild Greek Rule Prevails in Smyrna: Occupying Forces Permit Turks to Retain Their Civil Administration." *The New York Times* 14 June 1920: Pg. 15. Print.

Grigg, Joseph W. "Lloyd George May Try His Hand At Pacification Of Asia Minor: Expected to Make Move If Nothing Constructive Comes Out of the Genoa Conference- Will Work To The Last To Get Results." *The Sun* 14 May 1922: Pg. 2.

Harding, Gardner L. "Smyrna Delegates Declare Their Backs Are To The Wall: Autonomous Region in Asia Minor Endeavoring to Escape Tragedy of Being Handed Back to Turks" *The Christian Science Monitor* 5 August 1922. Print.

James, Edwin L. "Our Rights Ended, Ismet Pasha Says: We Can "Observe" at Lausanne, but That's All, Turkish Delegate Asserts." *The New York Times* 17 November 1922: Pg. 3. Print.

James, Edwin L. "Paris Acclaims Peace In Near East: Will Send Franklin- Bouillon by Fast Cruiser to Advise the Turks." *The New York Times* 25 September 1922: Pg.1 Print.

James, Edwin L. "Uneasiness In Paris In Near East Crisis: Kemal's Delay and the Proximity of British and Turks Cause Anxiety." *The New York Times* 30 September 1922: Pg.3. Print.

Newbold, John Turner Walton. "Greek Imperialism and Sir Basil Zaharoff" *The Living Age 7 October 1922: Pg. 10. Print.*

Price, Clair. "Mustapha Kemal Pasha, The Man." *Fortnightly Review* July 1922: Pg. 119. Print.

Reuters. "Fire Ravaging Smyrna: Outbreak Of Turkish Outrages Against Christians." *The Manchester Guardian* 15 September 1922: Pg. 9. Print.

Simonds, Frank H. "Near East Puzzle Almost Hopeless: Greek and Turk Armies Ready to Fight Again as U.S. Joins Probers." *The Hartford Courant* 5 July 1922: Pg. 4. Print.

Simonds, Frank H. "The Crisis In the Near East" *The Atlanta Constitution* 11 July 1921: Pg. 4. Print.

Snow, B. W. "As Snow Sees It: The Expected Happens." *Orange Judd Farmer* 1 October 1922: Pg. 12. Print.

Special. "700,000 Greeks Victims of Turks: Charge Made by Washington Legation, Which Puts Dead at That Figure." *The New York Times* 10 July 1921: Pg. 4.

Special. "Allies To Let Turks Remain In Europe And Keep Asia Minor: Paris Conference Decides to Maintain Sultan's Religious as Well as Secular Authority." *The New York Times* 27 March 1922: Pg. 1. Print.

Special. "Army Aviator Flies 450 Miles At Night: Lieutenant Bissell Makes Round Trip Between Washington and New York." *The New York Times* 5 August 1922: Pg. 10. Print.

Special. "Fiendish Tortures For Greek Prelate: Turkish Mob, at General's Order, Hacked Smyrna Metropolitan's Body to Pieces." *The New York Times* 18 September 1922: Pg. 3. Print.

Special. "Greece Denied Right To Seize Turk Capital: Allies Reject Athens' Plea For Occupation Of Constantinople." *The Baltimore Sun* 31 July 1922: Pg. 1. Print.

Special. "Greek Autonomy Granted in Asia Minor Disapproved: Seventy Per Cent of Population Are Turks- Franco-Italian Intrigue- Popular Rising Feared." *The Christian Science Monitor* 19 July 1922: Pg. 1. Print.

Special. "Greek Defeat InAsia Minor Laid To Curzon: Letter From Late Premier Gounaris Asking Aid Read In Parliament." *The Sun* 8 December 1922: Pg. 1. Print.

Special. "Greek Force Routs Kemalists and Rescues 1300 Christians" *The Christian Science Monitor* 8 August 1922: Pg. 3. Print.

Special. ""Mystery Man" Seeks Crown Of Ancient Ionia: Sir Basil Zaharoff, Millionaire Arms Maker, Reported After Throne." *The New York Times* 5 August 1922.

Special. "Must Curb Turks, Says Lloyd George: Allies Won't Make Peace and Leave Minorities Unprotected, He Declares in Commons." *The Sun* 25 August 1922: Pg. 1. Print.

Special. "New State Urged For Asia Minor: Autonomy Proposal by Greece Stirs Quick Protest." *The Christian Science Monitor* 21 July 1922: Pg. 1. Print.

Special. "Powers Will Take Up Near East Questions: England, France and Italy to Hold Conference With Greeks and Turks at Beikoh." *The Washington Post* 21 August 1922.

Special. "Praise U.S. Sailors For Aid At Smyrna: British Admiral and Head of International College Pay Tribute." *The New York Times* 11 December 1922. Print.

Special. "Saw Armenians Massacred: French Actor Declares Smyrna Slaughter Was Without Provocation." *The New York Times* 19 September 1922: Pg. 3. Print.

Special. "Says Lloyd George Misled The Greeks: Gounaris' Secretary Asserts He Urged Asia Minor Drive, Deserted When It Failed." *The New York Times* 8 December 1922: Pg. 1. Print.

Special. "Self-Government Given Asia Minor By Greek Council: Autonomous State is Planned as Solution of Riddle of Centuries in Near East." *The Christian Science Monitor* 18 July 1922: Pg. 1. Print.

Special. "Woman Pictures Smyrna Horrors: Dr. Esther Lovejoy, an Eyewitness, Tells of Terrible Scenes on the Quay." *The New York Times* 9 October 1922. Print.

Swift, Otis. "Rebels March On Athens As King Abdicates: Crowds in Capital Call Venizelos." *Chicago Daily Tribune* 27 September 1922: Pg. 1. Print.

Swift, Otis. "King of Greece Quits, Report: Constantine Gives Crown Prince Throne." *Chicago Daily Tribune* 28 September 1922: Pg. 1. Print.

Williams, T. Walter. "Says Greece Must Hold Gains in Asia: Lazzaro, Athenian Banker, Declares Withdrawal Would Mean Massacre." *The New York Times* 18 June 1922: p. 35. Print.

Williams, T. Walter. "When Greek Meets Turk: How the Conflict in Asia Minor Is Regarded on the Spot-- King Constantine's View." *The New York Times* 10 September 1922: Pg. XXII. Print.

Wilson, P.W. " The Case for Lloyd George" *The Independent* 11 November 1922: Pg.257. Print.

"Paddlesteamers.info" *PS Schobrunn* <http://www.paddlesteamers.info/Schonbrunn.htm>

"The Austrian Society for Railway History." *The Ship*. <http://www.oegeg.at/index.php/oegeg/english>.

Unpublished Sources

Official Documents

Lenser, Samuel David. 'Between The Great Idea and Kemalism: The YMCA at Izmir in the 1920s.' M.A. Dissertation, Boise State University August 2010.